# Our
# Little World

# Our
# Little World

A NOVEL

## Karen Winn

DUTTON

**DUTTON**
An imprint of Penguin Random House LLC
penguinrandomhouse.com

Copyright © 2022 by Karen Winn
Penguin supports copyright. Copyright fuels creativity, encourages diverse voices, promotes free speech, and creates a vibrant culture. Thank you for buying an authorized edition of this book and for complying with copyright laws by not reproducing, scanning, or distributing any part of it in any form without permission. You are supporting writers and allowing Penguin to continue to publish books for every reader.

DUTTON and the D colophon are registered trademarks of
Penguin Random House LLC.

LIBRARY OF CONGRESS CATALOGING-IN-PUBLICATION DATA
Names: Winn, Karen, author.
Title: Our little world: a novel / Karen Winn.
Description: New York: Dutton, [2022]
Identifiers: LCCN 2021015278 (print) | LCCN 2021015279 (ebook) |
ISBN 9780593184493 (hardcover) | ISBN 9780593184509 (ebook)
Subjects: LCSH: Sisters—Fiction. | GSAFD: Bildungsromans.
Classification: LCC PS3623.I66315 O97 2022 (print) |
LCC PS3623.I66315 (ebook) | DDC 813/.6—dc23
LC record available at https://lccn.loc.gov/2021015278
LC ebook record available at https://lccn.loc.gov/2021015279

Printed in the United States of America
1   3   5   7   9   10   8   6   4   2

Title Page Photograph: Summer Landscape © Val Shevchenko / Shutterstock
BOOK DESIGN BY ELKE SIGAL

*For Aimee and David*

# Our
# Little World

# Prologue

I SEE WHISPERS OF MY DEAD SISTER. I SEE HER WHEN I AM DRIVING, through the fogged-up window, her brown hair entangled in my windshield wipers. I am tempted to pull over and carefully remove each hair strand, as if untangling a knotted necklace—one, I suppose, that knotted due to my carelessness. I see my sister's small hands clasped around the same passenger pole I am clinging to in the crowded subway. We are all packed in, our fingers curling around the pole one on top of another in a tree-ring formation, but I instantly recognize the creases in her knuckles and the way her right pinky sits at an odd crooked angle—the result of a bike accident when we were young. I see my sister in the pile of still dead leaves from the red oak tree in our parents' backyard.

Audrina is a lurker, which surprises me. She is always there, on the periphery. Sitting, thin ankles crossed, in the waiting room of my being. When she was alive, in her short life, she was vibrant.

I can't figure out if death has subdued her, or if it has given her some sort of calming, new age wisdom. There is also the very real possibility that she is just confused, trying to figure out what happened to her. What happened to us.

# Part One

# Chapter One

MY SISTER ISN'T THE ONLY DEAD GIRL I'VE KNOWN, AND NOT THE first, either. Before Audrina, there was Sally. Little Sally Baker. My sister knew her, too. She knew her just as long as I did, which wasn't very long—not even the length of a summer.

It was June 1985 when the Baker family moved into the green-shuttered house across the street. I was twelve years old, the same age as Max, Sally's older brother. Audrina, my sister, was a year younger than we were, though you wouldn't have thought it. She was always acting older than she was, even back then: sneaking into our parents' bathroom to use our mother's makeup and perfume, pilfering her earrings and rings to stash away and try on later. My sister loved to get dolled up and gaze at herself in the mirror. "Pipiske," Father called her, an old Hungarian term of endearment meaning "girly" or "sweet."

I was not a tomboy but felt I needed to act like one. Audrina had stolen the looks in our family—a belief I knew didn't make sense but was convinced of nonetheless. She had Father's green eyes, and her hair was a shiny light brown that turned gold in the summer. My hair and eyes were so brown I thought of them as brown-brown, and my hair didn't change in the sun.

So to balance the equation, I acted tough, boy-like—the exact opposite of Audrina. I couldn't compete with someone who had managed to hoard all of the desirable genetics from our parents, so I cut my hair short even though I secretly wanted it long, and when I turned ten, I replaced my once-favorite faded pink unicorn shirt with a navy blue Cosmos one. The Cosmos were the New York professional soccer team that Father had taken us to see play at Giants Stadium, and I liked the way he smiled every time he saw me wear it.

The summer that the Baker family moved in across the street was the same summer that the Cosmos last played, after the North American Soccer League folded and Father's hopes for an American soccer craze were dashed. It was the summer Audrina and I befriended Max and Sally Baker, and it was the summer that Sally disappeared.

Sally was four years old, and I used to think about how I was three times her age when it happened. For years afterward, come each birthday, I would divide my age by three, even though I was aware it didn't actually work that way: *I am thirteen, and Sally would be four years and three months. I am fifteen, and Sally would be— should be—five.*

When we heard that the Bakers had moved to our sleepy New Jersey town from Boston, I instantly felt like they were special. In our sixth-grade class we'd read about the famous historic events that had taken place in Boston, like the Boston Tea Party and Paul Revere's midnight ride, and I envisioned that it was a bustling, exciting city, much like New York City, which we'd last visited the previous winter. The Baker family must have stories to tell, I decided, and I wanted to impress Max with my historical knowledge of his hometown.

"'One if by land, two if by sea,'" I'd uttered from atop my bike, the first evening we met. Our street dead-ended into a cul-de-sac, and we neighborhood kids would congregate there in the early evenings. Summer was in us and around us; we played kickball, tic-tac-toe, hop-scotch, and sometimes even made a makeshift shuffleboard with chalk and a marble. Other times we just twirled around on our bikes until the sky began to darken and fireflies started to appear.

I remember how Max and Sally had stood along the hickory-tree-lined edge of the cul-de-sac, waiting to be invited in. Max held Sally's hand as she buried her blond hair into his side.

He was cute, just about the cutest boy I'd ever seen. Long brown bangs that swept sideways across his blue-eyed face and a right-sided dimple when he smiled. Which he did, suddenly, at me. I remember how my hands grew wet on the clasp of my handlebar and how I wished I hadn't chopped off my hair a few months earlier.

"Paul Revere," he'd replied, his dimple growing even more pronounced. Sally put her hands over her face and then parted her fingers slightly so she could see. "Borka, right?" Max asked.

I flushed, surprised he knew my name, but then realized Mother had likely dropped off a welcome basket to their house on our behalf. "Yeah, but everyone calls me Bee," I quickly replied, wanting to erase the word *Borka* from his vocabulary. How I hated my name.

Audrina appeared next to me, and I wondered whether Max had actually been smiling at her instead of me. She wasn't on a bike; she hadn't been on one in a long time. Those days all she wanted to do was wear dresses and skirts and watch with a bored look while we horsed around. Nobody seemed to mind; in fact, I'd noticed how the Wiley brothers from up the street would glance over to see if Audrina noticed when they did wheelies and scored runs in kickball. I wanted to tell them they were wasting their time. Audrina noticed, but it didn't mean anything. She was used to people vying for her attention, perhaps too used to it.

"Hi there," Audrina said, moving toward Max and Sally. She crouched down to Sally's level, and Sally now removed her hands completely away from her face to look at my sister. Sally's arms and hands were thick enough to make her wrist creases a little pronounced, and the curve of her belly protruded from her pale, flowered strappy dress. A set of tiny red heart studs rested on her pierced earlobes. I'd only gotten my ears pierced two years earlier.

"Oooh," Sally said, thrusting one of her arms forward to rub the charm bracelet Audrina was wearing on her left wrist. Then she suddenly stopped, as if realizing she should have asked before handling it. She glanced at her brother, who slowly nodded, and she then turned back to Audrina. "Tho pretty," she said, with a lisp.

Audrina laughed. "You like it? Which charm is your favorite?"

Sally lifted her other arm up so both hands now encircled the bracelet. She leaned her face into the jewelry piece, as if she were smelling it. After a moment's hesitation, she declared, "This one."

From my angle I couldn't see which charm Sally meant, and I wondered if it was the jeweled box—the charm I had always coveted. Even in my self-appointed tomboy phase, I was enamored with it—with the entire bracelet, really. That particular charm was a shiny gold color and adorned with red, blue, and green stones. The box opened up to reveal a space so small it could barely hold the top of the pencil eraser that Audrina often put in it. Mother once called the bracelet "costume jewelry," a phrase I wouldn't know the true meaning of until later. At the time, costume jewelry conjured images of Halloween and other dress-up occasions, so I thought it sounded marvelous.

While I couldn't tell which charm Sally had identified as her favorite, I did clearly see how Audrina whispered something in Sally's ear, and how Sally then wrapped her arms around my sister's neck. The sun was starting to set, casting the sky with a warm dusky hue, and I remember being aware that Audrina had somehow just gained both Sally's trust and Max's admiration—as he looked on, smiling. It was supposed to be a feel-good moment, a happy one—like the ending of a Disney movie.

But not for me. Instead, I felt as if I were a puzzle piece that had accidentally gotten tossed into the wrong box. Audrina had a way of doing that—making me feel like I didn't belong.

*Borka, right?* I would always be a Borka. I would always be the hideous namesake of Father's Hungarian aunt who had died at age twenty-two from a brain aneurysm. I had never even seen a picture of her—Father had left everything behind in Hungary. I couldn't care any less that she died young. In my mind she was just an ugly, faceless five-lettered name.

And Audrina would always be an Audrina, always knowing what to do, how to act. Always belonging in beautiful moments. Creating them, really. Even now, it astounds me. We were so young, but everything came naturally to her. Mother had chosen Audrina's name simply because she thought it was pretty, which is the way one rightfully ought to acquire a name.

That day was the start of it all. Later I would decide it was somehow Audrina's fault, that if she hadn't captivated Sally, hadn't shown her the charm bracelet, then things wouldn't have happened the way they did.

❧

Audrina and I slipped into our usual pattern that summer. Summer days in the Kocsis household of our youth often meant spending lazy, unstructured mornings in pajamas, eating cereal and French toast with powdered sugar, and watching episodes of *Silver Spoons*. At some point we'd change into our bathing suits while we waited to see whether our mother or another neighborhood mother would be taking us kids to the lake or "the club"—Hammend's Tennis & Swim Club.

Soon after the Bakers' arrival, Mrs. Baker entered into the carpool mix, and because of their proximity to us—right across the street—she or Mother would often cart us around for the day. My sister and I quickly became close with the Baker kids, our friendships accelerated in the way that young summers and unstructured time allow.

If we woke up early enough and cajoled Max and Sally to join us, Father would drop us off at the club on his way to work. He owned his own roofing and siding business, and its storefront was located about thirty miles away from Hammend, in the city of East Orange. I always looked forward to breakfast at the club—they had a Taylor ham, egg, and cheese sandwich that came with a side of crispy fries, no matter the hour. Audrina equally enjoyed their toasted bagel drenched in butter and grape jelly. Max and Sally, who seemed to eat whatever kind of food they desired at their house, were less than enthusiastic about the early hour but usually acquiesced.

Father would get annoyed if we pulled up to the Bakers' house and they weren't ready—which happened often. One morning we waited for a good ten minutes on their circular driveway, and Father began muttering under his breath, his shoulders drawn sharply together. When the front door finally swung open, Mrs. Baker emerged in a pink satin robe, holding a robin's-egg-blue coffee mug, Max and Sally trailing behind her. As they climbed into the back seat alongside Audrina, Mrs. Baker leisurely strolled up to Father's rolled-down window like she had all the time in the world. She was a large woman with light brown wavy hair that she wore loose around her shoulders. As she leaned down to peer inside Father's window, her breasts pushed together and forward, creating a bumpy shelf. I was sitting in the front passenger seat, in full view, and averted my eyes in embarrassment. The other kids didn't seem to notice; I heard Sally giggling from the back seat while Max relayed a story to Audrina about some cereal mishap.

"Sorry," Mrs. Baker simply said to Father, who at first didn't respond; I think he was waiting for the explanation to follow, but none did. She just took a sip from her mug as she pushed herself up from the window, and Father stiffened, as if he'd just become aware of something unpleasant.

Mrs. Baker secretly fascinated me; she was so different from the other Hammend mothers, especially my own. I couldn't imagine Mother wearing her bathrobe anywhere other than inside our house, and she certainly didn't own a satin one. Mother's choice of dress was classic and tailored, her bathrobe safely muted, her skirts and high-waisted pants always paired with monochromatic shirts and blouses. At first it wasn't clear why the Bakers had decided to move to Hammend. There seemed to be an air of mystery surrounding their appearance in our town, even among the adults. One morning I'd overheard Mother whispering something on the phone to our neighbor Mrs. Wiley about "Fran"—Mrs. Baker—but before I could hear more, Mother had spotted me lurking outside the kitchen.

Dr. Baker was a big-time trauma surgeon, we learned, yet his new place of employment, our hospital, twenty miles away, was just a small community one.

"We lived in the city, right in the city, so my parents, er, dad could walk to work," Max once told us. "He was in charge of the trauma department, and his hospital was where all the really hurt people would go, like if you were in a car crash or something."

Max didn't share that his mother was a nurse—we would find that out later through the neighborhood gossip.

I'd assumed, because of Dr. Baker's career and since they came from Boston (which seemed fancy in itself), that Max and Sally— once she was old enough—would be going the private school route, like many of the kids on our street did: Mrs. Wiley's two sons, Andrew and Patrick, and the two older girls, Diane and Courtney, who lived at the very top of Hickory Place, around the bend. So I was pleasantly surprised to learn that Max would be joining me at Hammend's own junior high, Hillside, come fall.

Perhaps Mother was right about our good public school system. She often touted its qualities, like the number of high school graduates who went on to attend four-year colleges. Mother had grown up in Paterson, a nearby New Jersey city, and the only way to leave home in her neighborhood, she'd once told Audrina and me, was to get married.

I knew this was the reason why we lived in Hammend: Mother hoped for more for us. I also knew that even if we could have afforded private school, our parents still wouldn't have sent us. We didn't function in quite the same way as some of the other families in the neighborhood. There was a paucity of *things* in our house that didn't exist in other homes. It was evident in our cupboards that held just enough pasta boxes and cans, in the backpacks that Audrina and I were expected to use year after year, until the zippers broke or the material wore thin. Father was always repurposing furniture he picked up at yard sales; the now-forgotten playhouse in our backyard had come from such scavenging. Mother, meanwhile, nurtured our house like another child—cleaning it regularly, excessively even. "A place for everything, and everything in its place," she often said. She believed in orderliness, Father believed in practicality, and the combination ensured a stringent childhood upbringing.

Father had once told us he owned just two pairs of pants after immigrating to America that were donated by the local church; each evening he'd wash the pair he'd worn that day to school and then to the sausage factory, where he was an underage worker. Any money he received he gave to his struggling parents to supplement the small wages they earned from their day jobs at the chemical factory and their office-building janitorial duties at night.

Audrina and I certainly never lacked for anything—for clothes, or food, or toys; each year we received a sufficient but reasonable number of gifts under the Christmas tree. It's just that the things we had we were expected to take care of.

Our family "vacations" consisted of day trips down the Jersey shore to Point Pleasant. Father usually worked six days a week, except during the winter, when business slowed. The one time I'd been on a plane was two years earlier, before the Bakers moved in, when we went to visit my grandmother—Mother's mother—in Florida after her hip surgery. My sister and I also didn't attend camps—the exception being the one week of acting camp each summer Audrina had gotten our parents to agree to, probably only because it was a day camp, not sleepaway. Our parents simply didn't see the utility of spending money on camps since they'd already purchased a club membership, and since there was a perfectly good public lake nearby.

And it was, indeed, a perfectly good lake.

So when late July brought a week of heavy rain that closed the lake and forced us to spend day after day at the club, inside—Sally standing on a stack of books we'd dragged from the game room so she could peer through the glass at the racquetball courts below—we were all ready for a change.

As soon as Audrina and I awoke in our shared bedroom to find the sun's arms reaching through the shades, we snapped on bathing suits and raced to the kitchen. We half spooned, half slurped our bowls of Cheerios, milk dribbling down our chins, while gesturing to Mother to finish her call with Mrs. Wiley so she could figure out who would be taking us to the lake that day. "Mrs. Baker," Mother mouthed to us, and we quickly finished up eating.

I remember how the morning had that fresh smell that occurs after a summer rain as Audrina and I crossed the wet asphalt street. We always held hands, even though our house sat right next to the cul-de-sac and the only cars likely to pass belonged to us or to the Bakers, and even though we were too old to hold hands. We held hands because Mother told us to, and because I was the older sister, Mother had impressed upon me early on that it was my duty to make sure my fingers were firmly grasped around Audrina's anytime there was a street to cross. I often held on more tightly than I needed to, and Audrina often wrested her hand away a couple of steps before we reached the other side. This was the way we were, the way we always were: a push and a pull, a rib and a provocation. The distinction was often unclear.

At the foot of the Bakers' circular driveway, we saw a blue chalk drawing that cascaded the length of its pavement, past the parked station wagon squatting in the middle. We followed swirls of blue toward the garage, where they turned into an outline of a person and what appeared to be a house with a very tall, pointed roof. Only then did I realize what the drawing was supposed to depict: Rapunzel and her castle. The blue swirls, I supposed, were Rapunzel's hair.

"Audrina!" Sally yelled as she came bouncing out from the garage, Max following close behind. They were both already wearing their swimsuits—Max in blue trunks and Sally in a violet bathing suit with a heart on the front. Sally's hair was pulled into uneven pigtails and her fingers and cheeks smudged blue. Her earlobes were bare—no heart stud earrings today. But what really caught my eye was the gold charm bracelet that slid up and down Sally's left wrist as she moved. It was Audrina's. *Why on earth is Sally wearing Audrina's bracelet?*

"Look at my drawing!" Sally squealed, pointing to the ground.

"Sally," Audrina said, tugging one of Sally's pigtails, while I remained quiet. Processing. *Did Audrina give the bracelet to her?* Audrina continued: "Did you do your hair yourself?"

Sally smiled and nodded. "I helped Mommy!"

"And why are your fingers blue?" Audrina asked. "Were you eating blueberries this morning?"

Sally and Max laughed while I tried to think of something clever to add. Our uncle Arpad, Father's brother, often teased us like this. "Noooooo," Sally said.

"Were you eating blueberry pancakes?" Audrina added.

"Nooooo."

"Blueberry muffins?"

"No! I had Apple Jacks!" She flapped her arms as she spoke. "My fingers are blue from chalk!"

"Really!" Audrina feigned surprise like one of those actresses from the old-time black-and-white movies our parents watched on the VCR late at night, spreading her hand widely against her forehead and tossing her head back, nearly knocking Mother's wide-brimmed straw hat from her head. I wondered whether she had asked to borrow the hat or just helped herself.

Sally bent down and jabbed at the driveway with both hands. "Did you see the Rapunzel I drawed?" she asked. *Blueberry pie,* I thought. I should have asked her if she ate blueberry pie that morning. But the moment was gone; we gathered to inspect the drawing and muttered some oohs and aahs.

"Drina," I said in a quiet voice. "Did you give Sally your bracelet?"

"Yep."

"B-but *I* liked it," I sputtered. I couldn't believe it. Audrina had to have known how much I liked—no, *loved*—the jeweled box charm. I would often ask her if I could try her bracelet on, or at least if I could open the jeweled box. To give it to someone else, someone she barely knew, someone—*anyone*—other than her own sister, was insensitive. Wrong. "Why—why would you do that?" I said, in a more accusatory tone than I had intended, and I saw Audrina flinch.

"Welllll," she said, drawing out the word. "I guess I didn't know boys liked bracelets," she finally snapped back loudly enough for Max and Sally to hear, as she stared pointedly at my Cosmos soccer shirt.

"Are you a boy?" Sally asked in a curious tone, her eyes darting from the top of my head down to my feet.

I grew hot inside as I took a few steps away, onto the edge of the damp grass, which immediately engulfed my ankles. The Bakers didn't keep their lawn trimmed like the rest of us. Max had once explained that they didn't have a yard in Boston.

"No, no, of course not," I said, with an awkward laugh. "Audrina was just joking."

Just then, the front door opened, and Mrs. Baker materialized, wearing a silky floral purple-and-teal beach cover-up and carrying some towels. She tossed the towels into the back of the station wagon and instructed, "Max, go get the beach chairs."

Max walked over to the garage to carefully extract the folded chairs that were leaning against the inside wall, next to the Porsche I'd heard Father talk about with envy. I'd never seen Dr. Baker driving it—he left for work before I woke up and returned late. He must've still been home that morning. I was curious if Max ever rode in it; Mother had pointed out a Porsche was "useless" for a family, since it had only two seats.

We hopped into the station wagon—Max in the front passenger seat, and Sally in the middle back seat sandwiched between Audrina and me. The whole ride to the lake I studied the bracelet hanging from Sally's wrist. Sally twisted and tugged it, running her pink chipped nails over the cabled links and charms—a key, a heart, a bell, a flower, a star, a moon, and of course, the jeweled box. I knew every single one of those charms.

Mother had also bought me something "special" for Christmas the year Audrina received her bracelet, but it hadn't been a bracelet, or even a piece of jewelry. It was a New York Yankees jersey: Don Mattingly, number 23. "He's a lefty, like you," she'd said, as if that had explained everything. I was surprised; Mother had always created such thoughtful, personalized gift baskets for friends when they had momentous life occasions, like birthdays and anniversaries and showers. Indeed, Mrs. Wiley sometimes paid Mother to put one together so she could pass it along to someone else as a gift. But Mother's assessment of my interest in baseball was skewed. I couldn't remember ever saying I liked baseball, and I certainly had never played it—or softball—at least not on an organized team. So it seemed to me that the only reason my mother had chosen the jersey was because I was a freakish lefty, like Don, and because, since I was less *pipiske* than Audrina, I should like things like sports and sport paraphernalia more than—or even instead of—jewelry. But I liked both. To spare Mother's feelings, I'd pretended to be happy about the jersey and had even worn it occasionally—just around the house— so Mother would see. But then I stuffed it in the back of our closet, behind the suitcases we never used.

It took about fifteen minutes to get to Deer Chase Lake from our houses. Main Street eventually turned into Route 108, from which spit the turnoff for the lake's small dirt parking lot. The lake was located upon a hill, and it had a sandy beach, a fact I found ironic since the lake was as still as pool water, not at all like the ocean.

But surrounding the lake were dense woods, the trees so tall and busy that I'd once had the thought, as I stood on the lake's perimeter, that the lake itself was a sort of beach for the vast woods that crowned it. It was the kind of forest that seemed to hold secrets, that made you a bit dizzy if looked at too closely, or too long.

As soon as Mrs. Baker's station wagon chugged up to Deer Chase Lake, we could tell it was crowded, because there were no more open spots in the parking lot. Cars had now begun to line the road. Mrs. Baker pulled behind the last parked car, and we tumbled out to race up the stairs that led to the lake.

As we neared the top, summer sounds circled us like a swarm of bees. Children screaming and laughing, water being splashed, dogs barking, a cautionary two-whistle beep from the lifeguard's stand. I looked out to the lake, which appeared like a giant, nearly too-full bowl of water. People bobbed up and down, their bodies in constant motion. Kids raced in and out of the lake, chasing one another. In the far distance I saw two people swimming back toward the beach; they were much farther out than everyone else. That must have been the reason for the whistle blow, I realized.

The beach was shortened because of the recent storm, but we still managed to find a good spot not too far from the water. Mrs. Baker flung open her chair and angled it toward the sun, which meant facing a section of woods. She plopped down without stripping to her bathing suit and began fanning herself with her book. "Go ahead and play, kiddos. Keep an eye on your sister, Max."

I was secretly hoping that Mrs. Baker would remove her cover-up so I could see the way she looked in her bathing suit. Sometimes when it got really, really hot, she cooled off with a brief swim, though most of the time she was content to lounge in one of her colorful cover-ups, some of which looked more like fancy bathrobes than swimwear. She loved sunning herself, and I'd recently noticed that the inside of her arm—where the fat rolled over—was whiter than the rest of it. It was like the skin underneath my bathing suit, where the sun didn't hit. It always amazed me how skinny both Dr. Baker and Max were in comparison—like two tall asparagus. Even Sally, though sturdy, was not overweight. Once, when I'd asked Mother about Mrs. Baker's weight, she told me it wasn't nice to talk about such things and that everyone was created differently. Whether or not I brought it up again, I still thought about it. It was hard not to. It shames me now, how I thought about Mrs. Baker's size, how I viewed her as a curious aberration, though I tell myself my fascination was because of what eventually came to be.

Whenever our own mother took us to swim, I would marvel at how beautiful she looked. She favored a navy one-piece suit underneath an oversized Ralph Lauren white men's button-down bought at the outlet stores. Mother was glamorous like an actress, her eye-brows arched like perfect rainbows over circular, wide-set eyes. She often wore big glasses that someone said were like "Jackie O." At the time I didn't know who that was, but what I did know was that Mother's sunglasses seemed to protrude more than they should because they rested on two pronounced mounds of cheekbones. I wanted to be like her when I grew up, beautiful and elegant, but it wasn't looking so good. I'd inherited Father's large ears, which stuck out on either side of my head, and my recent short haircut did little to hide them.

Audrina had Mother's enviable cheekbones, though my sister would have been beautiful even without them. People liked looking at her, and they also liked being around her (I'd come to realize these things were connected), seemingly more so than being around me. The exception was my friend Leah. We were nearly the same exact age—April babies, born just a day apart—and had shared the same homeroom class for as long as we both could remember. I often felt like Leah looked up to me the way others looked up to Audrina: She'd bought the same pink jelly shoes as me; she began fastening a beaded safety pin onto the laces of her Keds once I started to. What I liked the most, though, was that she never seemed fazed when my sister was around. During the school year, Leah and I were inseparable, but Leah spent her summers in California with her father, where he now lived; her parents had gotten divorced when we were in fourth grade.

Sally began building a sandcastle "for Rapunzel," and Audrina took off toward the lake without me, while Max—after a brief hesitation and look in my direction—followed her. I frowned. Was Audrina still annoyed that I'd questioned her about giving Sally the bracelet? I felt I had more of a right to be upset, given the *boy* comment. Or maybe she was just being Audrina, doing whatever she wanted to do without considering me at all. I entered the water alone, letting my body bob in the gentle waves created by the other swimmers, while tears pooled in my eyes. No matter how many times I told myself I wouldn't let my sister get to me, she did. I still didn't understand why she would've given Sally the bracelet; had she done it *because* she knew I'd wanted it?

Then I heard Max yell out, "Hey, Bee! We're over here!" as he waved his hands in the air. I dunked underneath, so I could clear my tears, and swam over to him and Audrina. My sister grinned and splashed me with water, and I forcefully splashed her back. Audrina just laughed, and the edges around us softened, as they always did, even when I was sure they couldn't. We continued to play, eventually coming into the shallow water so Sally could join us, too.

For lunch the four of us had a picnic next to Rapunzel's sandcastle, munching on hot dogs and chips from the concession stand.

"Is this the country?" Sally suddenly asked, while surveying the lake and its surroundings.

"You mean the lake?" I replied.

"Everything," she responded, waving her half-eaten hot dog in the air, and Audrina and I giggled. To us, "country" might have meant Stilkes Farm, about an hour's drive away, where our family went each fall to pick apples and pumpkins and visit the barn animals. Or it might have meant Meg's Farm, where the third-grade class traveled on a field trip to see demonstrations of sheep shearing and butter making. But it certainly didn't mean Deer Chase Lake, or Route 108, or most of our town. Later, when I started dating my husband, who lived in New York City, I would realize that all of Hammend was indeed quite rural and possibly "country."

"No, Sally," Max gently replied over our laughter, as Sally's eyes widened with embarrassment. "It's not the country. Just a small town."

Small town or not, the beach continued to fill up throughout the afternoon, the sounds and amount of people becoming almost overwhelming. Back in the lake, I began diving underwater and lingering there, enjoying the sudden hush that the sound barrier of the water provided. The only noises were a thin humming that seemed to come from the water itself and the occasional bubble that would escape from my mouth. Every time I plunged underneath, it felt like the outside world was erased. All that was left was me. The lake was murky, so I had to swim fairly blindly. Sometimes I bumped into another kid, at which point I would pop up and yelp a small "Sorry!" before disappearing again.

It was during one of these accidental bumps and quick resurfacings that I realized people were exiting the lake. Everybody, in fact. It reminded me of when the lifeguards at the pool called for "adult swim" and the kids had to exit. I was momentarily disoriented. This wasn't the pool. And no lifeguard had blown a whistle. Or maybe they had, I realized as I sloshed toward the beach. I must not have heard it because I was underwater.

There was a frantic energy in the air. Some parents were reaching for children and picking them up, like they were toys. Others were whipping their heads left and right, frazzled. The older kids were running around or bundled in towels, hopping from foot to foot. Everyone was moving; it was as if we were all still swimming but without any water. In the chaos, I struggled to locate Mrs. Baker.

And then I saw her. I was surprised to find that even she was in motion. Up from her chair—standing, looking, twisting. One of the lifeguards stood in front of her and was grabbing every little girl who ran by.

"Mrs. Baker?" I asked as I approached. Her eyes just seemed to glaze over me.

"Is this her?" the lifeguard asked, another confused girl momentarily captured in his arms.

I suddenly felt sick, knots rolling in my stomach. A cool hand touched my back. "Bee," Audrina said in a hoarse voice. "Have you seen Sally?"

I shook my head. "No." Mrs. Baker looked as white as I'd ever seen her, as if the inside of her arm where the sun didn't hit had spread like a rash. "I was swimming. Did she go swimming?"

"I dunno," Audrina said. "I was swimming, too, with Max. I saw her playing in the sand. After we ate lunch."

We both stared at the lake, now quiet, and it felt like time had momentarily paused. Then a lifeguard punctured the surface, breaking the stillness, to take a deep breath before disappearing again under the water. Max paced back and forth at the water's edge, his gaze scanning the lake. The water barrier was pierced again by an older teenage boy, and another, and then by a man, and I realized there were a lot of people blindly swimming underneath, looking for Sally.

The sound of a siren boomed in the distance, and Audrina grabbed my hand.

The beach soon became saturated with cops and firemen and paramedics. It confused me why the firemen were there. There wasn't a fire. I understood why the paramedics were there; when they found Sally, she would need help. She might need CPR, as Mr. Beatty had last summer at the pool. I still remembered the way the lifeguard pounded his chest like he was mad at him, over and over again, and then opened his mouth and kissed his lips. "Eww," the boy standing next to me said, but before we could dwell on it, Mr. Beatty coughed awake, water sputtering from his mouth.

It had been a while now since anyone had last seen Sally, and I was getting more worried. How long could people hold their breath underwater?

*Two minutes.* The answer appeared to me, unwedging itself from a weighted bedrock of knowledge. Two minutes had long passed. I remembered, suddenly, how Audrina and I had a contest the summer before to see who could hold her breath longer. I'd easily won; I had always been a better swimmer than she was. I recalled how my lungs had felt warm, and then hot, like they were on fire. So hot it was dizzying.

Another two minutes ticked by, and then another, and at some point everyone was ushered into sections, with Max, Audrina, and I making up our own grouping. Mrs. Baker, who apparently had fainted and fallen flat on her back (part of me was sorry to have missed it in the chaos), was now being administered to by a paramedic in one of the ambulances. Max sat down, his head in his hands. His hair was dusty with sand, as if someone had sprinkled flour over him. His shoulders shook, and I realized he was crying. Police Chief Riley talked to him before moving on to Audrina and me. The chief was very tall, with dark hair and a stomach that protruded well past his trousers. He wrote down everything Audrina, who did most of the talking for us, said; I felt too numb to respond.

*Where's our mother?* I wondered once Chief Riley had turned his attention elsewhere. I wanted Mother. "Is our mother coming?" I finally asked a couple of cops standing nearby, my voice cracking. I tried to figure out where the nearest pay phone might be. I visualized the numbers I would punch on the metal phone faceplate when I reached it: 543 to start—those were the same three beginning telephone numbers that every household in Hammend used, and back then you didn't need an area code—but then, instead of the four unique digits that would follow, all I could see in my mind was the square number *2. Two minutes.*

"Don't worry, honey," a kind-faced cop said, crouching down to my level. He had short, light-brown hair and S-shaped eyebrows that slanted up on the inside corners. Sweat beads dribbled down either side of his forehead. I recognized him as the cop who often directed traffic at the entrance to Foodtown supermarket, where, I realized, the closest pay phone probably was. "We're going to take you home to your mom soon. We just need to talk to a few more people. You and your sister thirsty?" He wiped his forehead with the back of his hand, and it occurred to me that he was the one who looked a little thirsty.

I nodded.

"Hey!" he yelled over his shoulder, to a couple more cops who had just arrived. "Can we get these kids somethin' to drink?"

Talking to a few more people apparently meant interviewing every single other person at the lake. And the people were multiplying by the minute. I couldn't tell who had been at the lake to begin with and who was a new arrival. More men were swimming in the lake now. Soon a boat arrived and then another, which, after being hoisted into the water, dropped what looked like ropes into the lake's depths. The cops were also now coming in and out of the woods that lined the far side of the lake. The woods were thick, and I didn't even know where they ended. I'd never been in them. I tried to visualize what was on the other side—was it the road that led to the post office? No, it couldn't be, I realized, now gazing in the opposite direction, toward the main drag, where Mrs. Baker had parked her car.

The post office was near Main Street; we'd passed it on the way. My sense of direction was off. I stared into the woods as far back as I could, noticing how the brush and trees grew thicker with distance until they melded together to form one giant, dark blob.

"Pink bathing suit with a heart, blond hair," we overheard one cop say to a mother who was standing nearby with her girls, her arms protectively wrapped around them. The one talking was Jimmy, another young cop, who had brought us a couple of Dr Peppers. I suppose we should have thought of him as Officer Fort, but he was from the neighborhood and we'd known him for years, even before he became a cop. He and his mother, who had dementia, lived a block over from us, on Oak Street, in a Tudor-style house. There were only two Tudors in our whole neighborhood, including ours. A few days earlier his barefoot mother had approached our cul-de-sac kickball game, agitated and looking for her husband, who'd passed away years ago. Mother had gently guided her back home, over her loud cussing. It was the second time she'd been found wandering in our neighborhood that summer. She wore notes pinned to her clothes that stated her address and Jimmy's number at the police station, but they weren't necessary: We all knew who she was. We knew everyone in our neighborhood.

"No, no, no, that's not right, Jimmy!" Audrina shouted at him. "She wasn't wearing a pink bathing suit! It was purple." She pumped her fist. "Like we told the other policeman."

Worry sprang inside me. The police had to get it right; if they didn't know what Sally was wearing, how could people answer correctly about whether or not they had seen her?

Jimmy glanced down at the small notepad in his hands and frowned. "Yes, yes, that's right. That's what I meant. Purple." But the mother and two daughters were already shaking their heads. The girls were older, perhaps even high schoolers; they were not likely to have noticed a little girl playing in the sand. The kids I paid attention to were always older than I was.

Max, who hadn't moved from his spot in the sand, as if his bottom were glued to it, was now shaking more violently, and soon we could hear his sobs. "Don't worry, Max," Audrina said, slinging her arm around his back, and yet again I wished I knew how to act in situations like my sister did. I was the older one; I should have been the one comforting Max. "We'll find her," Audrina said. "She'll be okay."

Max lifted his head, and I saw that his face was splotchy, with red patches like a rash. "We should've—" He tried to finish, but his cries engulfed him. "We should've," he tried again, "been with her. I should've been watching her. It's my fault."

Audrina and I exchanged glances. We didn't say anything; we didn't know what to say. In a way he was right, although we all should have been watching her. But something didn't seem to add up. Sally never went into the water without us, and when she did, she only went just a little bit, so the water barely covered her knees. And why would she wander into the woods? There was nothing there.

The afternoon sun was now shining down with unabashed force, and I was beginning to feel dizzy. Some of the people whom the cops had talked to were now leaving, so I took the opportunity to wander away from where we had originally set up camp on the beach. Every few feet, I paused and looked around, as if I were expecting Sally to suddenly materialize. But all I saw were groups of people herding together, and a dozen cops moving about, their mouths firing into walkie-talkies. There was a remnant of a sandcastle I almost knocked over, and I wondered whether it was the one Sally had been working on earlier—it was hard to tell where exactly we'd been sitting now that everyone had moved around. I searched for Mrs. Baker's chair. Maybe it had been packed up. The ground beneath my feet was turning rougher, rockier, as I edged away from the lake, in the direction of the porta potties stationed next to the woods.

Suddenly I stepped on something sharp. Bending down, I picked it up. It was the charm bracelet, or part of it. A few links, from which were hanging three charms: the star, the key, and finally, the jeweled box.

I couldn't believe it; I'd wished so hard for that jeweled box, and now there it was. I glanced up; I didn't see anyone, so I slipped the bracelet piece under the elastic side of my bathing suit, against the skin of my hip. My heart was thumping against my chest as I swiftly walked to the area where my swim bag lay. I pulled up my shorts to cover the jewelry's bulge in the lower part of my suit, while telling myself: *I'm taking this for Sally, to return to her when she is found. That's all.*

# Chapter Two

It didn't occur to me at first that the bracelet might yield information about Sally. It was only a couple days later—after the kind-faced cop who directed traffic at the supermarket drove Audrina and me home from the lake; after I put the bracelet in my hiding spot, the small recessed space behind the toe-kick board of the dresser in our room; after the lake was dragged and the woods searched again and again by the cops; after we realized Sally had indeed vanished—that I realized I might hold a clue to her disappearance. A flyer with a picture of Sally, her measurements ("height: 40 inches, weight: 50 pounds"), appearance ("blond hair, blue eyes, pierced ears"), date of birth ("Nov 3, 1980") and a description of what she was last seen wearing ("purple bathing suit with a heart on the front and a gold charm bracelet on her left wrist") was slipped in our mailbox. In the picture, she was smiling, her hair pulled up on either side with bow tie barrettes. "Missing since Thursday, July 25th, 1985. Last seen at 2 p.m., at Deer Chase Lake. Persons Having Any Information Are Required To Call."

"What do they mean, any information?" I asked Mother, after studying the flyer that my sister had taped to the fridge, as if it were one of our art projects. In the days since Sally's disappearance, Hammend had shut, suddenly, almost with a sense of finality, the way my father snapped together his Robert Ludlum hardcovers when he was done reading the final page. The lake closed, our neighborhood kickball games halted, playdates were put on hold. Even Father was home, except when he left to help out with the search parties. What at first had been a mobilization of sorts led to an unspoken lockdown— every kid needed to be home, to be accounted for. It was as if we were under siege, hedged in by fear. Our parents told us it *wasn't safe* to be outside until we knew more. *Not safe* were two words that we kids were used to associating more with things like hot stoves and running with your hands in your pockets than with general life in our five-thousand-person town.

Mother paused scrubbing the island counter to eye the flyer. She tended to clean whenever she got worked up about something. "If anyone sees anything, honey," she replied. Lately our whole house looked like one of those homes on the covers of the *House Beautiful* magazines she occasionally bought at Mortenson's Drug Store: Our light oak kitchen cabinets smelled faintly of vinegar, the cleaning solution Mother used as her go-to, and the tan tile floors looked as immaculate as the cream-speckled Formica countertops she kept scrubbing invisible dirt off of. The mustard carpeting in the adjacent family room had precise vacuum lines stamped across it: long rows that extended from one mauve wall to the brick fireplace wall opposite it, even underneath the glass octagonal coffee table. I knew the Oriental fringe rug that lay in the foyer had been just as meticulously vacuumed, though you couldn't see the lines. We were not allowed to touch the large front-facing dining room window, which Mother had recently cleaned after finding smudges from our fingers on the glass, nor were we allowed to untie the gold braided ropes of its blue-and-pink floral double curtains, which matched the wallpaper border circling the room's perimeter.

Mother finished wiping the countertop and then added, "If anyone sees anything out of the ordinary."

"How is anyone going to see anything out of the ordinary," I asked, somewhat rhetorically, "when no one is even allowed outside?"

"Or if anyone remembers anything," she replied.

"Like what?" I pressed. I glanced out the kitchen French door, whose light oak frame matched the cabinets Father had built, like most of the cabinetry in our house. We had an awning-covered deck, also Father's creation, and beyond that was a small public pond that attracted smelly ducks in the summer and ice-skaters in the winter. I'd suggested to Sally and Max just a few weeks earlier, when they'd stopped by one Sunday morning and were peering outside at the pond, that we all go ice-skating come winter. Sally had started clapping her hands and stamping her feet, and Father, who emerged from his study to see what the commotion was about, said to her, with some amusement, "Do you even know how to ice-skate?"

Sally just frowned, like she had to think about it, and Max jumped in for her, "She's never been."

"Let me see those feet of yours," Father had replied, grinning.

Sally had stuck one foot out in front, balancing on the other, and Father peered down to look at it in an exaggerated manner, checking all around. "These look like some ice-skating feet to me," Father declared, while a trickle of jealousy worked itself through me—it was hard enough for me to get Father's attention. Maybe I'd just never been sufficiently cute like Sally or my sister. "We will just have to teach her," Father added.

I couldn't believe that conversation had been just weeks ago.

"I don't know what they would've seen. Perhaps a sighting of her, in the aftermath. Or an article of clothing." Mother shuddered and then glanced at me, as if worried she had said too much.

"She was only wearing her bathing suit and bracelet," I pointed out, stopping myself from regurgitating the word *purple* listed on the flyer. In my mind, *violet* was a much better word choice. Violet, after all, was what Crayola called the color. "So do you mean one of those two?"

Mother sighed. She was also sighing a lot these days. Sighing and cleaning. "Yes, I suppose I do."

Now I shuddered, the impact of what I'd taken at the lake finally beginning to sink in. My mother, her back turned to me while she scrubbed the front of the oven, didn't see my movement. "But why would they need to know that information?"

"It could hold a clue about what happened to her."

"What do they think happened to her?" The words were thick and difficult to get out. It was the question I'd been wanting to ask since Sally's disappearance a couple days earlier.

I braced myself for her answer, tensing, but Mother simply cleared her throat and said, "They don't know what happened to her. We don't know."

I frowned, unsure whether to believe her. When Father and Mother didn't want to divulge what they really thought, they claimed it was "grown-up business," which is what seemed to be going on now. There was an undercurrent I could sense—a silent uncertainty in the way they folded their arms, in the terse telephone conversations they had with neighbors, in the repeated glances out the window when there was nothing to see, or nothing new at least.

"Mother," I said, my voice shaking slightly, as I glanced again at the flyer on the fridge. "What would happen if someone knew something and they didn't say anything? Like if they found something of hers? Like one of those two things she was wearing?"

"Well, honey," my mother replied as she finally turned to look at me, "that would just be wrong."

"Why do you want to know, Bee?" my sister asked, suddenly appearing next to me, and I startled.

"Just because," I shot back, and then I added in a softer tone, worrying my response might have seemed suspicious, "I'm trying to understand how the police are going to find her. I just want to know what it all means."

Mother nodded thoughtfully, and I slunk away to our room so I could think. It was hard those days to gather my thoughts; my sister and I had shared a room forever, so privacy was scarce.

Although it was midday, and my bed was already made—my Laura Ashley bedsheets tucked in with sharp hospital corners the way Mother had taught me—I now tugged them loose and crawled in, pulling the covers over my head. The cocoon I'd created warmed with my recycled breath. What to do about the bracelet? I knew, had the situation been reversed—had I given Sally a bracelet that my sister then discovered at the lake—she never would have taken it. She would have promptly turned it over. She would never even think to have a hiding spot behind the toe kick of our dresser.

But it was done now. I'd taken it. *That would just be wrong.* It had been wrong—I saw that now—but I couldn't undo it. And I couldn't admit it; I'd be in so much trouble. It was too late. Now there was even documented evidence of what I'd done, the words on the flyer: *a gold charm bracelet on her left wrist.*

I scrunched my eyes, the way I saw Father do when he was trying to solve a problem. I'd found the bracelet not far from where Mrs. Baker's beach chair had been, I thought. Somewhere in the direction of the porta potties. No surprise there; that was where we'd all been playing, and I recalled Sally having used the porta potty that day. That wouldn't have been news to a policeman.

*So they don't need to know,* I decided, as I pulled the covers down from around my face to meet the cool air blowing from the wall vent. The sensation felt good, like a pressing on of reality.

Our parents weren't the only close-lipped ones in the neighborhood. Audrina and I had gotten on the phone with Andrew and Patrick a few times after our mothers were done chatting, but we'd soon realized there was not much to talk about. The Wiley brothers were also on house restriction and didn't know any more than we did. I began poring over the newspaper each day, but it simply reiterated the same, skeleton details we already knew: "A four-year-old has disappeared at Deer Chase Lake . . . The first time in Hammend's history . . . No leads . . . Police are conducting an investigation . . ." Even Diane and Courtney, the older private school girls who lived in adjacent houses on the top of our street, and who seemed to generally possess more knowledge about the world than they should, had no helpful gossip to offer.

In fact, Diane had tried to pump *me* for information when I answered her call.

"You and Audrina were there?" she'd asked, in an audacious whisper that seemed to imply that my sister and I were privy to some secret, not-yet-disclosed information. "I told Courtney we should've gone to the lake that day, but she insisted on the club." She sighed, almost regretfully. She and Courtney usually spent all their time together. "Because this kid James that she likes was supposed to be there. He wasn't, though. And she shouldn't even like him. He has a girlfriend!" she exclaimed. "Anyway," she continued, before I could respond, "I can't believe this. You have to tell me *everything* that happened that day. Everything." And then she added, almost as an afterthought, "Poor Sally."

"There's not much to tell," I said, and relayed the sequence of events that had occurred. When I got to the part of the story where I'd found the charm bracelet piece, I hesitated. I found myself with the urge to tell Diane, even though I didn't *really* want to. It was just, I realized, that I wanted to tell *someone*. The secret was getting heavier each day.

Diane cut into my thoughts, backtracking on the timeline to ask me a question she'd already asked, "Wait, so the last time you saw her was after lunch, next to the sandcastle?"

"Yeah," I replied. And the moment was gone; there was, of course, no reason to tell Diane—or anyone—about the bracelet. Besides, Diane was much more interested in the details of what had happened right before Sally went missing. That, and discussing the local television news van that was parked across the street from my house, which Diane couldn't see from the upper bend of the street.

"Yep," she confirmed, after pressing me to describe the van: white, medium-sized, blue and black lettering. "That's the same one I saw circling around. Not as often as it did yesterday, though. Did you see when the Bakers were on the news?"

"Yeah." I tried to sound nonchalant. I didn't want to reveal how it had secretly thrilled me at first when it occurred, how in fact I had run to grab Audrina to show her. My sister, too, had seemed excited, a slow, satisfied smile spreading over her face. We'd gotten so close to the TV that Mother, who had also come in to watch—likely alerted by whatever neighbor had just rung—told us we were going to hurt our eyes if we didn't move back a few feet. The reporter—the very one we'd spotted from our window earlier that day—was standing on the street in front of the Bakers' house, microphone in hand, reviewing the details of Sally's disappearance. Then the footage cut to Sally's picture from the flyer, and then to Deer Chase Lake, from the road, where four police cars and a few sedans were parked along the bank. Then back to the Bakers' house, where Dr. Baker stood on the front steps, alone, as he made a statement that had wiped the smile off Audrina's face and made me feel like I wanted to cry: "I'm the father of Sally Baker, who's been missing since Thursday afternoon from Deer Chase Lake. Sally is four and a half years old, with blond hair and blue eyes. If anyone has any information about Sally or has seen her, or even thinks they have seen her, please call the Hammend police or the missing children's toll-free hotline." Here he glanced down at a piece of paper he was holding. "The number is 1-800-THE-LOST. That's 1-800-843-5678. I'm—we, my wife and I—are prepared to offer a substantial reward for any information leading to the safe return of Sally." His voice broke, and he took a moment to compose himself before continuing: "Sally, if you are watching this, I just want you to know that Mommy and Daddy love you, and we won't stop looking for you."

"My parents thought it was kind of weird that Mrs. Baker didn't make an appearance," Diane confided.

"Oh yeah, us, too," I replied, even though we hadn't talked about it in my house, nor had it occurred to me that it might be weird. Now I wondered if it was indeed strange.

"But that's just like her, I guess. Remember how she didn't come to the Wileys' barbecue?"

Diane meant the Wileys' annual Fourth of July backyard barbecue, held just three weeks earlier. Most of the neighborhood usually went, or at least stopped by, and this year had been no exception: Among the attendees were Diane and Courtney and their families, the Garfields, the Johnsons, the Abbotts, and briefly, Officer Jimmy and his mother—until she'd yelled "Bitch!" at an aghast Mrs. Abbott, which might've been funny if we hadn't felt sorry for Jimmy. My whole family, of course, had gone for the entire time. As the Bakers were the newest to the neighborhood, everyone was anticipating their arrival. But only Dr. Baker, Max, and Sally had showed up, leaving the other parents to wonder what Mrs. Baker was so busy doing on a Saturday afternoon.

"Yeah, she wasn't there," I said.

"How many times have you seen the police drive up and down our street?" Diane continued. "I counted eight times yesterday. Or at least eight times that it went by on Oak." The front of Diane's house faced Oak Street, even though her driveway emptied onto Hickory Place.

"Uh, I don't know. A lot."

"But if you had to guess," she pressed.

I really had no idea how to respond, so I just picked a number. "Uh, ten, maybe?"

"Wow. You have the best view." She sounded envious, and I vowed to pay more attention to that metric. I was glad, suddenly, that I'd been the one—not Audrina—to answer the call.

It occurred to me then that Diane might also ask to speak with her, and so I quickly added, to keep her interest, "There's a cop there now, at the Bakers' house."

"Really?" Diane asked, her voice raising.

"Yeah, Officer Lark." I was feeling more important by the second. "He's been there for a while. Yesterday, too. My parents said it's probably just standard procedure, so they can communicate with the family and stuff." I always remembered Officer Lark's name because it rhymed with *park*.

"Oh," Diane replied, sounding disappointed I didn't have juicier details to disclose.

I didn't think what I had revealed to Diane about that day at the lake had been all that exciting, or insightful, but a few minutes after we hung up, Courtney called—clearly alerted by Diane that we had chatted—and asked me to tell her everything I'd just said to Diane. She, too, was especially interested in the last moments I'd seen Sally.

They had such different reactions than Leah. "I'm so sorry, Bee," she said the first time we spoke—shortly after Diane's and Courtney's calls—as the line crackled. "I wish I could be there. California feels so far away. My mom told me everything, so you don't need to. But if you do—do want to talk about it—I'm here."

"Thanks, Leah," I replied. But strangely enough, I didn't want to talk about it, at least not with her. My reticence surprised me; I'd always turned to Leah with any problems, and she'd always faithfully listened. And it was often I who had the problems, and she the listening ears. Truth be told, our friendship had historically leaned in my favor. Neither of us was part of the popular crowd of girls at school, but Leah usually acted more awkward than I did in social situations. I supposed I held a little edge over her, the way Audrina held an edge over me. But right then I didn't want a supportive reaction from Leah. What I wanted was to be sought out—to feel *important*—the way Diane and Courtney had made me feel.

I was beginning to realize that there was an unexpected power in being associated with a missing girl.

There were a couple more individuals who wanted to discuss Sally further with us: Officers Dittmer—who'd driven us home from the lake—and Jimmy. They appeared early on our doorstep one morning, dressed in their blue uniforms, which seemed loose on Officer Dittmer but perfectly fit Jimmy's broad frame. Officer Dittmer held out the newspaper he'd picked up at the bottom of our driveway, as if it were a prize.

I watched from the banister of the second-floor landing. It was a good spot to see people coming and going from our house without being noticed.

"Thanks," Father said as he took the newspaper, but I knew he was anything but thankful. He liked to get the paper himself, usually after he put on a pot of coffee, and then would read the paper in depth before beginning his day.

"We know it's been a rough few days," Jimmy said, as they stepped into the foyer, his short, reddish hair shining in the light, "but we just need to ask the girls a few more questions."

I shifted toward the opposite side of the landing, which was open to our family room below, so I could continue watching as the officers settled into chairs opposite the fireplace. Crouching down, I kept a low profile.

"Coffee?" Mother asked, as if this were a normal house visit.

"Please," Jimmy replied, while Officer Dittmer said, "Yeah, thanks."

"I'll get them," Father said as Mother disappeared into the

kitchen. Father moved back into the foyer and called up the stairs, "Audrina! Bee!"

"Coming!" my sister replied, in a loud voice, from our bedroom.

Even though I knew I'd have to make an appearance in a moment, I stayed put, curious to see what the officers would do once left alone.

Jimmy cracked his knuckles while Officer Dittmer glanced around our family room. Then Jimmy rose to approach our fireplace; he scanned the pictures on the mantel, and seemed to pause for a moment on the one of Audrina and me on our front lawn. I wondered if it was making him think of our neighborhood, of how it was *before*—when the idea of a missing girl was once inconceivable.

"Audrina! Bee!" Father yelled again, this time louder, and I heard our bedroom door open, and a moment later, my sister flew past me.

When Audrina and I took a seat on the couch, Officer Dittmer gave us a friendly smile that extended his S-shaped eyebrows into more of a gentle wave. Jimmy simply nodded over to us, his freckled face fixed in a solemn expression.

Father stood in the entranceway that led to the kitchen, his arms crossed. I noticed an uncharacteristic peppered-brown stubble on his face; normally he was so clean-shaven. Mother, meanwhile, scurried back and forth from the kitchen, bringing first the coffees, then cream and sugar, even though they'd said plain black coffee was just fine. Father finally put his hand on Mother's arm when she passed through a third time, carrying napkins. Mother nodded and then slid onto the couch on the far side of my sister and me, the napkins tightly clenched in her fist.

"So, um, we're going door-to-door, just trying to talk with all the neighbors," Officer Dittmer started, and then glanced down at his battered-looking notebook before he continued, "to get a sense of who Sally is and anything that might help us to find her."

Jimmy, too, had flipped open a notebook, but his, in contrast, looked nearly brand-new. Although I guessed both officers to be in their twenties, Officer Dittmer seemed younger, perhaps because he appeared less self-assured. Jimmy had always been so serious, which I'd just assumed was because he had to deal with his mother. It was interesting how personality and confidence could make you seem older. I was sure that to an outsider, Audrina appeared to be the older one.

"Girls?" Father prompted us.

"Yes," I replied, while at the same time, Audrina said, "Okay."

"And we wanted to review again what happened at the lake," Officer Dittmer said, while clicking his ballpoint pen on and off, "just to make sure we're not missing anything, and, um, I understand you guys were friends, so I wanted to find out more about that."

Audrina and I exchanged glances; we weren't sure how to respond. A few awkward moments passed, and then Father said, "Officer Dittmer and Jim—Officer Fort—it might be best if you ask the girls specific questions."

A flush crept up Officer Dittmer's neck, while Jimmy cut in to concede, in an even tone, "Good idea. Well, I know you already told Chief Riley at the lake that day what happened, and we don't want to make you rehash that, so is there anything else about that day that seemed unusual?"

"No," Audrina promptly declared, while a lump formed in my throat. Here, now—unexpectedly so—was my chance to reveal the charm bracelet. I wasn't prepared, though. I hadn't known that this opportunity would present itself. My heart raced. Was this the perfect situation to reveal what I'd done, to pretend I hadn't yet realized the bracelet's significance, or was it the worst situation? I swallowed, trying to think of what to say, how to begin. *If* to begin.

But before I could say anything, Jimmy nodded and said, "Okay," while Officer Dittmer scribbled something down.

"And I understand that you became friends with Sally just this summer?" Officer Dittmer asked, after reviewing the loose-leaf page peeking out of his notebook. There was text written on it, but I couldn't make out the words from where I sat.

I glanced at Father, still standing with his arms crossed, his face stern. Would he be angry, if I revealed this information now, that I hadn't told him first? Would I be embarrassing him, our family? My heart was beating so fast it made me feel a little breathless. I opened my mouth, but no words emerged. Then Audrina said, after a glance at me, "Well, Sally just moved here this summer."

"Answer the question, girls," Father instructed.

"But they already know that," my sister protested. "Especially Jimmy."

"Show some respect, Audrina. And it's Officer Fort," Father reminded her.

My sister had a point, though. Jimmy knew this, of course, from living in the neighborhood.

"It's okay, Mr. Kocsis. This is"—Jimmy gestured to their notebooks, and I noticed how the freckles that were scattered all over his face also extended down his arms—"what they tell us to ask, but these questions do seem redundant. We'll try to hurry it up. What's next on the list, Chuck?"

"Does she have other friends that you know?" Officer Dittmer asked.

We both shook our heads, and as the thumping in my chest slowed, I thought how the moment to say anything about the bracelet had passed. Later, I decided. I could tell my parents about the bracelet later, once Jimmy had left.

Office Dittmer pressed, "Did she mention other people?"

"Other people?" Mother questioned, and Father admonished her, "Shh. Let them do their job."

"Yeah, um. Other people," Officer Dittmer replied, as he scratched his forehead, which was beginning to acquire a shine. "Like friends or acquaintances or someone she might have mentioned a lot."

The word *acquaintances* hung awkwardly in the air, until Audrina pointed out, with her hands palmed outward, "Acquaintances? She's four."

"Audrina!" Father interjected, as the flush returned to Officer Dittmer's neck and now traveled up to his face. "Girls, you need to answer the question. Did Sally have friends that she mentioned?"

"No," my sister said, and I thought she'd answered for both of us until I realized that Father was waiting for me to reply as well.

"No," I added.

"Jimmy, are you two solely responsible for going through our whole neighborhood?" Father inquired. "Door by door?"

"No, no, Mr. Kocsis. We're all taking a section."

"Peter Emm—Officer Emmon, I mean—has Oak Street," Officer Dittmer piped in, "and Officer Lark is taking Maple. Me and Jimmy have Hickory."

"Ah," Father said.

Meanwhile, I took a peek at Mother; I knew she hated when people used incorrect pronouns. She hadn't moved a muscle on her face. Instead, she was tearing off pieces of the napkin in a slow and methodical manner. Audrina noticed this as well and nudged me with her leg, jutting her chin in Mother's direction. I smiled; my sister and I often bonded over Mother's peculiar habits. Audrina then coughed to cover an emerging laugh, and I had to quickly look away in the opposite direction so I wouldn't start giggling.

This small moment of comedic relief loosened any remaining tension I might've had about the bracelet. The truth was, I didn't want to tell Father about the bracelet *at all*; I was afraid I would be in serious trouble. Perhaps I could just wait and see what happened over the days to come.

"So, um," Officer Dittmer started again. He flipped through the notebook, as if he were trying to figure out what else to say. The only sound was the ticking of the grandfather clock, from the hall, and the turning of pages. "So . . ."

"So, why don't the girls think about it," Father said, with a hint of impatience, "and if they remember anything, we'll be sure to call you." He stuck his arm out and waved it in a gentle but ushering motion toward the front of our house.

"Yeah, yeah, that sounds great," Officer Dittmer said, flashing Father a grateful smile, as he closed the notebook and stood up.

Jimmy also rose. "Thank you."

"You're welcome," Mother said as she got up to see them out. "Jimmy, how's your mom doing?"

"Oh, she's having a tough time lately. Thanks again for bringing her home the other day . . ." Jimmy's voice began to fade as they moved toward the front door.

"Lord help us," Father said to himself, exasperated.

My sister and I looked at each other with widened eyes, unsure whether to be amused or alarmed.

We heard the door shut, and then Mother, who had reentered the family room, stood with a puzzled look. "Don't you think it's kind of odd they're sending around amateur cops for something so serious?"

"They're young," Father conceded, "but they're all amateur here.

It's not their fault. They're more used to handing out speeding tickets and breaking up high school parties than handling real crime."

*Real crime.*

Long after the police left, I kept wondering what Father had meant by that phrase. What did the police—and my parents—really think had happened to Sally?

I continued to contemplate this into the evening, when Father entered our room—the squeak of the door handle startling me, though Audrina remained fast asleep. Mother always said Drina and I were too rough with the handle; apparently it didn't used to make noise, but I couldn't remember a time when it didn't.

In the doorway Father simply stood, a dark, quiet silhouette against the dim hallway light, and I sat up in bed, slightly alarmed.

"Father?" I whispered.

His large shape made his way toward me, sinking down at the foot of my bed. "Borka," he simply replied.

"Is everything okay?" I asked, peering at him. His features appeared distorted, the dull light creating strange shadows. His nose looked too long, his ears too small. Then, gradually, his face righted itself.

"You don't ever go wandering off with anyone, you hear me, Bee?" he said, his accent suddenly thick. I had noticed that usually happened when emotions rippled through him, which he would quickly flatten.

I grasped the edge of my blanket. "What?"

"It's important you understand never to walk off with someone."

"Like a stranger?"

"Like anyone. Do you understand?"

"Okay," I said, wondering if he'd learned some new information.

"I'm going to tell the same thing to your sister," Father said. "It's important. Bad things can happen."

The next morning, I was mulling over all Father had said when I overheard Mother whispering on the phone, I supposed to Mrs. Wiley like usual. I was lurking in the hall, outside the living room, where Mother was likely curled up on the teal velour sofa.

"Janet said there was that weird guy who was painting her neighbor's place, and then he disappeared the day after Sally went missing," Mother said softly. "She went to the police about it but hasn't heard anything since."

A pause—and then Mother said, "Oh, really? That guy—the painter—was Bill's nephew? Bill from the fire department? Ooooh. Someone should tell Janet." Mother was silent for a few seconds, and then added, "Well, I will say this: My childhood friend Tessie, her brother-in-law is a detective in New York, and he said, in his experience, most murders are committed by someone the victim knows."

I inhaled loudly—louder than I had intended—so I quickly covered my mouth and held my breath. Is that what Mother—and people—really thought? That Sally had been *murdered*? And by someone she'd *known*? The horror of that possibility chilled me. Mother continued to chat, so I knew she hadn't heard my gasp. As I slowly exhaled, I reasoned: But if Sally had been murdered, wouldn't there be a body? She was still just *missing.* And it had been only a few days; there was still hope.

But *real crime* continued to weave its way into my consciousness, surfacing again a couple days later, when Mother surprised Audrina and me by gifting us with a set of diaries. She stuck them in new personalized school canvas totes that she placed on the foot of our beds (though, to my disdain, she'd unfortunately decided to use my full name, Borka, since Father usually preferred it). Our backpacks from the previous school year still had fully functioning zippers and were devoid of holes, so I knew this was an attempt on Mother's part to distract us.

My diary's cover had an image of a wicker basket filled with dogs even though we didn't have any pets, and Audrina's had little baskets of flowers scattered against a pink gingham background. Each diary had a little gold lock with a key. I surmised the diaries had probably been on sale at Mortenson's Drug Store. On the inside flap Mother had written, *Dear Borka, I hope you find this useful in recording your thoughts. Love, Mother.*

I glanced over to Audrina, expecting to commiserate on the silly choice of diary covers, but she was sitting on her bed, already stooped over her own diary, her hair falling down to obscure whatever she was furiously writing. What did she have to say? Was it about Sally or one of her many friends or acting—her favorite activity—or, perhaps, even about me?

As if on cue, my sister glanced up with a smile and said, to my surprise, "Love you, sissy. I'm glad we have each other."

"Me, too," I replied, caught off guard. And then I quickly added—in case my initial response hadn't been explicit enough—"Love you, too. And I'm happy we have each other, too." Whenever Audrina showed an unusual display of tenderness toward me, I felt the need to immediately respond so she would know it was reciprocated. Sometimes those special moments between us felt a bit too tenuous, liable to drift away.

Come fall, due to our one-year age gap, my sister and I would be at different schools for the first time. Hammend had one building for kindergarten to sixth grade—which Audrina would be entering—and then another building for seventh through ninth, on the other side of town, where I—and Max—would be. How would I manage a new school on my own, without the safety net of my sister? Was this a good or bad thing? As annoyed as I got with her—and she with me—we'd always been together. The idea of change was unsettling.

I looked at my own diary; I wished there were something pleasant I could write about, something in the same vein as the cheery sentiment the dogs emoted on my cover. But my friends were few in number, my one hobby was reading books. The last thing I wanted to do was write some sort of book report. And the only words that my pen produced, when pressed against the page, were *real crime*. That, and a quick scribble over *Borka* in Mother's note, replacing it with *Bee*.

If a "real crime" had been committed—if Sally had indeed been murdered—then who had done it? The police clearly weren't doing a great job; maybe I needed to do some investigating of my own. I mentally scrolled through people Sally had known, or might've known, during her short time in Hammend. Instantly, the white-haired pharmacist who worked at Mortenson's Drug Store popped into my mind. I couldn't recall his name, but his wire-rimmed glasses were creepy, and he always dressed up as a villain around Halloween time. I wasn't sure, though, if Sally had ever had reason to meet him. There was also Michael-the-mailman, who never smiled; he'd been coming around our houses for as long as I could remember, so Sally definitely would have interacted with him. Then there was Vittorio, the curly-haired middle-aged man who worked at Russo's Pizza and *always* smiled at me in a way that made me uncomfortable. Had Sally ever met him? Surely the Bakers must have picked up a pizza from there at some point this summer.

Then Mrs. Baker's face materialized in my head. I thought of the way she just didn't seem to care what others thought. The way she was different in a sense that was both fascinating and appalling. But then I immediately shunned the thought. She might be strange, but that didn't mean anything. Besides, she was Sally's *mother.*

As I glanced down, I realized that in my diary I'd begun to make a list.

I soon found another purpose for my diary: to write down a memory that had recently resurfaced. Thinking about the gold charm bracelet had dredged up a long-ago experience I'd had, when I was about four or five years old. The memory had rattled around in my mind, loosely defined for years, and I now wanted to make sense of it, to assign it a more definite shape. It involved another piece of jewelry: silver-colored hoop earrings.

I'd found the earrings in Father's study, tucked away in his desk drawer, underneath a yellow legal pad. Small round diamonds inside a fancy box that snapped open and shut. I don't remember why I went into Father's study in the first place, other than the fact that any and all drawers then were likely part of my daily exploration. The earrings caught the light of the nearby desktop lamp, reflecting sparkles onto Father's desk blotter like tiny stars. I played with the earrings and even tried to put them on my doll's ears because mine weren't yet pierced. Time melted in the hot glare of the desktop lamp, and then I recalled the thud of Father's heavy steps entering the room, and his big hands scooping in to retrieve the earrings from me. I froze, worried I was in trouble for snooping.

"Those," he'd said, his voice deep, "are not for you."

"Are they for Mother?" I remember asking, as her birthday was in a few days. Father just ran his fingers through his light-brown hair, which he kept shorter in the front and sides than in the back, and then he put his index finger to his lips, like it was a secret.

A few weeks later, after Mother's birthday had come and gone, and I realized I'd never seen her wear the earrings—nor Father give them to her—I asked, "Where are your circle earrings?"

We were sitting together at the dinner table, and Mother heaped more salad onto her plate from the serving bowl. "Circle earrings?" she repeated, almost absentmindedly, as she picked up a stray piece of lettuce that had fallen next to her plate.

Father's eyes widened, and I smiled at him, thinking he was pleased I'd remembered to ask about his special gift. "The silver circle earrings with the little sparkles that Father got you," I replied, as I made little circles with my hands and then held them up against my ears to demonstrate. I was proud I remembered all the details.

"Borka," Father now said, giving a slight shake of his head, and a strange, uncomfortable silence followed.

"Your father returned them," Mother finally said, bitingly. "They were not wanted." And then she abruptly rose and began clearing the table, even though we'd only just begun eating.

"She, uh, she didn't like the silver color," Father said quietly so that only I could hear. His face was strained.

Later that night, after Mother had put us to bed, I heard raised voices coming from their bedroom.

In my diary, I filled two pages with description of this memory, and then, finally, I put my pen down, a sense of exhaustion overcoming me. The experience, now more demarcated, remained disappointingly just as puzzling and unsettling as it always had been.

# Chapter Three

AS THE DAYS PASSED, THE MORE I THOUGHT ABOUT THE CHARM bracelet, the less I wanted to. I wished I'd never taken it, and I knew that if I admitted what I'd done, Audrina would be upset, and it might derail the closeness she and I were beginning to experience as a result of our house confinement. And this, I realized, I coveted more than anything.

Since we had to rely on each other for entertainment, my sister and I resumed activities from years earlier. Each climb into the attic revealed forgotten-about childhood treasures for us to once again pass the time with: the pair of Cabbage Patch Kids our mother had waited three hours in the rain for at Toys "R" Us, Lite-Brite, Fashion Wheel—which Mother had bought for me but then Audrina commandeered. We made Shrinky Dinks and sugar buttons in our Betty Crocker Easy Bake Oven; we used colored string to play cat's cradle and to create friendship bracelets. There was a comfort and history in the feel and manipulation of these old toys, even the way some of them smelled, like my Strawberry Shortcake dolls. We remembered not to reach too far into the Easy Bake Oven to move the cake tin, and that while six strands were adequate to make a chevron friendship bracelet, eight were preferable for a thicker weave.

When we tired of those toys, we played games like Risk and Scrabble, which were stored in the family room media cabinet Father had engineered at Mother's request. The Scrabble game, though, had been short-lived; once I'd started to beat Audrina by a large margin, she'd begun picking at her nail polish, and as I knew it was only a matter of time before she completely lost interest, I suggested we abort.

And when we tired of all the board games, we went into the basement and dragged Mother's trunk of old, fancy dresses up the stairs to our room.

"What do you think?" Audrina asked, holding up Mother's pale blue beaded dress, the one she once wore as a bridesmaid at her best friend Tessie's wedding. It trailed a foot beyond my sister's toes. "Should I try on this or the yellow one?"

"The bridesmaid one," I replied, loving that she was asking me what I thought. And then, to be generous, I added, "It kinda makes your eyes more green."

"You think?" she said, sounding pleased, as she checked herself out in our vanity mirror, meeting my eyes in the reflection.

I remember feeling, during that time period, the magic of being sisters once more. When our worlds were still small, defined mostly by the perimeter of our yard and landscape of our rooms—before grade school had started and external friendships formed—it was just Audrina and me. "We are sisters, and sisters are we," Audrina declared once, after we'd read Dr. Seuss's *Green Eggs and Ham*. Back then we played and fought and laughed and did it all again the next hour, the next day. We tried to synchronize our breaths when we slept, sometimes in the same bed. She would decipher what I said, when Mother and Father often didn't understand—I spoke too quickly when I was younger, one word falling into the next. When we used to play hopscotch, I pretended not to see when Audrina stepped outside the line, and during hide-and-seek, she would bypass my favorite hiding spot in the coat closet at least one time before flinging open the door. One night, I abruptly changed my favorite bedtime story from *Why the Sea Is Salt* to the much shorter—and therefore less desirable—*Corduroy*, because that was her favorite, and Mother read us only one story at night.

I don't know when it all changed between us, but it did. Maybe with the onset of grade school, or when Nikki, the neighborhood girl who briefly lived in the Garfields' house, declared she only wanted to play with Audrina. Nikki—who was my age, so technically should have been *my* friend. When Nikki's mother called the house asking if just Audrina could come for a playdate, Mother informed her that her daughters always played together, and so if Nikki wanted to see Audrina, she'd have to include me, too. And so I'd trotted along on their next playdate, but then, when playing "school," Teacher Nikki designated Audrina as the star pupil and me as the dunce.

So maybe it changed between us because our world got bigger, because others were drawn to my sister in such a way that I invariably got pushed to the side. But my sister, too, was responsible for the change that occurred. Drina grew into, simply, Audrina. She became independent, or rather, independent of me. One day she just didn't feel like translating my verbal jumble to our parents, so she pretended she didn't understand me. And another day she decided to change her favorite book without consulting me, which meant that *The Nutcracker* became our nightly read, since somehow Audrina's selection had become our default choice. Sometimes she even fished out the cereal-box prize without me. She grew her list of friends like she was collecting charms on a bracelet, each one further displacing me. And all those injuries gradually thickened into a scab of hurt until, at some point, I realized there was no longer Audrina-and-me. There was Audrina. And me. And always, it seemed, in that order.

If my sister wanted something, I came to realize, she simply went after it. There was a rationality to that kind of thinking—an ambition, even—that I admired, that I wished I could aspire to. If I wanted something, I first considered the circumstances and people surrounding it—I suppose I was guided by others in my decision-making, perhaps too much so, whereas my sister had a focus, an assuredness, a singularity.

My sister had laughed that day with Nikki when I was made the dunce. Not, mind you, because she was trying to be mean, but because she simply thought it was funny. Even so, I still wished she would've had my back. If the situation were reversed, I would have stood up for her.

It's also possible that I had changed somewhat in the last few years, that previously I'd been happy to go along with whatever my sister wanted, because I thought it was what we both wanted, until it occurred to me that it wasn't.

But in those beguiling days in the aftermath of Sally's disappearance, it was once more Audrina-and-me. Sisters were we. Early childhood had transposed to the present. We saw each other with four-year-old eyes: Sally eyes. Time slowed for us, daylight starting early and ending late, the hours to play elongated. When we woke up, we'd be unsure of the day, let alone the time, but realize it didn't matter. Our present consisted—subsisted—of us. The charm bracelet piece I'd found gradually (and thankfully) became buried in the back of my mind, as did my irritation about how my sister had chosen to give it to Sally over me.

I was beginning to realize that the sentiment Audrina expressed the day we'd received our diaries—of feeling lucky to have each other—had a profound truth to it. A deep sister-love resided—*still* resided—between us, of which we both seemed grateful and cognizant.

With distractions stripped away, our relationship had returned to a more natural state—a nod to its past—and, importantly, also became more consciously nurtured. My sister began asking me questions—my opinion—like she hadn't done for quite some time, perhaps because she wanted to know but also because she knew I would like it. I was the older sister, after all.

"Do you think that Sally left with someone?" Audrina asked one evening, while we were lying in bed. I could hear the vulnerability in her words, the way they were spoken at a slightly higher octave. We'd previously circled around Sally's disappearance, but this was the first time my sister directly addressed a sinister possibility. Our bedroom light was off, and the small pocket flashlights that we'd discovered in the attic were on; we made circles and loops on the ceiling above our respective beds.

"You mean, 'an acquaintance'?" I joked, and my sister laughed. I loved when I could make her laugh. "No, I don't think so," I said. "I mean, why would she?"

"I dunno." Her response had a weight to it that only night could produce.

I propped myself up on my elbows and tried to make out her outline in the bed, across the room. I saw her fingers clasped around the flashlight. "Did Father say something to you, too?" I asked. "Tell you not to go off with people?"

"Yeah, he did."

"We were there, though, Drina. Wouldn't we have seen that? If she went off with someone?"

Audrina sighed. "I dunno," she said again. "Are there even strangers in Hammend? I feel like we know everyone, or everyone we know knows everyone. Right?"

"Yeah, I think that's right." I settled back down onto my bed.

"So you think maybe she got lost?"

"Maybe," I responded. In my mind, I recalled images of some missing children the local news had mentioned when discussing Sally's disappearance: Adam Walsh, Etan Patz, Jonelle Matthews—whose pictures we were already well acquainted with, as they had been plastered on our milk cartons the last few months. Was Sally truly "missing," like these other children? It didn't feel like it; it had been only about a week—much too soon to be thinking that way—and things like that didn't happen in Hammend, anyway.

"But if she was lost," Audrina pressed, "wouldn't she have been found by now?"

I shrugged, though I knew my sister couldn't see me in the dark. "Those woods run deep. I heard that one side of them goes all the way through Etchers." This wasn't exactly true; what I'd actually heard was Father simply mention to Mother that the woods extended farther than one would think. But I wanted to impress my sister.

"Who did you hear that from?"

I stiffened, momentarily on the defense for what seemed like a snide remark, but then I stopped myself. Audrina seemed to be genuinely asking. "I don't remember," I fibbed.

"What do you think about the bear—bear *thing*?" she asked, her voice shaking slightly, while she made an *X* with her flashlight.

She was referring to the awful rumor we'd heard, earlier that day, when Mother took us grocery shopping—our first trip out of the house—after Audrina had pleaded with her, citing boredom. In the dairy aisle we'd run into our neighbor Mrs. Abbott, who lived in the house with overgrown weeds on Oak Street.

"I heard Sally wandered off into the woods," Mrs. Abbott began in her normal volume, which was louder than most people's, and then she stepped next to Mother to finish, in a loud whisper, "and was attacked by a wild animal."

Mother's eyes grew large, and she jerked her chin toward Audrina and me.

But Mrs. Abbott went on, oblivious. "There were more black bear sightings last year than in other years—"

"Grace!" Mother interrupted, and waved at us. "The girls."

"I'm whispering," Mrs. Abbott retorted defensively.

"Grace, they can hear you."

"Well, I'm just saying what I heard," Mrs. Abbott huffed before grabbing a gallon of milk and shoving away with her cart.

"What is Mrs. Abbott saying? Did a bear eat Sally?" Audrina had asked, as we'd both stared at Mother in shock. I suddenly felt cold, although I wasn't sure if it was from being in the refrigerated aisle or from what we'd just heard. I'd already been feeling on edge from seeing the posters of Sally—all of which mentioned the charm bracelet—stationed at prominent points in the supermarket.

"No! Mrs. Abbott is a busybody that should mind her own business. C'mon," she said, and yanked us along. "You can each pick out a special cereal," she added, and although we were aware she was changing the subject, we smiled at the thought of getting a box of

Lucky Charms, Cocoa Puffs, or perhaps even Mr. T. Our mother rarely let us buy "special" cereal.

"I think it's just a silly rumor," I now said to Audrina. Though I paused to consider if Mrs. Abbott's quickness to spread such a rumor made her suspicious. Perhaps I should also add her to my suspect list? "Besides, even if a—a bear ate her, there would be"—I paused, trying to erase the mental image of such a thing before I continued— "bones. And they haven't found any."

Audrina must have shivered, her flashlight making zigzag lines on the ceiling. "Really?"

"I think so. I mean, at least that's what happens with animals that die. Remember I told you about the owl pellet we dissected in science class?" A confidence was beginning to grow in me as I clung to my explanation. "You do that in sixth grade, so you'll do it this year. It was a mouse. And there were bones," I said, as I wondered if Max had heard the bear theory. There probably weren't bears in Boston. When our family had gone to New York City, we hadn't seen any animals—just lots of people and cars and buildings. I remembered the surprise on Max's face the first time a herd of deer had lingered near our cul-de-sac kickball game.

"Gross. I don't want to dissect owl poop," Audrina remarked.

"It's not owl poop; it's an owl pellet."

"What's the difference?"

"Well, an owl regurgitates the parts of its prey it can't digest, like the bones. And hair. It's not poop; it's more like throw-up," I explained, reveling in Audrina's interest. It had been a long time since she'd wanted to hear something I had to say.

"Yeah, like I said, gross. Have you heard anything else?"

I thought about what I'd overheard Mother saying on the phone, how most murders are committed by someone the victim knows. But

I wasn't about to divulge this information to Audrina. A protective streak surged through me; I didn't want her to consider murder. My sister hadn't been attuned to the news like I had: reading the paper front to back, listening to the radio on my Walkman—trying to collect as much information as possible. While my efforts were in vain, since nothing new about Sally had been reported, I was disturbed by the vast number of missing kids in our country. The bear theory, though unsettling, was in a way more comforting, easier for me to understand. Easier for both of us to understand. I wanted Audrina to avoid contemplating the even darker possibilities like I had.

"Nope, nothing else," I replied, and I clicked my flashlight off and then back on.

"I tried to ask Mother more about what she really thought happened," Audrina said as she made a loop with her flashlight.

"Oh yeah?"

"But she was just so weird. She asked me if I wanted to bake cookies, and then, even though I said yes, she just kept rearranging the drawer where we keep the baking stuff."

I laughed. "Did you bake cookies?"

"Did you see any?"

I didn't reply, instead I just wrote the word *NO* with my flashlight. After a few moments, I said, "Have you asked Father what he thinks happened?"

"No. Do you think we should?"

I made a question mark with my flashlight. "I doubt he'll tell us what he really thinks, but we could try."

The search parties seemed to be losing steam; Father joined them less and less. Hammend was small, as were the other nearby towns; how many times could they search the same locations? *Sally, I silently asked, where are you?* Would her picture eventually end up on a milk carton, if we couldn't find her? That thought made her disappearance seem so very real. Father had been right to remind us not to walk off with someone.

"He might not know what he thinks, Drina," I added.

"Yeah, well, even if he does have a feeling, one way or the other, he'll probably just get quiet. Because he doesn't want to answer us."

It was true that Father would grow silent and still when he didn't want to respond to things, as he did when we asked him about his deceased parents or his beloved late brother, Mihály, who'd apparently died from alcoholism when I was a baby. I often wondered about the hardships Father and his family had faced as Hungarian refugees; it was like all his past difficulties were embedded so deeply inside they were impossible to unearth.

"I miss Sally," my sister said, as she drew an upside-down *U* with two dots above it. "She's so cute, the way she loves Rapunzel and dress-up. She'd love all these old toys we've been playing with. Maybe we can give them to her when she gets back."

"Yeah," I replied. "That's a great idea." But a little knot of jealousy had formed inside. These toys were ours; they belonged to us, the way our sisterhood belonged to us. I was reminded that my sister had given Sally the charm bracelet I'd so coveted. A piece of which I still had in my possession. A feeling of discomfort returned.

"Sally's afraid of the water," my sister said suddenly.

"What?"

"Sally's super scared of the water. She knows how to swim, but she doesn't. Doesn't like swimming, I mean. She told me."

"Oh. I didn't know." I thought of how Sally always stood only knee-deep in the water, never going farther than that. "That makes sense," I conceded.

Audrina began to draw the letter *A* with the flashlight. "*A*," I said, before she was even finished. It was a game we used to play a lot when we were younger.

"How did you know? I wasn't even done."

"You always used to do *A*."

Audrina laughed. "I guess you're right."

I started to do the letter *K* and then had to add the *O*, before Audrina exclaimed, "Kocsis!"

Then my sister wrote out a word. I knew what it was but didn't want to say it aloud: *Sally*. When my sister had finished, she clicked off her light, and the word seemed to still hang in the air, like a shirt on a clothesline. I could hear the rustle of sheets as she repositioned herself in the bed.

I blinked and stared at the ceiling above, where my flashlight still emitted a single bright circle. Then, slowly, I drew a shape—a heart—to capture how I felt: happy despite the circumstances. My worry about the bracelet dissolved just as quickly as it had appeared. Because I was presently enclosed in this oddly comforting bubble that Sally's disappearance had created for my family. I knew where to find Mother each moment—around the corner, doing laundry, sipping her iced tea on the back porch, scrubbing the kitchen counter. And Father was home more than he'd ever been; we now had weekday breakfasts that mimicked weekend breakfasts, when he would be the one in the kitchen. Audrina and I were partners in crime. The Hickory Place Sisters, the main characters in our own little world. Safe in our family's Tudor with its nubby mustard-colored family room carpeting, glass octagonal coffee table scattered with *House Beautiful* magazines, a creaky swing set and forgotten-about playhouse in back.

Even now, my memories, my dreams, often take place during this time at 10 Hickory Place. I walk through the kitchen, light oak cabinets with brown knobs, a dent in the Formica countertop from where my father once dropped a mug. The answering machine flickers with a new message. I go to pull open the pantry door, but my mother stops me. *Your father already made breakfast,* she says. She says it matter-of-factly. Sure enough, when I turn around, the pan is sizzling. Western omelets. My father grins. *Cheese or no cheese?* He asks me every time. I always want cheese, but he does, too, so I like to make sure he is not giving me the last slice. Audrina is already eating, of course. Perched at the kitchen table, the pulp of orange juice sticking to her near-empty glass. Hardened cheese stuck to her fork.

Dreams have a strange way of mixing it all together. There's a fine line when you want to sleep too much, when your dreams are more comforting than your reality, when they mix the past and present. The dent in the Formica countertop, for instance. It happened later, after Audrina died.

# Chapter Four

"When can we see Max," Audrina asked one evening, about a week and a half after Sally's disappearance. Or, rather, she didn't so much ask as grumpily demand. She'd been irritable ever since our parents had decided to postpone her acting camp, "because of the Sally situation." "I don't get why," she'd complained to me, until I pointed out that at least she got to go to camp. But then she'd retorted that the reason why I'd never gone was because I didn't really have any strong interests, so that had been the beginning and end of that conversation.

Mother sighed before answering Audrina. "Let me see."

The next morning, after a few hushed conversations on the kitchen phone, our mother announced: "Okay, girls, you can go see Max. Dr. Baker thought it might be nice." Audrina grinned at me while I felt a wave of apprehension. What would we talk about? Would it be awkward? Mother continued, "I will watch from the window as you walk over. I only want you to stay for a little bit. It's a difficult time for the family. Remember to be quiet and respectful, and give your condolences." When Audrina looked blank, Mother explained, "Just say you're sorry."

Audrina and I nodded, already heading toward the door. It felt weird to step outside the house after all that time inside; the sun was so strong it almost hurt our eyes, the sky a large swath of blue. The first few steps we took were short, cautious ones, as if we weren't sure where we were going, and then our strides lengthened with each subsequent move forward.

But when we got to the Bakers' circular driveway, we stopped. A long river of faded blue curls, some areas rubbed out, snaked down the pavement toward our feet. The Bakers' station wagon squatted in the middle of the driveway, close to their front door, effectively blocking cars from driving down that half of the driveway, and I wondered if it had been done on purpose, to preserve the chalk drawing, but then I realized that I hadn't seen the station wagon budge in the past week. Most likely the Bakers hadn't used that car since the day Sally went missing.

"Oh," Audrina said as she surveyed the chalk drawing, and I shook my head, as if I could clear the discomfort it had produced in me. After a moment, we slowly followed the cascade of curls up the driveway to the station wagon, walking alongside the border, careful not to actually step on the drawing itself. There was a particularly congested area of curls that required us to pause and form a single-file line before continuing. Another spot—near a lopsided bow—necessitated a small hop.

The doorbell seemed to ring forever before Mrs. Baker cracked open the door. She had on a red-and-green plaid wool bathrobe, a sharp contrast to her pink satin one. It seemed like something meant to be worn around Christmas—not in early August. Strands of hair escaped from a messy bun, and her eyes floated above our heads, as though she didn't recognize us. It was the way she'd looked at the lake, while the lifeguard paraded different little girls in front of her in hopes she could identify one of them.

"Hi," Max called from somewhere behind her. He slipped next to his mother and pulled open the door to let us in.

The house appeared sad and dark—lights off, curtains drawn. We followed Max to his room, passing by a closed door adorned with heart stickers, which must have been Sally's room. Max lay down on his blue-carpeted floor next to a Star Wars pillow and crumpled blanket. A black-and-white poster of an old-fashioned airplane hung on his wall. Clothes were strewn across the room, and the shades were pulled down. I wondered what Mother would have made of this mess and whether his room was usually like this or if it was just because of Sally. We'd never been to either of their rooms. We'd only hung out in their family room or in their yard.

"I've been sleeping on the floor," he said, with a shaky voice. "Sometimes Sally would come sleep here when she had a bad dream."

"I'm sorry," Audrina and I, still awkwardly standing at the doorway, uttered in unison. What did that mean, though? How did *being sorry* help anything? Still—to this day—I'm struck by the futility of the expression. As it would turn out, *I'm sorry* was a phrase with which I would become well acquainted.

Max didn't reply at first. He tilted his head up toward the ceiling. "Sometimes I think she was faking it, just so she didn't have to sleep alone. 'Cause when I'd ask her to tell me about the nightmare, she couldn't."

I glanced at my sister, who was staring at the ground, her face lax. So I did the same. Max became quiet, and I wondered if this was it, if we would turn around now and head back home. Then he added, in a strained voice, "I miss her."

Audrina went to sit down next to him, and I followed. "So do I," she said.

"Me, too," I added. "Any updates?" I had heard my mother often use this phrase when talking with the neighbors.

Max rubbed his eyes. Was he crying? "My mom keeps hoping that maybe she wandered off," he said.

Audrina pulled at the carpet. "But to where? Sally wouldn't do that."

"I know," Max replied. "It's weird. It doesn't make sense. But I heard my mom talking to my dad about it this morning. It's so annoying; they don't want to tell me anything. I have to listen in."

Audrina and I nodded. "Us, too," I admitted.

"You know, we don't know our way around because we just moved here," Max said. "So my mom is just hoping that Sally's lost and just doesn't know how to tell someone how to get here."

"So Sally doesn't know her address?" I asked.

Max shook his head. "She knows the name of the street we used to live on in Boston. My parents made sure of that, living in the city. But here—I don't think so. The day we moved in, when we first turned onto the block and saw the street sign, my dad said, 'Welcome to Hickory Place,' and then Sally said, 'Sesame Place!'"

I gave a nervous little laugh, but Audrina didn't say anything, making me regret my response.

"I think my mom's even hoping Sally turns up at our old house in Boston."

"Maybe she will," Audrina offered, but I just puckered my lips. I knew that Boston wasn't nearby. I tried to remember if I had known my address when I was Sally's age; I wasn't sure. But it had given me an idea: What if someone who previously knew Sally took her? Came down from Boston to snatch her? Maybe I needed to add "Boston Person" to my suspect list.

"My dad said"—Max's voice shook—"they found her bracelet. The one you gave her, Audrina."

I suddenly tensed. What did he mean, they found it? Did my mother find the bracelet? Had I been found out?

"Where?" Audrina asked.

"In the woods somewhere. The woods next to the lake."

I let out the breath I didn't even realize I'd been holding. They must have found the other half of the bracelet. Phew. "So what does that mean?"

"Well, I think . . . it means . . . someone . . . took her," Max replied, in a stilted, halting manner, while Audrina and I stared at each other, our mouths parted. "But I think it made my mom hopeful, somehow. Like, that maybe she dropped it while exploring in the woods." Max shrugged. "Anyway, I guess they are checking for fingerprints and stuff."

Heat rose to my face while I replayed the way I'd taken the bracelet, and I bit my lip, hoping Max and Audrina wouldn't notice. When I finally glanced over to Max, I saw he had pulled the Star Wars pillow from under his head to cover his face.

I wanted to find out more about the significance of the discovery of the charm bracelet, but Max clearly didn't want to talk about it. So I was quiet, as was Audrina, who also seemed to not know what to say. Staring at Max's pillow-covered face, I ticked off, in my head, all of the Star Wars figures I saw: *Chewbacca, Darth Vader, Han Solo, R2-D2, Chewbacca—wait, I already got that one. Princess Leia.*

I wondered what characters, if any, Audrina would have been able to name. Father had decided, earlier that year, that we should watch all the Star Wars movies as a family; it had taken a couple of months to achieve, as every time he'd gone to the local video store, all three VHS copies of *Return of the Jedi* were already rented. By the time he procured a copy, Audrina had lost interest, as weeks had passed since we'd seen the first two, and she painted her nails during the viewing, to Father's annoyance. Mother also grew restless, taking the opportunity to reorganize the media cabinet upon which the TV sat. I'd felt sorry for Father, who ended up turning off the movie and moving abruptly to his study to watch something else. I'd joined him there, sitting on the floor in front of his small couch, but it had been hard to tell from his silence whether or not he appreciated my presence.

The Star Wars figures on the pillow moved as Max spoke from underneath, in a muffled voice: "I think I'm gonna take a nap. Thanks for coming."

We scooted out of his room, not sure whether we should say goodbye. As we walked past Sally's closed bedroom door, I ran my fingers across the heart stickers. We didn't see or hear Mrs. Baker, or Dr. Baker, for that matter—if he was even still home—so we just let ourselves out of the house. Audrina and I held hands as we crossed the street, and this time she didn't drop my hand until we got to our front door.

Although the idea of invisible fingerprints and found charm bracelets rested uneasily in my stomach, I was able to push those thoughts aside. I had a new focus, anyway, an exciting one that was shared with my sister: visiting Max each day after getting the okay from Mother.

Visiting Max was the only thing Audrina and I were allowed to do outside of our house, and since we were the only people he wanted to see, Diane and Courtney continued to call, peppering us with questions. Even Andrew and Patrick Wiley occasionally phoned to ask what we knew. I positioned myself by the phone so I could catch the good calls. I was so thankful we'd just gotten call waiting, so Mother didn't have an excuse to hurry me off. (Mr. Wiley, who worked for New Jersey Bell/Bell Atlantic, had clued my parents in on the feature.) When Leah phoned from California and then one of the neighborhood kids rang, I'd promptly end our conversation, pretending it was a call for Mother.

Though Dr. Baker had upped the reward amount to $20,000—an amount that then doubled between donations from Boston friends and Hammend neighbors, as well as a $5,000 pledge from our town's businesses—it hadn't produced any credible leads. I certainly hadn't been able to add any new notable suspects to my list, besides Mrs. Abbott and Boston Person. Even when Sally's disappearance briefly made the national evening news, the footage looked the same as what had already been shown on the local news—the lake, Sally's picture from the flyer, Dr. Baker pleading for information regarding Sally's whereabouts. So it was up to me to fill in the holes for the neighborhood kids, to provide the insider details the media didn't know about and wasn't reporting on.

Each morning I thought of a new detail I would release when the phone rang: the murkiness of the lake water in which we'd swum; the pile of dirty dishes in the Bakers' laundry room sink (once the ones in the kitchen sink had piled up); the last thing I remembered Sally saying to me in her lispy pronunciation ("Thorry, Bee" when she accidentally stepped on my leg as she ran by on the sand); the heart stickers decorating her bedroom door; the Christmas robe Mrs. Baker often wore; the private investigator from New York that

Max said his father had hired (though this person seemed like a ghost, since we never actually saw him); Sally's chalk drawing on the driveway. The chalk drawing.

Because there hadn't been rain, the chalk drawing—while increasingly faded—remained a lot longer than we'd expected it to. Audrina and I developed a pattern to avoid stepping on it, and I would tick off the directions in my head as we moved through: left here, right there, a hop by the lopsided bow. It was silly; we could have avoided it entirely by walking on the perimeter of the driveway, or the lawn for that matter. But we were drawn to it—this lingering piece of Sally. It was an unspoken agreement between my sister and me from the first time we went to see Max: follow the curls up to the castle but don't dare step on them.

At some point, the calls began slowing, and I was aware of an impending change: a moving-on. The drought in our town finally broke, and as the rains washed away the last of the blue curls and the bows, an emptiness settled within me. In my mind—and my memory—it signaled a turn of events. When we drove to the supermarket with Mother, we passed many kids playing in the streets, unsupervised, like the way they used to.

Everyone likes a happy ending, I suppose, so perhaps Hammend was growing tired of waiting for one. It seemed like people wanted this to be over, whether or not it truly *was* over. The disappearance no longer made the front page of the paper; there were days when it didn't make the news at all. A distance seemed to be occurring surrounding the Bakers. "The Boston Family," the paper referred to the Bakers one day toward the end of the summer, as if, while it was a shame Sally had gone missing, it wasn't really a New Jersey problem—at least not anymore. We, on Hickory Place, were not immune to this shift, where compassion was now starting to turn to critique.

"I wonder why Fran is so uninvolved," Mother said to Mrs. Wiley on the phone one late August morning, she in her usual spot on the teal velour sofa, and I in mine, eavesdropping in the hallway. A few mornings earlier, I'd unsuccessfully tried to listen in on her call from another phone—the old-fashioned rotary phone stationed on the sideboard in the dining room—but the audible click when I picked up quickly gave me away. Now I was back to eavesdropping on just one half of the conversation.

"It's so odd," Mother said. "The only one you ever hear from is Jack. He was the one who made the TV appearance, who organized the search effort. It seems like he's carried the whole load. When that Adam Walsh boy went missing, both those parents were all over the TV. They even went on *Phil Donahue*; do you remember that?"

I froze, trying to absorb all that I was overhearing. Mother, too, found Mrs. Baker unusual; I wondered if she also found her a little suspicious?

"Maybe she feels too guilty," Mother continued. "I don't want to point any fingers, but when the girls were little and I brought them to the lake, I always knew exactly where they were. At all times." Mother paused, and then said, "Yeah, I know you would, too. Look, I feel terrible about what happened—I couldn't even imagine, God forbid, if, if . . . Anyway, I just think something is off about that woman." Mother's voice lowered: "Did you hear the rumor about why they left Boston?"

Mother continued in a whisper now that was inaudible to me, even though I strained to hear. Gradually she returned to a more normal volume: ". . . some issues. Maybe she's depressed. Do you think we should invite her over for coffee?" Mother was quiet while

Mrs. Wiley seemed to be responding, and then she laughed. "No, you're right, she probably wouldn't come."

What had Mother revealed about the Bakers' departure from Boston? It seemed to have a stink of scandal to it, whatever it was.

"Well, I'll tell you one thing," Mother was now saying to Mrs. Wiley. "We've shown the Bakers a lot of support, and I don't appreciate how Jack is putting down the police department. We're a small town, but Chief Riley and our officers do a fine job. Oh—you didn't hear what he said?" Mother's voice rose: "He said the Hammend police should take a page from the Boston cops' book. And you know how he brought on that private investigator, right? . . . Well, a lot of good that's done. Can't be cheap, but I guess they can afford it. I wonder what he thinks about the FBI; I heard they are now involved. At any rate, I just simply don't like what he's saying about our boys. That's all. They're doing the best they can."

Mother's comments seemed to affirm, to me, that the Bakers somehow didn't belong. They were first newcomers and now interlopers; they'd brought tragedy and upheaval to our quiet town. It was easier to extricate ourselves from the unfortunate circumstances, to disassociate from them, if we thought of the Bakers as outsiders—not one of us. But I didn't want to think of Max that way.

When I read through the newspaper those last couple of weeks before school began, the world seemed large, vast. Christa McAuliffe would soon become the first teacher in space, and they'd just found the *Titanic*, seventy-three years after it sank. Ryan White was forced to remotely attend school, because of his AIDS, and 250 people died when Japan Airlines Flight 123 crashed near Tokyo.

Summer was ending, time was moving forward, and I felt our world opening back up. Little Sally, it seemed, was gone and not coming back. This realization was a powerful one, shocking in the way that only a dissolution of a childhood belief could be, like the time in third grade when Hope Rodale told everyone Santa Claus was not real.

Later it would strike me that Sally would belong in childhood, like a character in a timeless children's book. The summer of 1985 had claimed her, not allowing her to grow out of it. Some years later, the town began referring to her as "the Lake Girl," solidifying her disappearance to fable-like status, a story that had been passed down through generations instead of a real event that had temporarily paralyzed—and terrified—our town.

# Chapter Five

When the school year started, Max and I began carpooling—Mrs. Baker took us in the mornings, and Mother drove us home. Audrina was in a different carpool, one with some flexibility, so that Mother could still bring me to my school when Max chose to skip it, which happened at least once a week, sometimes twice, especially during those first few months.

The schoolyard where Mrs. Baker would deposit us was to the left of Hillside Junior High. I still remember the gradual hush that befell the crowd that first day as Max and I approached the many students already congregated on the outdoor basketball court. The silence traveled like the disorganized beginnings of a stadium wave; some kids quieted instantly, while others continued to talk and laugh until they caught on that something was going on. Eventually all heads—from those belonging to seventh graders to the eighth and ninth graders'—swiveled toward us. Bubble gum smacking silenced, basketball bouncing ceased, and all I could hear were small, isolated rustles of movement and scattered whispers. I'd never had that much attention before, but I was too self-conscious in the moment to appreciate it. Instead, I worried if my hair was growing frizzy with the humidity, whether my backpack—my old JanSport, which I'd chosen to use over the dreaded new *Borka* tote—looked too dated, since some of the girls we passed carried Esprit bags. Later, though, I would replay that walk over in my head, savoring it. Counting how many eyes were on me at once (probably close to one hundred; there were nearly forty kids in my grade alone) and relishing the rush I felt. Moments in childhood were often like that: too saturated to fully enjoy in real time, their pleasures spiking higher in subsequent recollections, once we had the space to consider them.

I steered Max, who had his face hidden beneath his Red Sox baseball cap, toward the far edge of the basketball court, where I recognized a grouping of fellow seventh graders, including Hope Rodale, the most popular girl in my grade. As we moved closer, I spotted Leah standing alone, a few feet away, her backpack at her feet. She'd flown back just two days earlier and looked the same as she had in June, the last time I saw her: skinny, with stringy blond hair that appeared uncombed, though I knew she'd probably overcombed it. She wore a purple romper, which, at quick glance, seemed out of place: None of the girls surrounding Hope were wearing rompers.

"Bee—" Leah began when I'd come closer, while at the same time, Hope said, "Hey, Bee! Come here!"

I stopped short, surprised Hope was summoning me. Flashing an apologetic smile at Leah, I changed course, nudging Max along with me toward Hope and her friends. Nobody ignored Hope Rodale; I hoped Leah would understand.

Hope looked me up and down, appraisingly, with wide hazel eyes set beneath a thick arrangement of bangs, and then shifted her gaze to Max. Her hair, a glossy and rich shade of brown, fell pin-straight down her back. She had a good three to four inches on me; her long legs were adorned in hot-pink leggings that extended beyond a blue miniskirt. I never would have thought to pair that skirt with those leggings, or even the oversized Hard Rock T-shirt she wore. I was also wearing leggings, yellow, underneath a stonewashed denim skirt. I felt denim was safe; everything matched denim. "Hi," I said, and nodded toward Max. "This is Max."

"I know," Hope replied, like they had met before, although they hadn't; she had spent most of the summer down the Jersey shore, at her family's beach house. "Hi, Max," she said, with a flutter of her hand. "I'm Hope." She smiled, revealing an enviable set of braces. I'd been deemed "lucky" by my dentist not to need them.

"Hey," Max replied, as he gave a half-hearted smile that briefly brought out his dimple. His hair had grown over the summer, and it now turned up at the ends under the baseball cap. I had an urge to touch it.

"I'm sorry about your sister," Hope said. "We've all"—here she gestured at the gaggle of girls who always seemed to be one to two steps behind her—"been praying for her safe return."

"Thanks." Max blinked a few times, more than he normally did.

"Do you want to go sit down over there?" I quickly said, gesturing to the remote set of benches beyond the court, which usually remained empty.

"Yeah." He started walking over, without waiting for me. The heads on the schoolyard turned once again as he walked past, though this time the chatter didn't stop.

As soon as Max was out of earshot, Hope said, "He's so hot."

"Totally," I agreed, in conjunction with affirmations from the other girls, although right then I was more concerned about his mental state. But before I could dwell on it, Hope and her friends encircled me, firing off questions about what Max and his parents were really like, how Max was doing, what Sally had been like, if I had any information about where she might be. As I answered them, I wondered if Leah was listening. I felt torn, pulled to her. She remained on the outskirts, flipping through a book, and only looked up once the school bell rang. Then she promptly tossed the book inside her backpack to speed ahead.

I managed to catch up with her as we squeezed through the double doors into the building. "Leah," I said, inadvertently jostling into her.

"Oh, hi, Bee," she replied, like it was the first time we were noticing each other.

"I'm sorry," I said as we spilled out into the hall and began walking toward the seventh-grade corridor.

"For what?" She gave me a quick side glance and tucked a strand of hair behind her ear. She'd gotten her ears double-pierced; a tiny gold ball stud rested above a dangling rainbow heart.

"I wanted to say hi, but then Hope, she . . ." I trailed off, unsure what to say.

"It's fine," she said, but I could tell it wasn't. We continued walking side by side, the loud conversations around us making our silence more obvious. Then, on an impulse, I reached over to squeeze her elbow; it was our old way of saying hello from our neighboring desks. We'd wait for the teacher to turn toward the chalkboard and then lean over and grab each other's elbow, because that was often the body part most accessible.

I could tell I'd taken Leah by surprise; she jerked her arm away and stopped short for a moment, Jay Flay nearly bumping into her from behind. But then she laughed and, relieved, I laughed, too.

But as the days went by, it was clear it wasn't going to be the same between us. And I knew this was because *I* wasn't the same. Growing up in a small town and going to school with the same kids since kindergarten, we were all friendly—or at least not unkind to one another—but there'd always been the popular girls, like Hope Rodale and whoever she chose to be in her clique, and then there were the rest of us. Now, for the first time, I was becoming part of the inner circle.

Each morning upon our arrival to Hillside, Max headed to the wooden benches, seemingly content to be left alone and shaking his head when Jay and the other boys asked if he wanted to join in on a game of H-O-R-S-E, or Butts Up against the brick wall, or even dodgeball. Meanwhile, Hope Rodale and her friends would advance toward me, fanning out in a circular fashion, as they peppered me with the same continuous questions about the Bakers—while Leah stood off to the side.

"What does Max say about Sally?"

"Have you seen Max *cry*?"

"What does Mrs. Baker say when she drives you guys to school?"

Unfortunately I didn't have much to reveal—Max didn't talk about Sally to me ("I'm sure you guys can tell, he doesn't really talk much"), I hadn't seen him crying recently (although I wouldn't have told them if I had), and the car rides to school were uneventful. Mrs. Baker had never been particularly talkative during those carpool rides in the earlier part of the summer, but now she would push in one of her ABBA 8-track cassettes immediately after I climbed into their station wagon, as if to signal she didn't want any conversation. Soon the songs would overtake the puttering noise of the engine. Prior to riding with the Bakers, I'd never been in a car that had an 8-track; Father had an 8-track in our basement stereo area, but all of our cars used cassette tapes.

"She has an old car," Father had said when I asked him about it. "Diesel engine, too," he added, and I'd just nodded, as if I knew what that meant.

I'd also never ridden in a car where the parent didn't say hello when I climbed in. Mrs. Baker would just nod—if anything—when I entered, and when we arrived at school, she would grunt and exhale cigarette smoke—our cue to tumble out. Before the school year started, I'd only been familiar with "Dancing Queen," but by the end of it I would be able to recite the lyrics to many ABBA songs, which was impressive given that the car ride to school took just seven minutes—or six, if we made the Main Street traffic light. "Mamma Mia" and "Fernando" became my favorites. When Mrs. Baker's 8-track player was on the fritz, playing two songs at once, Mrs. Baker would mutter, "Shit."

When Mother drove me to school, when Max was absent, the radio usually remained off; she didn't like the distraction of music. She drove much like she moved: forward, frenetic jerks and sudden stops. She'd glance over at me repeatedly, while quickly telling me how she had bought me a training bra, that I should use the Neutrogena orange soap bar to clean my face twice a day, that I should be expecting my period sometime soon (she'd already gotten it by the time she was my age). She covered matters of puberty in a militaristic and efficient fashion, as if it were her duty to impart that information during the concrete period of our car ride. She often got in her last words right as we pulled up to school, not giving me a chance to ask questions or respond, though I didn't want to, anyway. Sometimes it seemed as if Mother's sole purpose was to *function* as a mother (and, later, I would also include wife), but not necessarily to be one. There was a difference. Even the quiet, determined way Mother assembled her gift baskets seemed more about perfecting a skill than personal enjoyment. Once, at drop-off, I'd witnessed Leah's mother tenderly embracing her before Leah climbed out of the car. There'd been a gentleness, a naturalness, to their interaction that was foreign to me.

Even on the days I arrived solo to school, and even if I was tapped out of information about the Bakers, Hope and her friends remained patient and interested in me. It was so new, this idea that people wanted to talk to me, that they wanted to hear what I had to say. When they kept inviting me to eat at their lunch table—when it became a given I would sit with them—when they called me to chat about life in general, I realized my newfound popularity had surpassed any Baker gossip I might share.

And yet the story about the day Sally had disappeared did not grow old for them. It seemed like every few days, when we were in the schoolyard during morning drop-off, or at recess, Hope or one of her friends would beg me to retell it, like it was a dark fairy tale— the kind you want to hear over and over again, even though you already know the unfortunate ending. When this occurred, some of the boys in our class would pause their games to also listen in.

If Max had gone to school that day, I would make sure he wasn't close enough to hear before agreeing: ". . . And I must have been underwater because I didn't hear the lifeguard blow the whistle. When I came up, I just saw everyone leaving. Everybody was getting out of the water. So I followed them."

The girls would sigh at this and shudder; they were infatuated with this part of the story. Invariably one of them would press against me in a hug and say, "That's so scary. I'm sorry, Bee."

I remember how awkward I felt being hugged; I didn't routinely get hugs from people other than my mother—and even that was only on particular occasions, like, well, when she was feeling *motherly*, I supposed. But Hope and her friends hugged often; they hugged one another in the mornings and before leaving school. They hugged when they talked about their crushes and complained about their parents. They hugged when they accidentally dropped their lunch trays; they hugged when they traded food among themselves: Fruit Roll-Ups for Doritos, Twinkies for Hostess CupCakes, orange-flavored Capri Sun for fruit punch. They hugged the boys sometimes, too, as a greeting.

And so I practiced hugging; I hugged my pillow at night in my room when Audrina wasn't around or was already asleep. Of course it was easier with a pillow than with Hope or one of her friends. But I was determined: A few weeks later and I was a regular hugger, like all the popular girls.

Sometimes, during lunch, Leah—with whom I used to mock the way Hope and her friends constantly hugged—would watch me from her table across the cafeteria. I'd suggested Leah try sitting with me at Hope's table, and she'd acquiesced one time, but it had been awkward for everyone. So now we'd fallen into an unspoken agreement that we would walk with each other to lunch and then part ways as soon as we set foot inside the cafeteria. I always felt a little guilty once we entered the room and I pivoted toward Hope, but Leah had to understand: This was the way of seventh grade.

A distance also started to form between Audrina and me. In a way, it was natural: There were things that my sister, being a year younger and at a different school, was not privy to; what it felt like to wear a bra, how you should store a maxipad in your locker in case you get your period, what the "different bases" were. Audrina had stared at me the first time she saw me putting on my bra, but she didn't ask any questions.

But what was unnatural, or at least different, was that for the first time in my life, I encouraged this distance between my sister and me. I did not try to bring her into the fold; I was enjoying too much the stature I'd acquired as a bona fide popular seventh grader, the space I'd developed that belonged just to me. The day she'd stared at my bra, I didn't offer information, as I likely would have in the past.

One evening, the phone rang right when we'd sat down for dinner, and Audrina jumped up to answer, assuming the call would be for her. But it wasn't—it was for me: *Hope Rodale.* Audrina repeated Hope's name, and then, when a wide smile spread across my face, jabbed the phone at me with an unexpected roughness.

I didn't know whether Audrina had received the same level of attention at her school because of Sally that I had, but I didn't care enough to find out. There was a freedom in this I'd never experienced before, a distinct separation in our lives, likely more marked because of the time we'd spent together over the summer. In the past our worlds had been entwined, and mine even indistinct from hers—a shadow to her being. But now I was emerging, my own life, my own being.

One morning after school drop-off, I noticed Mother lingering in her car, watching from afar as I interacted with Hope and her friends, and later that afternoon, upon my return home, Mother commented, with a quiet pride, "It seems like you've made some nice new friends this year."

"Yeah," I said, trying to sound nonchalant when Audrina glanced up at us from the kitchen table. But the rest of the day, I replayed Mother's words, basking in them.

Even as I got wrapped up in my own social life, Max remained in the forefront of my mind. One morning, before we'd parted ways at the schoolyard, I spontaneously gave him a hug. I knew it had been a rough morning for him; he'd barely glanced at me during the car ride to school. I supposed this was how these things went; missing Sally was a yo-yo of emotions. He stiffened at first, a bit surprised, but then he hugged me back, and we stayed like that a moment longer than we needed. My whole body felt electric in a way that made the occasional hugs from other boys at school feel childish and annoying.

I tried to engage Max more after that, but it was difficult. "Want to hang out?" I would sometimes ask as we walked up to the schoolyard, as if the boys and girls in our grade did such a thing. Instead, the girls usually stood with the girls, one side of the chess board, and the boys were with the boys, on the other side, advancing every so often.

"Nah," he'd respond and then head toward his bench to wait out the morning bell. Max's answers were usually one-syllable, robotic.

"Are you going to soccer today?" I'd sometimes inquire. He was playing soccer that fall, although he often missed practices and games.

"Not sure," he'd reply. He seemed to make his decision every day come three o'clock, and no one questioned it.

Once a week Mrs. Fitz, Hillside's guidance counselor, pulled me out of class to check on me and ask about Max. Though she tried to collect me in an inconspicuous manner, my classmates always noticed. But I didn't mind—it added to my specialness factor.

"How are you?" Mrs. Fitz would ask, settling back into the chair across from mine, hands on her lap, waiting.

I would squirm, feeling that we were too still. I was used to my mother's cleaning compulsion, the nervous energy that manifested in constant motion. Mrs. Fitz unnerved me with her intense, unwavering focus. "Good," I always simply replied, and she always nodded.

By that point, I was used to adults asking how I was. Both Audrina and I got asked that question a lot that fall from all types of adults: teachers, neighbors, our parents' friends. Even the lady behind the checkout counter at Mortenson's Drug Store once asked how my sister and I were doing, and I knew, just knew, from the way she leaned over to inspect us, that she didn't ask the same question of the other kids who came in to buy gum and lip gloss.

"Okay," Audrina and I would answer at first, and then, after the first few times, we tried to outdo each other with our answers.

"Way cool," I'd jump in, before Audrina could reply.

"Rad!" Audrina responded another time, while I racked my brain for a response we hadn't yet used.

We had already seemed to go through them all: *gnarly, awesome, killer, stellar.* We'd learned the adjective *wicked* from Max, who often used it—at least, that is, he did before Sally went missing. One evening I asked Father's help in finding synonyms for *good* in the brown leather thesaurus that was kept next to the *Encyclopaedia Britannica*s in his study, and together we wrote down the possibilities: *well, exceptional, excellent, superb, marvelous, satisfactory, acceptable.*

"You, my student, are an exceptional, well, marvelous, excellent person," Father teased, with an authoritative tone, as he raised his hand in the air, his pointer finger extended.

I laughed; it was rare to see Father act silly. "And what about my sister, Professor Father?" I asked.

"Your sister is"—Father consulted the paper and then the open thesaurus—"superb, apt, worthy, and brilliant."

"And Mother?"

"Your mother is tremendous, extraordinary, amazing." Father smiled, and then he lowered his hand and gazed off with a wistful expression. "And she's beautiful," he said, his accent pronounced. "I'm lucky to have her," he added.

I'd overheard the two of them arguing the night before in their bedroom; lately, it seemed, that had been happening more frequently, about once a week, but only after Audrina and I were supposed to be asleep, as if they were scheduling their quarrels. The few times I snuck down the hall, lingering outside their bedroom door, I'd heard snippets of things that either didn't seem significant or I didn't understand: the Jeep windshield wiper that needed repair, a dinner that had occurred with the Wileys, the electric bill, something about a man named Casey Mitchell. I couldn't recall a friend of theirs named Casey, but I couldn't ask them; I didn't want them to catch on to my eavesdropping. I didn't obtain any information related to Sally, which was disappointing. I'd hoped there might be some progress.

After reviewing the list Father and I compiled, I'd crossed out *satisfactory* and *acceptable*—they were too banal. But even though I now had numerous possibilities, when Mrs. Fitz asked me how I was doing, I still stuck with *good*. I knew my fancy synonyms were not going to work on her.

Mrs. Fitz also spoke with Max on a regular basis, but she didn't need to pull him out of class. He found his way to her office several times throughout the day. In fact, when he wasn't in class, he was either there or at Nurse Vicky's office, occupying the small cot, the curtain drawn. More than once a teacher had gently asked me to collect him from one of those two places, which I was not always successful in doing.

"I'm sick," Max would sputter from behind the curtain.

"No, you're not."

"How would you know?"

That was usually the extent of our exchange, if Max even felt like talking. Sometimes he didn't respond at all, although if I waited long enough, he'd eventually slowly pull himself up and creep back toward the classroom with me, his face turned toward the ground. On these occasions, Sally's disappearance would suddenly seem so real, and I'd have to pinch my arm before reentering the classroom.

About a month into the school year, Hope Rodale and her friends also began making their way to Mrs. Fitz's office, allegedly to address concerns they felt about Sally—whom they'd never met—but I knew that they were doing it both to get out of class and because, suddenly, it seemed like the cool thing to do. I'd see them approach as I was leaving, Hope wearing a smug smile that unsettled me. Mrs. Fitz usually seemed less than thrilled with their arrival, a displeased look momentarily flashing across her face. Thankfully Max was too in his own head and skipped too much school to realize what was going on.

After Principal Dillon became aware of Mrs. Fitz's increasingly busy calendar, he hastily gathered the entire school into the gymnasium for an assembly. It was a day Max was absent, which I doubted was a coincidence.

As we took our seats in the bleachers, we spotted Chief Riley behind the podium; next to him were Officers Dittmer and Lark. Chief Riley told us, in a calm voice that projected over the microphone, that they were still looking for Sally, and that while they didn't know what had happened to her, they were doing everything they could and holding out hope she was safe somewhere. He also stressed, repeatedly, "You kids don't need to worry. You're safe. Just keep your heads up."

Then Officer Dittmer had taken the microphone and started off by saying, "But remember, don't talk to strangers," to which Chief Riley and Officer Lark nodded their heads in agreement. "Listen carefully," Officer Dittmer continued as he grabbed the microphone's cord and started walking toward us. "You never want to go off with a stranger. Or—or get in a car with a stranger. You shouldn't take food, or candy, or donuts, or any kind of sweets from a stranger, even if it's your absolute favorite candy, like Skittles or, I don't know, Sour Patch Kids—that's my favorite"—and then we students started to shift in our seats, looking at one another, unsure whether to feel uncomfortable or amused.

Officer Lark scratched his head while Chief Riley strode toward Officer Dittmer to abruptly grab the microphone out of his hands. "Uh, thanks, Chuck," he said, clearing his throat, and the noise echoed throughout the gym, which generated a nervous flurry of laughter. "What we're trying to say is, just be aware of your surroundings, kids."

Hope Rodale made fun of Officer "Up-Chuck" that day during lunch, sticking her finger down her throat in a vomiting sign, causing the other girls to giggle. Meanwhile, I had to force myself to smile. Seeing Officer Dittmer took me back in time to the car ride home from the lake, when I'd kept my hand pressed against the bulge of the bracelet piece in my bathing suit, and to the missed opportunity I'd had to confess when he stopped by our house. I wondered what Chief Riley and the FBI were doing with their half of the bracelet, whether they believed Sally had been lured by candy, as Officer Dittmer's speech implied. Were any of the people on my suspect list, which I continued to revisit in my diary, on their radar? I'd often seen my sister writing in her diary, too, but I doubted she'd been using it for the same purpose.

Later, when I got home from school, I locked the bedroom door and fished the bracelet fragment out from its hiding spot for the first time in nearly two months. It hadn't been touched; it seemed a safe place to hide things. The dresser was one of the few larger furniture pieces in our house that Father hadn't built, and I'd discovered by accident that the toe kick detached, when I once dropped my earring backing on the floor. As I stared at the bracelet, running my finger over it, I was awash in guilt. I pictured the flyer that had circulated about Sally in the days following her disappearance, as clearly as if someone were holding it up for me to read: *Purple bathing suit with a heart on the front and a gold charm bracelet on her left wrist.* Max's words from the day Audrina and I visited ran through my mind: *They found her bracelet. The one you gave her, Audrina . . . In the woods somewhere. The woods next to the lake.*

I involuntarily shivered and gripped the piece so tightly in my hand that it hurt. And I grasped on to one thought, one sure-as-hell thought, that temporarily soothed my guilt: Audrina should have given it to *me* in the first place. She knew I'd wanted it. But she had to act all special and beautiful and get Sally to adore her, as if she hadn't already had enough people adoring her.

# Chapter Six

By mid-October, the trees at the end of the cul-de-sac had mostly turned golden yellow, and Mother started her annual sewing of Halloween costumes. Audrina wanted to be Madonna from her recent "Like a Virgin" MTV music video, but Father wouldn't let her, saying she was too young to dress like that, so she settled on being a pink ballerina. Meanwhile, I strategically chose to be a strawberry so that the green stem hat would hide my shaggy hair, which seemed like it was taking an extra long time to grow out.

Father usually took us and the Wiley boys trick-or-treating around the neighborhood, but this year, despite all that had happened with Sally, my sister and I were finally allowed to go on our own, as long as we stayed in the neighborhood.

As we set out, I noticed only one dark patch of street, belonging to the Bakers, who'd gone to Cape Cod for the weekend. Kids suddenly sped up to pass it, like the house was haunted or had cooties. We also moved quickly beyond it, but only because we were eager to hit the other houses. When I glanced up at Max's darkened bedroom window, I thought about the school winter dance that was coming up in a little over a month. It was the first dance we seventh graders would have the opportunity to attend, and it was all Hope Rodale and her friends could talk about. Hope told me Alex Tricket was planning to ask me to be his date; she'd said I was lucky, since Alex was cute and dressed well in Izod shirts and smelled nice—and apparently had never asked out a girl before. But I didn't want to go with Alex, so I'd been trying to avoid him. I wanted, of course, to go with Max, but I hadn't had the confidence to ask him yet if he was planning to go.

Our neighborhood was otherwise Halloween festive: Lit-up houses were adorned with pumpkins and jack-o'-lanterns, and the Johnsons, who always went all out, had turned their front yard into a spooky cemetery with glowing tombstones and skeletons. The neighbors were extra generous that year, allowing us to double-dip into the treat baskets, and the Garfields gave pennies and dimes along with their treats. Officer Jimmy's mother held out a filled-to-the-brim basket of candy that shook a little too violently in her hands, making us scared to approach, until Jimmy appeared in the doorway behind her. As usual, Mrs. Abbott was an orange grinch, simply leaving a bowl of peanuts and Sun-Maid raisin boxes on her doorstep, which naturally no one touched.

While we made our way through the streets with the Wiley brothers, whom we'd quickly run into, I lagged a little behind, keeping an eye out for Hope Rodale. She'd told me she and the girls would try to swing by once they were done with their own neighborhoods.

"Who are you looking for?" Audrina asked as I paused to check out another group of trick-or-treaters we had passed.

"No one," I lied, surprised that my sister had noticed. "I was just looking at the costumes," I added as I walked along in a balancing act on the stone edge of the sidewalk, one foot directly in front of another. I thought it better not to mention anything in case Hope didn't end up coming.

"Diane and Courtney went trick-or-treating with their Canter Prep friends," my sister remarked.

Even though I'd already known that, I replied, "Oh!" Then the heavy pillowcase I was grasping in my left hand suddenly tilted me off-center, and I stumbled onto the street. *Serves me right for not telling her the truth,* I thought.

Just then, a car's light shone from behind as it approached; when it pulled up alongside, Hope's teasing voice projected from the front passenger window, "Hey, has anyone seen a strawberry?"

"Oh, hey, Hope," I said nonchalantly as my sister whipped around.

"I guess these are the friends you weren't looking for," Audrina bitingly remarked, low enough that only I could hear.

"We'll get out here, Mom," Hope said, and then she and Gwen, another member of her group, climbed out. Gwen wore a giant Rubik's Cube, and Hope was dressed as Madonna. I cringed, instinctually empathizing with my sister.

Up ahead, the Wiley brothers loudly beseeched us from where they waited at a doorstep. "Slowpokes! Let's go!"

"Coming!" Audrina called out, giving me a look I couldn't interpret.

Hope adjusted her pearl necklace and then pointed in the opposite direction. "I think we should go this way."

I hesitated a moment too long. My sister marched ahead. "Drina, wait—" I started to say, but she kept going.

As I continued trick-or-treating with Hope and Gwen, Audrina no longer in sight, an irritation began to kindle inside me. This hadn't been premeditated; I didn't even know if Hope would show up. It wasn't fair of my sister to make me feel bad. She should be *happy* for me that I was developing friendships with girls other than Leah. Besides, it was usually the other way around; I would be hopeful that Audrina and I could do something together, but she would already have plans with one of her myriad friends—to go to the mall, see a movie, hang out at someone's house. Had Audrina ever had second thoughts when ditching me for her friends? It seemed doubtful.

Maybe this would finally make her realize what it felt like to be on the other side.

A few days later, after a weekend of me being ignored by my sister, my father was sitting in the car at school pickup instead of Mother. It was a day Max had decided to skip, so I was alone.

"Father?" I said as I tossed my backpack into the seat and leaned into the Jeep to look at him. My chest felt a little tight. He hadn't ever picked me up, not as far as I could remember. He couldn't—he was always working, especially during the fall and spring, which were his busiest seasons. "Is Moth—is Mother all right?"

"She's fine," he replied, his tone sharp as he looked at me with a grim face. "She's home. Get in," he commanded, and turned to face ahead.

I swallowed as I climbed into the car. It almost felt like I was in trouble, though I didn't know why I would be. Then I remembered how Audrina had stayed home from school that day because she was sick, and my chest grew tight again. "Is Drina okay?"

"Yes. She's home, too." He didn't elaborate, and we drove a few streets in silence. It was a warm day for November, almost sum-merlike. The bright sun angling through the window seemed at odds with the half-barren and brown-leafed trees. And with the seriousness of Father's mood.

I waited until we paused at a stop sign to ask, "Father . . . What's going on?"

"We'll discuss with your mother when we get home," he said, not at all reassuringly. I went through the different possibilities: Someone had died; someone was sick. Not immediate family, because it was clear that Mother and Audrina were okay, but maybe it was Uncle Arpad, Father's still-living brother, or one of his daughters, my cousins. They lived in Ontario, so we didn't see them that much. The oldest daughter was already at university, and Father often said she took after his late mother; I had never met my grandmother, but I imagined she'd been a heavyset woman, much like my cousin Nora. Or maybe something had happened to Mother's family: her mother, the one who lived in Florida. She was my only remaining grandparent. There was also Mother's brother, Uncle Mike, who lived in New Mexico. Yes, it would make more sense that it would be either my grandmother or Uncle Mike, because otherwise Mother would have picked me up. Poor Mother, I thought, already feeling an enormous sense of grief.

And then a thought gripped me: Sally. What if this was about Sally?

When we entered the house, Mother was sitting at the kitchen table with her hands clasped together. She had the same look on her face she wore when trying to balance her checkbook: concentrated, eyes narrowed, lips pulled together. But there was no checkbook in front of her—not even a single piece of paper.

"Mother?" I said, the tightness that was in my chest now spreading over my whole body. "Mother, what happened?" I put my hand on her arm as I slid into the chair next to her.

Father dropped the car keys on the counter—not in the designated key drawer—and sat down at the table, too. Mother just stared at me, eyes unblinking, as she unclasped her hands. There, on her palm, lay the charm bracelet piece.

"Where did you . . . ?" I started to ask, but I knew exactly where they had gotten it. From the toe kick. I'd been found out. Mother must have discovered it during one of her cleaning sprees. It wasn't entirely uncommon to see her using her entire body weight to shift large pieces of furniture that looked much too heavy to even budge, just so she could vacuum an extra couple of inches. Since I'd previously observed her vacuuming near the dresser but not attempting to move it, I'd foolishly thought I'd been safe.

My parents exchanged looks. "Borka, we need you to tell us how you got this," Father said in an even, serious voice.

"That's not mine," I said, because I didn't know what else to say.

"Bee," Mother said, "please."

"That's Audrina's bracelet."

"But Audrina gave—" Mother started to say as Father cut in, "Shh—Clara, please," he said, holding up his hand. Mother nodded. Father continued, "Audrina gave it to Sally, right?"

"Yes," I whispered.

"And Sally was wearing it the day she went missing."

I nodded. "Yes."

"So how did you get this?" Father demanded.

I gazed down at the kitchen table. It had a wood border that encircled a large rectangle of white and blue tiles, and I remembered how long it had taken Father to make it.

"I got it at the lake," I admitted. "That day, when Sally went missing. I found it." Mother exhaled sharply, and the chair creaked as Father shifted.

I chewed the inside of my lip as I began counting backward in my head: November to October, October to September, September to August, August to July. Four months had passed already since Sally went missing.

Father took out a folded piece of paper from his pocket. I knew what it was before he even opened it. The corner was a light yellow, from where Audrina had spilled apple juice on it. The flyer had lain on our kitchen counter for a while, once Mother had taken it down from the fridge, and then one day it disappeared. I'd incorrectly assumed it had been thrown out. I didn't need to look at the words on the paper Father now held out in front of him; I had them memorized. *Purple bathing suit with a heart on the front and a gold charm bracelet on her left wrist.* Father shook his head, and with each shake, I felt time shrink, the seconds rooting me to the chair. Trapping me. It was a grave situation, getting in trouble in childhood. Once you were there, the divide between *being in trouble* and *not* felt too great, insurmountable even. "Where did you find it?" Father finally said.

"At the lake," I repeated.

"But where at the lake?"

I closed my eyes briefly and then reopened them. "It was in the sand. I found it after she—after the police came."

"Why wouldn't you tell us?" Mother asked, and Father shot her a look that meant, *Let me handle this.*

"Borka," Father said. "Why did you take it? Instead of giving it to the police?"

I shrugged. "I don't know. I guess . . . I thought I would just take it for Sally, to hold on to it for her. Until she came back."

"And you never told anyone you had it?" Father's gaze was piercing.

"No."

"You saw this paper then, right?" He shook it in front of me. I nodded, but Father said, "Answer me."

"Yes, I saw it."

"So you knew the police were looking for it?"

I frowned. Had I known the police were looking for it? Yes, but they were really looking for Sally. "Well, sort of. I knew that they were looking for Sally—"

"So you've had it this whole time," Father said, interrupting. "You found it, and you didn't tell anyone. And then you hid it."

"Yes," I admitted. "That's right."

"You took it, and you hid it." Father's tone cut through me. "I don't know what to say, Borka. Even if you didn't know it was wrong at the time, you must have realized, after you saw the flyer—"

"I remember you asked me about the flyer," Mother interjected, her voice cracking. "You asked me—asked me if someone had information, what they should do." The bracelet piece, which now lay next to her on the table, looked more brownish and less shiny than I had remembered. Why had I wanted it so badly?

"You should have turned it in," Father continued. "What if it could have helped somehow? I'm not saying it would have, but we won't ever know now, will we?"

"I'm sorry," I whispered. "I'm so sorry. I know it was wrong. I'm sorry." I laid my head on the table, now eye to eye with the bracelet. The tiles felt cooler on the side of my forehead than the wood. I wished for the superhero power to reverse time, imagining myself standing up and walking backward, through the garage door, to slip on my sneakers and climb back into the car. Maybe I could travel back to that day at the lake, and let the bracelet slip into the sand and withdraw my foot to avoid stepping on it.

*What if it could have helped somehow?* Father's voice echoed inside me. Audrina never would have done this, I thought, not for the first time. Audrina—wait, Audrina. Where was she, anyway? Wasn't she supposed to be home sick? Father had said as much. So where was she?

"Get your shoes on," Father said, standing up suddenly.

"Where are we going?"

"To the Bakers'."

Father made me say it three times that day: once to Mrs. Baker, once to Max, and then once more to Dr. Baker, when he returned home from work.

I tried to curl my toes as I recited the first apology, to Mrs. Baker, but it was difficult to do wearing Keds—we hadn't needed to take off our shoes, like we did in our house. "I'm sorry," I started. "I . . . I should have turned it in . . . Found it that day, in the sand . . . I stepped on it . . . I didn't realize that it might have helped . . ." It was hard to get this last bit out, so I pressed the tip of my thumbnail against the flesh of my index finger so hard it hurt for several seconds afterward.

Mrs. Baker immediately walked into the adjacent dining room to the bar cart that was tucked into the far corner. My father and I followed and watched as she fished out a cigarette from a pack lying on top of the cart, which was filled with liquor bottles and a scattered assortment of glasses. I'd never been inside their dining room before, and I was surprised to see the cart; from the front foyer, it was hidden from view. Mrs. Baker lit the cigarette, and then, keeping it propped in her mouth, she popped open a liquor bottle and began pouring it. When she turned, she held her robin's-egg-blue mug in her hands.

She walked over to collapse in a green velvet dining chair, flinging the pack of cigarettes onto the wooden dining table beside her and then chugging from the mug as if she were very thirsty. The air was now tainted with cigarette smoke. I tried to discreetly turn to the side and wave it away, but it was useless.

Mrs. Baker's crying came in spurts; there were quiet periods and then big, heaving sobs that made her shoulders and breasts move. Father awkwardly bent over her from the front, trying to soothe her. "It's . . . it's okay," he said, patting her shoulder. I'd never seen my own mother cry, not even a little. Crying, it seemed, would be a waste of energy for my mother. She'd rather channel that discomfort into motion—picking up miniscule crumbs from the floor, Windexing the windows, even polishing the fancy silverware. She'd once told me that in her former life, she was sure she had been a parlor maid.

Mrs. Baker's sobs and Father's patting motions made me uncomfortable, and I began to shift my weight from one foot to the other. She was certainly having a strange reaction to my confession. Although I had my questions about Mrs. Baker, I felt terrible for her; it was hard not to. Her emotional outburst was in such contrast from her usual indifferent attitude that it made me realize how tough this must be for her. I supposed she wasn't like the other mothers in Hammend, but she was still a mother. I wondered if any of the neighbors had made a real, genuine effort to get to know her—not just one propelled by pity—and I felt bad I'd ever considered putting her on my suspect list. Clearly she was way too upset to have been behind Sally's disappearance.

Max entered the room, carrying a shiny pink Matchbox car and a half-filled metal ashtray that I'd seen before on their kitchen counter. I promptly dug my heels into the ground.

"Max, Bee has something to say to you," Father said, momentarily straightening up to stand next to Mrs. Baker, whose cries abated with her son's appearance.

"Okay," Max replied as he placed the ashtray on the table next to his mother, who nodded. He still held the Matchbox car firm in his grasp; it must have belonged to Sally.

Max didn't blink as I repeated the same thing I'd said to his mother. When I was done, he began pushing the car back and forth on the table. I winced every time his arm moved, thinking how my own mother would be worried about scratches.

"Okay," he repeated as Mrs. Baker sniffled. She still hadn't said anything, and Max slowed down his car to glance up at Father. "It was my fault, you know. Not Bee's."

There was a silence, and Father frowned. Mrs. Baker used the end of her cigarette to light a new one and then put out the stub in the tray among the others.

"Max?" I said, in a high-pitched voice as I gripped onto the back of one of the dining chairs. "What do you mean? That's not true."

"It is my fault. I was the one who should have been watching her," he said.

Mrs. Baker just blew a ring of smoke and didn't say anything. Her face was splotchy and swollen, her eyes like narrowly opened window slats.

"Max?" I said again as he continued driving his car on the table. "Father?" I added, unable to believe that this was what Max still thought—and that his mother would just let him say it. The pity I'd started to feel for Mrs. Baker instantly vanished.

But my father didn't say anything, just placed his hand on

Mrs. Baker's shoulder and stood there, like they were posing for an old-time family portrait. His face was hard, like an unripe fruit. I'd never seen Father touch another adult, other than Mother, like that. A sudden pride flashed through me. He was not a father like Mr. Wiley, who would sling his arms around Patrick and Andrew while they played basketball on their driveway, who would hold Mrs. Wiley's hand during their neighborhood strolls. My father was not affectionate, yet here he was, as awkward as it was, trying to console Mrs. Baker.

"Max, that's not true," I said, feeling it was my duty to comfort Max. "We were all watching her. Your mother—" I stopped myself short of saying that Mrs. Baker should have been watching her. We were kids, after all. Why would it be our fault? Even Mother had insinuated, on the phone with Mrs. Wiley, that Mrs. Baker should have kept a more watchful eye on Sally.

As if hearing my thoughts, Mrs. Baker glanced briefly at me and then squinted her eyes shut. I gave Father a pleading look, but he shook his head slightly and remained silent.

Max nodded at me, as if to say goodbye, and headed back upstairs. I heard a loud noise and quick succession of steps, as if he'd accidentally dropped the car and scooted to collect it.

The three of us remained in the room, silent. Father removed his hand from Mrs. Baker's shoulder and sank into a nearby chair. I remained standing, counting the number of repeats in the wallpaper and wondering if I was supposed to say something. Mrs. Baker sniffled, and when I dared to glance at her, she closed her lids again, avoiding my eyes. Her hair hung limply around her shoulders, the top part flat and shiny, like it needed washing.

I was about to ask Father if we could just come back later, and then Dr. Baker arrived. He stood in the doorway, his eyebrows lifted in surprise. Father explained why we'd come over—that I had something to say. Dr. Baker nodded, removing his glasses and rubbing them on the bottom of his blue scrub shirt. He seemed tired, slow in his movements. What had he done that day—what type of people had he seen, what kind of surgeries?

As he placed his glasses back on and smoothed out his shirt, I noticed a red stain on the upper part of his scrub pants, over his right thigh. Was that blood? For a moment, I wondered whether I should put Dr. Baker on my suspect list. But he was a surgeon, I reasoned. He was bound to have blood on him. Right?

Father, who'd come to stand next to me, now nudged me, and so I recounted what I'd done, how I was sorry. Dr. Baker simply nodded, but the information seemed to physically overcome him, his shoulders slouching, his body shrinking inside his scrubs. When I was done, he said, "Can you explain again where you found it?"

"In the sand."

"Did you see anything else?" He glanced over at Mrs. Baker, who was still sitting at the dining table. I wondered why Dr. Baker hadn't gone over to stand next to her. Or even to give her a kiss. Father always gave Mother a kiss when he got home from work.

"Uh, no."

"Nothing unusual where you found it? Are there any other details you can remember?" he inquired.

I bit my lip. I wanted to be helpful, but I didn't know what more I could offer. "I'm not sure."

"And you found it when everyone was looking for her?"

I'd already said that. "Yeah." Father gave me a look. "I mean, yes."

"Do you remember exactly where in the sand you were?" I must have looked blank, because Dr. Baker expanded, "If you were to go back, could you identify the spot where you found it?"

I slowly nodded. "I think so."

"You'll have to go to the police station," Dr. Baker replied. "That's the first step. And tell them. You need to see Chief Riley."

At the mention of police, a sick feeling came over me. Police. Did that mean I was in trouble, like trouble-trouble? And what did he mean, the first step? Would I have to talk to other people, like the FBI, or the private investigator he'd reportedly hired?

"Thank you, Betty, for telling us," Dr. Baker continued in a tired but gentle tone, and his graciousness surprised me. "It's always good to be honest."

"Bee," I corrected him, surprising myself with my boldness. Father leaned into me, as if to say, *Just let it go.*

"What was that?"

"My name is Bee, not Betty. Well, it's really Borka, but I go by Bee."

"Aha," Dr. Baker said. "My apologies."

"You don't have to apolo—" I started to say, while Father began steering me toward the door.

"Borka, head outside," he commanded. "I'll be there in a sec."

I stepped through the threshold, into the autumn night air, which was now crisp and cool. The conversation felt unfinished, although I wasn't sure why. A minute later, Father rejoined me. As we made our way down the front steps and onto the driveway, I knew: I'd wanted to tell Dr. Baker how Max felt responsible for Sally's disappearance. Dr. Baker should know so that he could reassure Max. Because Mrs. Baker sure as heck wasn't doing anything about it.

But now it was too late.

I'd driven by the police station nearly every day of my life—it was on Main Street, on our way to school—but had never had reason before to be inside. Mother and I waited for Chief Riley the following day in the station lobby. It was nearly empty: just us and the blond-haired, middle-aged receptionist, who reminded me of my third-grade teacher, Mrs. Nowak, so much so that I almost smiled at her. They had the same pointy jaw and puggish nose, an unusual combination that felt wrong, mismatched, like the features should instead belong to two different people. The woman's hands moved quickly across a typewriter. One line done, and then she would pull the arm back to reset to the next line.

My backpack rested at my ankles; Mother was planning to drop me off at school afterward. The timing that morning had worked out well: When we'd entered the front door of the police station, school had already started, and thus none of my friends spotted me during their own drive to school. You had to be careful in small towns with just one main street.

I was still unsure whether Audrina, who had felt well enough to return to school, knew about the bracelet. She'd been watching TV in the family room when we returned home from the Bakers', and then, while we'd readied for school, she hadn't said anything, so neither had I.

The title *Chief of Police* sounded so serious, making me nervous. "Mother," I whispered, not wanting the receptionist to hear, although the typing was fairly loud. "Do they have a jail here?"

Mother lowered the *Reader's Digest* magazine she'd picked up from an end table to thumb through. "No."

"Oh." No jail made me feel a little better. Plus, I still had my backpack with me. Backpack equaled school.

Leah, I realized, might want to know the reason for my late arrival. She'd been trying to hang out with me more recently, suggesting activities she knew I might find attractive, as if feeling desperate she was losing me. The next time we hung out, she'd recently promised, we could go through her mother's old piles of *Cosmopolitan* and *Glamour* magazines.

Dentist appointment. I'd tell Leah—and anyone else who asked—that I'd had a dentist appointment. Right as I wondered how much longer this would take, Chief Riley appeared in the hallway entrance. Either he was taller than I'd remembered or the ceiling was short—his head was less than a foot away from it. His dark brown hair was combed over to the side, his tie neatly knotted around his thick neck.

"Borka Cock-sick—" Chief Riley beckoned us with a wave of his hand.

"Kocsis," Mother and I corrected at the same time, while I scooped up my backpack and imagined an *X* crossed through my name. First and last name—a giant *X*, replaced with the most boring of names: Jane, or maybe Ann, or possibly even Mary. Last name could be the runner-up, like Jane Mary, or Ann Jane. I certainly hoped none of the boys in my class would ever mispronounce my last name like Chief Riley just had.

We followed him past what looked like a meeting room, where we spotted Officer Jimmy sitting alone with his feet propped up on a large table. "Jimmy," Chief Riley simply said, pausing for a moment in the doorway. His tone was one of parental disapproval, and Jimmy quickly removed his feet; he seemed surprised to see us and gave Chief Riley a questioning look, but Chief Riley continued on.

He led us into his office, which was the very last one at the end of the hall. It didn't seem much different from the office of my pediatrician, minus the bulletin board with kids' pictures and drawings. There were windows with crooked white plastic blinds, framed documents hanging on the wall, and a desk with a few photos. One of the picture frames was angled enough that I could make out a dark-haired child.

"So, Borka," Chief Riley said, leaning back in his chair. His face had scattered bumps on it, almost like zits without the redness. The ones on his cheeks faded into his face muscles when he spoke: "Your parents mentioned you have something to tell us related to Sally Baker."

A heat spread over me, and I began to tap my feet on the floor. It seemed so real all of a sudden. "Yeah," I muttered, and then corrected myself before Mother could say anything, "Yes, Chief Riley."

Mother reached into her purse to pull out a plastic bag containing the bracelet. The kind of bag she used for my apple slices and Goldfish snacks. She handed it to the chief, who looked at it for a moment before laying it down on his desk and reaching for his pen.

He didn't seem surprised by the story I was there to tell; he just nodded every so often and occasionally scribbled onto a notepad. He did press me on the location of where I'd found the bracelet, although I had trouble putting it into words. "The sand . . . but it was the gravelly part of the sand. Like if you were going to the porta potty."

Chief Riley cocked his head. "You found it by the porta potty?"

"It was in the sand," I repeated, and realized how unhelpful that sounded. I tried again: "I mean, how the sand turns gravelly the further away you get from the water."

Jimmy popped his head through the door just then and glanced around at us. "Do you need anything, Chief?"

"No, Jimmy, we're all set."

Jimmy nodded and looked around again, seemingly narrowing in on the bracelet bag, before he disappeared. Had he been eavesdropping? I supposed all the Hammend police were naturally going to learn of my mistake; my cheeks burned at the thought.

Chief Riley picked up the bag and looked at it for some time, turning it over, examining the bracelet from different angles. His big stomach protruded so much it created a shelf he might have rested the bag on. "We'll have to take a ride out there, and you can show us the spot where you found it, okay?"

"Okay," I automatically replied. And then, "When?"

"No time like the present. That okay for you, Mrs. Coat-cheeks?"

I saw Mother flinch, but this time she didn't bother to correct him. "Fine," she said, her lips pressed together. I could tell she liked the idea of taking a ride to the lake about as much as I did.

I'd never been to Deer Chase Lake except in the summer, and of course I hadn't been back since Sally went missing. Without the concession stand and the lifeguard and the people, things looked different, felt different. Subdued, tired. The trees—of which there were so many—were tall and naked, wearily exposed. *Look*, the trees seemed to say, as they extended their bony branches and rheumatoid fingers, *we have nothing to hide*.

They had seen it, I remember wanting to absurdly point out to Chief Riley, when he asked me to show him the location where I'd found the bracelet. The trees knew.

Because I didn't. The porta potties were no longer there, and even though Chief Riley showed me where they had once stood, I had trouble remembering where I had been in relation to them when I'd come across the bracelet. I pointed to one sandy spot, where there were bits of gravel mixed in, and Chief Riley took pictures, but when he asked me, "Are you sure?" I nodded while at the same time, admitting, "No."

"Bee," said Mother, who'd been pacing up and down the sand, her arms forming stiff perpendicular angles, like a toy soldier, with each step. Her movement annoyed me. "This is really important."

"I *know*," I snapped, and then quickly added, "Sorry," when Mother paused her walking to glare at me.

Her eyes softened a bit, and she nodded. "It's okay. Take your time."

But I couldn't take my time. It was now late morning—well past the time it would have taken to go to the dentist—and I worried about what excuse I could offer to Leah and others when I finally arrived to school. Morning attendance and first-period English were over, and likely second-period social studies was nearing its end.

"I think it was here," I said, returning to the patch of sand that Chief Riley had already photographed. He'd inserted a small red flag, like the kind landscapers used to indicate when grass had been fertilized. Only the ones on our neighborhood lawns were usually yellow, fitted with warning symbols. "It's just hard to know," I admitted. "I remember it was in the sand but the rougher part," I said as my gaze drifted down the beach—whose entire outer edge, I now realized, was gravelly.

"Were you walking toward the water or toward the porta potties?"

"The porta potties," I replied as I watched Chief Riley make a note. "But I wasn't going to the porta potties."

"No?"

"No, I was just walking around. Looking for Sally."

"Were there people around you at the time?"

I frowned, frustrated at my inability to more precisely recall the information. "I don't really remember. I didn't see anyone."

"You didn't see anyone, or you *couldn't* see anyone?"

When I paused, Chief Riley added, "I'm trying to figure out if you were in an area that was obscured from view."

"I didn't see anyone," I said. Was that really true? Perhaps it had been the other way around. Perhaps I had been hidden from view, concealed by the porta potties I had been walking toward.

"Okay, Borka," Chief Riley said. "I was just wondering if being here would jog your memory further, if you might recall something else."

I looked at the lake; it was still, like the end of an exhalation. It seemed that at any moment the surface would break, expelling a lifeguard who'd been swimming underneath, searching for Sally. "Why would they even think Sally drowned, anyway?" I wondered aloud. "Why would that have been what was searched first?"

Chief Riley crouched down to my level, but he remained a few inches taller than I was. "What do you mean?" he asked, his light brown eyes blinking a few times. He shoved his hand into the ground for balance, glancing down as he did so, and I noticed a shiny, hairless patch on his head. Standing so close to him made me feel self-conscious, and I took a step back as Mother came to stand by my side.

"Just, like, why would they search the lake first? Instead of the woods?"

"Well," said Chief Riley, whipping his head suddenly toward the lake as if he, too, had spotted someone swimming in there. "Why wouldn't they?"

"I mean, it's not like she drowned."

"Why not?" Chief Riley pressed, now turning to face me again.

I sighed. "Because she didn't like to swim."

"That may have been true, but she still could have drowned. It happens very quickly, it can happen very quickly even for people that know how to swim." The beeper attached to his belt began buzzing, and he rose and unclipped the beeper to examine it.

"Are we done here?" Mother asked.

Chief Riley snapped the beeper back on his belt. "Yes, I believe we are. Borka, thank you for helping today."

I kicked the ground hard; it didn't really seem like I'd helped at all. I wished I'd been able to remember more detail. Before we left, I had one more question, one lingering question that was festering inside me. Had been since the first time I'd seen the flyer on our fridge door; maybe, if I was being truthful, even earlier than that. It was the same question Father had asked me. "Um, Chief Riley," I began, my voice already faltering—it was so difficult to utter the words. "Would it have helped if I'd told you—told someone—sooner? About finding the bracelet?"

Chief Riley glanced at Mother, who had a pleading look on her face, the kind that she used when she wanted Father to do something. He looked at her, and then down at the sand, and then toward the lake. And then, for a good long moment, he stared off at a section of the woods where there were tall, naked trees, and I suddenly wondered if that was where they had found the other half of the bracelet. Chief Riley hadn't said anything about its discovery to us, and I wondered if Mother knew, though I wasn't about to ask her. Chief Riley took a moment too long to respond, and that moment sank me. He did meet my eyes when he finally said, "No, I don't think so," but there was a thinness in his words, almost as if they were translucent.

# Chapter Seven

"Borka!" Father hollered from downstairs later that evening when he came home from work. "Come to the study!"

I was alone—Mother had taken Audrina somewhere. I slowly made my way down the stairs and paused at the threshold. Getting called into the study by Father was never a good thing, and this time I knew exactly what it was about.

Father sat at his desk that smelled of wood and leather, his back turned. After a few seconds he glanced over his shoulder and noticed me. Rolling his chair around, he jerked his head toward the dark tan leather couch. "Come in, have a seat."

I sank into the couch, my insides feeling unnaturally tight.

"So, Borka," he said. I couldn't wait to go back to being just Bee. I'd been called by my real name so many times that day.

Father gave me a long look. "You met with Chief Riley."

"Yes, Father."

"And you went to Deer Chase Lake? Did it help at all?"

I wasn't sure what Father meant, but I assumed he was asking whether it would help find Sally. "Um . . . I don't think so."

My father nodded, slowly. He folded his hands onto his lap, and I noticed how thin his waist was in comparison to Chief Riley's. "You did the right thing, the hard thing, by going over to the Bakers' and telling them," he said.

"Yes," I replied.

"Well. Well, I hope you learned your lesson."

"Yes, I did," I said, averting my eyes to look down at the rug. And I meant it. I would have done anything to change what I did. I couldn't bear to think that my foolish, split-second decision could have potentially had an impact. I just had to believe Chief Riley that it wouldn't have mattered.

The chair squeaked as Father leaned back into it. "Good."

When I glanced up at him, I could tell, by the absence of lines on his forehead, he wasn't upset with me—at least not too upset. I waited for him to continue, but he didn't. It seemed we weren't going to discuss it further. I gave him a tiny smile. When he returned it, I felt my insides begin to unstick themselves a bit, which gave me the courage to ask a question. "Father, did you ever do something like that, you know, when you were younger?"

He crossed his ankles together and scratched his chin. It was smooth; the facial hair he'd temporarily sported when Sally went missing long gone. "We all make mistakes, Bee. I didn't steal a bracelet when I was younger because, well, as a boy I wasn't interested in bracelets." He chuckled. "But I did other things . . ." His eyebrows drew together, and a long, deep slice now appeared across the skin of his forehead.

"Like what?" I prompted.

He swatted at the air, like he was shooing away a fly. "Well, one time I stole a loaf of bread, when I was a boy in Budapest—"

"Really?"

"—because I was hungry."

"Oh."

"I stole it from my friend, from his father's bakery," Father continued.

"Oh."

"They were struggling—we all were, once the Russians came. They took everything from us—the Communists. Everything we all had worked so hard for."

I remained quiet, still—not even wanting to satisfy an itch on the inside of my thigh. I was well aware of Father's view of the Russian Communists, but I hadn't heard this story.

"And so, when I stole it, it was bad. They needed it. They needed the money; they needed the food. We all did. Everyone was in the same position; we were all hungry. The last thing I should have done is steal from a friend." He began rotating his gold wedding band around on his finger. "So, we all make mistakes. Kids, even adults."

"Oh?" I repeated for a third time, wanting him to continue. When he didn't, I pressed, "Did you get caught?"

"I sure did. My father found out. I got in a lot of trouble." Then, to my disappointment, he glanced at his watch and said, "It's getting late. You have homework to finish?"

"Father?" I asked, ignoring his question and rising from the couch.

"Yes?"

"Did you ever know anyone that just disappeared?"

"Well, not in this country, not in America," my father replied. "Can't say that I did. Sally will turn up."

"Really?" Excitement trickled through me. "You think so?"

"Well, what I meant was, I think we will eventually find out what happened to her."

"Oh." I exhaled slowly. *Most murders are committed by someone the victim knows.* "Father?" I said again.

"Yeees?" Father replied with a grin.

"Do you think that someone who knew her tried to hurt her? Someone we—we know?"

Father's grin was gone. There was a strange look that now came across his face. He squinted his eyes slightly, and his jaw stiffened. I waited, but he didn't respond. "Father?" I prompted him.

"No, I don't think that. It's late, Bee."

"Okay," I said, starting toward the door, "Father, one more thing." He nodded, so I quickly continued, "Well, um, I feel bad that Max feels like it's his fault. About Sally. Remember he said that, when we were there?" Father nodded again. "Well, I just wish his mother would tell him otherwise."

His face softened. "You're right, Bee. Thank you for pointing that out. I'll have a talk with Fran—Mrs. Baker."

Now that I'd been forced to face my choice, the shame I felt about stealing the bracelet was like a prickly brush I needed to get by—if I moved a certain way, if I moved the *wrong* way, the shame would pierce me. But if I navigated slowly and skillfully, then I could clear my way around it. Move past.

So I was careful. In the days following my meeting with Chief Riley, I avoided my sister, which turned out to be easy because she'd signed up for the local theater production of *Peter Pan*. Play practices ran in the evenings. And at night, my sister stayed up late in the kitchen, studying her lines, crawling into bed once I'd already fallen asleep. Because the director's daughter was already playing Wendy, they of course wrote in a whole new role for Audrina—an added sister—which Mother proudly filled me in on during a car ride home from school.

As the days passed with limited contact, I began to wonder if *she* was actually avoiding *me*. I didn't think Audrina knew what I'd done, but I didn't want to find out. I worried she would take a magnifying glass to my poor decision, further enlarging my shame, creating more prickles. She'd probably want to probe why I'd done it, finding the notion herself inconceivable. But whether she examined it or didn't, whether she confronted me or remained silent, the end result was the same. She wouldn't have done it; I did. Plus, I didn't tell her, which could only add insult to injury.

It seemed that Audrina had always been the better sister. The one our parents favored, the one who did the right thing, the one to whom things came easily. I'd had to rely on the association of a missing girl to match her popularity status. And even that I couldn't do right; it was possible I'd messed it up now with the stupid bracelet.

Trying to lie low, I was careful to act normal, so no one at school—as well as no one in the neighborhood gang—would learn about what I'd done. Max certainly wasn't going to say anything; he still barely spoke to anyone. I wished, strangely enough, that he would address it with me—just me. I wanted him to react, to get mad. Then, at least, he wouldn't blame only himself for his sister's disappearance. How could his mother have just let him believe that?

I was beginning to realize that Mrs. Baker was not a very nice person. She seemed to do whatever she wanted—a trait that reminded me of Audrina. During rides to school, Mrs. Baker would eat, in between puffs of her cigarette, Lay's potato chips from a large bag—not the snack size Mother occasionally bought for our lunches. She'd hold the steering wheel with her left hand—red nails curled around a long, skinny cigarette—while she dipped her right hand into the bag, pulling out generous fistfuls. Crumbs would fall down like flakes of dandruff, which she would wipe off her box of Virginia Slims to grab her next cigarette. When we caught the red light on Main Street, the smoky air pooled in the station wagon instead of escaping through her cracked window, making me cough. I didn't understand how Mrs. Baker could even find the chips appealing—I imagined they must smell and taste like the film of ash I spied on the center console. I soon began to trade my snack size of Lay's chips for Leah's Doritos on our way to the cafeteria. Leah hesitated the first time I asked her to make the switch, but she acquiesced, like I'd known she would. From that day forward she brought two bags of Doritos to school and traded one away, while depositing the un-opened Lay's into her backpack.

With that prickly brush always just a smidge away from scraping me, I didn't tell Mother about the smoking, about how Mrs. Baker waited until pulling out of our driveway to light her first cigarette, or how once she was almost done with it, she used it to light up the next one. I knew Mother wouldn't like it, and I didn't want to draw any further attention.

I wondered what compelled Mrs. Baker to behave so strangely; did she blame herself for Sally's disappearance, like some of the people in town did? Did she know something about it? Closer scrutiny was shifting her back toward my suspect list. It was odd how mismatched she and Dr. Baker were. If there were a police lineup and I had to choose which suspect Mrs. Baker was married to, never in a million years would I select Dr. Baker. I couldn't ever remember a time when I'd seen them physically next to each other.

I couldn't help but ponder whether an ulterior motive kept them together. Perhaps they were harboring a secret—a secret about Sally.

The thing was: How does one lose a daughter, like she's a toy? It just didn't make sense.

I could usually smell the smoke on my clothes during the first few periods of school, but it must have dissipated by the time I came home at night or Mother surely would have caught on. Since our morning with the chief, it seemed like Mother was noticing everything about me. She hadn't mentioned the bracelet again, nor did she seem upset with me. If anything, she seemed to hold more compassion toward me. I knew this in the way she scrutinized me more than usual, checking to see if my shirt was adequately wrinkle-free, if my nails were cut short enough, if the part in my hair was straight, if I'd completed all homework assignments to her satisfaction. This last precaution she and I both knew was unnecessary: I was a good student, the much better one. I was well on my way to earning straight As, maybe even all A-pluses. Though I didn't have a hobby like Audrina's acting, my grades were historically one of the only edges I held over her. When I wasn't studying, I loved curling up with an L. M. Montgomery novel. In particular, I loved rereading the Emily of New Moon series; there was a lingering darkness in Emily with which I strongly identified. Sometimes I fantasized about possessing a psychic ability like she'd had. Perhaps then I could locate Sally, maybe even by harnessing the power of the bracelet fragment.

My sister read only when she had to, if then. Already that fall I'd overheard a conversation between Mother and Father, after they received a call from Audrina's teacher: Instead of participating in class, my sister doodled hearts and rainbows. She wasn't keeping up with her assignments, couldn't master her fractions, and misspelled common compound words. The teacher had added, apparently aghast, "Audrina doesn't seem to care." I'd had to stifle a laugh when I heard this last bit; I found it somewhat satisfying to know that someone else—an adult, no less—found Audrina frustrating. The thing was, you just had to accept that what my sister deemed important was important—to her. Audrina had clearly decided at some point she didn't care about getting good grades, so no amount of tutoring, extra help, or teacher reprimands was going to change that. Mother must have realized this, too; despite Audrina's teacher's complaints, Mother remained more meticulous in checking my homework than my sister's.

And I secretly loved this extra attention—proof that I, too, was special.

# Chapter Eight

MOTHER USED TO WARN AUDRINA AND ME TO BE CAREFUL ABOUT writing things down on paper. "Once you write it, you can't deny it," she would say. This was before the widespread use of the Internet and any social media. Writing was both our tool and weapon— allowing us to pass notes in class, to record our thoughts, to fill out homework worksheets. It was how we identified ourselves, from initials scratched into wood desks, to gossip penned on the back door of the girls' bathroom stall, to our signatures, both in cursive and print, uppercase and lowercase.

I used to believe Mother about the danger of the permanence of written words, but then something happened that led me to believe that spoken words are just as powerful, as undeniable, as written ones. Perhaps more so, even, because they don't have a landing pad like their written counterparts. There is no thrice-folded-up note or bathroom stall door on which to be scribbled. Instead, the spoken words—the hurtful ones—float around in you, without a substance on which to anchor. The hurt shifts like water, sloshing around in your insides, rising up when you tilt certain ways, sometimes unexpectedly so. Just to remind you it is still there.

A week had passed since my meeting with Chief Riley, and nothing more about the bracelet came up, so the prickly brush thinned. I hadn't talked at length yet with Audrina, who continued to spend late evenings with her play script in the kitchen. We'd had a few curt exchanges in the morning, but I chalked it up to her crankiness or to her perhaps still being sore about the Halloween incident. I reasoned, logic prevailing, that if she knew about the bracelet, she would have said something. Or I would have been able to sense that she knew, even if she'd kept quiet.

When the weekend arrived, Mother announced that we were finally going to go apple picking, our fall family tradition. Normally we went in September or October—not mid-November—but Father's business had been particularly busy on the weekends that fall; he'd been making up for time he took off after Sally went missing.

As we climbed into the back of the car, I was surprised when Audrina scooted all the way over, as far away as she could get from me, as if I were a contagious disease.

"Drina," I said, and when she didn't reply, I leaned over and jabbed her side with my finger, hitting the middle of one of the squares on her green plaid flannel shirt. "Drina."

"Stop," she replied brusquely, and shifted toward the door.

*Is she really still mad about Halloween?* I wondered. And then the unsettling thought took ahold of me: *Does she know about the bracelet after all? Did Mother or Father tell her?* "Drina," I tried again, as I swallowed.

But she didn't respond.

"Drina," I said, a little louder.

"Leave me alone."

"Girls," warned Mother, as she turned around, pointing a finger at us. Mother, in particular, hated when we bickered. Father would usually ignore it until things escalated and Mother asked him to intervene.

The whole ride to Stilkes Farm—about an hour—Audrina and I didn't talk, and I became increasingly uneasy. I replayed recent events in my mind, trying to figure out what was wrong. I kept returning to the possibility that she knew about the bracelet, but I also kept rejecting it, not wanting it to be true. I gazed out the window at the passing scenery, counting the endless telephone poles. There were farms that were much closer, a couple even located in our town, but they didn't have apple orchards as extensive or farm animals and tractor hayrides. So we always went to Stilkes, though we went so late that year that Red Delicious—my favorite apple variety, because it reminded me of Snow White—was picked out, and the only pumpkins left were bruised and sad-looking.

But we didn't need a pumpkin; Halloween had passed. And despite the tension between Audrina and me, as I bit into a juicy Granny Smith—almost as good as a Red Delicious—I found myself enjoying the crisp day. The sun shone brightly, the earth smelled fresh, and Mother and Father walked along holding hands—a rarity. I filled my collection bag with GoldRush and Macoun apples, and Father held the ladder as I climbed up to grab more Granny Smiths. I laughed when he pretended I'd dropped an apple on his head. Audrina kept her distance, exploring an adjacent row, but I barely noticed; I was having too much fun.

After our bags were heavy, we stopped at a farm stand for warm apple-cider donuts. Audrina and I silently munched on the last of them while waiting in line for the next hayride. I didn't even enjoy hayrides anymore—finding them boring—but Audrina did, so of course Mother and Father expected us to still do it together.

When the dusty green tractor pulling the wooden crate returned, my sister waited for me to board first and then tried to sit as far away as possible, on the opposite end, like she had in the car. But then a group of six boys scrambled on, forcing her to move down, directly across from me. As the tractor pulled away and we began to bump along, each on opposing haystacks, the breeze of the late afternoon intensified. We both pulled the wool blankets pooled at our feet over our legs.

A few of the kids began laughing as they started a curse-laden verse of "Old MacDonald Had a Farm"—with a pig who went *"oink shit here."*

"Drina," I said, leaning forward. She couldn't avoid me like she had that morning; we were face-to-face.

She stared at me, hard. Her cheeks were slightly reddened from the wind, and her hair was pulled back into a loose ponytail that kept getting slacker. "What," she finally responded, in more of a statement than a question.

"Why are you being like this?"

"Do you really have to ask why?" She shook her hair free of a pink elastic and pulled it onto her wrist.

"Yes," I simply replied, unsure how else to respond.

*". . . and on that farm he had an ugly owl . . . ,"* sang the other kids.

"Because of the charm bracelet," she said.

Her words slapped me. *So she knew.* "I . . ."

"I mean, I just can't believe you took it," my sister said, raising her voice. "And then you hid it? What if it was a clue or some-thing?"

"It—it wasn't," I replied. "Chief Riley said so." But of course he had said no such thing. I momentarily drew my knees up to my chest but then had to place them quickly down again because the crate was wobbling too much, and the prickly brush was now on me, in me. "I had to meet with the chief," I added, because I wasn't sure what she knew and didn't know about what had transpired.

Two boys at the far end of the hayride, on the same side as Audrina, got louder, now switching to—and tainting—another nursery rhyme. "*There's a goddamn hole in the bucket, dear Liza, dear Liza,*" they sang. They seemed at least a year or two older than me, and I noticed how they kept leaning forward and glancing at Audrina.

My sister ignored the boys and gave me another long, hard stare. I finally had to look away and instead gazed out at the rows of apple orchards around us. From where we were, I couldn't see their uneven limbs, their mesh of intertwined arms and disproportionate number of apples. I saw only orderly lines of green trees, uniformly placed, decorated with red dots. The way Mother would like it. I wondered if that's how Audrina and I appeared to a faraway spectator: neat, spaced perfectly apart from each other, deceptively harmonious. "Just please don't tell anyone," I finally pleaded, now looking back at my sister. "Please."

Audrina picked at the edge of her blanket, extracting nubby pieces. "If my barrette hadn't fallen on the floor, I wouldn't have found it. Like probably never."

It took me a moment to hear what she had to say. *Really* hear it. "Wait—*you* found it?"

Audrina kept talking: "It was so wrong of you."

"*You* found it? You told Mother and Father?" A chill went through me, as though the sun had disappeared behind a cloud. But the sky was clear, and it was still bright.

"Of course." Her tone was matter-of-fact. She let the blanket fall from her hand like she had no use for it anymore, like she was dropping something into the garbage. "They had to know. I didn't know what to think when I found it. I'm so scared for Sally—"

"Why didn't you say something *to me*?" I cut in.

"Because."

"Because why?"

"Because—because *this*."

"What do you mean?" My voice got louder, and now the boys in the crate turned to stare.

"Because—because I knew you were going to be like this." She waved her hand around us, and I felt my face grow warm.

"Whatever, Drina." I knew she found me defensive, and I was— but rightfully so. She'd betrayed me. She was my sister; she was supposed to look out for me. Instead, she'd done the exact opposite. The ground below me began to blur, as my eyes filled with tears.

". . . Then get a clue, dumb Henry, dumb Henry, dumb Henry," the boys continued to bellow.

A couple minutes later, after I had managed to squash the burgeoning tears, I said quietly, "I don't even like hayrides. They're childish and stupid. I wouldn't even be doing this if it wasn't for you."

"Yeah, well, same here," she said, though I knew she was lying.

"It may have been 'so wrong' to take the bracelet, but it was 'so wrong' of you to give it to Sally in the first place."

"It was my bracelet. I could give it to anyone. Anyone I want."

"But I'm your sister," I protested, as anger flared inside me. "You knew how much I loved that bracelet." I kicked the back of my leg against the haystack; it was surprisingly firm and itchy, and pain shot across my calf. "You should've given it to me," I added, my voice shaky. "Then this wouldn't have happened. I feel like maybe you didn't just because you knew how much I wanted it." It was what I'd been wanting to say for months.

"Besides," Audrina continued, like she'd hadn't heard me, "Sally was just a little girl. *Is* just a little girl. It was nice of me to give it to her."

"So you care more about being nice to someone else than to your sister?" I spit out. The back of my leg started aching, and I had a weird desire to thrust it again against the haystack, perhaps even harder this time.

Audrina leaned forward, her eyes tagging mine, like a laser. "You mean, like the way you care more about Hope than you do about me?"

"That's not true."

"Yeah, it is."

"Is this all because of Halloween?" I asked incredulously. "Because a friend of *mine* happened to show up that night? Am I not allowed to have friends like you do?"

"No. I'm just pointing out the facts."

The boys were done singing, and now one of them said loudly, "This message will self-destruct," and then they snickered. But I no longer cared whether or not they heard us.

"The facts?" I repeated. "The facts are that you always are doing things with Lindsay and Vanessa and—and all your other friends, and I never give you a hard time. Do you have any idea what it's like, how awful *I* feel, when you always choose your friends over me? Or what it's even like to be your sister? Everything comes so easy to you—and you don't even realize it. So why would you resent that I now have my own life, my own friends? Do you not want me to be happy?"

"I would think," Audrina sneered, again ignoring my points, "you'd be *happy* Sally got something nice before she disappeared. You really are terrible."

"Yeah, well, so are you!" I shot back.

"I wish you weren't my sister," she said forcefully, now settling back into her seat and staring off above my head. A moment later, she added, in an almost wistful tone, "I always wish that." Her face relaxed, her eyes turning glossy, almost doe-eyed. A second later, maybe even half a second, she shifted and turned to the side. It was the type of movement you do when you're uncomfortable, when you feel too exposed.

That was it—those were the words: *I always wish that.* Time stilled then, and the moment caught me like a net. Noises of the outside world hushed, my breathing paused, and the rush in my head grew louder.

We might have said hurtful things to each other in the past, but never in this way. There was an undeniable truth to Audrina's words: Anger might have unearthed them, but she didn't say them *only* because she was angry. The words seeped into me, a density of shame.

She didn't want me as her sister, confirming a long-held fear I'd harbored: I was not worthy of her.

But it wasn't always so.

This is us at four and five: Wobbly-legged on our bikes, training wheels off for the first time. We are positioned at the top of our street, Father standing behind us.

*Go, go!* he says.

I know he's talking to me. But I can't go. My heart pounds as I stare down the hill. My knee still smarts from the tumble I took on the cul-de-sac. Wordless, I shake my head.

Father grows impatient; it's hot out. His forehead glistens with sweat. *Go,* he says again.

*I can't,* I say.

*Yes. You can.*

*No, I can't.*

*You did it already.*

*But that was down there. This hill is scary.*

*Borka, if I have to push you down the street, I will. You know how to bike. Now go!*

He's angry now, I can tell. His face is red. I hate when he gets this way. Tears fill my eyes.

Suddenly Audrina pushes past us. *It's okay, Bee,* she says. *I'll go first.*

But she hadn't mastered the cul-de-sac. Not like I did. Father didn't even want her up here. Before I can say anything, she's off, flying down the street, much too fast.

*Use your break!* Father shouts. *Slow down!*

But she doesn't do either. She hits the curb, and she soars through the air before crashing hard on the sidewalk. My sister is in a heap, not moving. Father and I rush over. I'm shocked to see her crying. She never cries. She holds out her right hand: her pinky is bent the wrong way, like someone has tried to yank it off.

*It's okay,* Audrina says, smiling through her tears. *I'm okay. You can do it, Bee.*

This is us.

This is us—when it was just us.

# Chapter Nine

FATHER MUST HAVE TALKED TO MRS. BAKER LIKE HE SAID HE would, because she began to take more of an interest in Max—and, by default, me—during our morning car rides, at least on the days she was in a "good" mood. It gave me a chance to observe her more, to try to figure out exactly who Mrs. Baker was. Whether or not she deserved to be on my suspect list. Luckily she never brought up the charm bracelet piece, or Sally for that matter.

"Which song do you want?" she asked Max one morning, after lighting her first cigarette halfway down our street.

I could tell Max was surprised she'd asked; his eyebrows went up, and he took a moment to respond. "Uh . . . um . . ."

"How about you, Borkette?"

"Borka," I replied.

"Kinda awful name, isn't it?" She looked at me in the rearview mirror as she took a puff of her cigarette. She laughed and added, "But I guess Borkette is worse. Are you the one who came up with Bee?"

I nodded. It was sort of true; in third grade I'd begun drawing a bumblebee for the first letter of my name, followed by the *orka*, but then the boy next to me had noticed. "Bee. That's a good nickname," he'd said, and from then on I'd used it, though it had taken a while for people to catch on.

"Cat gotcha tongue? Which ABBA song do you like?" Smoke floated up from her cigarette, clouding her face.

"'Fernando,'" I replied promptly, and then I turned to Max, who nodded.

"Good song," he said. Then he looked down at his lap. "Sally used to like that one, too."

Mrs. Baker cranked up the music loud, louder than she normally did.

I found myself wanting to inch my fingers over, across the empty seat between us, and grasp Max's. I wanted to comfort him, but I also just wanted to physically touch him. Mrs. Baker couldn't see our hands from the rearview mirror, but I had no idea whether Max thought of me that way. He didn't seem to mind that I'd taken the charm bracelet, unlike Audrina, which made me feel safe. Like we were on the same side—a team. I knew a lot of girls in our seventh-grade class had a crush on Max, and Hope had mentioned, more than once, how lucky I was to be able to carpool with him. But I already knew that; I didn't need her to tell me. I hadn't told anyone how I felt about him, the way the days he wasn't at school seemed long and colorless. At least, I reasoned, I was the girl he talked to the most, or at least was around the most. And he did always sit in the back seat of the car, when he could've easily taken the front seat; that had to mean something.

But beginning one early December morning, Max could no longer sit in the front seat, even if he wanted. When Mrs. Baker rolled up to my house, I opened the station wagon door to find a pile of boxes stacked high on the middle seat.

"Hey," Max said, from the other side.

"Hi," I said, boxes tumbling into my lap as I climbed in. I grabbed a few, noticing the words *Mary Kay* written on them. I searched for a place to toss them, but the front seat was also occupied with boxes.

"You can throw those in the way back," Mrs. Baker said, barely turning around, and I could already tell it was going to be one of *those* days—the kind when she seemed bothered by any sort of interaction.

I peered in the back, but that area, too, was pretty full. I looked over at Max, who just shrugged and crossed his feet on the boxes he'd placed underneath like a footstool, so I followed suit.

"What are these boxes?" I asked once I'd made sufficient room for myself. Mrs. Baker didn't reply, so I leaned forward, curiosity getting the best of me, and tapped her on the shoulder, asking again.

"Mary Kay," Mrs. Baker said dryly.

"Makeup," Max clarified.

"Yeah, but what are you doing with it?" I asked, still leaning forward toward Mrs. Baker. "Are you selling it?"

"Ding-ding."

I settled back into my seat, puzzled. It seemed like every week that went by, Mrs. Baker became more of a mystery instead of less. I simply couldn't figure her out, and I didn't know if her peculiarities made her more suspicious. I hadn't made any headway on any of my other suspects, either, except for the white-haired pharmacist, who'd fallen off my list, quite literally. He'd suffered a deadly heart attack and collapsed at the store. When I heard about it, I was sure of two things: One, he'd clearly been too frail to pull off a kidnapping, and two, I was very glad I hadn't revealed my list to anyone.

Keeping his voice low, under the sound of the music, Max explained, "She was thinking about doing this before Sally . . ." And then his voice trailed off.

I tried to envision Mrs. Baker putting makeup on someone, like the way Mother sometimes got her makeup done at the Epstein's beauty counter, but I couldn't. "Cool," I finally mustered.

"Yeah, she's making a home office and everything."

"Oh yeah?" I flicked my eyes to the rearview mirror, but Mrs. Baker was staring straight ahead.

"Yeah, don't you already know? She's converting part of our basement into an office."

"How would I know that?"

"Because your father's going to do the work."

"Oh, right," I said, like I'd known and just forgotten. It wasn't unusual for Father to do side projects for our neighbors; he did the Wileys' kitchen cabinets, a toolshed for the Abbotts, a bookcase for Diane's father, and he once even constructed a playhouse for a family who lived on Maple Way. I must've not been paying attention when he'd mentioned it. I'd never seen the completed playhouse on Maple Way, I suddenly realized. I'd have to bike by sometime, before the weather got too cold to check it out. I'd been so wrapped up in my own newly packed social life. It was exhausting, especially since I'd been trying to ward off Alex's attention. He'd recently put a note inside my locker, asking me to the winter dance (he'd drawn a *yes* heart-shaped box, next to a broken-heart *no* box). I had yet to respond, but I had no desire to go to the dance with him, or at all. I'd finally gotten the courage to ask Max if he was planning to go, and he'd said he wasn't up to it.

"The basement's gonna be cool," Max said, with a lightness to his voice I hadn't heard in months. "We're making part of it the office, and then for the rest of it my dad said we could eventually create a rumpus room. With a pool table and everything."

"That does sound cool," I admitted.

"Your dad had some really good ideas, but actually your sister thought of the best idea: an old-fashioned soda fountain, like from a diner."

"My sister?" I replied, surprised.

"Yeah, she was with your dad when they stopped by to look at the space."

"Oh," I said. She hadn't mentioned anything to me, but why would she? Since the day at the farm, we'd had an uneasy truce, marked by a lot of silence between us. I never brought up the hurtful words she'd said, and she never brought up the bracelet. We both felt wronged, and I only hoped that our history of fighting would repeat: Eventually we would get over feeling slighted, or angry, or betrayed, and the weirdness between us would dissolve to the point where it would be hard to remember when it had ever existed.

But this fight had been a particularly terrible one, and now there seemed to be a shift in our relationship, a new mistrust. When she couldn't find something she'd misplaced, like one of her shirts, she would ask me in an accusing tone, "Do you *happen to know* where it might be?" When Mother would praise me for scoring 100 percent on a test, Audrina would sniff, as if I were somehow undeserving of her praise. It was almost as if she now thought less of me—her opinion of me as a person had diminished. It bothered me, deeply.

No matter how popular I'd become at school, nothing could erase the sting of my sister's reactions.

"What soda flavors do you think we should get?" Max asked. "I like root beer, Sprite, and Coke, but I'm not sure how many we can have."

"Those are good ones," I said. It was cute how excited Max was; I hadn't seen him like this before. He almost seemed *happy*. "I also like Mountain Dew," I added.

"Right! I forgot about that one." Max smiled and opened his mouth to say something else, but then closed it.

"What?"

Max shook his head. "Nothing."

"C'mon, tell me."

"It's nothing," he said, but then he continued to smile at me.

I wrote Alex a note, declining his invite to the dance, but thanking him nonetheless, and saying I just wanted to be friends. I slipped it into his locker early one morning, before he arrived at school. I didn't tell anyone I was doing it, but by lunchtime everyone knew. He and Jay Flay pointedly sat on the other side of the lunch room, and when I tried to give Alex a small smile from across the way, he'd simply turned away.

"Why would you do that?" Hope grilled me as Gwen and Michelle stopped munching to intently listen. Peanut butter oozed from the sandwich Michelle had pinched tightly between her hands.

I shrugged as I looked down at my own sandwich: ham and cheese with a generous amount of mayonnaise, though you would know only once you bit into it. Mother was meticulous about lunch presentation; she often wiped the edges of the sandwich before carefully placing it into the container. "I don't want to go to the dance."

"He was really upset," Hope continued, almost in an accusatory tone.

"Well, there's nothing really I can do about that."

Hope tapped her fingers against the table. "You could go to the dance with him, even if you only like him as a friend."

Again, I shrugged. I felt embarrassed, being put on the spot.

"So why don't you?" Hope now asked.

"I don't want to go to the dance," I reiterated, "and I don't want to go with him. He should go with someone that wants to go with him."

"I thought you would make a cute couple," Michelle piped in, and I sighed, looking away. Leah was sitting a few tables away; she caught my eye and smiled wistfully. I wished suddenly I were sitting there instead; I was tired of always trying to fit in with Hope and her friends.

Max was also a couple tables away, sitting with some of the boys from the soccer team. But his back was facing me, and I could only see a portion of the hair on his head. I stared at it, willing him to glance back, but he didn't.

When I turned my gaze back to the girls, I realized, to my surprise, they were waiting for me to speak. What more was there to say? "Look," I replied, now a little irritated but trying to mask it. "Alex is a nice guy. And yes, he's cute. But I just don't like him like that."

"That's too bad," Hope said condescendingly.

"Hope," I retorted, "if you care so much, then why don't *you* go to the dance with him?"

There was a beat, while Hope and the other girls stared at me.

Nobody spoke to Hope Rodale like that. I scrambled for something to say, something to soften the situation. "I just want to be his friend," I retreated, slowly reciting the words I'd written on the note to Alex.

"If you don't like him, then who do you like?" Hope interrogated.

"Nobody," I lied. I'd had a suspicion for a while that Hope's interest in Max extended beyond the disappearance of his sister, so I wasn't about to reveal my feelings. Perhaps, I suddenly realized, Hope was pushing me to be with Alex so that I wasn't an obstacle to Max.

"Are you still gonna go to the dance?" Michelle asked.

"I don't think so."

"Well, we don't have dates, and we're all going," Gwen said, gesturing to our table. Of the three, she seemed the nicest, often trying to compensate for Hope's behavior.

"My mom just told me that she and my dad went to a seventh-grade dance together," Michelle cut in, in a dreamy kind of voice. "Can you imagine that you might have already met the boy you're going to marry? Here at Hillside? He might be in this very room!"

"My parents went to school together, too," Hope said. "They lived across the street from each other."

"Not mine," revealed Gwen, a bit regretfully. "How about your parents, Bee? Isn't your dad from Germany?"

"My parents met in high school, in Paterson. Father grew up in Hungary, actually. His family left during the '56 Hungarian Revolution. They were refugees and eventually came to the States. Mother grew up in Paterson."

There was a beat, and then Hope snorted, "'Mother'? 'Father'?" causing Gwen and Michelle to laugh. "That's so . . . formal. What are you, from the 1950s? Who calls their parents that?"

I could feel my cheeks burning. I knew it was unusual, but it was just the way it was in our family; I couldn't ever remember calling them something different. "I—I don't know. We just do."

When the bell rang, Hope took off toward the door, not waiting for the group, like she normally did. The others scrambled after her, Michelle scoffing to Gwen, not so subtly, "I hope 'Mother' still lets me go to the mall with you later."

I stayed put, looking at the space where Hope had just been sitting and wondering if I had just undone everything.

The night of Hillside's winter dance, Leah and I spent the evening together at my house watching *Carrie*. When I asked my sister if she wanted to join us, she said no without bothering to offer up an excuse. I tried to reassure myself that this was how it worked between us, that it just took time to move on. But I was also aware of the gravity of our most recent fight.

When I called Hope the next day to find out how it went, she wasn't home, and for the first time in months, it occurred to me that she might not call back. I then tried Michelle and Gwen and, of the two, only reached Gwen.

"The dance was fine. You didn't miss much," she assured me. "Except Jay Flay pulled down one of the banners, and Señora Flannigan jumped out of the way, and then she fell into the table, and the whole thing collapsed."

I laughed, grateful for Jay's inadvertent diversion that had hopefully made the girls forget about my rejection of Alex. But as I waited by the phone the rest of the afternoon without it ringing, I began to feel worse and worse. In retrospect, I shouldn't have been surprised I was getting frozen out; I should've known, based on how things had played out at lunch—and then in the days afterward, when Hope stopped paying attention when I talked.

Peering out my front window, I spotted Andrew and Patrick tossing a baseball in the cul-de-sac. I threw on a coat to join them; I needed some physical distance from the phone.

"Mrs. Baker keeps a cart full of liquor in her dining room. And she smokes," I announced as we played catch, wanting to reveal something that would make me seem interesting and special again. I grasped the ball and threw it as hard as I could; the feel of it in my hand—real, tangible—was reassuring. I glanced over to the Bakers' house, even though I already knew that nobody was home—they had gone to Cape Cod again for the weekend—and added, "Every morning. Like, chain-smokes, when she drives us to school. She doesn't care that it's all smoky or anything." I'd just learned the phrase *chain-smoking* in the *Cosmopolitan* Leah had brought over the night before.

Patrick threw the ball to Andrew, who caught it and nodded. "Yeah, we see her, sometimes, on the yard," Andrew replied. "I heard she's into things like that, so I'm not surprised." Then he tossed the ball to me, and the force of the throw stung my hand through the mitt, but it felt good. They had asked me if I wanted to use a softball instead, but I'd said no.

"What do you mean, Mrs. Baker is 'into things'?"

Andrew and Patrick looked at each other before responding. Both brothers had dark brown hair, pale skin, and freckles. From profile view they looked very much like the same person—they even wore similar North Face parkas, and I suddenly had the distorted sense of looking into a mirror within a mirror, where image fragments multiply.

"You have to promise not to say anything," Patrick said, "'cause our mom would kill us." He was my age; we were both two years younger than Andrew. But unlike my own sibling dynamic, Patrick actually seemed to listen to his older brother, taking his lead.

After Andrew nodded in approval, Patrick continued, "We're not really supposed to know. We heard our mom talking about it, and we begged her to tell us, but she doesn't want us spreading it around, especially since we don't really know the whole story."

Andrew added, "And 'cause of everything that the Bakers have already been through."

"Promise," I replied. I picked up the ball and pitched it hard at Andrew, as if to prove I really meant it.

"Our mom said she was caught stealing drugs," Patrick divulged.

"No way," I said as I tried to process the information. Drugs? At that point in my life, my knowledge of drugs was limited to the fact that they were bad, and that people I knew didn't do them. Mother once said that Father's brother Mihály had drunk himself to death, but alcohol was different from drugs, wasn't it?

"She was a nurse in Boston, and she lost her job because she was stealing drugs. Like from the patients," Patrick added.

"Oh," I said, feeling confused, as I dropped a ball that was thrown to me. I thought about the bottle of blood pressure medication my father kept on his bedside table. "So it wasn't really drugs? But medications? Because aren't drugs illegal?"

"No shit, Sherlock," Andrew said. "We know drugs are illegal."

I was surprised he swore but decided to act like I hadn't noticed. "But he said she was 'stealing drugs,'" I replied, nodding toward Patrick. I wondered when I would finally learn all the things I needed to know: Vibrators, drugs, chain-smoking, what else was there? I remember feeling like every time I learned something adult, something forbidden, it meant there were at least ten more things I didn't know about. Could there even be enough *Cosmopolitan*s to cover all the topics? Sometimes I worried that when the time came to be sexual with someone, I would mess it up because I had no clue what to do. I'd never even kissed a boy yet.

Andrew sighed. "Whatever. She was stealing *medications*, then."

"Why would she do that?"

Andrew shrugged, and then so did Patrick. "Dunno," Andrew said.

Then I blurted out, "Do you think it's weird that she and Dr. Baker are married to each other?"

The brothers laughed. "Yeah, we do. They're both weird," Andrew replied.

"Dr. Baker is weird?" I stood with my mitt in one hand and the ball in the other.

"Yeah, we always hear him racing his Porsche through the neighborhood, late at night, when he's coming home from work," Andrew revealed. "Up and down Oak Street. And even sometimes on Maple Way."

"I've never heard anything," I said, frowning.

"Our bedrooms face the back of Oak," Patrick explained. "And sometimes we sleep with our windows open."

"And then, once he turns onto Hickory, he goes as quiet as a mouse. I've even seen him cut his lights, like he's a spy in stealth mode or something," Andrew said.

"That is weird," I remarked, at the same time that Patrick said, "He *thinks* he's all stealth."

Suddenly I remembered how his Porsche had been parked in the garage the day Sally went missing. With everything going on, the memory had escaped me until now. Had Dr. Baker stayed home from work that day or just gone in late? Did that constitute a reason to cast suspicion on him?

"Our mom says he must be stressed from his job," Andrew said. "You know, being a trauma surgeon and everything,"

"Stress might be the doc's excuse for being weird," Patrick said, holding up his mitt to indicate I should throw to him. "But what's Mrs. Baker's?"

I aimed the ball at him, but Andrew stepped in front of his brother to catch it, remarking, "Well, I wouldn't blame Mrs. Baker nowadays if she stole shit. She's probably pretty fucked up because of what happened to Sally."

"What happened to Sally . . . ," I repeated. "But we don't know what happened to her."

I wondered if anything had come of my turning the bracelet in to the police. If it had, I figured I would have heard something by now. Perhaps I'd ask Jimmy about it the next time I saw him—as long as he wasn't with his mother. Her dementia was getting worse; now, when she wandered through the neighborhood—which was happening much more frequently—she'd call out, "Sally! Sally? Sally, pretty girl," as if she were looking for a lost kitty.

"Sally's obviously dead," Andrew declared as he threw me the ball, and Patrick nodded in agreement.

It didn't matter that I'd had the same thought about Sally; what they said still bothered me. I was quiet as we continued to toss the ball. So were they, waiting for my reaction. Finally I said, "You don't know that."

"C'mon, Bee," Andrew said. "A three-year-old goes miss—"

"Four-and-a-half-year-old," I interrupted.

"Whatever. A four-year-old goes missing in our little town of

Hammend, where like no one ever has ever gone missing. And you don't think something bad happened to her?"

"I didn't say that," I retorted. "Obviously something bad happened. She's missing. But that doesn't mean she's dead."

Patrick nodded. "That's true, Drew," he said.

"Well, either she's dead, or she's locked up in some basement somewhere with some old pervert. Not sure which one is worse."

"Pervert," Patrick repeated, and snickered.

My heart started bouncing in my chest, like the ball was inside, hitting against my rib cage. "But there's no—nobody ever found her body. Is that what most people think, that she was murdered?" I kicked a loose stone on the ground and watched it skid. "No one really talks about it anymore," I confessed, but these words were quiet, as if I were saying them to myself.

Andrew and Patrick looked at each other. Our catch game had paused; Patrick now had the ball and began tossing it to himself, from his right hand into his left glove, over and over. "Some people think that," Andrew said.

"But who would do that? Who would do that to someone? And why?" My voice was rising now, and then I blurted out, "Fucking why?" The swear sounded weird coming out of my mouth, almost like I'd mispronounced it, even though I hadn't.

Both brothers shrugged. "Beats me," Andrew said. "There are some baaaaad people. Anyway, don't tell anyone about Mrs. Baker."

"I won't," I said, not really paying attention anymore; I was too preoccupied with what had just been said about Sally. I looked over once again at the Bakers' house, now searching Sally's empty bedroom window. I fiercely willed her to appear, even though I knew it was impossible.

✤

Though the implications of Sally potentially being murdered continued to weigh heavily on me, the new Mrs. Baker information was too useful to ignore. I would need it; over the next few months I would watch my specialness factor—the thing that had made me popular for the first time in my life, the thing that caused grown-ups to ask repeatedly if I was okay—slip to the ground and get buried under the snow. Vacation tales and weekend plans would now command the indoor gymnasium where we gathered in the cold weather before school, although it was always *Hope Rodale*'s weekend plans and vacation tales, like her Disney trip, that everyone talked about. In February, we would watch in our classroom, via satellite, with stunned silence as the *Challenger* shuttle exploded. It would remind us that there was a world much bigger than ours, but by March, my universe would shrink again, when Hope held the birthday party that topped all others: a fancy dinner, where we wore ruffled dresses and sat around her parents' cloth-covered dining room table while her mother served us sparkling cider in real wine-glasses. I would feel lucky at first to be invited, that she still considered me close (only ten girls were there), but then later I would find out how a select few of the girls were asked to stay afterward for a sleepover. After that I would unfairly avoid Leah for a few weeks, certain that my association with her was at least part of the reason why I wasn't included in the sleepover, even though I knew deep down I was the one to blame. I'd acted uncool, and the aura of Sally's disappearance had long since worn off. It was as if I had just borrowed my new life the past few months, like a library book, and now it was time to return it. Like it was overdue, really.

When the warmer weather came and the earth was completely uncovered, when the last small white blanket of snow melted away, my specialness factor would be completely gone. But my sister—Audrina, always-special Audrina—would have somehow managed, without my noticing, to tie hers onto a kite and let it soar into the wind, where it was going up and up.

*Peter Pan* ran that spring, and we sat in front-row seats that Father made us go early to snag. I turned around to see people's faces during Audrina's scenes. Nobody noticed me looking at them; they were too enraptured with my sister's performance: with the way she glided across the stage like she had on magic slippers, the way the words she spoke in the dark theater hung for a moment before descending, the way her beautiful face glowed like a lantern. There was a transfixed look on all the upturned faces, a stillness of their bodies, that wasn't present when the other actors and actresses performed. It didn't matter in the slightest that Audrina was an extra sibling they'd added on. She was a lead, perhaps even the main lead, or at least the main star, though technically the program listed her as a secondary character. Nobody, I realized then, could ever outshine my sister.

Shifting back around, I saw that my parents were even more mesmerized. Father's jaw was slightly open, as if he'd wanted to say something but had forgotten to speak; Mother was as motionless as I'd ever seen her. I knew, in my heart of hearts, I would never be able to do something that would elicit that kind of response from them; I didn't have any special talents, and even if I did, I wasn't Audrina.

I remember wondering what it would be like if Audrina weren't my sister, or if I were an only child, like Leah. Would my parents pay me more attention? Would they be prouder of me? I would have my bedroom to myself; I wouldn't have to share my clothes or my friends. I wouldn't have to compete with anyone for anything.

And then a dark thought seeped into my consciousness: What if Audrina had been the one to disappear, instead of Sally? It was a horrible notion, and I instantly took it back, although you can't really reverse thoughts like that.

At visiting day that spring, when my sister and her sixth-grade classmates came to see what Hillside would be like for them come September, I would watch from the corner of the schoolyard as Audrina greeted and easily hugged her friends as if she hadn't seen them in months, when she had seen them all just the previous day. I would watch as the boys—boys in both her grade and my grade—smiled and ignored her in equal parts—a sure sign of interest. I would notice Hope Rodale eyeing her from afar and how a circle formed around my sister like it had formed around me the previous fall. But nobody would ask her about Max or Sally—Audrina was interesting enough herself. I would know then that it was no longer my school, that it might not even be *our* school. I would feel empty, as if the attention previously paid to me had filled me like sparkling cider bubbles—now gone flat.

# Part Two

# Chapter Ten

THE SUMMER OF 1986, THE HOT WEATHER ARRIVED—SWIMMING weather—but Deer Chase Lake remained closed. "They found bacteria in the lake," Mother told Audrina and me one June morning over breakfast, "so it's not going to open for a while. They have to clean it."

I nodded, feeling relieved, and swirled around the milk in my cereal bowl to douse the remaining Cheerios that were still partially dry.

Audrina snorted. "Who'd want to go there anyway?"

I glanced up from my bowl of cereal, surprised that we were in agreement on this, albeit silently, when we still felt so far apart.

My sister grabbed the box of Cheerios to pour more into her bowl, even though she wasn't nearly finished with her current helping. She filled the bowl so much that some Cheerios spilled out the top. Then she picked up the sugar dispenser, also for the second time, and turned it almost completely upside down, unleashing a storm of white crystals. Mother didn't say anything like she would have had I been the one doing that. I was still on my first—and only—lightly sugared bowl. My jean shorts were snugger than they'd been the previous summer. Mother had frowned the first time she saw me wearing them, muttering, "We'll have to go shopping soon." Lately she'd begun setting the table with our meals already proportioned on the plate, like TV dinners, with my ration less than Audrina's. My Cosmos shirt was also tighter, but for a different reason: two mounds swelled underneath. Over the course of seventh grade I'd gone from training bra to regular bra, and now this one was feeling too small.

My sister was able to eat whatever she wanted and never gained weight. In fact, her jean shorts seemed to ride down more so than usual, now resting below angular hip bones. "You must have your mother's metabolism," Father said to her one day, his voice brimming with pride, unaware I'd just walked into the room.

His comment prompted an urge I'd developed over the past couple of months, a shameful compulsion that helped to release some of the tension inside me: I wanted to pull out strands of my hair.

I found that pulling my hair helped to provide a buffer against hurtful words, to soothe those tender spots created by the prickly brush. It helped fill the void—the rift—in the relationship between my sister and me. It eased the sharp edges of my fall from popularity and blunted the painful memories of how captivated my parents had been during Audrina's theater performance. Pulling my hair created an umbrella for the raindrops of guilt that showered down on me whenever I recalled Chief Riley's response when I'd asked if turning in the bracelet the day Sally went missing would have made a difference.

Each hair extraction would feel good, but the next one would feel better. And the next even better. It wasn't painful at all—quite the opposite, like the pleasure you get from finally giving in and scratching an intense itch. But also like itching, the pleasure of pulling a hair strand was temporary; the urge to do it again would shortly recur. I needed to get the root of the hair strand for the pull to feel complete; when the hair accidentally came out mid-shaft, I felt cheated, and needed to pull several more hairs properly—by the root—to "right" it.

I was careful not to pull too much. I started performing periodic checks to make sure this was the case, and I discovered that using Mother's white plastic handheld mirror—which was normal on one side and magnified on the other—was best. When Mother went out, I would sneak into their bathroom and angle it against their large bathroom mirror so I could see the back of my head, lifting up different sections of hair. If there was a suspicious spot, I would flip to the magnified side, climbing up on the bathroom counter for a closer look. My last haircut had been shortly before the Bakers moved to town the previous summer, so my hair fell midway down my neck. A thorough inspection took a fair amount of time.

Only once, in early June, after overhearing a worrisome conversation between my parents, had I pulled so much I'd created a very small thinned-out patch above my left ear.

"Sammy from the jeweler's called," Mother had said as soon as Father walked in the door from work.

I was nearby, in the family room, reading a book—*A Wrinkle in Time*. Audrina, meanwhile, was reclining on a lawn chair on the porch and listening to her Walkman.

"He said you accidentally gave him an extra twenty," Mother continued.

"Oh yeah?" Father said, and I heard him drop his keys on the floor. "Whoops."

"Whoops about your keys, or whoops about the twenty?"

Father glanced over to the family room, and I quickly put my head back down in the book, like I wasn't listening. "It was going to be a surprise," he said in a low voice. "For our anniversary."

"Our anniversary was last month."

"It took a while to get. It was special order."

"Oh, yes," Mother said, and at this point I didn't need to strain my ears to hear; she was speaking in a normal, if not even louder, voice. She must have assumed I was outside with Audrina. "Sammy told me. A white-gold heart pendant. White gold—my favorite. I pretended to know what the heck Sammy was talking about because I didn't want to look like a fool."

I couldn't believe Audrina was missing this; I could see her through the family room window. An open Coke and bag of Doritos lay next to her, and after each orange bite she licked her fingertips and reached back into the bag. I wanted to get my sister's attention, for her to hear as well, so we could discuss what this all meant, but she couldn't see me. I supposed we wouldn't have discussed it anyway. Though the previous few months had naturally smoothed our tensions, things between us just hadn't been the same since she discovered the bracelet—and since the hayride fight. But at least now we could peacefully coexist.

Father didn't reply for a few seconds, and then he said, "Well, you have so much yellow gold already. I thought it might be nice to do something different."

"I'd like to see it." Mother spoke sharply.

"Now?"

"Yes. Now."

Father strode past me to his study, and then returned about a minute later. I didn't look up until he had already passed; then I saw him holding open a black box for Mother, who was fingering its inside contents. I was brought back, suddenly, to the black box containing the diamond silver hoops I'd found in Father's study drawer, years earlier.

"It is nice," Mother said, in a much softer tone. "But as you know, I like yellow gold. And have for some time now." She paused here; there seemed to be some sort of implication. "So why don't you return it—I'm sure Sammy will honor a return—and you can get the same thing, but in gold."

"Yes, of course," Father said, and I heard the box snap shut.

Over the following couple of weeks, I'd observed Father, peering in on him when he watched TV in his study, in the evenings. I even rifled through his drawers from time to time. I waited outside my parents' bedroom door late at night, expecting to overhear an argument, but to my surprise, there was none.

But even though I never told Audrina about the white-gold heart pendant, I couldn't shake the suspicious feeling about Father that had now arisen within me. One day I flipped back through my diary to read what I'd written about the diamond silver hoops. Had Father bought these items for someone other than Mother? It was hard to believe; Mother was so beautiful. Should I be worried about my parents' marriage?

I knew, from my friendship with Leah, how one's world could change when your parents got divorced. She'd gone from living with both parents in a big house with a lot of toys, to sharing a small, cluttered home with just her mother. Leah never confided in me why her parents divorced, though I wondered if her father's girlfriend, with whom he lived, had anything to do with it. With summer upon us, Leah would be leaving again for California.

No, Father wouldn't betray Mother; he loved her. I closed my diary firmly. At any rate, the Bakers had finalized their basement renovation plans, so Father would be starting work on that soon. I could continue to keep an eye on him.

I was also hopeful that Father's upcoming time at the Bakers' would allow me to remain connected to Max. I no longer felt like Father needed to check in with Mrs. Baker about how Max was doing, since the answer was obvious: His absences decreased over the course of the school year, he laughed a lot more, and he'd made some good friends, both at Hillside and in the neighborhood, like the Wiley brothers, with whom he'd spent many a spring afternoon, riding bikes and shooting hoops. But our time together as fellow classmates had come to an end. As it turned out, Max would be switching to the Wiley brothers' school, Ludlow, come fall.

When Max had told me, during the last week of school, I'd tried to act cool, but I'd been devastated. "That's great," I'd lied. "How exciting. And you already know Andrew and Patrick."

"Yeah, I'm glad about that."

"Did you not like it here? I mean, I know it was a rough year, obviously, but . . ." I stopped talking, feeling like an idiot. *A rough year* was an understatement.

But Max just laughed. "Yeah, you could say that. Nah, I liked it. Everyone's so nice. Present company included." He smiled, and I smiled back, and I'd wished that we were not standing in the middle of the hall, with just a minute to spare before the final bell rang, but rather somewhere alone. "My dad went to private school—well, a boarding school, actually—so I think he just likes the idea of it."

"Oh." I couldn't really say much to that.

"It's too bad we won't see each other anymore because we don't live across the street from one another," he teased.

I laughed. "Right. If only we lived closer."

But even our proximity offered no guarantees, because Max had just departed for Massachusetts, where he'd be spending the first half of the summer with his aunt.

Other neighborhood families and kids were leaving unusually early for vacations and camps, as if they didn't want to stick around for a repeat Hammend summer. For the first time since I could remember, the Wileys wouldn't be holding their July Fourth party.

I looked at the summer ahead with anxiety, wondering what it would be like with half the swimming options, half the friends, and the anniversary of Sally's disappearance pressing in on us.

Before Leah left for her dad's, she invited me over to do something that we'd been talking about for a while: double-piercing my ears. Ever since my relationship with Hope and her friends had died out, I'd been hanging out regularly with Leah again.

"You have to get it really numb," Leah instructed, as I held a paper-towel-wrapped ice cube against my ear. We were sitting in her bedroom with the supplies laid out in front of us: rubbing alcohol, a bag of cotton balls, cups of ice, multiple sterling silver ball-stud earrings we'd bought earlier at Claire's at the mall.

"So numb you can't feel it," Leah continued. "And then you'll hold your ear down and I'll push the earring through."

Her instructions made me wince. "Are you sure you know what you're doing?" I hadn't discussed this endeavor with Mother, anticipating her refusal, and I didn't think a shoddy job would go over particularly well.

"I already told you, yes. The girls in California at my dad's country club do it all the time," she replied, waving her hand in the air like it was no big deal, but I could tell by the way she kept looking to see my reaction that she wanted me to be impressed. I was indeed impressed but kept my face expressionless. "They would get bags of ice from the club restaurant and do it in the bathroom," she said. Then she smiled and added, "Until they got in trouble."

"Sally had her ears pierced," I said suddenly. With the summer now upon us, I'd been thinking of her a lot. "Did you know that?"

Leah nodded. "Yeah. I saw on the flyer."

"That must have been weird for you, returning to Hammend, after she went missing."

"Yeah, it was," Leah said, nodding. "My mom was scared. We talked about it a lot."

I was curious about the conversations Leah and her mom had surrounding Sally—from what I knew, they were very different from the conversations I had with my own mother. Had she revealed any juicy gossip to Leah? "Do you ever think about who did it?" I asked. Funnily enough, we'd never discussed our personal suspicions, whether it was because we'd drifted apart when Sally first disappeared, or because I had sensed that Leah's purer nature would inhibit her from freely discussing such matters.

Sure enough, she now shook her head, not meeting my eyes. It was obvious she felt uncomfortable. She began rapidly shredding one of the cotton balls. A mean streak settled into me; I enjoyed seeing her discomfort, perhaps because I was used to being in her position. After a few seconds with no response, I repeated, in a very deliberate manner, "Do you ever think about who might've killed Sally?"

"We—we don't know she's dead," Leah replied as she dusted her hands, remnants of cotton wisps floating down. Then she picked up another intact cotton ball.

"C'mon, Leah," I said, and then I parroted the Wiley brothers: "A four-year-old goes missing in little Hammend, where like no one has ever gone missing. And you don't think something bad happened to her?"

She just stared at the ground and shrugged her shoulders. "Do you?" she finally responded.

"Maybe," I admitted.

Leah reached up to fix the barrette in her hair. I don't even know why she bothered to put anything in her hair—it was so fine that barrettes were always slipping out. One night, when sleeping over at her house, I'd touched her hair after she fell asleep, curious how it would feel in my fingers. The strands had been so slight, so soft, they seemed to melt in my hands the way a snowflake would.

"So?" I prodded. "Who do you think could have done it?"

Leah shrugged. "I don't know."

"If you had to name someone," I pressed, while I considered my own list. It had been a while since I'd examined it. "One person," I added.

"Sometimes I think Mr. Hoosier is creepy," she disclosed. He was the science teacher.

"Hairy Hoosier?" That is what the students called him behind his back.

"Yeah," she replied. "I dunno . . . he just seems . . . off."

"Interesting." I thought about Mr. Hoosier's clunky black-rimmed glasses, and his dark, hairy knuckles that were so obvious every time he pointed to an element, like oxygen or nitrogen, located higher up on the large periodic table pinned to the wall. I thought of the life-size skeleton Mr. Hoosier had nicknamed Harvey that stood in the corner of the science room. There was a palpable, clinical feel to the room—and, perhaps, to Mr. Hoosier—that felt slightly disturbing. "I could see why you would think that," I conceded. "But Mr. Hoosier never even met Sally," I pointed out.

Leah shrugged again. "Like I said, I don't know, Bee."

Now I picked up a cotton ball, but instead of ripping it apart, I pushed it in to make it more compact. The further we got from Sally's disappearance, the more confused and uncertain I was of my suspect list. The same people were still on it: Michael-the-mailman; Vittorio, the pizza guy; Mrs. Abbott; and Boston Person. Mrs. Baker continued to pop on and off the list. I hadn't been able to rule any of them out; in fact, Michael-the-mailman was sporting a mysterious black eye, and the Abbotts had just put their house on the market, so they could retire for some unknown reason to Vermont, where they didn't have any extended family. Both of these things seemed somehow suspicious. And I couldn't help but recall the Wiley brothers' reveal about Mrs. Baker stealing medications as a nurse, and the way Dr. Baker raced around the neighborhood late at night in his Porsche. "What about Sally's father?" I asked.

"Dr. Baker? Seriously, Bee? No way." Leah blinked her eyes in quick succession.

"Why not?" I countered. "You name Mr. Hoosier, who's a teacher, but not Dr. Baker, who's a trauma surgeon? So he's . . ."

"So he's what?"

I wasn't sure exactly what I was trying to say. "So he's good with knives, right? And knows stuff. Medical stuff." I thought of the bloodstained scrubs he'd worn, when I had to apologize for taking the bracelet.

"But that doesn't make him a murderer," Leah said, frowning. "He's a doctor."

I bowed my head. "The almighty Dr. Baker!"

"C'mon, Bee," Leah said, tugging at my arm so I looked up. "Cut it out. I was just saying that there's a reason for him to be good with knives—surgical instruments."

"Yeah, I guess that's right," I conceded. I decided not to reveal the other tidbits I had on him.

"Is there anyone else you think is suspicious?" she asked, rather shyly.

Based on her reaction to Dr. Baker, it didn't seem like a good idea to share the rest of my list. So instead I said, "Hey, how come you only have your ears pierced once? Not double, like you said the girls in California have?"

Leah flushed, but before she could answer, her mother entered the bedroom. She carried a tray with a large plate of baked goods and two glasses of milk.

"I brought you girls some treats," she said. "I made both plain brownies and cream cheese brownies, because I didn't know what kind you liked."

Leah turned even more red. "Mom, we're too old for milk and cookies—I mean, brownies."

Suddenly I remembered that Leah had indeed had double piercings at the beginning of the school year, but then one of her holes got infected, so she'd let them both close. She'd worn a Band-Aid over the affected earlobe for a few weeks, clearly self-conscious. Now I felt bad for bringing it up.

"Wow, thanks," I said as Leah's mother simply smiled, placing the items down. She closed the door behind her as she left. I couldn't imagine my mother asking me what kind of brownies I wanted, let alone bringing me any kind of food. In my house we weren't allowed to eat anywhere other than the kitchen; Mother said she didn't want crumbs all over. The only time Mother had asked for my opinion about dessert was after I showed her my seventh-grade final report card, in which I'd earned A-pluses in six of my eight subjects—the only As being in art and music. Given Mother's scrutiny over my eating habits, I'd known she was really proud, even though her options had left something to be desired: "We could get you a small-size ice cream cone, no toppings, or an orange popsicle. You choose."

The piercing hurt much more than I thought it would, even though my earlobe was supposedly numb, so I lied and told Leah I only wanted to have one of my ears double-pierced instead of both. Hope Rodale had both, but Gwen had only one, so I knew it was still acceptable.

Audrina spotted my second piercing immediately. When she asked Mother if she could have a second piercing—and Mother said no—she kept my secret safe, to her credit. Mother, of course, eventually noticed as well, but she allowed me to keep it—after dousing my earlobe with rubbing alcohol and inspecting for any signs of infection, of which luckily there were none.

Over the first few weeks of summer vacation, Audrina and Mother thankfully *didn't* notice the most important thing: my hair-pulling. Since Audrina didn't say anything, I knew I was in the clear. Because she usually noticed everything about me: if I had a zit (I'd been getting quite a few lately), whether my shirt and pants were acceptable shades of matching turquoise, if I was wearing her lip gloss—which was just a tad lighter shade than my own. And we were spending a lot of time with each other: As June turned into July, and the neighborhood emptied, we were thrust together, much like the previous summer, albeit without the confines.

"Do you think we should ask Max when he gets back from Massachusetts if he wants to come with us?" Audrina asked one day as we lay, stomach-down, on pool lounge chairs at the club, where Mother dropped us off nearly every day.

It took me a moment to register what my sister had said; it felt like the muggy weather was creating a haze inside my brain. I propped myself up on my elbows, noticing how my chest generously filled in the space against the chair. "Ask Max to come with us where?" I responded after a moment.

Mother had recently swapped out my bras for some larger ones in my underwear drawer and, the same day, stocked our bathroom under-sink cabinet with several more boxes of maxipads. Audrina was still as flat as the chair slats themselves, though she didn't seem to mind. I had to admit that I liked the way the boys were noticing me more, but Audrina's complete nonchalance about her own lack of assets made me wonder if I shouldn't like it.

"Duh. To the club."

I rolled my eyes beneath my sunglasses. "Sure," I said cautiously. I didn't like my sister's interest in Max. But things had been slowly getting better between Audrina and me over the past couple of weeks, and I didn't want to ruin it. I'd been making an effort; I asked her a lot about acting—for instance, whether she ever got nervous performing ("No"), the next play she wanted to do ("I'm hoping I can land a role in Hillside's spring musical, whatever that will be"), and which character she'd want to play on certain TV shows. I didn't tell her that seventh graders never participated in the musical, and I held my tongue when she said she'd probably be Blanche in *The Golden Girls,* and I'd definitely be Dorothy.

I also tried to ignore how Audrina had begun waking me up nearly every night when she got up to use the bathroom. After several disrupted nights, I'd finally asked, "Drina, can you go to the bathroom now so you don't wake me up later? It's so annoying."

She hadn't replied, and then that night she'd gotten up even more than usual, which made me question our recent truce.

"Do you think Max would come?" I asked. Part of me wished I had the courage to share my feelings for Max with her, but I just couldn't bring myself to completely trust her. Not yet.

"I think so," my sister replied. "It's not the lake."

"Good point. Why do you want him to come?" I tried to casually ask.

Audrina now propped herself up, her jelly bracelets slipping down her arms. Her nails were painted a blood red—Mother's nail polish that she'd used, as always, without permission. She'd also begun wearing Mother's blue eye shadow, but I didn't dare point that out. I myself wasn't that interested in makeup and only occasionally wore a light gray shadow that was more of a shimmer. "Why would you ask that? What do you even mean?" she replied, sounding annoyed, but I could've sworn that her cheeks and neck grew pink, like someone had just put a drop of pink dye into her skin.

I instantly felt hot in a stifled way, like the time I'd first stepped out of the Florida airport when we visited my grandmother a few years earlier, and the humidity had been so thick and smothering. I'd reached out with my hand, almost expecting to be able to scoop it up in my fist, like an object. Now I flipped over to my back, taking a big, deep breath. Thank goodness I hadn't divulged my feelings about Max. We didn't talk again until we needed to pack up.

At the end of each club day, my sister and I would collect-call Mother from the pay phone inside. She never accepted the charges, but this way she knew we were ready to be picked up. Sometimes we even gave a fake name, like Ima Nerd or Penny Less or A. Boogie, to be funny. When Mother would arrive, she'd pretend like she was looking for that person.

"Sorry, what's your name?" she'd ask, while Audrina and I rolled our eyes. "I'm supposed to be picking up Ima Nerd. Do you know her?"

"Moooom," one of us would finally say, drawing out her name.

"Hmm. Maybe it's a him?"

"Mother!"

Yet we would still go through the whole routine with her the next time.

One night it was not Audrina opening our bedroom door that woke me up but something else: the pressure of something weighing down on my bed—specifically on my feet. I pulled my head up to take a look, and it took me a moment to focus and to believe what I was seeing: Audrina was sitting on the edge of my bed as if it were a toilet, her pink-and-white-striped pajama bottoms and underwear pulled down to her ankles. Her face looked relaxed, like she was in a trance.

"Drina, what are you doing?" I yelled. "Are you pee—?" I didn't need to finish the sentence; a warm wetness flowed over to my foot, and I jerked my foot away and scrambled to a seated position. "Gross! Stop, Audrina! Stop it!" She did stop then, apparently done, and hopped off my bed to pull up her pants and underwear.

"Mother!" I screamed. "Mother! Father!" I huddled my knees toward my chest. "Mother!" I started crying as Mother rushed into our room, Father behind her.

It was hard to get the words out. Audrina had just used me as a toilet, squatting directly on me. Why would she have done that? Was she getting back at me because I'd asked her to use the bathroom before she went to bed? My voice stuttered as I relayed what had happened. Mother sat down on my bed and gathered me in her arms as I spoke. When I was finished, I wiped my runny nose and wet face with the back of my sleeve and finally looked over to my sister's side of the room. But she was gone, as was Father.

"It was an accident, sweetie. She didn't mean it." Mother began stroking my hair, and I almost let her, but then I remembered about my hair-pulling secret, so I pushed her hand away and then stretched, as if that was the reason why I hadn't wanted her to touch my hair.

"It was strange," I said. "She looked weird—had a weird look on her face. Almost like she was sleeping, but she wasn't."

"She may have been sleepwalking," Mother said.

"Where is *she*?" The *she* came out harsher than I'd intended, and Mother's face tensed, the hollow space beneath her cheekbones suddenly more depressed. "She, Bee, is your sister. It was an accident. She is with your father."

*She* was gone the whole night, through Mother changing my bedsheets, through Mother giving me a good-night kiss. I knew *she* was gone the whole night because in the morning her bed looked the same: Her pillow was askew in the middle of it, her yellow-and-blue comforter crumpled toward the end. Had she slept on the couch? The next morning, I waited for her apology. Even if it had been an accident, she owed me one. I kept waiting while we passed each other in the bathroom, while we ate breakfast, while we climbed into the back seat of our Jeep to go to the club.

In the car, when my sister finally looked at me, *really* looked at me, I thought the apology was coming. But instead, her eyes drifted to the side of my face, then beyond to the car window, and she said, "Mother, I was listening to that song from *Guys and Dolls* you like: *I love you, a bushel and a peck . . .*" She punched the air with her arm with each syllable.

I grabbed Audrina's wrist the next time she raised it into the air. Her wrist was small in my hand, smaller than I had remembered, making my hand feel big and clumsy. "Um, hello, Drina," I said. "Do you have something to say?"

"Borka," came Mother's warning from the driver's seat.

Audrina wrested her arm free and continued singing, as if she hadn't even heard my question. When we pulled up to the club, Mother said, "Bee, stay here for a minute. I want to have a word with you." Audrina hopped out of the car, which is when I noticed her wearing a neon-pink belt that Leah had given to me as a birthday gift, but like so much of my stuff, Audrina had blurred the lines of its ownership. "You share everything, girls," Mother always said to us, but the problem was that once Audrina wore something of mine, it belonged to her in a way that it had never belonged to me. My shirts fell on her just right, my old dresses looked new on her body. And I couldn't even claim those clothes anymore, because most of them no longer fit me.

"Sweetie, accidents happen," Mother said as she turned in her seat to face me. "Audrina didn't mean it, obviously. Your father and I are going to make sure your sister uses the bathroom before going to bed and doesn't drink so much water beforehand."

I waited, but she said nothing else, only gave me a smile that revealed she'd uncharacteristically smeared plum lipstick on her teeth. "That's it?" I finally replied. "She's gonna use the bathroom and not drink so much water?"

"Do you have a better solution?" Mother snapped, her plum lips smacking closed. I knew not to push it and let myself out of the car.

The solution actually seemed to work, temporarily, but then Audrina would occasionally wake up in the middle of the night to drink water because she was so thirsty. I would hear first the bedroom door creak open, her feet scamper across the hall, and then the water sprinkling out of the sink faucet. "Please don't tell Mother," she whispered to me one night when I got up to use the bathroom. Her face looked pale as she brought a plastic cup to her lips. Her nightgown hung loose like a blanket. "I'm sorry I woke you up."

"It's okay, Drina," I said. To my surprise I had an urge to hug her, but I didn't know how she would respond. For the first time, it occurred to me that something might be wrong. "Are you okay?"

She took one last big gulp, the water trickling down the sides of her mouth. "Fine," she replied curtly, turning off the faucet. She pushed past me on her way back toward our room, and the suddenness of her movement surprised me. She wasn't acting like herself; perhaps she wasn't feeling well?

As I moved around in my bed, I relived the scene in the bathroom, trying to understand if I had done something to annoy her.

"Quit moving, Bee, you're making too much noise. I'm trying to sleep."

I couldn't believe, after all she'd put me through during the night, she would suggest that *I* was the one keeping *her* up. An anger rose swiftly inside me, and I wanted to direct it at her. "Eat shit and die," I spit out.

Audrina gasped. We never swore at each other. In fact, it was well-known how an eighth grader named Ryan Lampa uttered those exact words to his teacher during the last week of school and got expelled. I don't even know why I said it to my sister; I was just tired of trying to figure Audrina out, tired of her being nice one moment and, well, being Audrina the next.

I waited for her to respond, but she didn't, and soon a growing satisfaction worked its way over me. Now I flung my covers off and then pulled them back on in loud, exaggerated movements. I turned this way and that in the bed, as disruptively as I could. As sleep overtook me, I felt justified. I'd stood up to my sister; she had no right to treat me the way she did—the way she always did.

In the morning, though, when I went to awaken Audrina, any satisfaction I'd felt vanished, and all that remained were the terrible words.

At first Mother and I just assumed Audrina was being a sleepyhead; sometimes, especially lately, she stretched how long she could sleep in. She'd been so tired recently. But when I finished breakfast and my sister still hadn't made an appearance, Mother sent me to wake her for our dentist appointments that morning. I took my time as I climbed up the stairs to our bedroom, imagining with pleasure the chaos that would ensue as Audrina scrambled; Mother hated for us to be late for anything.

My sister was still in her bed, and curled up, her face turned into the pillow, her brown hair splayed like a doll pushed facedown. "Audrina," I whispered. She didn't move. Was she ignoring me because of what I'd said to her last night? "Audrina," I said louder. But I was in no rush. In my head I counted, *One-Mississippi, two-Mississippi, three-Mississippi* . . . all the way to ten. "Audrina." I pushed her body, but still she didn't react.

"C'mon, Drina," I said, getting a little annoyed. Still, no response. "Drina." When I tried to turn her head toward me, my hands slipped on her face. It was wet, like she had just misted herself with a spray bottle. It dawned on me that something was very, very wrong. "Drina,"

I said again, and finally succeeded in repositioning her toward me. Her skin looked ashen, and she was breathing funny, panting almost, but in a regular rhythm. There was a sweet fruity smell coming out of her mouth, like she'd just eaten a lollipop.

"Mother," I screamed, and Audrina's eyes fluttered. "Mother!"

# Chapter Eleven

I REMEMBER STUMBLING OVER A SMALL CLEAR PLASTIC HOSE ON the rug near our front door. Someone said it was oxygen tubing, and then I worried it had fallen off Audrina when the paramedics had carried her out to the ambulance. The tubing was rubbery like a plastic band but stronger. When I pulled it, it didn't get longer.

I remember how Officer Jimmy sat in our family room drinking a hot-pink can of Tab. He looked different; now he had a reddish mustache and was heavier than when he'd last been here asking us about Sally. Like then, I watched him from the banister of the second-floor landing. He must have been jostling the can around because when he opened it, brown soda erupted and sprayed over our tan couch. He looked around to see if anybody was watching before using our decorative yellow flower pillow to mop it up. When he glanced up and noticed me, he pretended he was fluffing the pillow.

Time warped during the days following Audrina's hospitalization—minutes elongated, hours stretched out like Silly Putty, and even though it released for nighttime, time remained bumpy, misshapen. Skewed.

One sleepless night, I saw Father in his study very late, sitting at his desk, with a shadow of a beard. He and Mother needed my help, he said. Needed me to be responsible because Audrina had become a diabetic. Like Grandpa Joe, he'd added, meaning Mother's father. The silence that followed wasn't silent at all—it was actually quite loud: loud in my head, loud in my body. At night, when I lay in my empty room with my index finger entwined around a piece of hair, images of Audrina—her white face pressed into a glass of water, her thin body drowning in her nightgown—swept through me. I remember rolling the word *diabetes* around and around in my mouth as if I were chewing a piece of gum—*di-a-bet-es, die-a-beat-ease*—and thinking it cruel that it had the sound *die* in it. But Grandpa Joe had died from a stroke, not diabetes, so there must be hope for Audrina.

I missed my sister with an intensity that surprised me. We'd always been together, even when we fought, sleeping in the same room, brushing our teeth in the same mirror, reaching into the same cupboard for cereal bowls. Now, without her, the house felt strange. She was not here, but her stuff was—her clothes, scrunched in the hamper and suspended on hangers; her toothbrush, with toothpaste remnants, sitting in its holder, beside her crimping iron; her bathroom drawer, scattered with makeup and hair ties and bandanas. It was a tangible inconsistency, these things that placed her where she was not. I was keenly aware of her absence and the way it made me feel like I, too, was somewhere I shouldn't be. We were sisters, and we were young; we were supposed to be together. I had a terrible thought that chased me each day: What if my sister never came home?

Mother stayed mostly at the hospital, only coming home at night to shower and collect clean clothes. Often I'd wake to the sound of her rustling through Audrina's drawers. She'd snatch a couple Audrina-items to bring back with her: her glittery headband, a white flowered nightgown my sister had worn so often it grew fuzzy nubs on it. When I'd call out to Mother, she'd come over and kiss my forehead, whispering "I love you," and then in the morning she'd be gone, the house again eerily quiet. Sometimes I'd wonder if I'd been dreaming, but then I'd realize yet another piece of Audrina was missing from our room. One morning I noticed Audrina's yellow-and-blue flower comforter had disappeared from her bed.

Grandpa Joe had died in a hospital. I remember Mother had answered the phone in the kitchen, and then suddenly run to the bathroom. Audrina and I, who had been playing nearby, followed, confused. We knocked and tried to open the door, but it was locked. We were worried, not understanding what was wrong. Finally the door creaked open, and Mother, with a red but dry face, kneeled down to our level. "Grandpa Joe went to heaven," she said, and I began to cry, as my sister simply walked into the family room to lie down on the couch. As Mother hugged me, she said, "Shhhh. It's okay. He's dead now," as if that should make me feel better, when that was exactly what upset me.

Mother's absence also weighed on me, especially in the mornings when I poured myself Lucky Charms, sitting at the kitchen counter alone, since Father left so early for work. This was not how the middle of July was supposed to be. I surprisingly missed Mother's watchful eye. Nobody was there to even care whether I was eating a lot of "junk cereal." I finished off the cereal box, and then another one Father bought at my behest.

There were crumbs on the kitchen floor and dirty dishes in the sink that stayed for days until I cleaned them. The fringe on the rug by our front door was uncharacteristically tangled, and I walked over it several times before finally taking the pink wide-toothed comb my mother kept in one of the kitchen drawers and combing the fringes straight, like I had seen her do before guests came over.

I didn't understand exactly what to make of Audrina's diagnosis. Father hadn't disclosed much, and I was hesitant to ask Mother during her brief appearances. Would my sister have diabetes forever, or was it like a flu that she would eventually get over? It was weird that she had gotten it; it seemed an old person's disease. As far as I knew, no kid we knew had it. Nobody at school—not even, surprisingly, Hope Rodale—had called me to ask about Audrina, which only added to my guilt. She'd called often the previous fall, in the aftermath of Sally's disappearance. Perhaps no one wanted to speak to me because they somehow knew what I had done—what I'd said to Audrina. *Eat shit and die.* The only other possible explanation I could come up with for Hope Rodale's lack of interest was that she simply didn't care about my sister, which didn't make a ton of sense. During Audrina's school visiting day, Hope had already pegged her as a very important person.

One evening, a few days after Audrina had been gone—although it felt much longer—Father casually said, over pizza dinner, "You know, the reason why Audrina was so thirsty was because of the diabetes." I was mid-sip of soda, and I'd had to force myself to continue swallowing it. The cold drink ran down my insides, guilt rising up to meet it. Our parents always instructed us to look out for each other, and I knew, without him explicitly saying it, that because I was the older sister, he had expected more from me. But I had let Audrina down; I had dismissed her symptoms and then taken so long that morning to wake her up, just so I could see her flustered when she realized she'd overslept. What kind of sister was I?

Maybe, I later thought, as I twirled the leftover oxygen tubing around my fingers like it was a strand of hair, if I had let her drink more water, maybe if I hadn't complained about how often she was peeing, she wouldn't have gotten diabetes, or at least she wouldn't have been so sick that she needed to go to the hospital.

One thing I felt for certain: If I hadn't told Audrina to *eat shit and die*, then this wouldn't have happened. I'd somehow cursed her; I was sure of it. This dark knowledge lived in me. At times, it almost overcame me. Audrina had said she wished I wasn't her sister. Was what I'd said to her the equivalent? Or worse, even? Were we slowly severing the bond of sisterhood with our unforgivable words? Our unforgivable actions?

I started drinking tons of water and consequentially urinating a lot, hoping, in a remote way, that I, too, could become a diabetic. I deserved it more than Audrina did. But the only thing it did was make me need to use the bathroom in the middle of the night. One night I dreamt of a storeroom full of toilets, and I eagerly plopped down on one, only to awaken to the spread of wetness beneath me. When I went to change the sheets, I couldn't find a new set. Where did Mother keep them? I climbed into Audrina's bed, where I lay, unable to sleep.

Often, when I found myself staring at the dark ceiling at an unknown hour, I felt the immensity of life: how the minutes throbbed with uncertainty, how we were all mortal—how Sally could already be dead—and I'd reach into my scalp for release.

About a week after Audrina had been hospitalized, Diane and Courtney returned from camp and took me for ice cream. Just like the previous summer, I found myself a source of interest. We rode our bikes to the store, which I'd never done before—I'd only ridden to the park. Diane and Courtney were used to independently riding their bikes around town. But I didn't need to ask permission; there was no one around to ask. Father was at work.

We sat at the counter on the red swivel stools, me in the middle. They seemed much older, or at least much more experienced, than the summer before.

"My cousin has diabetes," Diane informed me, her mouth full of vanilla ice cream and hot fudge, after relaying how she and Courtney, who'd bunked together at camp, had played a game called Spin the Bottle one night and kissed two and three boys, respectively. "Diabetes sucks."

I nodded, as I wondered how Spin the Bottle worked and who I could ask without looking stupid. Maybe Leah would know, and if not, maybe we could find out in one of her mother's magazines.

"I don't know anyone who has diabetes," Courtney admitted, a bit wistfully, as if she wished she did.

"How is Audrina doing?" Diane asked.

"Much better," I said, although I really had no idea. My parents hadn't said anything either way, and I was still afraid to ask. My sister and I had spoken just once on the phone, briefly. Our conversation had been flat, as if we were strangers. I hadn't known what to ask her other than how she was doing, and she hadn't inquired about my life, which, I suppose, wasn't out of the ordinary. She also hadn't brought up what I'd said to her the night she'd gone to the hospital; perhaps she was waiting to do it in person.

"Well, tell her hi," Courtney chimed in, as she took another spoonful of her small, plain vanilla ice cream. It was the ice cream that Mother would have wanted me to get, but I was deep into my strawberry banana split. I'd wanted sprinkles, too, but when the boy behind the counter asked, "Rainbow or chocolate?" I was unable to answer, shaken by a sudden memory: Sally once calling sprinkles "freckles."

"Okay, sure. I'll tell her," I replied, and twisted on my bar stool, a little to the right, a little to the left, and back again. I thought about asking my parents if I could visit, but then I dismissed that idea. What if Audrina said she didn't want me there? Then my parents would learn about what had transpired between us. I dreaded disappointing them again.

"Courtney, you're so boring." Diane sighed, pointing to Courtney's ice cream. "When are you going to drop this diet?"

"When I lose five pounds," Courtney moaned, and then I glanced down and noticed how much smaller her thighs were than mine. I stood up for a moment and tugged down on my jean shorts before sliding back down, wondering if this was how all older girls talked. Hope Rodale had never mentioned weight or diets.

"You're fine, Court. You know, Audrina won't be able to eat things like this," Diane said, gesturing to my own ice cream.

"Like bananas?" I asked, confused, as I scooped another spoonful into my mouth.

"Like ice cream."

"She won't be able to eat ice cream?" I said, smiling. I thought Diane was kidding, but she nodded, and my smile disappeared.

"Oh," I said, and then I found myself unable to take another bite, even when the ice cream got runny and mixed with the hot fudge, the way I liked.

Staring down at the floor, I noticed a loose cigarette on the ground, and I hopped down to quickly grab it and pop it into my bag, while pretending I'd dropped my napkin.

Later that night, I put the unlit cigarette in my mouth and then pulled it out and tapped it, the way I'd seen Mrs. Baker do. What was it about smoking that was so appealing to her? I considered whether Diane and Courtney had ever tried a cigarette; they probably had, I concluded. The cigarette wasn't long and skinny like Mrs. Baker's were, and it had a little dinosaur on it. A camel, I realized, upon closer inspection. The wet cigarette, now bent in half, had lost its shape. After tasting a small, loose piece of tobacco—which I immediately spit out, repulsed—I flushed the cigarette down the toilet.

At night Audrina's bed looked half dressed without her comforter, and it unsettled me in a way that could only be undone when my fingers had had their fill of hair plucking. The tension that arose within me prior to my plucking was now as familiar as a hunger pang; it was a deep urge that only intensified with time. Once I began pulling out hair strands, relief came in gasps and waves, my skin and heart and mind eventually rolling into quietude, into pleasure.

One night, looking for a distraction, I went through my sister's stuff. I found her diary in the desk drawer, stored underneath some notebooks, and her key tucked in the back of her pants and jeans drawer. I hesitated, running my fingers over the diary cover, before finally unlocking it. Flipping open to the first entry, I began reading.

> *Dear ~~Diary~~ Sally,*
> *I'm so worried!! What happenned? I hope your okay.*
> *You were with us at the beach and then you weren't. We*
> *looked every where for you. Everyone looked for you. The*
> *whole town!! Everything here is the same except people are*
> *worried and scared but try not to show it. Bee's acting like*
> *its all fine and so I am too because I don't want to know*
> *her how worryed I am. Mom bought me this ~~dieary~~ diary*

*because she said she's worried about me and Bee but
I think she just wants me to practice my handwriting
and and grammer and spelling (EYE ROLL). I'm not a
good speller, not like Bee. I hope you're okay. Are you
hungry? ~~Scarred?~~ Scared? Are you alive? (I'm sorry. I had
to ask.). I feel like you must be because I feel like I would
like know if you were dead. Like something would change
somehow. Nothing has changed here except we are all just
~~weighting~~ waiting. Please come home soon. I miss you.
Love,
Audrina*

*P.S. Max is ok. For now.*

The first entry took my breath away: my sister's keen worry about Sally's well-being, the way she'd addressed the entry to Sally. And I felt guilty for reading what were clearly such intimate, personal thoughts—but not enough to stop. The chance to finally understand Audrina was just too enticing. I decided to just skim through, noting only entries that involved me.

*Dear Sally,
Today I was fixing my hair and dropped my barrette. And
then guess what happened?!! I found ~~my~~ your bracelet
under the dresser. Bee must have hid it. I think she found
it at Deer Chase Lake. Why else would it be there? I don't
know what to do. I don't want to get her in trouble but I
think its a BIG deal. Maybe she found it at your house?
That doesn't really make sense but I hope it's something
like that. I worry about what this means for you. I think I*

*need to tell someone. Do I tell Mother and Father or do I
say something to Bee? I'm kind of mad at Bee. She doesn't
pay any attenttion to me. All she cares about is Hope
and her new friends. When Hope calls the house Bee acts
all special, like it's President Reagan calling. I don't even
know if Hope really even care about Bee but I can't tell Bee
that. I don't know what to do about the bracelet. I think I
need to tell because I think it could help you. I hope you
are ok. I think about you a lot.*
*Love,*
*Audrina*

*Dear Sally,*
*Bee and I are in the longest fight ever!! It's so long that it
went from a big short fight to a never ending one. Did you
ever fight with Max like that? She got mad at me for
telling my parents about the bracelet. That is not fair! I
had to tell them. It was the right thing to do even though
it didn't help to find you. (I'm the one who should be
mad. She took your bracelet!!) But then I got mad and
said I wished we weren't sisters. It was a really mean
thing to say and I feel badly. I didn't mean it. Bee got
very hurt. Ever since it hasn't been the same with us. I
love Bee and she is a great sister.*

I paused here, tears unexpectedly filling my eyes. The memory
of the day at the farm was still raw, and to hear my sister say that
she loved me—despite things not being the same between us—was
overwhelming.

*You don't have a sister so you might not understand what its like having one. Take my word for it it's hard!!! Sometimes its like Bee only remembers what she wants to remember. Like how she borrows my shirts thinking they are her's. And she didn't tell me I did a good job with Peter Pan. She didn't say anything at all which was really mean. I worked SO hard to memorize all my lines. (I'm not smart like Bee is.) Every time I think we are going to make up she acts like a snot again. ~~Sometimes it makes me hate her as much as I love her.~~ Anyway, summer is coming soon. I'm not going to go swimming at Deer Chase Lake, even if it does reopen. I hope you're okay, but I'm not sure anymore.*
*Love,*
*Audrina*


*P.S. Brian Roslin gave me flowers after the play!!! He is SO cute.*

Instead of feeling closer to Audrina, like I'd hoped, after reading those entries I felt more conflicted. And even more guilty about everything I'd done. I hadn't been supportive of her; I hadn't treated her well. I hadn't been a good sister; the root of our problems was me—even if she, too, sometimes hate-loved me. I realized Audrina had just been trying to do the right thing by telling our parents about the bracelet. She clearly missed Sally, continuing to address the entries to her. I'd hurt my sister with the way I'd gotten caught up in my own social life, the way I hadn't praised her *Peter Pan* performance.

It was difficult to digest.

Yet I kept reading. I told myself: *Just one more entry; just one more.* And then, at some point, I'd read through the entire diary, through her concern about having to pee so often and her worry that she was too skinny and too flat. I'd had no idea.

Afterward I felt terrible. And nothing made me feel better except pulling my hair. Even when I started to hear Father's laughter again, when Mother began sleeping at home, when my parents told me with strange, puzzling smiles that after a week and a half of my sister being in the hospital, I could finally visit—that, in fact, if I didn't visit soon I'd miss the opportunity since *Audrina Was Coming Home!*—even then, the urge persisted and my fingers misbehaved. Most mornings I just stuffed my stray hairs into my pillowcase. (The extra sheets had, of course, been neatly organized in the hall closet.) I realized I was going to have to clean up before Audrina returned home—empty the pillowcase, flush the hairs down the toilet, make sure that there were none on the mattress.

The day of the hospital visit, I walked with my father down the corridor. Mother had gone to Mortenson's Drug Store for supplies that Audrina would need at home, so it was just the two of us. I'd felt vulnerable and reached for Father's hand as soon as we'd entered the hospital, and he'd hesitated for just a moment—long enough to make me feel foolish. Mother was the more affectionate one, though neither of them were particularly physical. But—still. Still. I suppose we hadn't held hands in a long time, perhaps years, so maybe I'd caught him off guard.

I recalled when he had put his hand on Mrs. Baker's shoulder, during my confession, and how proud that had made me at the time. Now, though, the memory just made me angry. Why was it that he could offer comfort to a stranger but waver when it came to holding his own daughter's hand?

But it was too late to take back the gesture, so we trudged down the hall, our hands clasped awkwardly together, and I stared at the people we passed to avoid looking at him.

The walls of Audrina's hospital floor struck me as childish, like a kindergarten room, painted with zebras, monkeys, and other zoo animals holding red and blue balloons. The nurses we passed smiled at me with their whole faces. As my shoes clacked against the linoleum floor, making tiny echoes, I could feel my hand growing sweatier, slipping in my father's grip.

Even though it had been only ten days since my sister and I had last seen each other, it felt much longer. What would she look like? How would she react when she saw me?

I knew I had to apologize. More than anything, I wanted to make things right—to get us back to how we once were.

"Father," I suddenly said, wondering if I could verbalize the question that had been sewn up inside me since the moment Audrina had first gone to the hospital. "Father, will Audrina . . . die from this?"

"No," he was quick to answer.

But I felt like he hadn't understood my question. "*Could* she die? Not now, but later?"

"No, no, of course not," he replied, his Hungarian accent coming through. It seemed I wasn't the only one feeling nervous.

When we entered Audrina's room, she was sitting up in the bed and painting her nails, dressed in her white flowered nightgown, the one with the fuzzy nubs. Her hair looked the way it did after we spent a summer at the club—gold-tinged, loose with a little wave.

Her cheeks were rounder than I'd remembered. She didn't look sick at all. There were more real balloons in her room than there had been fake ones on the outside walls. Between the balloons, cards, flowers, and baskets, there was no bare space left. I spotted a piece of oxygen tubing strewn on her table, atop a Mad Libs book and a *Seventeen* magazine.

"Father! Bee!" she exclaimed with a smile. She pushed aside the items on her table to make room for the nail polish bottle and then opened up her arms, keeping her fingers spread wide so as to not smudge the polish. I paused for a second, unsure who she meant to hug, but when she continued to smile in my direction, I realized she wanted me. I bent down and gave her a weak pat, afraid I might hurt her. But she pulled me in and squeezed me hard with her palms. It was the type of solid hug I always wished my sister would give me, though she rarely did. "I missed you, Bee," she said, to my surprise. Instead of savoring the moment, though, I pulled back.

"Drina," I began, feeling a little dizzy. "I'm sorry," I said, my voice hoarse. I hadn't meant to say it in front of Father, but I was overcome with emotion, with a desire to right my wrong, then and there.

"Sorry?" Both Audrina and Father questioned, confusion in their voices. Audrina's eyebrows were furrowed in a way that reminded me of Mother.

"For what?" she asked, while Father shrugged.

"You know, what I said to you that night." I looked down at the large gray-speckled floor tiles.

"What night?"

"The night you were home. I mean, before you went to the hospital."

"You're sorry for the night I went to the hospital?"

I shifted. "I'm sorry for what I said to you that night."

"What did you say?"

"You don't remember?" I said, my heart tugging upward just a little. "Really?"

Audrina laughed—her confident, high-pitched laugh that I'd nearly forgotten. "I don't remember anything about that night. I don't remember anything about that whole time."

My shoulders relaxed. "Oh," I said, relieved and unsure what else to say. It had never occurred to me that she wouldn't remember.

"How you doing, Pipiske?" Father interjected. "Ready to go home soon? Your mother's out shopping now, getting everything ready. The food Dr. Carlogie recommended. All that stuff."

"So what did you say?" my sister pressed, ignoring Father. I glanced around her hospital room as I tried to come up with a response. I was curious who all the cards and presents were from—our neighbors? Family? Then I noticed a Polaroid of a few girls taped on the wall behind her bed, and I leaned in close to take a look. It was a picture of Audrina, Hope Rodale, and Michelle. Audrina was wearing another set of familiar pajamas, her pink-striped ones, and they were all sitting on a bed. This bed. I recognized the pale blue drape that hung from the wall like a shower curtain.

"I don't remember," I managed to utter. "Hope Rodale visited you? And Michelle? Here, in the hospital?"

"Uh-huh," my sister replied, and then turned her attention to our father. "I'm so excited, Father. The nurse said if Dr. Carlogie comes around in the next hour to sign the paperwork, I could even go home today."

I heard my sister talking, but it was like she was far away, an echo. Hope had visited my sister; I felt weak with the knowledge.

Scanning the rest of her wall, I tried to read the signatures of hanging cards and see if I could spot any more pictures. Had others come to visit her?

"When—when did Hope visit you?" My voice cracked.

Audrina picked up the nail polish and began shaking the bottle to mix up the contents. "I dunno."

"I think it was a couple of days ago, right, Audrina?" our father said.

"Father, how come . . . ?" I started. "Why didn't I visit earlier?"

Father laughed, as if it were a funny question. But something about his laughter was weird. It was short, forced. Like he was embarrassed.

Audrina had noticed, too—she furrowed her brows again, and said, "Yeah, why didn't Bee visit before?"

"I—your mother," he started, and then he took a deep breath. "Borka, I—I thought your mother asked you if you wanted to visit, and she thought I asked you."

Now Audrina laughed. "You mean, you guys forgot to ask Bee if she wanted to visit?"

I bit the inside of my cheek as something deep inside me flared.

"You could've asked us, too," Father said.

"But I didn't know—" I started to say, as Audrina suddenly stopped shaking the nail polish bottle and cocked her head at me.

"Did you do something different to your hair?" she asked.

My hand automatically reached to the back of my head, where I'd been plucking hairs lately to avoid the sides. "No," I said loudly, more loudly than I intended to. Had I been pulling out too much hair? Was it obvious? I'd started wearing a new part, one that was off center. It seemed to provide the most coverage for my thinned-out sides.

"It looks . . . different," my sister said, staring at me oddly. I shook my head.

"It does look different," Father agreed. "Did you get a haircut?"

"No," I replied. I should have worn a hat. "I have to go to the bathroom," I mumbled, anxious to get away from the attention.

But as I started to leave the room, Father called out, "Bee, there's one right here," and pointed to a closed door on the side of the room that I'd assumed was a closet. I nodded, disappointed. I'd been hoping to flee down the hall to the bathroom we'd passed by the nurses' station. After I scooted inside the tiny bathroom and locked the door, I stared at myself in the mirror, trying to objectively view my hair. But the mirror was small, the lighting was poor, and I wanted to cry.

Everything seemed upside down; Audrina was in the hospital but didn't look sick, I'd pulled out so much of my hair it was now noticeable, and because my parents hadn't asked me, and I hadn't known to ask myself, I was the last one to visit my own sister in the hospital. *They had forgotten.*

How could they? Mother—that was somewhat understandable, since she'd been basically living at the hospital. But Father? I wished I'd never reached for his stupid hand.

Now I remembered the funny look Gwen had given me when she stopped by the other day, to my surprise, with a plate of cookies. We hadn't spoken since school ended, but even when Hope dropped me, Gwen had still gone out of her way to make small talk when she saw me in the hall.

"I haven't seen her yet," I admitted, from the doorstep, when Gwen asked how my sister was doing.

"Oh, really?" she'd said, raising her eyebrows. Her mother was waiting in the car in front of our house, her window down. She waved when she saw me looking at her.

"We've talked on the phone," I replied, and then I'd added, "We've talked, like, a lot," which wasn't true. But her questioning look made me feel funny.

"Okay," Gwen finally said, and opened and closed her mouth like she was about to say something but then changed her mind.

I felt so foolish. Yes, I realized, surveying my hair: My sister and father were right. My hair did look "different." I'd gone too far. The only consolation was that it was difficult to tell what was different. There was my new part, obviously, but it was more than that. The overall texture was different. There was an uneven spattering of density that reminded me of a tree just beginning to lose its autumn leaves. Why did I feel so compelled to pull my hair? Were there other freaks like me? Or was I the only one? I took a few deep breaths and then flushed the toilet, even though I hadn't used it, and then ran the faucet as if I were washing my hands. Over the sound of the running water, I could hear Audrina and Father laughing.

Suddenly I understood why Hope Rodale had never called to ask about Audrina. It wasn't because she hadn't cared about her; it was because she hadn't cared about *me*. Hope hadn't needed me for information because she had gone straight to Audrina. I needed to know who else besides Hope and Michelle had come to visit, I decided. And who had sent cards. I would pretend to admire the cards and see if I could read the messages, see if I could recognize any names or spot any more photos.

But when I came out of the bathroom, Audrina had what looked like a small pen in her hands. "Bee," she said, thrusting it toward me. "This is my insulin syringe. I have to give myself injections with it. Twice a day."

I took the syringe from her to examine it. It was about the same length as one of Mrs. Baker's cigarettes but much skinnier. I was surprised; I didn't remember Grandpa Joe having to take shots.

"They had me practice on an orange at first," Audrina said. "And then Nurse Christie even let me practice on her!"

"Does it hurt?" I asked.

Audrina nodded slowly. "A little. They say it gets easier. I also have to prick my finger to check my sugar levels." She turned her hands over to show me her fingertips, which were red and swollen. A few were speckled with red dots. Father sighed as he looked away.

"Ouch," I replied.

"I'm not good at it," she confessed. "Actually, I hate it. But I want to go home, so I pretend like I'm okay with it."

"How long do you have to do this for?"

"Forever," she said, "or at least until they find a cure. Dr. Carlogie said they are going to find a cure for diabetes in about seven or ten years." She smiled, and Father smiled back hesitantly in a way that made me doubt whether it was really true. "She said I'll need help at first," she continued. "From my family."

My plan to gather intel on who had visited her suddenly no longer mattered. She needed me, I realized. She wouldn't be able to eat banana splits and candy, she would probably still have to pee a lot, and she had to give herself shots, had to prick her fingers. She needed my help.

"Yeah, Drina," I replied. "I can help you." And Father then broadly smiled, the type of smile that appeared when he got the rare chance to watch Manchester United, his favorite soccer team, play in a European Cup game on the family room TV, and it suddenly seemed like it was all going to be okay.

As it turned out, I didn't need to figure out who else had visited or reached out to Audrina just then, because later that day she was discharged from the hospital—along with her skinny injection needles and her plethora of balloons, cards, and stuffed animals, all of which were crammed in our room, on display where I could look at them anytime I wished. And even when I didn't wish to.

# Chapter Twelve

WHEN AUDRINA CAME HOME, SHE HATED EVERYTHING ABOUT HER
diabetes, and I, at first, loved everything about it. Checking her
blood sugar, which was required twice a day, sometimes more, reminded me of a science experiment. There was unusual equipment:
a machine our mother called a guillotine and thin pieces of paper
known as chemistry strips (or "chem strips," as Audrina said Nurse
Christie called them) that we would either read against a color chart
or run through a digital blood glucose meter. And, of course, a logbook to record the information, since a good scientist always has to
document her data.

Audrina refused to check her blood sugars herself, so Mother or
I would have to do it for her. I never confronted Mother about how I
hadn't been taken to visit Audrina earlier in the hospital; I didn't
want her to feel bad, and I'd decided I was most likely to blame for
not having asked. Besides, I could tell Mother was trying hard to
make sure I felt included. "Ready, teammie?" she would ask me when

it was time to check Audrina's sugar, and I'd roll my eyes, though secretly I enjoyed the nickname. The guillotine, used to prick Audrina's fingers, was shaped like a tape measure; we had to load it like a rifle, cocking it back while forcefully holding Audrina's finger. As we pressed the button top, a spring-loaded needle would blast through the plastic hole onto Audrina's finger with a loud whacking noise, outmatched only by her scream. It was a horrible device; one day I tried it on myself to see if it hurt as much as Audrina said it did—and as much as it looked like it did. It did not disappoint; the tip of my middle finger was bruised for a few days afterward.

"Thank you for your help, Borka," Mother would murmur in my ear when she came into our room at night to check on Audrina.

I would swim in Mother's whispered *thank you,* float in it, really—the uncomfortable feelings I'd had about being forgotten sinking like dive rings in a pool. Finally I had a chance to do something right, to make up for past mistakes.

Audrina detested the logbook where we recorded her blood sugar levels; at the end of each day, she'd toss it into our closet and close the door so she didn't have to see it. As a surprise, I bought the scratch-and-sniff stickers Audrina used to like at Mortenson's Drug Store—even daring to approach the corner of the store where the pharmacist had reportedly collapsed—and used them to decorate the cover of her logbook. I knew it was a childish gesture, but for some reason I thought she'd be excited about it. Audrina had indeed smiled when she first saw the stickers, but then she'd started anxiously picking at them, using her nails and then whatever finger bed hadn't been stuck in a while to rub off the remaining bits.

Father avoided the testing and the needles; Mother said it was because he had a sensitive stomach. But it seemed like Father didn't really want anything to do with diabetes at all. He'd ask the same questions over and over, simple things like *Is that a good number or bad number?* about the blood sugar result, and *How many times a night do you need to do that?* when he'd see us drawing up the nightly dose of NPH insulin—the only injection she took at bedtime. I remember how Audrina would just look at him, silent, as if he were speaking Hungarian and she didn't understand.

Mother, on the other hand, managed Audrina's diabetes with the same gusto she used to comb the Oriental rug fringe. Carefully, in her neat penmanship of square-like letters—each so perfect that it looked like she had used a tracer—she recorded my sister's life: her blood sugars, what she ate, when she began and ended meals, the sites of her insulin shots. The KitchenAid mixer that usually sat on the counter disappeared, and in its place became an area dedicated solely to Audrina's diabetes: labeled bins of insulin syringes, lancets, chem strips.

Audrina always took a while to emerge for her thrice-daily injections, slowly trudging in as if she were wearing a pair of too-small, uncomfortable boots.

"Reality has set in," Mother remarked to Father when Audrina threw her insulin syringe against the wall one night.

Surprisingly, my sister didn't want any friends visiting, now that she was home.

"Why?" I'd asked.

"I just don't want it."

"But you saw your friends when you were in the hospital," I remarked, trying to understand, and then it struck me that *your friends* sounded funny, since Hope Rodale was technically in my grade and used to be my friend. "Your visitors," I corrected, but Audrina was already shaking her head.

"Yeah, but it was different there. It was like, like not-real yet. Like

I was just sick. But now I'm home, and I still have this stupid diabetes."

"I get it." Looking around at all the diabetes paraphernalia, I nodded. It was quite the life change, and I felt a rush of sympathy. "It's okay, Drina," I cooed, in a gentle tone I had recently perfected with her. "You don't have to see anyone you don't want to. Not until you're ready."

"I hate diabetes," she just snapped in response.

"Should we get rid of all the sugar in the house?" I asked Mother one day, after opening the fridge and immediately noticing a bottle of Hershey syrup, maple syrup, and a liter of Coke. I could only imagine how Audrina felt when she was the one peering into the fridge.

Mother smiled. "That's considerate of you to ask. Dr. Carlogie said we didn't need to. Audrina needs to learn to make smart eating choices."

There was one exception, one time my sister was allowed—required, even—to have sugar: when she got "hypo." Hypoglycemia, I learned, was the big worry; if Audrina's blood sugar level dropped too low, she could die. An emergency jar of sugar cubes soon lined both the "diabetes area" on the counter and Audrina's bedside table; an orange juice I wasn't allowed to touch sat in the fridge.

With my sister home, I didn't pull my hair nearly as much—I couldn't do it so openly. I also found that I didn't have urges as frequently. And when the desire did rise within, I'd recall Audrina's stinging, offhand remark—*Did you do something different to your hair?*—which would sufficiently swat down the urge. I'd found an old thick pink plastic hairband under our bathroom sink; it miraculously covered the thinned-out spots on either side of my temple. Mother still hadn't noticed, probably because she was so consumed with Audrina's care. It would help, I thought, that it was summer. I'd always heard that hair grew faster in the summer.

But that summer, once Audrina came home, nothing was fast. My days were long, organized around diabetes—learning about diabetes, managing diabetes—with intermittent escapes into the Sweet Valley High book series.

We hadn't gone to the club, or anywhere else—she didn't want to, so I didn't go anywhere, either. I didn't mind; it's not like I had concrete plans I was missing, and my sister needed me—that was the most important thing. I wanted to make up for lost time, for the awful way I'd treated her in the past. I wanted her next diary entry to be one that reflected how good of a sister I was being.

Even when Max—whose face had tanned dark, making his eyes look even more blue—and Andrew and Patrick stopped by the house (all three having returned from their various vacations), asking me to join them at the club, I said no.

"Can't," I'd replied, from the inside of my doorway. The early August heat blazed through the door like flames emanating from a grill, and I could sense the summer I was missing.

Andrew and Patrick had shrugged. "Suit yourself," Andrew said, and they hopped back on their bikes. Max lingered for a moment before getting on his bike, as if he wanted to say something, causing my stomach to flutter. When I closed the front door, I had to lean against it. I'd been right to say no, I told myself. Being with Audrina was more important than going to the stupid club . . . right? But I wondered whether they'd ever think to ask me again. Me—not Audrina—I realized. They'd asked *me*.

Father's work at the Bakers' house, which had temporarily halted during Audrina's hospitalization, started back up, and I consoled myself with the fact that his project would likely extend into the beginning of the school year—plenty of future opportunities, therefore, to see Max. For now, I'd continue to help my sister.

One day I asked Mother which food on Audrina's plate was part of which exchange group—the diabetes diet she was following.

"Audrina needs to understand, honey. Not you."

"Ugh," Audrina said in response, setting her fork down on the table, defeated.

A tiny feather of relief dusted over me. It had been a big responsibility to be so involved in Audrina's diabetes, bigger than I had anticipated, especially since she refused to have anything to do with it herself. "Really?" I asked, and then cleared my throat when my sister frowned. "I mean, I can help you, Drina, if I need—I'm happy to help . . . I just don't—"

"You are not the one with diabetes," Mother said. "You are a big enough help as it is. Your sister needs to start to learn how to take care of this herself."

"Oh," I replied.

Audrina breathed out loudly, as if she were blowing out a candle.

"Do you hear me, Audrina?" Mother continued. "You need to start learning how to take care of your diabetes yourself. Like Dr. Carlogie said."

My sister nodded. "Yes," she replied, through gritted teeth. "I know, Mother. You've told me. A million times."

"That is why you are going to diabetes camp."

"Diabetes camp?" Audrina and I said at the same time.

"Yes," Mother said. "There is a camp right here in New Jersey. It's a sleepaway camp, like Diane and Courtney go to. But everyone at this camp has diabetes. So you'll learn a lot."

Sleepaway camp? A diabetes sleepaway camp? "When?" I asked, as Audrina shoved her plate away—her fork scattering across the table, a piece of chicken plopping next to me—in order to bury her head in her arms.

"I was warned about this. One of the girls in the hospital warned me," Audrina mumbled from beneath.

"The last two weeks of August," Mother replied to me, ignoring Audrina's comments. "We were lucky that we were able to get in last minute, otherwise we would have had to wait a whole year."

"She said I could forget about regular camp," Audrina continued. "Just diabetes camp from now on. Everything friggin' diabetes."

"The last two weeks of August," Mother repeated. "Which is coming up."

"Last two weeks of August . . ." Audrina moaned into the table, and then suddenly looked up. "That's, like, next week!"

"Exactly," Mother replied. She glanced at Audrina and then looked away, bringing a cup of water to her lips, and I realized that she meant business.

Audrina's pleas did not deter our parents from shipping her off.

"It sounds awful," she'd complain, time and time again over the next few days, though her complaints were largely ignored. "What about acting camp?" she'd say. This, too, was ignored, since the answer was obvious: Acting camp was not happening this summer. I knew that she didn't really want to go to acting camp, since she hadn't brought it up until now—she just didn't want to go to diabetes camp.

"I hate diabetes!" she'd yell when she felt like nobody was listening. And then I'd quickly jump in to ask her if she wanted to paint our nails or sunbathe in the backyard. She always said no, and sometimes in a mean, curt way, though I overlooked it—she was tired, overwhelmed, maybe even had low blood sugar. There were a million reasons why. I knew this was not easy for her.

One night while we lay in bed, she said, "Bee, thanks for everything. I don't know how I could do all this without you."

"You're welcome, Drina," I said as my heart swelled. "Love you."

"Love you, too, sissy."

Our hayride fight was distant history, and I knew my sister hadn't meant those words she said—or, at the very least, not anymore. I only hoped that she would continue to feel that way.

A couple days later, Father loaded my sister's suitcase into the trunk of the Jeep as she, resigned, watched alongside me. "Just think," Father said, "it's actually a pretty good time to have diabetes. One hundred years ago, Pipiske, they didn't have insulin. They didn't have anything. Certainly not diabetes camps."

"See, Drina? It's a good thing," I repeated like a monkey, as I imagined what it would be like for the two weeks she'd be gone. I couldn't stop thinking of the way Max had lingered on his bike, and at night, when the urge to pull my hair rose, I switched focus by imagining what it was he had wanted to say to me, why he'd lingered. *I wish you could come, Bee.* Or perhaps: *Want to hang out later?* I thought of his ocean eyes, and how his damp hair had pressed against his tan forehead.

"One hundred years ago, they didn't have a Bee, either," Father said, and ruffled my head like I was a dog. His affection surprised me. This was confirmation that I had done the right thing that summer. That perhaps I'd even made up for my mistakes the previous summer. I'd been a good big sister, putting Audrina's needs ahead of my wants. But maybe, I thought, as my heartbeat quickened, sometime over the next two weeks *I* could be the one to invite Max to the club.

Two weeks. Two whole weeks. Two weeks in which I wouldn't have to watch Audrina for hypo episodes; I wouldn't have to use the guillotine or give her shots—I wouldn't even have to see any of that stuff. It was packed in a Clinique cosmetic case Mother had given her.

"I'll miss you, Bee," my sister said. She had an earnest look on her face, a vulnerability about her that made her seem younger. "Please write." Then she climbed into the passenger seat and turned her head down, toward the dashboard.

"I will," I promised, shouting through the window. I vigorously waved as the Jeep backed out of the garage. And I swear I meant it.

# Chapter Thirteen

THE NEXT DAY, MOTHER KNOCKED ON MY DOOR TO ASK IF SHE could enter—something she never used to do. I guess it meant I was growing up; I was, after all, about to enter eighth grade.

"Deer Chase Lake just reopened, Bee. Today," Mother said. She sat on the edge of my bed. Though her tone was matter-of-fact, I could tell she was nervous from the way she folded and unfolded her hands. Her wedding band slid up and down as she moved—she was thinner than she used to be. Audrina's diabetes had taken its toll on her, too.

I'd forgotten about the possibility of the lake reopening—the conversation Audrina and I had had with Mother about the contamination seemed so long ago, even though it had been only a couple months earlier. Since then, so much had happened.

"You don't have to go if you don't want to," my mother continued, her right hand now atop her left. "But you can, of course. There's no reason not to go. No reason to be scared to go."

"Okay," I replied. It felt weird to be alone together, without Audrina. I couldn't remember the last time it was just the two of us. The quiet privacy tempted me to broach something. "Mother, can I ask you a question?"

"Yes, you physically can."

I rolled my eyes. "*May* I ask you something?"

She smiled. "Yes, honey."

"Did you and Father . . ." My voice trailed off. "Did he get you a heart necklace?" I finally mustered. I'd recently peeked into her jewelry box, and I hadn't seen it. I think half of me wanted to talk about it with her so that she could assuage my worry, and dismiss my concerns, but the other half of me simply wanted to know the truth.

Mother tilted her head, giving me a quizzical look.

"I—I heard you," I explained. "A few months ago, you said Sammy from the jeweler's called. I heard you talking with Father about it in the kitchen."

"Big ears. Yes, you don't need to worry," Mother said, then adding, "Honey," in afterthought. She spoke in a stiff manner, like she was trying to figure out how to respond. "It was an anniversary present." She smiled, but it didn't reach her eyes.

"It was?" Now I cocked my head.

"Yes, it was a very nice gift. Very generous of your father."

"Did you get it? The gold one? Instead of the white gold—"

"Bee, why are you so curious about this? I just said I did." She wasn't smiling anymore, but she didn't seem mad, either. Just a little weary, maybe. A thin blue vein under her left eye appeared more visible than usual.

I wanted to know more: Where did she keep the pendant? Had she worn it? If so, why hadn't I ever seen her wearing it? But I also didn't want to know. "That's great, Mother," I forced myself to respond.

Mother rose from the bed. "You can bike to the lake, you know," she said, as if she wanted me to know that it really, truly was okay if I wanted to go to the lake. So far she had only allowed me to bike to the town park and back, but Deer Chase Lake was much farther away, and on the part of Main Street that became Route 108, which meant the road was usually pretty busy. I didn't mention how I'd already biked along there to the ice cream store with Diane and Courtney. "Just be careful on 108," she advised before she left the room.

Slipping on a yellow bikini that I thought was the most flattering of all my suits, I wondered if I dared to go. Suddenly the sound of the lake being sliced by rescue divers the day Sally went missing reverberated through me, and my body grew hot. The room turned blurry, like it was filled with squiggly heat waves.

When it cleared, a memory that had been folded inside me suddenly opened: Sally, standing in the shallows, her feet barely covered by water. She looks out to us—Max, Audrina, and me—who are already swimming in the deep part, several feet away.

All the courage I'd worked up to ask Max to go swimming was for naught; Max was pretty firm that he didn't want to go. "Nope," he said, cutting me off mid-question and then shooting a basket on his driveway. When the basketball swished through the netting, Max looked over to see if I had been watching. "Not today. Sorry," he added, with a half-smile as he retrieved the ball and began dribbling around me, as if we were playing one-on-one.

I was perched on my bike, spinning the pedals backward as I

tried subtly to pull down my shorts, which kept creeping up. They matched my favorite coral-and-white-striped Gap shirt, so I wore the shorts despite their tendency to ride up when I moved. The August sun was hot, and sweat dripped down my back. Max stopped pretending I was an opponent and moved toward the hoop.

I took the opportunity to tiptoe my bike toward the shade that Max's garage provided as I wondered if his reluctance had anything to do with the fact that Deer Chase Lake was reopening. Why else wouldn't he want to go swimming today? When I'd checked the back page of the newspaper, where the weather was always printed, there'd been a yellow sun with *90 degrees* next to it for today's forecast. Maybe he thought I was asking him to go to the lake? "But we could just go to the club," I tried, once more spinning the pedals backward.

Max suddenly stopped moving, mid-pose for a shot, and gripped the basketball with both hands. He lowered it and looked down at it, as if he were reading the ball like a book. "What do you mean, we could *just go* to the club?"

*Uh-oh*, I thought. "I mean—" I started and then stopped.

"Are you going to the club or to Deer Chase Lake, Bee?" His voice had the tone that my mother would use when she was trying to suss out whether I'd done something mischievous.

"Club," I quickly answered. Max was quiet, and then other words spilled out of me: "I guess. I mean, I don't really know."

"You *want* to go to the lake?" Max asked as he began bouncing the basketball against the ground. He seemed to push the ball down harder with each bounce. "You'd actually go there?"

"It's confusing," I admitted, and then my mother's words tumbled out of my mouth. "There's no reason not to go, right? I mean, we—I shouldn't be scared to go."

Max gave a sound that was a cross between a scoff and a snort. "I'm not scared," he said. "I just don't want to go that place. Ever."

I felt like an idiot. This was not how I'd envisioned asking him to go swimming with me. "I'm sorry," I mumbled, staring down at the black shininess of the Bakers' driveway. Their driveway had been repaved just a few weeks ago, and when I'd looked out our dining room window to watch the machine noisily rolling out the black tar, I imagined Sally hunched over, her fingers smudged with blue chalk.

"For what?"

"I dunno. For asking if you wanted to go swimming, I guess. Today, of all days—with the lake reopening. I'm stupid."

Max used the bottom of his T-shirt to wipe the sweat off his forehead, and I glimpsed his stomach. "Don't be sorry. I like the club; I'm the one that asked you to go the other week. I just don't want to go today. I feel like everyone there would be looking at me, and talking about me, because of the lake reopening."

It was the first time I'd ever heard Max express that he was self-conscious of people talking about him. It must be difficult on so many levels, I thought. My heart felt heavy for him.

The ball, which was at his feet, began rolling away toward the edge of the driveway, but instead of fetching it, he walked toward me and said, "Can I ask *you* something?"

"Sure," I said. My stomach started to fold on itself, the way it always did when Max came close.

"What do you think of Patrick?"

"Patrick?" I repeated. "Why?" I asked, confused.

"I think he likes you," Max said. He stared at me, his pupils dark dots against blue saucers.

"Likes me?" I repeated again. Patrick Wiley liked me? As in, like-liked me? Patrick-with-the-freckles who never paid me any attention? Patrick, as in Patrick-and-Andrew? I couldn't even think of the two of them separate—they were the Wiley brothers. As I ground the handlebar in my hands, more sweat accumulated; now the back of my shirt felt like a wet towel. Max opened his lips slightly as if he was going to say something else but then decided against it, and my gaze fluttered to his lips and then back to his eyes. We continued staring at each other. Something was rooting us to the moment. It was like the world around us had melted away in the heat of the sun and it was just us—right there, right then.

"You have an eyelash on your cheek," he said, and I touched my face. "Other side," he instructed, and I moved my hand to the other side and began dusting it. "I'd get it for you, but . . ." He trailed off, and I stopped moving, keeping my hand still against my face, my eyes in his. It was difficult to breathe; the air in my chest felt like liquid.

Then the sound of the car next door—the Garfields' car—rumbled to life, and we both glanced in that direction. Max went to retrieve the basketball, which had rolled onto the grass.

"Come over to Andrew and Patrick's house tonight," Max said as he began dribbling again. "Their parents told them they could have people over. Diane and Courtney will be there. We can watch a movie or something."

As I pushed down on the bike pedals, my thoughts felt jumbled, chaotic, and I pedaled faster and faster. What had just happened between Max and me? And what would have happened if the Garfields' car hadn't started, if we hadn't been interrupted? I reached the part of Main Street that sloped downward, and now I coasted, my body still but my mind busy. And I was surprised that Patrick liked me, although I knew I was definitely not interested in him.

But Max. Max. I liked him. Did he also like me? There was something—a moment, between Max and me—that had occurred, even though he'd been talking about Patrick. There had been a couple of moments like that between us in the last year, but this one had felt especially powerful. A warmth burned inside me as I imagined what it would feel like to touch Max, to press my lips against his. I wished I could talk to Audrina about what had happened. Maybe I'd write her a letter. But what would I say? I couldn't put into words the moment that had occurred. And would Audrina even believe me?

It was only once I pedaled to a stop in front of the bike rack at the base of the stairs leading to Deer Chase Lake that I realized the sub-conscious decision I'd made. I stared at the hill in front of me; I couldn't see the lake from where I stood. And then, automatically, my body took over as my mind recessed, as if trying to protect it: Hands easing the bike into the rack, legs pausing at the bottom of the stairs. Fingers tugging down at shorts, lungs filling with a deep breath. Then my body moved forward, my feet moving up each step, one Rainbow sandal in front of another. My mind was in the past, remembering how we'd raced up the stairs the day Sally had gone missing. When I rounded the top, the sounds of the lake wrapped around me like a childhood blanket: people laughing, water splashing, dogs barking. A déjà vu feeling. I had the thought for a moment that perhaps the lake had never closed but I'd just been away for the past thirteen months.

Sally. Where was she, right now, at this moment? I started to imagine potential scenarios: Alive, maybe being kept too high up for anyone to hear her cries, like in an attic similar to the one we had, alongside rigged mousetraps. Or she might be belowground, in a space without windows—locked up in a basement with a *pervert*, like the Wiley brothers had once speculated. Or dead, of course—that was a very likely possibility.

A dark, disturbing feeling replaced my initial euphoria as I spread my towel across the sand, choosing a patch of the beach that wasn't as crowded.

I couldn't believe how many people had come to the lake—mothers with children, lifeguards, people from my school—and it was early yet. I recognized a few boys at the far end of the beach who would soon be high school freshmen. Hope Rodale, I noted with relief, had not decided to come to the lake, at least not yet.

I dragged my feet up from the sand, tucked my knees in, and looked down through my billowing shirt at the outline of my breasts against my yellow bikini. Max's words, *We can watch a movie or something*, rinsed through me, and I straightened out my legs and raised my head.

Two little girls with dark hair and pink bathing suits ran in and out of the lake, yelling as they splashed each other with water from their heels. They looked like sisters close in age, perhaps four or five years old, both with the same oval face.

Suddenly I recalled what Audrina had said about Sally, shortly after she went missing: "Sally's super scared of the water," she had said. "She knows how to swim, but she doesn't like to."

*Audrina should have told people Sally wouldn't be in the lake*, I thought. Then they wouldn't have wasted all that time searching it. I took the bracelet, which might have led the police in the direction of the nearby woods, but Audrina withheld important information that also would have propelled the search toward the woods. Wasn't that kind of similar? So how were Audrina and I so different? Weren't we both guilty?

A long, shrill sound brought me back to the present—the life-guard on the red platform was standing, whistle in mouth. I recognized him from school. Dennis Gallen. His younger brother John, one year ahead of me, had once quietly asked me in the hall, when no one else was around, if Audrina had a boyfriend. Dennis blew his whistle again and gestured to a few kids in the water, something about staying on one side of the buoys. It all seemed so normal, a normal summer day, like nobody had ever disappeared on this lake, like no one ever *could*.

# Chapter Fourteen

THERE WAS A RED OAK TREE IN OUR BACKYARD THAT I USED TO climb while Audrina watched from below. She must have climbed it at least once, though, because I have one specific memory of the two of us examining a small hole in the trunk on the back part of the tree, an area not readily visible from the ground. Likely I came across it first and convinced Audrina to take a look.

I remember how the cavity looked like a porthole, with a thick ring of bark encircling it, and how the dense branches of red leaves overhead felt like giant sails. "Arrr," I'd exclaimed, like a pirate, and Audrina laughed. We took a closer look—as close as we dared. The hole was dark inside, which caused that displaced sensation you get when you stare too long at the sky. My sister and I took stock of our hands and arms, and we reasoned we could have stuck at least our fists into the hole, if not potentially our entire upper limbs, had we tried.

But we weren't going to try. In fact, I think that was one of the last times I climbed that tree, because a dark hole in a tree is a scary thing. Who knows where it leads, or how deep it is, or what creatures may lurk within? There are secrets inside a tree trunk, secrets that never leave. They are trapped inside the trunk's fortress walls.

When Peter Scoffer and Jonathan Smalls, two eight-year-old boys from Etchers—the town adjacent to Hammend—came across a long, skinny bone sticking out of the generous cavity of a large silver maple tree, on the outskirts of a local farm in the summer of 1986, they were understandably nervous about what they'd found. Was it human? Were there other bones to find? What had happened? Was a ghost inside the space? Peter and Jonathan, best friends since preschool, did their secret handshake—two fist pumps, a high five, and eight consecutive finger snaps (one for each year of their lives), and made a pact never to tell anyone about it.

It would last for a while.

The Wileys' tan front door had grooves forming rectangular borders. Three rectangles carved across and five down, I counted, taking a deep breath. It was the first time I would be going to a boy's house at night. Mother had smiled, pleased, when I told her of my plans. My outfit had been carefully picked—after trying on many options, I'd settled on jeans and a pink cotton sweater.

After another breath, I pushed in the Wileys' doorbell. It was sticky, so it rang for longer than I'd intended. I took a step back, embarrassed, and immediately made sure my hair was pulled in front of my ears on both sides, even though I had barely touched it since Audrina's return home from the hospital. I heard a few footsteps, and then Mrs. Wiley opened the door. Mrs. Wiley always made me a little nervous because she and my mother talked on the phone almost every morning, "like teenagers," Father said. So I was aware she knew a lot about me, probably more than I wanted her to know.

She wore a white polo shirt and khaki shorts and was carrying a bowl of Doritos, as if I had just rung her doorbell to trick-or-treat. I almost expected to see the cordless phone attached to her ear, with Mother on the other line.

"They're downstairs," she said, handing me the Doritos and ushering me toward the basement door. Unlike us, the Wileys had a finished basement, which meant wood paneling, stiff gray Berber carpeting, a wet bar, TV area, and game space. Whenever my parents had drinks at the Wileys' house, my father would return with enthusiastic ideas about finishing our own basement, and my mother would just smile, knowing that Father would soon become distracted by another project. Plus, Father used the basement (as well as part of the garage) as workshop space, so we knew he would never actually give it up. I wondered how the Bakers' basement would look when it was done; from what Father had said, it sounded like the office portion would be boring, but the rumpus room would be pretty amazing.

Downstairs, Max and Andrew were playing Ping-Pong while Patrick fiddled with his father's stereo system in the corner. Diane and Courtney were already there, helping themselves to the soda and potato chips on the plastic card table. I recognized the wicker basket holding cocktail napkins; it was one of Mother's gift-basket creations, with a red ribbon that threaded around the perimeter of the basket and ended in a giant bow. I was the last to arrive, unless more people were coming. I placed the Doritos on the table next to the potato chips and smiled at the girls.

"What's up?" Diane said, and she and Courtney each gave me hugs that I felt I adequately returned.

"We heard about diabetes camp," Courtney said, crossing her arms. "That really stinks."

"Thanks," I said, unsure how else to respond. My sister had now been there for more than twenty-four hours; I hoped it wasn't too bad, and that she was settling in. Father said she'd looked pretty miserable when he was leaving. I poured myself a Coke in one of the red plastic cups and then scooped some Doritos into another.

"How long's the camp?" Diane asked.

"Two weeks." Steve Miller's "The Joker" began emanating from the floor speaker, and Patrick caught my eye from across the room and waved. My arm felt jerky as I waved back.

"I didn't even know there was such a thing as diabetes camp," said Courtney.

"Neither did I," I admitted, holding a Dorito in my mouth until it grew soft and then chewing it.

Diane leaned in slightly and asked, in a soft voice, "So, how are *you* doing?" while Courtney uncrossed her arms.

"Okay," I said slowly. I felt the familiar warmth of being the center of attention; it had been a while since I'd commanded interest like that. I needed to give them a compliment to return the goodwill. Any compliment. "You look so pretty!" I said to both of them. "I like your shirt," I said to Courtney, and then to Diane I said, "And yours, too!" There was a moment where they didn't say anything in response, and I worried that my compliments had been too much, too forced. But as Diane gestured downward, I realized she was wearing a dress, and not a shirt and skirt like I'd assumed. "I mean—" I started, trying to figure out how to fix what I'd just said. But then they just laughed, easy laughter that came quickly, and I felt like they were laughing with me, not at me.

Diane lowered her voice. "Hey, did you hear what the boys want to do?"

"No," I replied as I glanced over to them.

"They want to play Spin the Bottle."

"Really?" I nervously slurped my Coke, and just then, Max gave me a wave from the Ping-Pong table that made me feel warm inside. "I thought we were going to watch a movie."

"This will be more fun," Diane assured me, while Courtney asked, "Have you ever played it before?"

I shook my head, wishing I had asked Leah about it when she called me from California a couple weeks earlier. But our conversation had been brief and mostly focused on Audrina. "I don't even know how to play," I admitted as I tried to subtly pick out, with my tongue, the piece of Dorito chip that was now stuck in the ridge of my back tooth.

"We just played for the first time—a few weeks ago, at camp," Diane confided, and I nodded, like she hadn't already told me. "It was fun, right?" Diane asked Courtney, who nodded. "Don't worry," Diane said to me. "It's a lot of fun. We'll show you. We can add Truth or Dare to it, which will make it better. We did that at camp, too. And we—the three of us—need to decide on a key word, in case there's anything we don't want to do, like *Lego*."

"Anything we don't want to do?" I asked.

"Don't worry," Courtney replied, smiling. "We'll explain everything."

I smiled back, but my mouth felt contorted. "Okay, great." The whole thing seemed like anything but a good idea. A thread of anxiety knitted through me.

I got through an awkward hello with Patrick, who then procured one of his father's glass Heineken bottles from upstairs without his parents noticing. We formed a circle and took swigs to empty the bottle. I had to force myself to swallow the beer; it was gross. I'd never had beer before, although once I took a sip of the red wine Mother left on the kitchen counter when she went to use the bathroom.

Diane gave me a quick rundown of the game: You spun the bottle, and whoever the bottle landed on, you had to kiss. Or challenge that person to a truth or dare. I'd never kissed anyone before, and I wasn't entirely sure that I wanted to. At least, I admitted to myself, my heart quickening, not anyone but Max.

"My father drinks this brand," I said, my voice shaking a little.

Patrick snorted. "Our father drinks whatever he can get his hands on."

"Sounds like my mom," said Max, and everyone went quiet for a moment, unsure how to respond.

We decided to play clockwise beginning with Patrick, which meant I would be the third person up. Mercifully, when Patrick spun the bottle, its neck landed on Diane. She and Patrick stood up and gave each other a quick kiss on the lips, the type of kiss my mother would give me. I was relieved; I could handle a peck. Then it was Courtney's turn, and when it landed on Max, I looked away as they kissed, digging my fingers into the stiff carpet. My fingers were still a little orange from eating the Doritos, and I accidentally stained the gray fabric, which I tried to rub in without anyone noticing.

Then I was up, and my heart thudded in my ears. This meant I'd have to kiss someone, I realized, as my hands swatted at the bottle. It was a bad spin, much too hard, sending the bottle off-kilter. Eventually it stopped and pointed at someone. But the someone was an in-between, as in in between Andrew and Patrick.

"Closer to Andrew," Diane declared, to my relief. The last person I wanted to kiss was Patrick. "Okay, Bee," Diane said. "Remember the rules: You have to kiss Andrew. Or you can challenge him to a truth or dare." My head felt mushy. So far no one had chosen the truth or dare option.

"And a dare could be anything," she gently continued. "You could dare him to hug you or run naked through the room." We all laughed, but I felt grateful to Diane, who was clearly reminding me of the rules so I'd have an out if I didn't want to kiss Andrew. Which, of course, I didn't.

"Okay, truth or dare, Andrew," I said while I formulated the question I'd ask when he replied, *Truth.* I'd ask him if he'd ever French-kissed a girl, I decided.

But to my surprise, he replied, "Dare." His face reddened so that his freckles looked like seeds on a strawberry.

"Um," I said, trying to think, and then Diane's words floated through my head: *You could dare him to hug you.* "I, um, dare you to hug me."

"Okay," he said. My legs felt unsteady as I stood up and made my way outside the circle toward him. He turned even more strawberry-ish as he pushed himself up, and as we reached for each other, I could feel Max's eyes on me. It was the most awkward of hugs, even more awkward than I remember feeling prior to mastering my social-hugging skills. I don't even know if you could call it a hug; it was more like a quick squeeze, like the kind you give a ketchup bottle.

Somehow I made it back to my spot in the circle, and as I settled to the ground I felt Diane's hand on my back. "You okay?" she whispered, and I nodded.

Diane was up next, and as she shared a peck with Andrew, I wondered if anyone thought I was lame that I had dared Andrew to only give me a hug. A peck wasn't a big deal, I convinced myself. Next time I would just kiss the person the bottle pointed to.

On Andrew's turn, the bottleneck stopped at Max, and we all laughed. The Coke I'd drunk felt heavy in my bladder. When would it be an appropriate time to use the bathroom?

"Um, as much as I like you, Max," Andrew said, "I think I'll challenge you to a truth or dare."

"You don't want to kiss Max?" Diane teased.

"Okay," Andrew said, drumming his hands against the floor. "So, truth or dare, then?"

"Truth," Max replied.

Andrew took a long look around the circle. I grew hot as his gaze passed over me. "Who do you like?"

Max uncrossed his legs to stretch them out in front. "No way, dude. Not answering that."

Andrew rolled his eyes. "Fine. Do you like someone in this room, or maybe someone related to someone in this room?" I wondered why Andrew was asking this question. Did he know something I didn't? The Wiley brothers didn't have any sisters, nor did Diane. Courtney had a stepsister who was around my age—she was actually quite pretty, though she primarily lived with her mother, in Etchers. Did Andrew mean her? And there was Audrina, of course. Always Audrina.

Max slowly nodded. "Yeah." I cleared my ears, the way I did when I went swimming. I felt like I hadn't heard him right—he'd said yes. That meant, I realized, he liked either Diane, Courtney, Courtney's stepsister, Audrina, or me. *Or me.*

I excused myself to the bathroom, unable to hold it in much longer. When I rejoined the group, Andrew was up again—this time asking Courtney who she liked. It dawned on me that everyone had rotated through, and I'd missed Max's first turn. At least I'd gotten to skip a turn. Had Max kissed anyone while I was gone?

"Lego?" Diane mouthed at me as I settled down next to her. I knew she was asking if I was okay.

I nodded, grateful for her concern.

"You didn't miss much," she whispered. "Good timing, though." She crinkled her eyes as she gave me a big smile, and I wasn't sure why, until I realized Max was now up. Did she know I liked Max? I wondered, as I watched his hands give the bottle a push. The bottle twirled fast and then started to slow, and I kept my eyes on it, hard, willing it to stop in front of me.

Magically, it did, the little red star on the bottle front directed at my midline. My eyes traveled across the upside down Heineken letters, but reading left to right, so going from the lowercase *n* to the uppercase *H*. I felt my face get hot as I finally looked up to meet Max's eyes. Instead of rising to move toward me for a kiss, though, he just stared at me and said, "Truth or dare."

"Truth or dare?" I repeated, feeling a little confused.

"Truth or dare," he confirmed. His eyes filled mine as if there were no one else in the room.

I swallowed. "Dare," I answered, surprising myself. The others seemed surprised as well. Courtney made a clucking noise, and Patrick let out a whistle.

"I dare you to go into the closet with me for one minute."

I wasn't sure if I'd heard him correctly. Somehow, the words finally made sense: Go into the closet with Max. For one minute. I got up from the circle to follow Max into the closet the Wileys used for their surplus of coats, near the bottom of the basement stairs. Diane smiled again at me but this time didn't mouth *Lego*, as if she already knew I'd *want* to go into the closet with him. Max's arm brushed against mine as we entered the dark space. We had to squeeze in, moving aside a few long coats that hung from the rack on metal hangers that I knew were metal from the way they scraped when we pushed them aside. We made a clearing in the coats, a cocoon-like space on the inside. My mouth felt dry, and I wished I had some water to drink. There was a mustiness in the air, like the way my unfinished basement smelled.

I heard Max breathing as we faced each other. His features gradually became more recognizable in the dark as his right hand found my left. It sent tingles through me and made my mouth feel even drier. I was aware that a coat behind me had inched forward on the rack and now covered my shoulders like a cape.

"Do you think sh-she's okay, Max?" It was something I suddenly needed to ask, and he didn't question who I meant.

"I hope so," he answered without hesitation, and before I knew it, his lips touched mine, and his tongue was in my mouth, probing, as if looking for something. I pushed my tongue back against his, and my head traveled to a place it'd never been.

The next day, while sunning myself in the yard, I tried to relive the moment I'd had with Max. The sun was fierce. Instead of moving to the shade of the oak tree, I cast a shirt over my face, creating a small pocket through which to breathe. The muted sounds of the neighborhood filtered through my cotton barrier: the rumble of distant car engines, the growl of a lawn mower, the air—a gentle whisper that entered and exited my nostrils with each breath.

Drifting back in time, I recalled each moment, each sensation. I hadn't known I could feel that full, that something like a kiss could pad my body in all the right places.

I wanted to confide in someone about what had happened with Max, and I wished I had a friend the way Diane and Courtney had each other. As friendly as they had both been to me lately, they were still older than I was, and I knew they had their own Canter Prep school friends. Private school seemed to me like a foreign country, an intimidating place with its own code: special uniforms, acronyms, random vacation weeks, even sports—I'd heard Diane and Courtney talk about whether they should take golf or field hockey. I hadn't known that kids could play golf.

Leah would be returning home soon, but I wasn't sure that I could talk to her about this—at least not yet. She didn't have any experience with boys, so she wouldn't be able to relate. I also wanted to wait to tell her until Max asked me out, and we became officially boyfriend and girlfriend. I was a little embarrassed about how I'd kissed him without first being in a relationship. It would clearly happen soon, I reassured myself. But would Leah be hurt when she realized I'd waited to tell her? She'd once asked me who my best friend was, and I automatically replied, "Audrina."

"Oh," she'd said, looking down at her stonewashed jeans—the ones she'd bought after I got a pair—and then I realized she'd asked because she was hoping I would say her. That would be crazy, though. Audrina was my *sister.* Sure, Leah and I were close, but she wasn't family. Since she was an only child, she didn't know what it was like to have a sister, to be a sister. Mother and Father had impressed upon Audrina and me early how important it was to be loyal to family. "You only have one another," Mother often said, while Father would simply say, "Family is everything."

But now, with the Max news on my mind, I wondered if this was actually true. I was proud of how Audrina and I had mended the cracks in our relationship over the past couple of months. We'd proven our mutual loyalty to each other: I'd sacrificed most of my summer to help her with her diabetes, and Audrina had chosen me—not her friends—to rely on when she came home from the hospital. My sister hadn't meant what she said at Stilkes Farm—she'd said as much in her diary—yet despite all this, I found myself now reluctant to tell her about Max. There was a half-written letter to her, sitting on my desk, which I couldn't bring myself to finish. Why? Was it because I hadn't told her about my crush to begin with? Maybe it was because I desired something of my own: something not linked, like all things in my life, to my sister.

I wondered what Audrina would answer if someone asked who her best friend was; perhaps someone was asking her right then, at that moment, at camp. She'd always had so many friends, so many girls who vied for her attention. I hoped she would say it was me.

Keeping my eyes closed, I reached alongside my chair into my bag and felt for a piece of Trident gum. The gum was soft from the heat, and I slid it into my mouth. I popped bubbles and decided not to think about Audrina for the time being. I had other things to focus on—to savor. After the kiss, while we were still in the dark, Max had smiled at me. A smile you give someone you like. He'd said he liked someone in the room, or someone's sister. Now I knew it was me.

Sometimes I wish, now that it's all over, that I could have just stayed in that lawn chair, the day after my first kiss. The day when I was a subject of the sun, when the heat formed sweat beads between my breasts like condensation on a glass. It was the day that melted the forgotten fuchsia-colored lipstick in my bag, the day of daydreams, when I swam in near-perfect possibilities—free, for a brief moment, of my sister's shadow.

# Chapter Fifteen

At the end of August, before the start of third grade, Peter Scoffer and Jonathan Smalls decided to go back to the silver maple tree, to see if the bone was still there. Each boy had wondered, over the last few weeks, if they had perhaps been mistaken about what they'd found. Maybe, they thought, it had been a stick. Maybe their eyes had been playing tricks on them. After combing the edge of the farm, they finally located the tree. They approached it in unison, neither wanting to pull ahead of the other one.

Jonathan spotted the bone first; he sprinted away, abandoning Peter, who instantly froze and squeezed his eyes shut. After a few moments, Peter tried to crack open just one eye, but he could never wink, not like his older brother, Sean. So he blinked open both his eyes, and a chill traveled through him that made the hair on his arms prickle. There, jutting out from the tree in front, was the bone, like a witch's arm reaching for him.

He scrambled to catch up with Jonathan, and they once again did their clandestine handshake, to cement the secret. But Peter was beginning to wonder if they were doing the right thing, now that they were certain it was a bone. He considered confessing to his brother. Can secrets still be secret when you tell one more person?

Audrina returned home from diabetes camp on the Friday of Labor Day weekend, rattling off girls' names I'd never heard of. "Misty's had diabetes ever since she could remember," she told Mother as they unpacked the clothes from her suitcase. "Like since she was a baby. Can you imagine? She's been going to that camp for years. Priscilla's like me—a newbie. So it was her first time there, too."

I sat on my bed and fingered my hair while I wondered what had happened to my sister over the last two weeks. She was Audrina like she used to be, prediabetes. She was tan and thinner. But she was also different—separate from me, somehow. Perhaps it was her new experiences, new friends.

"Kate gave me this," Audrina announced as she fished out a brown beaded necklace from her namesake tote. "She was one of my bunkmates—remember I told you about her? Anyway, I told her I liked her necklace, and then she gave it to me. Moth—Mom, can you believe that?"

I noticed she kept calling our mother Mom, or trying to. Had someone shamed her, the way Hope had done to me?

"That was nice of her," Mother said, smiling with her whole face. She didn't seem to mind the change in her name. She pulled out the laundry basket from our closet to toss Audrina's dirty clothes in it. "So I take it you liked camp?"

Audrina laughed loudly in affirmation as she glanced at me.

"We're going to have a reunion this winter, Mom. The girls do it every year. They meet up in New York City for lunch. Can we go?"

My finger wrapped around a single hair; I attempted an inconspicuous, quick pluck, the first in weeks. As the urge to continue grew stronger, I hopped up from the bed, trying to dampen that desire. Audrina and Mother paused their unpacking to look at me, but then continued talking as if I didn't exist.

"Yes, we can go. What a lovely idea. I'm so glad you met some nice girls," Mother replied. "Do they all live in the area? New York or New Jersey? Or is that just the central meeting point?"

"Most of them live in New York. Kate lives right in New York City, can you imagine? She lives in a building with a doorman, all the way up on the twelfth floor."

I sank back down on the bed, defeated. The first thing Audrina had done when she got home was show us how she could prick her own finger to check her blood sugars, using just the lancet itself, instead of the guillotine—followed by a demonstration of how she could give her own insulin injections. "I know how to do it all now," she'd said to me, matter-of-factly. Dismissively, even. "Misty showed me and Priscilla. She even let us practice on her." Something had shifted; it was like old Audrina magnified, like at least three times.

Even though I hadn't missed attending to her diabetes when she was away, I'd naturally assumed I would return to a helping role— and I wanted to. I wanted us to be how we were before. It made me feel empty—and hurt—to not be needed. In a matter of just two weeks, my sister had somehow once again slipped out of my grasp. As if all the time I'd previously spent helping her was now erased.

But I was different, too, I thought. I'd had unique experiences that didn't have anything to do with my sister. I'd gone to Deer Chase Lake on the day it reopened. I'd kissed a boy. And not just any boy, but Max. I'd French-kissed him. His tongue had been in my mouth, and my tongue in his. My sister didn't know about those experiences; she didn't get to know about them—they belonged to me.

I recalled the way Audrina's skin had turned pink earlier that summer when discussing whether we should ask Max to come to the pool with us. It still bothered me, even though I knew from reading her diary that she liked Brian Roslin. At any rate, *she* hadn't been around to ask Max, and *she* was not the one who had kissed him.

Audrina turned her tote upside down, and a stack of letters fell out. "Thanks for all the letters, Mom," she said. "Barbara—you know, my camp counselor—asked me if I had a fan club or something." She grinned as she picked up one of them. Then shot me a look that I couldn't read. My eyes traveled to our desk, where I'd stuffed my half-written letter to Audrina—my one and only attempt—under the desk blotter.

"Thanks for the letters, too, sissy." She enunciated each word fully, her voice teeming with sarcasm.

"Whatever. You could have written *me*," I replied, in an automatic defense, but then I realized it was true: She also hadn't written to me, and she could have. Why would she expect me to write her when she hadn't done the same? *Because she's Audrina*, I reminded myself.

My sister ignored me and turned to Mother. "Me and the girls are going to write letters to each other now."

"The girls and I," Mother corrected, while I considered what would have happened had I told her about Max. She probably wouldn't have believed me. Or she might've decided to say something to him, the next time she saw him, against my wishes.

Sometimes it seemed like that kiss hadn't even happened. Since the night at the Wileys' house, now nearly two weeks earlier, I'd hardly seen Max. Only once had I spotted him, from our front window, as he played basketball on his driveway. But by the time I'd walked my bike out of the garage, he'd gone back inside his house. It made me wonder if he was avoiding me, and so I'd asked Father later that night if he'd seen Max around. "Borka," he'd replied, "I'm working in the basement. Max doesn't come down there."

So much for the benefit of my father working there, I'd thought. He'd been putting in more and more time at their house, too, sometimes even going early in the morning before work. At least I hadn't seen or heard any more cause for concern about my parents' marriage that summer—though we'd all been distracted with Audrina's diabetes.

The first full morning of Audrina's return, the phone rang constantly, between her new friend Kate and her old school friends. I had to periodically lock myself in the bathroom just to escape the sound of my sister chattering away in our room. Even Father got annoyed.

"Hello?" Father barked into the kitchen phone, when yet another call had interrupted his coffee-and-newspaper weekend ritual. Audrina flew into the room to try to grab the phone out of Father's hand. He held it up high, out of her reach. I paused eating, cereal spoon in my mouth, to watch.

"You want to speak to Audrina?" he said. "Who is this? Kate? Kate, again? Kate, do you how many times this morn—"

"Thanks, Fath—Dad," Audrina cut in.

"Jeez, Audrina," Father snapped. "What do you even have to talk about?"

I was surprised by his tone, but Audrina just brushed it off.

"Diabetes, *Dad*," she answered, as she switched to the cordless phone she was carrying in her other hand and then went upstairs.

Father stared after her. I wasn't sure what was going on with him; he'd been acting short lately—even with Audrina, with whom he usually was never displeased. "Father?"

"Yes?"

"Are you okay?"

Father gave me a quizzical look. "Why do you ask?"

I shrugged. "I dunno. You seem . . . I don't know."

"I'm fine, Borka. Everything's okay. I guess, I'm just tired, maybe." Father rubbed his eyes, and I thought about how hard he'd been working. He'd been at the Bakers' late the night before, and since his store was closed for the holiday weekend, he'd likely be heading back there soon.

"How's the Bakers' basement going?"

"Good."

"Are you almost done?"

Father laughed. "No, but I've been able to make progress lately, with the house pretty much empty."

"Max isn't there?"

"No, he's in Chicago."

"Chicago? Really?" That would explain why I hadn't seen him around. I frowned; Ludlow would be starting soon. What was he doing in Chicago? And who had he gone with? Mrs. Baker's station wagon remained parked in front of their house.

"His father had a medical conference last week," my father said, as if reading my thoughts. "So Max went with him. They'll be back in a couple days, on Monday."

"Oh, okay." I sighed, disappointed, and Father must have heard it in my voice because he said, "Borka, you should think about getting some more friends, like your sister has."

"I have friends," I replied indignantly, my face growing hot. Did my own father think I was a loser? "We just don't talk on the phone," I grumbled.

The rest of the day dragged; I felt like I was just waiting. Waiting for Labor Day weekend to pass, for Max to return home, for school to begin. For my sister and me to get over this new tiff we were now somehow embroiled in. For that warm, sticky end-of-summer feeling in the air to disperse so that the cool fall breeze could arrive, with its reason and rules.

*Max likes me*, I told myself over and over. I simply needed to get through two more nights, and then he would be back. Maybe he'd been feeling just as awkward about the whole thing as I had. Maybe he'd been waiting for me to make the next move.

As soon as Max got home, I decided, I would go over and ring his doorbell. I didn't need Father working there as an excuse. We would hug hello, and he would know that I liked him, because I'd come over. And because of the way our bodies felt when they touched. And then he would ask me out. He had to.

I pictured myself with a smug smile, strolling past all the Hope Rodales standing at our beige-colored lockers; I would have a private school boyfriend. Even Hope herself had never had one. It was the best scenario: I could concentrate at school and not have to worry about the way I looked. And then we would see each other on the weekends. He could come to the winter dance with me; I'd heard some kids did that—invite private school friends.

I didn't need more friends, like Father had suggested. I only needed Max.

After dinner, as Mother made her weekly grocery store run, Audrina retired to our room, cordless phone in tow, so I retreated to the bathroom. There was a generous nook by the bathroom window, where Mother had placed a basket with towels. I shifted the basket forward and moved the fuzzy floor mat from the bathtub to line the floor against the window. I ran the bathtub, as if I were taking a bath, but instead just sat in the nook, my back against the wall, with one of the towels covering me like a blanket.

I peered out the window at Max's house, willing him to magically appear, even though I knew that was impossible. It was half past seven, so the sun was well into its retreat, darkness fast replacing the reddish sky. I saw a figure walking across the street: Father, en route to the Bakers'. From my angle above, I couldn't see the entire front door of their house, only the bottom half, even with the porch alight. The odd view allowed me to later question what I saw: Mrs. Baker flinging open the door as Father approached. She pulled him tightly against her, her hand grasping his behind, before they vanished inside.

I quickly ducked beneath the windowsill and hid under the towel, as if I'd been the one who had just gotten caught.

Once, when I was younger, I found a Hungarian book in Father's study. It was tucked into the shelf above the volumes of *Encyclopaedia Britannica*.

The book was slim, about a quarter the size of the Robert Ludlum and Tom Clancy novels it was wedged between—it was so slight, in fact, that it had probably been there for years, and I never noticed.

The title, *Magyar Közmondások*, was written in block letters against a gray faded cover that reminded me of old, worn carpeting, the kind you might find in an elderly relative's apartment. I knew *Magyar* meant Hungary, and I surmised it must be a book of poems or quotes, since each right-sided spread of the yellowed pages contained a few sparse sentences accompanied by an illustration.

The one that caught my eye depicted a giant, white-petaled trumpet flower with bright yellow pollen. The flower leaned from a vase; a dark, disproportionately large and shadowy blob extended from its base across the middle binding and onto the left page. It was the only illustration in the entire book that ran onto the other side.

"*A fehér liliomnak is lehet fekete az árnyéka,*" the words above the illustration read.

Once I saw that image, I couldn't get the shadowy blob out of my mind. For a few weeks afterward, I saw it everywhere: along the corner of our bedroom wall, after Audrina turned off the lights, in the maple syrup that pooled on my plate of pancakes, on my ink-stained third-grade art class smock.

The next time I spotted Father sitting at his study desk, I fished the book off the shelf and presented it to him. "What does this mean?" I asked, jabbing at the foreign words above the flowers.

"Where did you get that?" he replied, frowning at the book. He took it from me and closed the cover so he could read the title. "Hungarian Proverbs," he said. "I haven't seen this in years."

"It was over there. On your bookshelf."

Father opened the book to the page I'd first shown him and rested it on his desk. He tapped the eraser end of his pencil against the book a few times before answering. "'*A fehér liliomnak is lehet fekete az árnyéka.*' It means: 'Even a white lily can cast a black shadow.'"

"'Even a white lily can cast a black shadow,'" I repeated. "That's funny."

"It means even something beautiful can be ugly."

Over the years, I repeated the foreign saying to myself so often that it stayed with me. I still think about what it means, about beauty having two sides. Or maybe it's just one side: the facade you show the world, and what's really lying beneath.

The moment between Father and Mrs. Baker happened much too quickly for me to be confident about it, I at first told myself. Afterward, I remained at the bathroom window—long after Father emerged again on the Bakers' front porch to return home. I studied my view of the Bakers' door. I rose up and bent forward; I leaned to the side and sat back down. The image before me didn't change: I could still clearly see a portion of the door, the part that someone's lower half would occupy. So try as I might, I couldn't reason away what I'd seen—the realization anchoring heavily within me.

I thought of Mrs. Baker's chain-smoking, how she lit one cigarette with the next. The way she consumed Lay's potato chips like the mindless popcorn you inhale in a movie theater. *I heard she's into things like that,* the Wiley brothers once said. *She was caught stealing drugs.* It all added up, these blocks of bad behavior.

How stupid I'd been, admiring Father for touching her, comforting her, those months earlier.

And then I thought of the white-gold heart pendant necklace—and even the diamond silver hoops I'd found years earlier. Had the necklace, perhaps, been for Mrs. Baker? I tried to remember when Mrs. Baker's birthday was; it had come up on the way to school a few months ago. It might have been around that same time, I now realized.

How could Father? How could he? It made me physically ill. My stomach was tightly braided in emotion: one strand anger, one strand disbelief, one strand sadness and disenchantment. I couldn't believe he would betray Mother, betray our family. Did Mother know? Did she suspect? And now a familiar feeling: guilt. Maybe *I* was the reason why this whole thing between Father and Mrs. Baker had started. They wouldn't have interacted to begin with if I hadn't taken the bracelet. They would have just been friendly at-a-distance neighbors, like Father was with other neighborhood mothers. Maybe a little more than that, I conceded, because Father had been involved with the search efforts. But I'd asked Father to follow up with her about Max. Maybe this was all my fault.

The following day, I closely watched Father: He acted exactly as he would on any given Sunday. He prepared a large Western omelet and then left it covered with Saran Wrap on the kitchen counter, so we could help ourselves. He carried his newspaper and coffee mug into the family room, where he sprawled across the couch and turned on the recording of his favorite weekly show, *Soccer Made in Germany*. In the afternoon he drove to Channel Lumber to poke around the hardware and tool department and in the evening complained about Mother's cordon bleu.

"It's a little too salty," he said, as he took another generous bite.

"Sorry, dear," Mother replied in a conciliatory tone, and Father nodded, as if he had been expecting the apology.

I glanced over at Audrina to gauge her reaction, but she was too busy pushing around the pieces of the plain baked chicken Mother had made her. She shoved a few pieces to the right, and then a couple to the left, and then mixed some with the steamed broccoli.

It wasn't unusual for Father to criticize Mother's cooking, and while it had occasionally irritated me, it had never made me feel so angry as it did at that very moment. *Who is he*, I thought, *to talk to Mother this way?* Beautiful Mother, with her large brown eyes and high cheekbones that made girls like Leah remark she was the prettiest mother. Father, on the other hand, had ears that stuck out too much, and he chewed too loudly with his mouth open.

Father, who gave Mrs. Baker *that hug*, and whatever else had occurred afterward. How many others had there been? And why Mrs. Baker? How could he like *her* over Mother?

"Good girl," Father now said, as he surveyed Audrina's plate, which contained a deceptively cleared area. He popped the toothpick Mother had aligned next to his plate into his mouth, and I had an urge to yank it out and scratch his face.

Explain away as I might, I still knew what I had seen, the image that was now inked like a tattoo onto my consciousness: Mrs. Baker's arms greedily wrapping around Father, engulfing him as if he were a piece of ham-stuffed chicken.

# Chapter Sixteen

MOTHER ALWAYS TOOK PICTURES OF AUDRINA AND ME STANDING on our front steps on the first day of school, and years later, when I looked at pictures from the morning I officially became an eighth grader, I saw Audrina, beautiful Audrina, smiling in a knee-length, red flowered dress that would later elicit a whistle from a ninth grader hanging out in the school parking lot. Next to her was a chubbier, almost unrecognizable version of myself—two big wooden-log thighs protruding from under ill-fitting shorts, my lips pushed firmly together as if I had taken a vow of silence, eyes looking somewhere beyond our mother. My heart—if you could have looked inside to see it, past the breasts I suddenly hated, that now felt heavy and cumbersome—had a dead spot. A small area where it was necrotic, diseased by adult knowledge, by things it was not yet ready to learn.

❧

As soon as Audrina and I stepped onto school grounds—the first time in a year that we were back together as students on the same campus—she became surrounded by a bevy of girls. I wasn't surprised. They wanted to know all about her diabetes, her hospitalization, her camp, the shots she had to give herself. She wore her diabetes like an accessory, I thought, as she waltzed across the schoolyard, waving around her swollen finger beds as if showing off a new manicure, her metal medical bracelet slipping up and down in an ostentatious manner. With each additional comment and smile thrown her way, I felt worse and worse. Popularity is such a funny thing, I thought. You want it until you have it—at which point it feels imperfect—and then, when you lose it, it feels worse than if you'd never had it at all.

Faithful Leah, her ponytail shiny with hair spray, came to stand next to me, knowing better than to ask how I felt about Audrina being at our school. Instead, she talked about California, filling my silence with details about the road trip she and her father took up the coast—things she hadn't yet revealed to me on the phone: Hearst Castle, Big Sur, the Golden Gate Bridge, Alcatraz. She even gifted me a pair of pink hoop earrings that she'd brought back as a souvenir.

It was impressive, all the stuff she'd seen and done. Perhaps, I thought, there was at least one perk of divorce: two different residences, each with its own affiliated attractions. Although in my situation, I supposed, Father and Mother would stay in the same town, or at least in New Jersey.

"Maybe next time I go to California, you can come with me," Leah suggested shyly.

I wondered if at some point I could reveal to her all I was feeling inside: the complicated dynamics with my sister, the kiss with Max, my hair-pulling, the situation between my father and Mrs. Baker. Would she understand it, though? Would anyone?

I decided I couldn't say anything to Mother or Audrina about what I had seen transpire between Father and Mrs. Baker; I didn't want them to be hurt like I was. It would have destroyed Audrina; she had always idolized Father. And it seemed possible that Mother might not have wanted to know, based on the way she had acted about the white-gold heart necklace. Or maybe I was just telling myself that, but the simple fact was, I didn't want my parents to get divorced. I didn't want our family to break up.

*Casey Mitchell.* I kept coming back to that name, the person whom Mother and Father had argued about months earlier. Who was he? I needed to know; he felt like a missing piece of Father's new life of which I was now aware. I opened Mother's personal address book and scrolled through until I found him. Then, fingers shaking, I dialed his number; I didn't know what I was planning to say.

"Hello?" a woman's voice answered, which caught me off guard. Mother always listed both the husband and wife's name in her address book, so I'd just assumed Casey was single. "Hello?" the woman repeated.

"Uh, is Casey there?" I managed to reply.

"Speaking. Who's this?"

"Casey? Casey Mitchell?"

"Yes. Who is this?"

I promptly hung up, crestfallen. Casey Mitchell was a woman, which meant she could have been another one of Father's transgressions. I wished I hadn't called.

Knowing Father was still going to work at the Bakers', I couldn't help but be obsessive, even though Max and Dr. Baker were now around. As often as I could, I kept a corresponding watch from the perch in my bathroom window when he headed over. If I continued to keep a lookout, then perhaps I could prevent things from happening between them again.

There was nothing else I could do, was there?

I was also desperate to see Max, who'd been at Ludlow for a week and a half already. I couldn't believe we hadn't talked since our kiss; he did wave from his driveway when I'd passed in the car coming home from school a few days earlier, but then he disappeared inside his house. I doubted Max had any idea about our parents.

A few hours into "my watch" on a Saturday, I glanced up from reading *To Kill a Mockingbird,* which Mrs. Hatcher, the town librarian, had recommended when she noticed me checking out another Sweet Valley High book. There was movement on my periphery: The Wiley brothers strolled up to the Bakers' front door, soccer ball in hand. Max soon emerged, wearing his yellow-and-black-striped shirt—the one I'd thought of in seventh grade as his bumblebee shirt. They began passing the ball back and forth in the front yard.

After smoothing my hair in the mirror, I scrambled downstairs. It wasn't ideal that the Wiley brothers were around, or that they were all in the vicinity of Max's front door, where the *incident* had occurred—but I didn't want to let the opportunity slip. Finally we would see each other. Finally we would talk.

My shorts stuck to my sweaty legs as I exited the garage and hurried across the street. I walked fast but also tried to casually widen my walking stance to air out my legs.

"Hey, Bee," Max sang out. He paused with the ball at his feet, flanked on either side by the two brothers.

"Hi, Bee!" Andrew and Patrick chimed in.

"Um, hi, Max. Hi, guys." The sound of my heart amplified in my ears as the steps between us shortened. The moment was here; they were mere feet away from where I stood on the sidewalk. Max was so close I could have reached out and touched the yellow stripe on his arm.

"How you doing?" Max asked.

"Good." I opened and closed my mouth. Would he be the one to say the next thing? Or should I? A couple of possible words formed on my tongue, but then Patrick began dribbling the ball, toward the other side of the lawn, and Max and Andrew followed. Andrew's laughter cut through the air, and Patrick said something I couldn't make out, and then all three laughed. Not at me, I knew. They were no longer paying attention to me.

I kept on walking up the street, as if that had been my intention all along, and the space between Max and me now grew larger. He clearly didn't like me. I went past the Garfields' and then the Johnsons', whose *Happy Labor Day* banner still hung from their porch. Each step I took further pounded in my embarrassment. I passed the Wileys', and then Diane's and Courtney's houses, wondering if the two girls had later discussed my kiss among themselves. Turning onto Oak Street, I strode past Officer Jimmy's house. His mother's dementia had gotten worse, Mother said, so she'd moved into a nursing home over the summer.

How does a moment affect one person but not another? The moment of slipping Sally's bracelet into the inside lining of my bathing suit (while initially easy) had created coarse reverberations; the embrace Father had shared with Mrs. Baker would gut me for years. And while my kiss with Max had irrevocably changed me, thrusting me into a teenage awareness of my body, it seemed like it hadn't made a bit of difference to him.

When I reached the turnoff for Maple, I remembered how I'd wanted to check out the playhouse Father built for one of the families on the street. Suddenly I realized it was very important for me to locate this structure, to know that it hadn't been a lie on Father's part. About halfway down the block, I spotted it, to my relief.

I exited Maple back onto Oak and continued along, beyond the Abbotts', whose house remained on the market. I cut through the Greens' backyard, past the grill we often smelled from our back porch, and alongside the pond so that I could return to my house from the rear. The boys, whose voices in the distance grew louder as I approached, couldn't see me from this angle.

Why had Max dared me to go into the closet if he didn't like me? He hadn't dared anyone else. In fact, no one else was dared to go into a closet; no one else had French-kissed. So why had Max done that with me?

Suddenly I felt dirty and used, and I half ran, half walked to the far side of my house against the woods, where no one could see me, not even from inside my house, and I let my cries freely flow. Maybe Diane and Courtney hadn't been dared to go into the closet because they wouldn't have gone. Maybe I was the only dirty-filthy-disgusting girl who would have done it, who would have let a boy put his tongue in her mouth, and then would have put her tongue in his. Dirty-filthy me. Dirty-filthy-disgusting me. And then a thought occurred to me, one that made me kneel to the ground. What if I had been a bad kisser, and that was the reason why Max didn't like me anymore?

I wished the kiss had never happened; I wished I had never gone into the closet, never even gone to the Wileys' that night. I wished the Bakers had never come to Hammend.

As the fall weeks passed, it appeared that Audrina had fully adjusted to her new reality—even flourished. The attention paid to her swelled; the girls at school who marched behind her like a pack of ants once even waited outside the hall bathroom while she used it. My sister auditioned and won a small part in our school production of *Annie*—unheard of for a seventh grader—and she was always on the go, as much as our parents allowed: to play practice, doctor appointments, hangouts at friends' houses, weekend movies. Mother seemed determined to provide Audrina a "normal" experience, nearly always acquiescing when my sister asked to do something social. But perhaps unbeknownst to Audrina, Mother would call the friends' houses in advance, reviewing with the other mothers the signs of hypoglycemia of which they should be aware and my sister's dietary limitations. Once I even saw Mother create small "diabetes baskets," replete with a jar of sugar cubes and typed instructions, that she then loaded into her car—presumably to drop off at the friends' houses.

With Audrina often gone, I was usually the only one who Mother needed to pick up at the end of the school day. Sliding into the car, my backpack heavy with books, I'd be cognizant how my grades constituted my one "talent." My reality was this: I was no longer popular and didn't think I would be again. I wasn't Audrina. Max didn't like me, and my father was a cheater—a secret I had to hold inside.

"I'm so glad Audrina has accepted her diabetes," I overheard Mother say to Mrs. Wiley on the phone one morning. "And she's really doing so well with it. Her doctor's happy with her progress."

But I wasn't the only one with a secret. One night, I walked in on my sister holding a chem strip under the faucet sink in our bathroom. The faucet was nearly turned off; a few drips periodically squeezed out.

"What are you doing?" I asked, and she jumped. Her diabetes logbook lay open on the counter, its sheet scattered with eraser crumbs. Next to it was a pencil with a nubby top and a number of used chem strips, some of which had been cut in half lengthwise.

"God, Bee! Quit creeping around."

"Audrina," I said, concern trickling into me. Something didn't seem right.

My sister looked at me with a serious expression, barely moving a muscle in her face, until I frowned and looked away. Then she sighed and admitted, "I'm experimenting. Seeing how I can water down my blood or use old chem strips and get a lower number, okay?"

"Get a lower number?" I repeated.

"Yeah, you know, so it looks like my blood sugars aren't so high, if Mother checks."

"Oh," I replied. "But isn't that—"

"Isn't that what?" Audrina put her hands on her hips.

"I mean, you have to be honest, Drina."

"Oh, really? Why?" She waved her arm as she took a step closer, and I noticed how Audrina's finger beds were dotted red like little freckles. "Why do I have to be honest?"

I didn't reply; I just bit my lip and stared over her shoulder at the blue flower wallpaper pattern, suddenly wanting to tug my hair.

"Look, don't tell Mother and Father, okay? I don't—won't—do this all the time. Just once in a while." When I didn't say anything, she pleaded, her voice soft, "Promise, sissy?"

"Okay," I choked as the blue flowers blurred together.

"I mean, could you imagine if you were told you could never eat sweets again, except for one piece of cake on your birthday each year? It's so unfair."

"No," I said. I couldn't imagine it, but it didn't make what Audrina was doing right. "Is that why you do this? So you can eat sweets sometimes?"

Audrina didn't answer but instead said, "Look, if Mother and Father are happy, and the doctor's happy, then I'm happy, okay?"

"Okay," I said again, unable to hold my tears in.

"Why are you crying?"

"I don't know," I admitted as my sister pulled me in for a hug. It felt like the hug she'd given me when she saw me at the hospital. A real hug—it was nice. But was it a real hug? Or was she just trying to ensure I'd keep her confidence?

She pulled back and looked at me. "Stop crying. Your pretty brown eyes are going to get all red. Tomorrow morning I'll show you how I do my makeup, okay? Mascara, eye shadow, eyeliner? We can do it together before school."

"You think I have pretty brown eyes?" I was surprised.

"Of course."

"Does Mother know about all the makeup you're wearing?" I asked, suddenly suspicious. I'd only seen her wear Mother's blue eye shadow, and nail polish, but nothing else.

"No. And you'd better not tell her, either."

"Okay." I wondered when she put it on, since each morning before school and each evening I hadn't noticed her wearing any. "But when do you—"

"I put it on in the bathroom at school, and then wipe it off by the end of the day."

"Oh." That made sense.

"Here, why don't I show you now, so you can see if you like it." Audrina rummaged through her bathroom drawer and retrieved a handful of makeup items. "Close your eyes," she instructed, and I obeyed. I wanted to believe she wasn't doing this just to distract me. The brush swept across my eyelid in small strokes; it was a strange, tickling sensation. "Sometimes I don't—" she started to say, her voice trembling, and then she halted. I tried to keep my face expressionless, my eyes closed. Like Mother, Audrina never cried. The only time I could ever remember her shedding tears was when she'd fallen off the bike and broken her pinky. She still couldn't completely straighten it.

Audrina gave a little cough and then started again. "Sometimes I don't take my insulin. Not like I'm supposed to."

"You don't take your insulin?" I concentrated hard on the back of my eyelids, trying to see a bit of color, any color. But all that was there was a film of brown mud.

"I just don't want to take it all the time. It's hard, okay? It's just hard. Sometimes I just don't want to think about it every day. Every single freaking day."

I was about to chastise her, but then I stopped. I didn't want to ruin this close moment between us, make her regret trusting me. It felt dangerous, though, what she was doing. "Please, Drina," I finally managed. "Be careful."

My sister ignored me, now brushing something cool against my lips with her finger. Then she streaked some onto my cheeks and rubbed it in. I blinked open. With Audrina so close, I noticed how her eyelashes covered her entire lid, all the way down to the almond tips, like they were leaves of a flower.

"Why are you telling me all this? And why—why are you helping me?" I asked.

She squinted as she applied a brow pencil to my eyebrows. She didn't look at me as she replied, "You're my sister."

Later I would pinpoint this as the exact moment in time I would want to revisit: when my sister stood so close that I could feel her quiet vulnerability; when her thin, cool fingers pressed against my face, and I could easily reach up to touch them. I would stand there, not questioning her motives, even if I knew they were at least a little crooked. Instead, I would just bask in that glorious Audrina-adoration, the sensation all those girls waiting outside the hallway bathroom door craved. I would breathe it in and feel lucky. I would tell her how much: how much she meant to me, how much I loved being her sister. How amazing it was, even when it wasn't.

"Nice," my sister said, smiling, as she stepped back to assess me. "Hang on." She left to return a moment later, her Polaroid camera in hand. "This way you can copy what I did. Cheese," she instructed. Then she clicked before I could respond.

The makeup did look nice, I had to admit, as I shifted my gaze to the mirror. My cheeks were tinted pink, like I'd just been running, and my eyes much more distinct. My lips were glossed like the girls on magazine covers. I looked . . . dare I say pretty? I started to smile, and even that looked different: almost coy, with my shiny lips turned up at the edges; my cheekbones two small apples, defined in a way they had never been before.

Audrina stopped waving the picture in the air, its image now developed. She brought it close to her face, remarking, "You're actually really photogenic, you know. I'm not photogenic like you." It was true that Mother always said I took a good picture, even if I didn't necessarily agree with it, but before I could say thank you, my sister added, "You know, you look even better in photos than you do in real life. It's so annoying."

I rolled my eyes; it was so like my sister to make some sort of cutting remark without realizing it. I was going to point out her insensitivity, but then I noticed, within the makeup pile, the gold cursive writing on the lip gloss container: *Mary Kay*.

"Where did you get this?" I demanded.

"The lip gloss? Mrs. Baker."

"She gave it to you?"

"Yeah. Why?"

The memory of Father and Mrs. Baker closed in on me in a suffocating fashion, and I took a deep breath. "When did she give it to you?"

"I dunno. A couple weeks ago?"

"When did you see her?"

"She gave me a ride home, after the movies."

"You went to the movies with Max?"

"No, I went with Lindsay and Vanessa . . . and Brian"—she paused here for a moment before continuing—"but Hope and Gwen were there, and Max and Jay, too. A bunch of people. And his mom offered me a ride. She had all these boxes in her car, and one fell over, and everything spilled out. There were a bunch of these," Audrina said, aiming her finger at the lip gloss, "and she said I could keep one."

I looked at myself in the mirror; all I could see was lip gloss. I wanted it off. Immediately. "I need a tissue."

"Why?"

"I just need a tissue."

"Why? You don't like what I did? I think you look pretty."

"There's too much—" I used the back of my hand to begin rubbing off the lip gloss. "There's just too much. I—I want to take some off."

Audrina put her hand on her hip. "You don't like her, do you?"

I stopped rubbing. "What?"

"You don't like Mrs. Baker. I can tell. Why?"

"That's not true. I just want to take off the lip gloss." I spun around and grabbed some sheets of toilet paper. Returning to stand in front of the mirror, I attempted to remove the gloss while my sister watched. Some of the toilet paper stuck to my lips, like little pieces of lint, and suddenly I thought of Mrs. Baker's plump lips, the way she outlined the perimeter—even slightly outside the perimeter—with a darker color and then used a lighter one to fill them in. It was so odd; was that considered attractive? Did Father find that appealing? Mother didn't wear her lipstick like that. I ran the faucet and cupped water in my hand to rinse off the remaining bits of toilet paper. "I never said I didn't like her," I reiterated. "Why do you think that?"

"You don't have to say it. I can just tell. You just get this look on your face whenever anyone mentions her."

"That's ridiculous," I replied, because I felt caught off guard. I hadn't realized my feelings were so transparent; I'd have to be careful. I threw the toilet paper into the trash can and turned to my sister, who was standing there with her large circular hairbrush, the kind she used to curl the ends of her hair. "Thanks for the makeup, Drina. I'm sorry; I guess I'm just not used to wearing—"

"Now your hair," Audrina interrupted, pulling me close.

"No—" I started, but she ignored me, yanking a brush through the side of my hair. "Please—Drina, I don't—"

"Is there a side that is better?"

"Better?" I questioned.

"Better—more hair."

"What do you mean?" I replied, my heart beginning to knock against my chest.

"You know what I mean."

"I . . ." I didn't know what to say.

She grabbed a barrette and held it between her teeth as she continued brushing my hair. "I'm not going to say anything. But you should tell Mother. She's gonna figure it out if you keep doing it."

"How did . . . Is it obvious?" I finally managed to get out. In the mirror, I could see how my entire face was now the color of pink lip gloss.

"No," Audrina replied after a long moment. "You do a . . . good job hiding it. I just saw you pulling it one time."

"You did?" I exhaled, feeling the tiniest bit relieved.

"Yeah, one night, when you were in bed. And I can tell. 'Cause how you look. I don't think others can," she was quick to add. "But when I saw you in the hospital, I could tell it had gotten bad. It's much, much better now."

We were quiet for a moment, and I wondered what she thought of me, and of it. Then I admitted, with a sense of shame, "I don't know why I do it."

"So which side is better?" Audrina probed. "Meaning, which side has more hair? Your right?"

"Yeah," I said, wondering what she was getting at. "Why?"

"'Cause we gotta show it off, then." She snapped the barrette into my hair and then peered all around my scalp, reminding me of the way Mother would inspect us for lice when we were younger and there were school outbreaks. "Good," she said, apparently satisfied, and then added, "Why is your right side better? Because you're a lefty?"

"Yeah," I replied, surprised she'd put that together. It had taken me a while at first to figure that out.

"It's like me," she said.

"Huh?"

Audrina fanned her left hand in front of my face. "My right side is better, too. Because I usually prick my left hand for my blood sugars."

"Oh. I'm sorry, Drina."

"Yeah." We looked at each other in the mirror, and she crinkled her eyes as they traveled over my face. "Much better. You know, my friend Kate—my bunkmate from camp—her cousin pulls her hair."

"Really?" There were other girls who pulled their hair? I'd always wondered—and hoped. To hear it aloud the way Audrina had just casually said it, too, like it was a normal thing, buoyed me. But then, suddenly, an awful thought snaked its way in. "How—how did that come up? Did you talk about me . . . about how I do it?"

We were still, staring at each other in the mirror, and a few seconds passed before my sister shook her head, mumbling, "No."

I didn't believe her. I thought of all the times the phone had rung in the past month and a half, all the times I'd answered and Kate had been on the other end. All along Audrina had known, and talked about me, probably at camp, even. Her whole entire bunk likely knew that Audrina's sister was a weirdo who pulled her hair.

"Anyway, your hair looks much better now." Audrina shrugged. "You should always wear it like this."

Peter Scoffer kept the secret about the bone in the tree for as long as he could, but its existence had started to weigh on him. What if, he wondered, it really was a witch? Or what if they'd accidentally awakened some tree-demon? Even though Peter mocked his third-grade classmates who believed in such things, he was secretly beginning to worry that if he didn't tell someone about the bone soon, harm might come to him and Jonathan—and maybe also to their families. His stomach had begun to hurt a lot—sharp, stabbing pains, occurring often when he thought about the bone—and the memory of the bone grew larger and more menacing by the day.

"It's probably just a piece of wood. A stick," his sixteen-year-old brother, Sean, assured Peter when he finally burst with the news.

Peter closed his eyes as the now-sizable bony image that had haunted him for weeks reappeared. "I don't think so. It looked different than a stick."

"Maybe someone's getting ready for Halloween," Sean laughed, and then his laugher turned into a growling noise. He made a clawing motion with his hands.

"Stop it!" Peter said. "It's not funny!"

Sean dropped his arms and shrugged. "Relax. I was just kidding."

"You don't believe me," Peter said. A tremble appeared in his voice.

Sean sighed. "Look, I believe you. Maybe it's a bone; it's possible. It could be an animal bone. I don't think it's anything to get worked up about."

"Can I show you? Can you come with me to see it?" Peter looked hopefully at his brother.

Sean shrugged again. "Sure." And then, as Peter started smiling, Sean added, "But not right now, okay? I've got some stuff to do."

"When?" Peter pressed.

"Soon, little bro. Okay? I promise."

Peter nodded, but as soon as Sean left the room, Peter crunched over, gripped once more with stomach pain.

# Chapter Seventeen

MOTHER DISCOVERED THAT AUDRINA WAS CHEATING ON HER sugars without me having to say something. She came across Snickers wrappers folded inside a piece of Audrina's stationery when emptying our bedroom trash. Unlike my sister, I didn't like chocolate with nuts.

Even before finding the wrappers, Mother had been growing suspicious of how Audrina was managing her diabetes: She'd had one hypoglycemic episode during the month of October and then two more, shortly after Halloween. Despite opting not to trick-or-treat that year, Audrina apparently still helped herself to my Halloween stash, then likely overcompensated with extra insulin.

When her blood glucose levels dipped, my sister would act goofy, like one of those confused cartoon characters with stars encircling its head. I could usually tell, even before she reached that point. There would be something different in the way she moved or talked; she'd be a bit slower to respond, on a half-second delay, sometimes noticeable only to me. Anytime I confronted her, offering an orange juice, she'd deny her sugars were low and vehemently refuse the drink, as if I were trying to trick her into taking poison. She'd narrow her eyes, swat at me, and spit, "Get away!" Often the episodes would end with Mother or me shoving a sugar cube in her mouth, and when she returned to a normal state, she'd have no recollection of how she had just viewed me as the Evil Queen. The next day my sister would be off to see Dr. Carlogie, even if it wasn't time for her monthly visit. I didn't know what transpired during those appointments, but when she returned home, she'd smile to herself in a smug way, and nothing too dramatic would change with her treatment: another unit of insulin added here, or subtracted there, as if the diabetes were an equation that could be so easily solved.

As fall progressed, I saw Max and the neighborhood kids only every once in a while, when we passed one another in cars, and occasionally on the streets. Everyone, it seemed, was busy with their respective lives. The older we got, the less our history on Hickory Place seemed to hold us together. Audrina focused on her friends and play practice, and my time was split between hangouts with Leah and getting lost in a book—an escape I continued to relish. Mrs. Hatcher now allowed me to check out three books at a time from the town library, and once had even let me take four, when I couldn't decide which ones to pick. "Don't tell anyone," she'd said, with a wink. With her advice, I alternated between classics, like Hemingway and Fitzgerald and Orwell, and young adult fiction, like Norma Klein.

One Saturday evening in early November, while Audrina was sleeping over at a friend's house, I curled up with the novel *1984* and a bag of Doritos. Suddenly loud noises erupted from outside: the sound of broken glass followed by a shrill yell. I ran over to the dining room window, where I saw a patrol car parked on the street in front of the Bakers' house, and then beyond that, on the yard, Mrs. Baker being held back by an officer. She appeared to be screaming at Dr. Baker, who stood on the front porch, Max behind him in the doorway. Max stumbled a few steps toward his mother, but Dr. Baker's arm shot out, stopping him.

I dashed to the front door and bumped into Mother, who had a puzzled look on her face. "What in the world?" she said, cracking the door open.

The sounds hit us full blast, like someone had just cranked up the volume.

"Asshole!" Mrs. Baker screamed. "It's all your fault! It's your fault Sally is gone!"

Dr. Baker was silent, his grim face hard. Max covered his face with his hands.

"Fran," Officer Lark was saying in a firm and authoritative voice as Mrs. Baker kept trying to break free. "Fran, calm down." But all that did was ignite Mrs. Baker.

"I'm not fucking calming down. You tell him to calm down!" she screamed, pointing at Dr. Baker, who was turned, as if he was saying something to Max, and then I saw the back of Max's head as he disappeared inside, the front door swinging shut behind him.

I scanned the house, but I didn't see what had made the breaking-glass noise, and then I looked farther up the street, where I saw the Garfields' outdoor light flicker on. More and more people on the block were gathering at the edge of their own front yards, trying to understand the commotion. Another patrol car sped down our street, toward the Bakers'. I wondered if the noise had also roused the neighbors at the very top of the street, like Diane and Courtney.

Dr. Baker slowly walked down the front steps, in the direction of his wife. He had his hands up, the way they do in the Western movies when they surrender.

Mrs. Baker continued her tirade. "We should've stayed in Boston! I didn't want to come here; Max and Sally didn't want to. You could've taken that job at Bay Memorial, and we could have stayed put, but you were too embarrassed by me. And that job wasn't *prestigious enough* for you. You couldn't be 'just' a surgeon. You had to be in charge, running another surgical department. *You* made us come here, to this shit town! This fucking shit town! For what? For what? So you could impress the small-town people with what you know? So you could work all the time? So you could get your fancy fucking car and be a fancy fucking head surgeon?!" she screamed, louder than ever. "Congratu-fucking-lations! You're real important now, aren't you?! An important doctor and—and a famous father!" And then, glancing behind her, she yelled to Officer Lark, "Let me go!"

Father's low voice spoke from behind, startling Mother and me. "Borka, that's enough. This is not our business. Let's go inside." Annoyance surged through me; Father had no right telling me what to do when it came to Mrs. Baker.

When I didn't move, Father barked, "Borka, I said inside! Now!" And then, in a less sharp but still commanding voice, he said, "You, too, Clara."

I promptly moved to our front-facing dining room window, defiant, and Mother slid behind me. Father shook his head, but he remained at the entrance of the room, close enough to still get a look. We watched the scene outside as if it were a silent movie: Officer Jimmy was now also there, standing near Dr. Baker, who was still several feet away from his wife. Mrs. Baker managed to wrench herself free of Officer Lark, and she lunged toward her husband, but she stumbled and fell down instead. She lay in a heap, her body moving in waves, and it was clear she was crying. I snuck a peek at Father, but he had left the room. After a few seconds had passed, Dr. Baker moved toward his wife, with Officers Lark and Jimmy cautiously positioned on either side, as if she were a dangerous animal. Then Dr. Baker crouched over her, his arms spread across her backside. They rocked together, and the officers nodded at each other, their bodies going a bit slack. At some point the Bakers stopped moving, but remained in an embrace, and it suddenly felt like too intimate of a moment to witness. Mother must have felt similarly because she put her hand on my arm to finally draw me away. As I pulled back, I looked beyond the lawn, to the front windows of the Bakers' house, trying to find Max's face peering back at mine. But their house was dark.

Later that night, I couldn't get that image of the Bakers wound together on the yard out of my mind. Relationships between adults appeared to be just as complicated as those between siblings—perhaps even more so. As dislikable as Mrs. Baker was, sympathy was now reluctantly creeping into me. Maybe there was more to her than I'd realized. Just like I felt I had many more layers than most people knew.

I wondered what had made the fight between the Bakers become so ugly. Sally had been gone for more than a year. Why tonight? When my parents argued, they did it behind closed doors, and it never would have escalated to that level.

I briefly considered whether it might have anything to do with Father, but that didn't feel right. No—this fight was congested with the Bakers' own history.

Sleep escaped me, and I went downstairs to stand again by the dining room window. The Bakers' front porch light was still on, and to my surprise, I saw Max, bending down behind the shrubs that lined the front of his house. He picked something up and put it into a trash bag he was holding, and then he moved a few feet away to repeat the same gesture. I took a quick peek at the kitchen clock: 11:14 p.m.

I quietly donned my shoes and fleece, and snuck out the front door.

"Can I help?" I asked Max, standing in front of his shrubs, shivering. It was chilly; I was wearing just my cotton striped pajamas beneath my jacket.

Max gave me a subdued half-smile. He didn't seem surprised to see me. "Sure, thanks," he replied. "Don't cut yourself," he added, as he bent back down.

Mrs. Baker—or Dr. Baker, though I doubted it—must have thrown something against the house. I picked up one of the glass pieces; a strong liquor smell emanated from it.

"Did everyone see us?" Max asked after we'd worked quietly for a bit.

"I don't think so," I lied. "We just, you know, live across the street."

Max smiled, a little more genuinely this time. "Yeah, I guess that would've been hard to miss."

I glanced up at his house, which remained dark. "Is she asleep?"

Max nodded. "Yeah. She passed out." We were quiet again. Then he paused and said, "I know what people must think of her."

I wasn't sure how to respond, but I knew I should say something. "What do you mean?" I replied.

"She's had a rough time, Bee. Her sister, my aunt Helen, had cancer a few years back. And my mom—she was a nurse; did you know that?"

I shook my head; I wasn't about to admit what I'd heard.

"Yeah, she worked in the ICU. And my dad was one of the surgeons. When Aunt Helen got sick"—Max took a second before continuing—"my mom stole pain pills from the hospital. To help her sister, because she was . . . really in a lot of pain, I guess."

I nodded to show Max I was following along, and I was glad when he continued talking because I still had no idea what to say. The rumors were true, then.

"And then, when she died," Max said, "my mom kept stealing the pills. But for herself. Because *she* was in a lot of pain."

I cleared my throat. "I'm—I'm sorry to hear that, Max."

"So she had a problem. Has a problem, if you can't tell." Max took a depth breath. "That's why we're here. She got caught stealing the pills, and she lost her job, and because of my father, it was a big scandal. So, we moved, for his new job. So he could have a fresh start. She didn't want us to."

"Wow. I—I'm sorry, Max. I didn't know."

Max laughed bitterly. "Yeah, but stuff clearly followed us here."

I pursed my lips; it was too much. I felt so bad for Max, I wanted to cry. Instead, I picked up another piece of glass that had caught my eye. It didn't seem fair that Max had to shoulder all of this himself.

"I'm pretty sure I'm the only thing still keeping my parents together," he continued. "And now she's drinking, obviously." Max held up the larger piece he'd just retrieved. It clinked against the other glass as he dropped it in the bag. "She shouldn't be, but it's hard. My dad's not around a lot, so she doesn't really have anyone. Anyway, maybe it's hard to understand unless you've gone through it."

"No!" I said quickly. I didn't want Max to stop confiding in me. "I understand. Well, I don't understand everything, but my uncle Mihály—my father's brother—was an alcoholic. I never met him, though. He died when I was a baby. I think it killed him." Instantly I regretted that last bit; I didn't want Max to think that that could happen to his mother.

But then, looking at the trash bag Max was holding, I realized I couldn't really relate. Mother and Father were not perfect, but they'd given us a life that was steady, predictable. I couldn't imagine enduring even one fraction of what Max had to go through.

He took a step closer to me and put his hand on the upper part of my arm. It felt like the current from his fingers traveled through my coat and shirt and directly into my heart. I held my breath. "Thanks for listening," he said in a low voice.

"Thanks for telling me," I half whispered back.

"You're so nice, Bee." Our gazes were locked on each other. "I'm sorry we haven't hung out lately. I've—I've been dealing with all this." Suddenly we heard the front door open, and Max dropped his hand from my arm.

"Max?" Dr. Baker called from the front porch. "Are you out there?"

"Yeah, Dad. Over here. I'm with Bee." Max moved toward his father, and I followed, standing next to him.

"Hi, Dr. Baker," I said, as if seeing each other right then was the most normal thing in the world. He wore a white T-shirt and flannel pants, and I quickly looked down, because it felt a bit improper to be seeing him in his pajamas.

"Hello, Bee."

"She's helping me clean up."

"That's very kind of her," Dr. Baker replied. "But it's late, and I'm sure that her parents want her home."

"Okay, um, I'll see you later, Max. Good night, Dr. Baker." I could still feel Max's hand on my arm as I walked away.

Father never again set foot in the Bakers' house after Mrs. Baker's meltdown. I wondered if it was because he'd found her public scene unappealing, and her too unstable, or if he'd realized the emotional repercussions of his actions: There were two families—two spouses, two sets of children—involved. Beginning the day after the incident, and for two consecutive straight weeks, Father sent over Scott and Gary—two of his long-standing employees—until the project was finally complete.

I wasn't as happy that it was over between Father and Mrs. Baker as I thought I'd be. My discontent lingered because I still knew—the memory of what I'd seen remained within me, despite my best efforts to expunge it. To make matters more confusing, after everything Max had told me, I'd begun to see Mrs. Baker in a new light. She was no longer simply the bad mother or the greedy temptress. She was human and she was sad. I could relate to that. Might we all be excused for one or two of our actions, based on extenuating cir-cumstances? I was even beginning to wonder if Mother was at least partly to blame. Perhaps, I thought, she'd driven Father away with her obsessive-compulsiveness, her desire for control.

Looking at the sweat on Audrina's contorted face when her sugar levels dropped, the terrible way the Diabetes Beast tormented her during those moments, I'd almost wish I could go to those depths, too. Then, perhaps, I might be able to purge my knowledge of the affair. Because once we'd excised the Beast from Audrina, it would be long gone, its presence not even a memory.

Peter Scoffer kept pestering his brother to go with him to the maple tree, but Sean kept putting him off.

"If it's a bone, it's not going anywhere," Sean replied. "Already dead; nothing we can do about that," he said another time.

Finally, the second weekend in December, after Peter—with tears in his eyes—accused Sean of never keeping his promises, Sean nodded and put on his jacket.

The landscape looked different with the foliage having shed, and Peter had trouble locating the maple tree. Sean kept looking at his watch; he had plans to meet up with his friends at the arcade. "C'mon, little bro. Put your thinking cap on."

Peter glanced around, and then led them to a different area of the farm's perimeter, where they finally stumbled upon the tree.

"Holy shit," Sean said as they stood in front of it.

With his brother beside him, Peter felt bold, and he poked at the bone with a stick. "Told you so!"

"No, no, don't do that," Sean quickly said, putting his hand over Peter's arm to lower the stick.

"What do you think it is?

Sean had a bad feeling. It didn't really look like an animal bone. Maybe he should have listened to Peter months earlier. "I'm not sure."

"What do we do?"

"We gotta tell Mom and Dad."

# Chapter Eighteen

"ARE YOU OKAY? DID YOU HEAR?" LEAH ASKED, SLIDING INTO THE seat alongside mine during third-period class—social studies. It was four months into eighth grade, winter break just a week and a half away.

It was an odd combination of questions, and I grew concerned as I shook my head, my pink plastic hairband sliding forward. I quickly eased it back into place; it was covering a new problem area. Since Mrs. Baker's disconcerting breakdown, I'd resumed pulling more frequently. "Hear what?"

The bell rang, and students who had been lingering by the door and in the hall scrambled to their seats. "Good morning," Mrs. Dongle announced as she stood up from her desk. She wore pearl strands, and a feather boa wrapped around her shoulders. Behind her, on the chalkboard, were the underlined words: *The Roaring Twenties.*

She rapped on the surface with a wooden pointer. "Students,

I want you to pretend that you are living in New York City in the 1920s. It's a time of growth and creativity—a new 'consumer society.' People are buying automobiles and radios en masse. Going to movie theaters! Jazz music explodes; the flapper is born. Women, as of 1920, when the Nineteenth Amendment is ratified, can finally vote. But while some rights expand, others shrink. Prohibition . . ."

Leah mouthed "Sally" to me with a tight half-smile, her lips pressed closed—the way she did when she was nervous. Then she turned to face the teacher, while I was left gawking at her profile.

Sally? What on earth did she mean? I swallowed, the tension immediately rising within me. And how could Leah just say that and nothing else? Leah's lips remained clamped, and I gazed at her until I realized I was staring. I jerked my head forward to listen to Mrs. Dongle, but I couldn't focus on anything she was saying, despite the interesting subject matter. So I glanced out the window. The trees were nearly bare, exposed, their leaves now part of the mulch in the ground.

As the class continued, I grew more anxious and more annoyed with Leah, at the way she'd left me hanging. Finally I scribbled a note—*What do you mean???*—and tossed it to her when Mrs. Dongle had her back turned.

Leah stared at me before picking up her pen. She started to write something on the paper and then crossed it out and, after a pause, wrote something else. She folded the note into careful creases, and the next time Mrs. Dongle turned toward the chalkboard, Leah placed it firmly on my desk, her hand lingering for a second, like she didn't want me to have to know.

I fumbled opening the note: *They found Sally's bone.*

❧

"It was an arm bone," Leah gently informed me, when we spoke after social studies. And Audrina said the same thing, as we waited in the lobby after school for Mother to pick us up.

"But which bone?" I pressed my sister.

"An *arm* bone, like I just said." She sounded drained. Was her blood sugar okay?

"Bye, Audrina," a group of girls exiting through the front doors called out, and my sister waved, somewhat absentmindedly.

"I know, but you have three bones in your arm." I shifted my backpack off one shoulder and rested it on the opposite hip as I pointed to my arm. "There's the ulna, the radius, and the humer—"

Audrina cut me off: "Bee, I dunno." She briefly shut her eyes. "I just can't believe it."

I took a small step toward her. "I know," I commiserated. It actually didn't seem real to me yet, but my sister's reaction made it more so.

Audrina gave me a thin smile and then, to my surprise, pulled me in to rest her head on my shoulder. Her hair was fragrant with Agree shampoo and Aqua Net hair spray. She seemed small, vulnerable. I remembered how I'd once wanted to protect her from a scenario such as this.

"Hey," interrupted a familiar voice from behind. We pulled apart to find Michelle. "I heard about Sally. How terrible. I'm so sorry." Her eyes flickered over me to settle on my sister.

"Thanks," Audrina said.

"You must be so upset," Michelle continued, her gaze still focused on her.

"Yeah," Audrina said, and I almost snickered. My sister usually commanded all the attention, but as this concerned Sally, it equally related to me. I pulled my backpack up on both shoulders, hoping the movement would make Michelle realize I, too, was standing there. Plus, I was annoyed how she'd just disrupted our sisterly moment without any hesitation.

"Well, let me know if you need anything. You can call me if you feel like talking." She leaned in to give Audrina a hug, and then looked at me and simply said, "Bye, Bee."

"What am I, invisible?" I asked once she'd left.

"She saw you."

"She saw me, but she didn't hug me."

"Why would she hug you?" Audrina asked. "You're not friends with her."

"First of all, I was friends with her before you were. Last year, we were friends. And since when are you two friends, anyway?"

"Don't be jealous, Bee."

I sighed. "I'm not, Audrina."

Back on Hickory Place, cops swarmed the Bakers' residence. There were patrol cars parked both on the street and in their driveway. Some of the cars had their engines running, officers sitting within. Chief Riley briefly emerged from the Bakers' house to speak to one of the officers and then disappeared back inside.

Mother sat Audrina and me down at the kitchen table to tell us what she knew. But her responses were calibrated, as always.

"They may have found evidence of Sally," she started.

"Was it her arm bone?" Audrina jumped in.

"Yes, but . . . there were other bones, too," Mother said, using her nail to pick at a piece of old, dried food that lay in the table groove. Then she paused and peered carefully at our faces. We were quiet, stationary, like Mother had always wished we could be during long car rides years earlier, when we'd fight and shove each other. Now we couldn't move, even if we wanted to.

"The whole skeleton?" Audrina inquired, but Mother just looked at her without saying anything, which made me feel like that was a no.

After a period of silence, Audrina asked, in a squeaky voice, the question I was also wondering, "How do they know it's her?"

"They don't for sure," Mother replied. "They'll do some investigation, of course. But I think there was a piece of clothing—" Mother abruptly stopped, as if worried she'd said too much.

"When did those boys find the skeleton?" Audrina pressed. "Did it really happen months ago, like we heard?"

Mother sighed. "It was sometime in the summer, I think. Bad news travels fast, I see."

"So why wouldn't they have told anyone?" my sister asked.

"I don't know, honey. The important thing is that they eventually told their parents. Or one of them told their brother, I think, who told their parents? Anyway, I don't know why they waited . . . Maybe they were scared. Or thought it was an animal bone, with all the deer we have around here." It was not unusual to see dead deer, casualties of car accidents, on the side of the road. Father always reminded Mother to drive slowly, especially at night.

"Do deer have arm bones?" I finally piped in, and Audrina gave me a look. "What?" I said to her.

"Girls," Mother warned. "Bee, I don't know what kinds of bones deer have. It's okay to ask questions, though. I don't think there is a correct way to respond. It's a . . . strange situation."

"Does Max know?" I inquired, my voice wavering. I felt like I was only just starting to absorb the gravity of what Mother was telling us.

"Of course he must know," Audrina replied, but her voice now had a funny lilt to it.

Mother confirmed with a nod. "Your father is going to stop by there later this evening, after work." I looked sharply at Mother when she said this. The last thing I wanted was for him to see Mrs. Baker.

"Are you going, too?" I asked.

Mother drew her eyebrows together and gazed over our heads, in the direction of the street. "Well, I wasn't planning to, but on second thought, you know, maybe I should."

"Wow," Audrina said, slumping back in her chair. Her face was drawn. "This is so warped."

"Where did they find . . . it?" I asked.

"I believe at one of the local farms," Mother replied.

"Do they know what happened to her?" I probed. "Have they talked to the farm owner?"

"We don't. And yes, of course." Mother had said it was okay to ask questions, but her responses indicated otherwise. Later I would reflect on the clinical way in which she had delivered the news. Her tendency to avoid disturbing matters did the exact opposite of what she likely intended; instead of protecting me from harsh truths, it always just made me fret more with the possibilities. "The police are investigating all angles," she continued. "Which is why they were— are—at the Bakers' house. A forensic anthropologist is on the case," she finished.

"A forensic anthropologist," I repeated, while Audrina slowly pushed back her chair. I knew what an anthropologist was, and the term *forensics* sounded familiar, but I definitely had never heard the two words put together.

"Wow," Audrina said again. She rose, almost hesitantly. I could tell she didn't know what else to say. I glanced up at her, then at

Mother. I could sense our window of conversation was closing, but I wasn't ready for that.

"Can you tell me—us—more about what happened?" I quickly asked, panting slightly. It felt like my breath was getting trapped in my throat.

"Which part?"

"After the parents found out about the, um, the bones?"

"They called the police," Mother replied, pushing back her own chair to stand up. "And now the forensic anthropologist is involved, like I said. That's all we know."

"But—" I didn't know what I was going to ask. I just wanted to talk more, to know more. I was tired of the way Mother always handed me just scraps of information that she'd deemed sufficient. We were older now. I'd seen the open and tender way Leah's mother spoke with her, the conversations that seemed like actual conversations. Why couldn't it be like that in our house?

Mother stood with one hand leaning against the table, waiting for my full response. Even Audrina, who had started to shuffle toward the hall, turned back around to see what I had to say.

I swallowed and returned to the timeline. "But what happened then, after the parents called the police? I mean, what did the police, or how did the police get the b-bones? Like, how did it get to the forensic anthropologist? This—this has to mean Sally's dead, right?" I inhaled deeply.

"Beeee," Mother said, drawing out my name. Her voice was now softer, but still with an edge. "Look, I know this is hard to hear. Somehow the forensic anthropologist obviously got involved—where or when it doesn't really matter. In terms of what it all means, well, we have to just wait and let them do their jobs."

When I'd overheard Mother talking about the New York

detective—who'd suggested that most murders are committed by someone the victim knows—the thought that had occurred to me at the time was: *If Sally had been murdered, wouldn't there be a body?*

I realized now that even though I'd been making *the list* for months, even though I had been watching those around me with a slight suspicion, it hadn't seemed entirely real because there hadn't been any evidence.

But now there was: a bone. *Bones.* So it mattered. This could be Sally—all that was left of Sally—and it mattered very much.

During the following weekend, the Bakers' house seemed to transform into a prison: Visitors, like the police and neighbors and our parents, entered, but the family who lived there didn't come out. Only once had I spotted Mrs. Baker: She was on her lawn, in her bathrobe, cigarette smoke curling up from her fingers. She walked a few steps in one direction, and then backtracked the other way, before repeating the process. A police officer appeared to steer her back inside.

There'd been no sign of Max, though. Mother told us he wouldn't be returning to Ludlow until after the winter break. I frequently stared out the window, trying to send mental signals to Max to look out at the same time, but it never worked. Every minute that passed, I felt my heart break a little more for him. Every minute that passed, I grew more desperate for information. Answers felt elusive, stuck in some hard-to-reach place, as if buried in the trees lining Hickory Place.

"We don't know anything yet," Father reported, after he and Mother returned home from a visit and I pounced on him.

"We have to wait and see," Mother added.

But I didn't want to wait and see; I couldn't. I needed to know more; I needed to understand more. I ran my hands up and down my arms, thinking: *Ulna, radius, humerus. Humerus, radius, ulna.* I kept seeing the image of an arm bone, a single arm bone, stuck in a dark tree hole. I saw the arm bone everywhere—in the half-broken Cheerio floating in my cereal bowl, in the dollop of toothpaste that squirted on the bathroom countertop. When I closed my eyes, the bone moved slowly across the shadowy part of my lids.

I'd held—*taken*—the bracelet piece that had slid up and down that tiny arm. That tiny arm that was no longer an arm in the way it should have been. I felt sick thinking about it.

I wondered why people felt so certain it was Sally. Had the piece of clothing Mother alluded to been Sally's bathing suit? That was the only thing she'd been wearing when she disappeared. But if the article of clothing they'd found was something else, like a shirt or pair of shorts, then it would have to belong to someone else. Or what if the bones actually were from a deer or some*thing* else?

On Monday morning, after the final bell rang, I waited until the halls were deserted and then snuck into the empty science lab to examine Harvey, the life-size skeleton in Mr. Hoosier's classroom. Harvey hung suspended on a pole, his feet dangling above a metal stand. I dropped my backpack at his feet and stood straight. My head reached the top of his rib cage. He was an adult male, I remembered Mr. Hoosier telling us. I picked up Harvey's left arm and then realized another thing that I didn't know. Which arm bone of Sally's had been found, the right or left? Perhaps both? So I also lifted Harvey's right arm and held the two in front of me, studying them. The arms were light in my hands, and I wondered with a chill how much heavier bone was than plastic.

"Can I help you with something, Bee?" Mr. Hoosier's voice

boomed from behind as he entered the lab, and I jumped, dropping the arms.

"Sorry," I muttered, turning to face him. "I was just, um, I just wanted to see something." I picked up my backpack and slung it over my shoulder, ready to leave.

Mr. Hoosier pushed his black-rimmed glasses up on his nose and ever so slightly moved between me and the classroom door. "Do you have a question, Bee?"

I just blinked and took an instinctive small step back. I did have a question. I had many of them, but I wasn't sure how to begin. "Um, well, I was just wondering, um, like, you said this is a male skeleton, right?" Mr. Hoosier nodded, so I continued: "Right, of course, because his name is Harvey. But what makes this skeleton male? I mean, if you were to find it, like on an archaeological dig or something, what makes you know that it's male?"

"Good question." Mr. Hoosier moved close to the skeleton and bent down to grasp the pelvic bone. I spied thick tufts of hair covering his knuckles and wondered if he knew of his nickname, "Hairy Hoosier."

"Look here," he pointed out. "Adult men like Harvey have narrower pelvises, and adult women's pelvises are more spacious, to allow for childbearing."

"Okay," I nodded, as I felt a heat flush over my face. He must have noticed because he stood up and took a step back.

"But you have a more specific question." His gaze was big, probing, from behind his glasses. I noticed his eyebrows were the same unruly thickness as his knuckle hair.

"Yes," I admitted. I glanced over at the enlarged periodic table of elements hanging on the side wall. My eyes traveled to the letters of my birth name: $B$ for boron, $O$ for oxygen, $R$ . . . I couldn't find an $R$.

"I do. I, um, wanted to know what if you found just one or two bones, like an arm bone, maybe." Then I added, as I spotted *Be*, like Bee, for beryllium, "Hypothetically speaking." I didn't want Mr. Hoosier to know what I really meant, though given our small town, I'm sure he knew exactly why I was asking these questions.

"Yes, hypothetically speaking. Of course. An arm bone," Mr. Hoosier said. "Perhaps like the ulna or humerus?"

"Yes," I said, my voice suddenly scratchy, and randomly chose the latter: "Like the humerus."

"Well," Mr. Hoosier began, as his eyebrows drew downward, and it struck me that it was the first time I'd ever witnessed him searching for how to respond. He rubbed his nose and replied, "When you find individual bones, there are certain attributes the bones can reveal: stature, or height of the individual, sex, ethnicity, and age at death."

"Really? You can know all of that from one bone?" I stared at Harvey.

"In theory. It depends on which bone you find. The humerus won't tell you if the deceased was male or female. Not like finding the pelvic bone would. The humerus won't tell you the ethnicity of the deceased, either, at least not with our current research. But because it's a long bone, you can estimate the height of the deceased based on the size of it. Longer bones mean larger, older individuals; smaller bones mean smaller, younger individuals."

"Okay," I replied, folding my own arms together. That made sense.

"Now, if we find the humerus of a young adult or child, hypothetically speaking—" Mr. Hoosier paused here, and I nodded. "If we find that, we might be able to estimate the age of death based on something called the epiphyseal fusion."

"Epi-what?"

"Do you remember learning in class that babies are born with about two hundred seventy bones?"

I nodded in a hesitant sort of way. I didn't really remember and hoped he wasn't going to ask me a follow-up question about it.

"A lot of those two hundred seventy bones fuse together over time. Harvey, here, is an adult; he has two hundred and six bones. That's about sixty-five fewer bones than he was born with."

"Wow," I replied. "That's a big difference."

Mr. Hoosier smiled—unusual for him—and again pushed up the bridge of his glasses. "It is. When you're born, you're still 'in parts.' Long bones, like the humerus, have a main bony shaft, and then their ends, or epiphyses, are unattached, separate pieces. Over time, as you grow into adulthood, those ends fuse with the main shaft. And we know roughly when these fusions occur."

I nodded, appreciating the comprehensive and serious manner in which Mr. Hoosier was speaking with me. He was admittedly strange, but he was harmless—no, he was more than harmless. He was actually quite nice. I felt bad that Leah and I had discussed him as a potential suspect.

I turned to stare again at Harvey. "So, if someone finds a humerus that doesn't have the ends attached yet, we know it's a child?"

"Exactly."

I swallowed as my eyes traveled up one of Harvey's arms, from his bony fingers—phalanges—to his ulna and radius, and then I paused at the humerus, before glancing beyond that at his scapula. A chill passed through me as I tried to imagine a humerus on its own, separated from those connecting bones on either side and dripping with unattached, loose endcaps.

Mr. Hoosier approached Harvey, placing his right hand in

Harvey's left one, as if they were about to shake hands. "People say, 'If these walls could talk,' but I say, 'If only these bones could talk.'"

As we approached winter break, news about Sally spiraled. School was where I learned from Leah, who'd heard from her mother, that the remains were scattered between two areas: the tree with the hole and then the dirt nearby, an animal having likely pulled them there.

School was where I learned from Jay Flay, whose cousin was a classmate of Sean Scoffer's, that the place where the bones had been found was Wicke Farm.

I knew of Wicke Farm. I'd passed by it perhaps a hundred times in the year and a half since Sally went missing. It was off a small dirt road that intersected Main Street, toward the town of Etchers. The same Main Street that turned into Route 108; the same Main Street we took every time we went to see a movie, or to go to the Shop-Rite in Etchers—which had a bigger selection than Hammend's Foodtown—or to get on the highway going north. Wicke Farm was roughly two miles from Deer Chase Lake; when you traveled north from the center of Hammend, the turnoff for it was actually a few streets before the lake.

All those times I'd passed by this turnoff, not even registering the farm's small wooden sign perched at the corner intersection: the words *Wicke Farm* painted above a picture of a cow, a carrot making up the letter *i*, an apple for the *a*. All those times I'd passed by, and Sally could have been there the entire time.

I wondered if she'd wandered around the farm, if she'd been lost, and hungry, and tired. If, once it had gotten dark, she'd been afraid. Or if the animals had scared her. Or maybe she had never seen any of that; perhaps she'd just been brought there—afterward.

"I bet Mr. Wicke did it," Jay Flay said at the beginning of Spanish class midweek, when our teacher, Señora Flannigan, was occupied at the doorway, engrossed in conversation with another teacher. "That crazy man shot his BB gun at my brother and his friend when they were just walking down the road one night." Jay's brother was older, in high school. "They weren't even on his actual property. But the man lied and said he thought they were deer." Jay smirked.

The only interaction I'd had with Mr. Wicke occurred a couple years earlier, when he stopped by a garage sale in our neighborhood, on Maple Way. When Mother went to pay for the twenty-five-cent sequined purse Audrina was insistent upon getting, she realized she'd left her wallet at home. Mr. Wicke kindly stepped in to give Mother a quarter, saying he would be insulted if Mother tried to pay him back.

"Guilty," murmured a few other kids, and a terrible feeling washed over me. How could we already be accusing Mr. Wicke when we didn't know the whole story? But then again, wasn't that exactly what I had been doing with my own list? My suspicions hadn't been founded on anything that *actually* counted. With a sinking feeling, I acknowledged that I couldn't trust my—or anyone's, really—instincts.

"What was your brother doing at his farm?" The question burst out of me before I could grab ahold of it.

"Huh?" Jay glanced over at me like he was surprised I could even talk.

I took a moment before answering, conscious that everyone around me was waiting to hear what I had to say next. My heart loud in my ears, I turned my head down toward the Spanish textbook on my desk and replied as if I were talking to the book cover: "You said your brother was there in the middle of the night."

"I didn't say the middle of the night. I said *at night*. What are you getting at?"

I didn't know what I was trying to say, so I didn't reply, instead just flipping open the textbook.

"Like I said," Jay sneered, "he was *walking* there. Last time I checked, that's not against the law, Borka."

Laughter rose up around me, and I pushed my head further down into the book, cowering. The page blurred, but I managed to stop my tears from slipping out. As my vision cleared, I focused on the story at hand. There were two illustrations: the first, of a little girl riding a bike, and then next to that, the girl was crying and holding her arm, the bike now in tatters on the ground. The description read: "Maria se cayó de su bicicleta. Tiene mucho dolor en su brazo."

Maria fell from her bicycle. She has much pain in her arm.

*Brazo.* Arm.

# Chapter Nineteen

It would take five weeks, long enough for the ground to be coated with a thick layer of snow, before the police tracked down an X-ray Sally had the prior year in Boston (when she'd caught her finger in the bedroom door). The X-ray confirmed the bones belonged to her.

By then, my sister would be dead, too.

But we knew it was Sally long before that. We knew once the newspaper reported, shortly after the bones were discovered, that the police had, in fact, also found part of a child's purple bathing suit at the scene. And we knew Sally had been *murdered* once the forensic anthropologist determined that a piece of skull showed blunt-force trauma. Little Sally was killed first, then discarded.

The news hit our town like a main sewer line break—the terrible underbelly of humankind suddenly unearthed, exposed. The stench of evil drifted into every Hammend home, paused over every family dinner table.

It settled deeply over us on Hickory Place.

I remember thinking how different it was, *murdered* versus *missing*. A child's murder, I would learn, permanently fractures a five-thousand-person town. A missing child—yes, that has an effect, but it is temporary, or eased by hope that the disappearance is not due to nefarious circumstances. A missing child brings together parents and neighbors and search parties and hot casseroles. It's an ongoing story, with characters and plots and subplots, grief and faith in equal proportions. But a murder is over as soon as it begins. It dead-ends, isolates people; it brings a finality stamped with distrust.

I remember worrying we might not ever know who killed Sally. That even though her murder was now a fact, there were no further answers to be had. No culprit to bring to justice. It was a silencing sort of realization. One that whisked you away from the island of childhood. Because in childhood fairy tales, the bad guy was usually caught, made to own up: Rumpelstiltskin, Maleficent, Cinderella's evil stepmother.

This was 1986, well before we realized that even a single piece of clothing could contain hidden DNA clues.

"I still can't believe it," Audrina reflected as we added some homemade ornaments to our Christmas tree. It was a Monday afternoon, just three days before Christmas. An overnight storm had granted us a school snow day, and we were using some of the art supplies Mother had purchased from Mortenson's Drug Store over the weekend. To take our minds off Sally, she had gone overboard with craft projects, as well as holiday decorations.

We had not one but two trees: the real one in our family room, and a small, new artificial one in the living room. We had garlands lining our fireplace mantel, cascading down our stairs, even framing the entranceway between the kitchen and family room. There was the usual Nativity set displayed on the foyer table, but this year Mother had added nutcrackers on either side of the stable. A three-foot wooden reindeer now stood next to our main tree, which was adorned with a new host of ornaments, including the papier-mâché snowman and candy cane Mother had helped us make earlier. A poinsettia wreath hung on the inside of our front door, as if our house were inside out.

"Why is this here?" Father had asked the night before, pointing to the wreath.

"Because we can't hang it outside. It's too . . . festive," Mother had replied, glancing in the direction of the Bakers' house. Father strolled over to the dining room window and looked out at the street; the other houses in our neighborhood still seemed to have lights and decorations, although the giant-sized, light-up Santa with his sleigh had been removed from the Johnsons' lawn.

Father nodded, and then questioned, "But why put it up at all, then?"

"Because it's Christmas," Mother had briskly replied.

"Are you glad Mr. Wicke was cleared?" my sister now asked, rifling through our pile of paper cutouts to pull out a snowflake. Mr. Wicke, we'd learned, had been in Alaska during the time of Sally's disappearance—first attending his military son's wedding and then going on an extended six-week vacation.

"Glad?" I responded, a little puzzled. "I'm not not-glad or glad." I assessed the gingerbread man cutout I'd decorated with googly eyes and stickers. It looked juvenile, like something a six-year-old would make, not a thirteen-year-old.

"Oh, I thought you wanted him to be innocent."

I sighed in response; it was clear Audrina had heard about my Spanish class incident.

"I still can't believe that Sally was murdered," my sister reflected, then drew in a sharp breath. "That sounds so weird, *murdered*."

"Yeah," I agreed. "It does." We were silent, working on our respective ornaments. Unspoken questions surrounding Sally lingered, creating an air of discontent. For the umpteenth time, I wondered how Max was; our parents said he'd been quiet when they saw him. That it would take time for him to register everything.

But how would time help? Sally was dead.

Audrina hung her snowflake, now adorned with glitter, and began sifting through a box of old childhood toys she'd dragged down from the attic to repurpose for tree decorations. "So?" she finally said, pulling out a Barbie doll. "What do you think about it?"

"I don't know," I replied, taking a sip from the water glass next to me; I'd woken up with a sore throat. "It's strange, right? We know more about what happened to her, but we still don't know anything."

"God," Audrina said as she shuddered. "Do you ever think about how it could have been one of us? You or me?"

I chewed the inside of my lip. "No," I lied, and as I swallowed, my throat burned. I took another sip of water and asked, "Do you?"

"No," my sister was quick to answer, but it seemed almost too quick. "Oh, shoot!" she then exclaimed. I glanced over: She was attempting to loop a string around Barbie's neck, but it kept coming undone.

"Are you serious?" I asked, a little aghast.

"What?" she replied as she finally tightened the loop.

"You're, like, hanging Barbie."

My sister tilted her head as she held up the string, Barbie dangling below. "You're right," she giggled. "Oops."

"That's macabre, Drina."

"What's macabre?"

"How you did that, with the noose. You know, because of Sally." Audrina just stared back, so I added, "I know you didn't mean it. I was just saying that the timing—"

"What does *macabre* mean?"

"Oh! Sorry. It means, um, gruesome."

"Sally didn't hang. Someone hit her head."

I sighed. "I know that. I was just saying—forget it."

"So do you think the murderer is someone in Hammend?" my sister asked.

I thought about how I'd returned to that possibility, time and time again, with my suspect list.

"Well, Mother's childhood friend Tessie—" I began, and then stopped, glancing toward the kitchen, but no one was there. Mother was not back yet from dropping off Christmas cookies to the neighbors. She'd dead-bolted the kitchen garage door behind her, as she'd begun doing ever since Sally's bones had been found, so we certainly would have heard her return. "Her brother-in-law is a detective and he said"—I took a deep breath here—"most murders are committed by someone the person knows."

"Really?" my sister said as she loosened the string around Barbie's neck. "That makes sense. Because you would need to have a reason to kill—to do that to someone, right?"

"Right." I was surprised by her logical response.

"So who do you think it is?" my sister probed.

"I really don't know, Drina."

"Like who?"

"I just said, I don't know." I picked up another Barbie from Audrina's box and fingered its hair. "Isn't it kind of fitting that the last time we pulled out these toys was when Sally went missing? And now here we are, almost a year and a half later, and they found her?"

Audrina shrugged, like she didn't think much of my observation. "Do you think it was someone there, who was at the lake that day?"

*Should I tell Audrina about my list?* Maybe it was okay to talk about it now since I knew it had been baseless.

"What?" she said, as if she knew I was holding something back.

"Nothing."

"Bee, tell me."

"There's nothing to tell."

"C'mon, Bee." My sister raised her eyebrows so that her green eyes appeared even larger. "I know you're not telling me something. Please."

"Fine." I sighed. "But you can't say anything to anyone, okay?"

"Okay."

"I—I made a list." I started to braid the hair on the Barbie, but it kept coming undone.

Audrina tilted her head. "What?"

"I made a list. Of suspects. But I don't think it's right anymore."

"Who's on it?"

I placed the Barbie back into the box before answering. "Do you really want to know?"

"Of course I want to know." My sister rolled her eyes. "Why would you tell me you wrote a list if you're not going to tell me who's on it? Why are you being so mysterious?"

"Fine. Well, there's Vittorio, or he *was* on the list, but not anymore."

Audrina looked at me blankly. "Who?"

"Vittorio. You know Vittorio, from Russo's Pizza? The guy with the curly hair?"

"The pizza guy's on your list?" Audrina asked in an incredulous tone. "Why?"

I shrugged. "He kinda gives me the creeps. He smiles at me all the time."

Audrina laughed. "He's nice, Bee. That doesn't make him a murderer."

"I know, Drina," I replied stiffly. "Anyway, he's not on my list anymore, because—" I recalled how the last time I was there, his wife and young daughter had walked in, and he lifted his daughter up into the air and laughed. I'd realized that just like Audrina said, he was simply friendly. But I wasn't about to give her that satisfaction. "Never mind."

"Who else?" Audrina prompted. She rapidly pushed her Barbie's legs forward and back, as if she were walking in a brisk manner.

Michael-the-mailman's face came to mind, but I opted against mentioning him. I was sure she would think my reasoning about his never smiling was as silly as my suspicions about Vittorio's constant smiling. Instead, I offered, "Dr. Baker, 'cause, you know, he's a surgeon and good with knives—I mean sharp surgical instruments—and knows the human body."

Surprisingly, my sister nodded. "Okay, I get that." She straightened Barbie's legs and then turned her over, surveying her backside.

"Also," I continued, "do you remember how he was home that morning, when we went to the lake? His Porsche was in the garage."

Audrina shook her head. "I don't. Huh. Maybe he just hadn't gone into work yet?"

"Maybe."

"Who else? Do you think it could've been Mrs. Baker?" Audrina asked evenly.

I swallowed. The memory of her embrace with Father continued to rattle me. "Why do you ask?"

"I know you don't like her."

"Well, just because I don't like her—*if* I don't like her—that doesn't mean I think she's a murderer."

"So you just admitted you don't like her."

I blew the air out of my lips in a puttering fashion. "God, Audrina. Why are you being so annoying?"

"Why don't you like her?"

I looked over at the stockings that lined our fireplace. Father's stocking was the longest, then Mother's, and then Audrina's and mine were the same length. Technically, mine should have been a tad longer than my sister's. "I didn't say that," I repeated.

"I think you think she's guilty," my sister said, shifting her position on the floor and giving me a hard look.

I paused, considering. I might not like her, but after all that had happened—after all I had come to realize—did I really think that? "No," I replied, with certainty.

"Then why don't you like her?"

*How did she know?* I would later wonder. *How did she know?* I reached into my scalp, a reflex reaction. My sister's eyes immediately traveled to my hairline, and I quickly pulled my hand back down.

"Bee," she said after a moment, "I need to tell Mother."

"You promised you wouldn't!"

"It's gotten worse."

"Then I'll stop! You can't tell, Drina!"

"I don't think you can stop."

As we stared at each other, anger seethed inside me. It wasn't her business to tell Mother. It was my hair, my body; I should be the one to tell—when I was ready. But more importantly than that, Audrina had promised to keep my secret safe. She was going to break her promise. Because she always just did whatever she wanted, without regard for anyone other than herself. "Fine. Do you really want to know why I don't like Mrs. Baker?"

"Yes. Tell me." She blinked at me, waiting.

"Something happened between her and Father. I saw them from the bathroom window."

"What do you mean?" My sister's face scrunched up like a raisin.

"You know how Father was doing their basement stuff?" My sister just nodded slowly. "Well, over Labor Day weekend, I was in our bathroom, looking out the window—it was at night—and I saw Father walking over there. And when Mrs. Baker opened the door, she . . . she pulled him in for a hug, like a hug-hug."

Audrina opened and closed her mouth, and then she opened it again but took a few seconds before she spoke. "So you *think* you saw them *hug* from the window in the bathroom?"

Something in her tone gave me pause, and I took a moment before replying. "No, I know I saw them hug. Something happened with them. Between them." I examined my sister's face: She had a spacey expression, looking through me. "There were others, too. Well—at least I think there were. I'm sorry, Drina." And I did feel sorry all of a sudden; perhaps I shouldn't have said anything, but I realized that while my initial intention was to provoke her, I was also desperate to confide in someone, and who better than my sister. "I didn't want to tell you—"

My sister's eyes suddenly laser-focused on mine. She rose to a standing position, while I remained on the ground. She bent forward so that her pinched face was over mine, looking down. Her color was a little flushed, like she'd just exercised. "You're a liar. How dare you say that about Father!"

A cold hand cupped my heart. "I—I'm not lying, Drina."

"You're a liar. You just can't stand the attention other people get, can you?"

"What?" I could feel my sister's breath on me—she was that close.

"You can't stand the attention other people get—like me, or the Bakers—so you have to make up rumors."

"That's not true." My voice was shaky.

Audrina took a step back, like she was considering something. "Or maybe it's the bracelet," she muttered.

"Huh?"

"The bracelet. You feel bad about stealing it—that it could have helped to find Sally." My sister nodded while she spoke. "It's why you pull your hair. Guilt. It's why Kate's cousin pulls her hair—she has guilt about shutting the garage door on their dog. You're guilty."

The cold hand squeezed my heart now, without warning. It was painful, freezing up my whole chest. My sister was right; I knew it. My past mistakes continued to return to me like a boomerang. I had guilt. Guilt was what drove me, at least initially, to pull my hair. Perhaps not anymore, though. Now it was its own demon. "I didn't do anything wrong," I protested weakly. My voice sounded far away.

Audrina didn't respond; she was just looking at me with her lips pulled up at the end corners, like she had it all figured out.

Then I remembered something. "You knew Sally was scared of swimming," I said.

My sister put her hand on her hip. "Yeah? And so what?"

"You should've told them. That day at the lake, you should've told them that, that Sally couldn't swim and that she was scared of the water." I couldn't speak fast enough; the words burst out of me, like they were trying to run one step ahead of the cold trickling throughout the rest of my body. "Then they wouldn't have wasted their time in the water. They would have looked in the woods, like right away."

My sister's mouth dropped open. "Are you kidding me? Are you trying to make yourself feel better for what you did? Don't blame me. Of course they were going to search the lake. She was four; she could've drowned, whether or not she knew how to swim. Whether she loved swimming or hated it."

We heard the dead bolt of the kitchen garage door turn with a click, and then, in succession, the creak of the kitchen door, Mother's footsteps, and the rustle of a bag. "You're sick," my sister whispered with a sneer.

"How is that different?" I said as I scrambled to stand. I grabbed the side of my head, hiding the patchy spot. "How is what I did any different from what you did? Audrina? Drina?"

I walked backward, quickly, out of the family room, before Mother could see. Then I turned and sprinted up the stairs, into our bathroom. Locking the door, I pushed against the counter and stared at myself in the mirror.

I saw a girl with big ears and thinned-out areas on her scalp. It was obvious. Of course. Of course everyone must know. I looked like a liar. Like the type of person who would steal a dead girl's bracelet, who would pull her own hair because she was grotesque, who was a bad kisser, who would make up stories to sully her father's reputation.

Throwing my back hard against the wall, I slid downward, until I'd disappeared from the mirror, until the cabinet was in front of my face, and then the tile floor hit my bottom.

I wished I could just keep going, pushing farther and farther down, against gravity. My sister had unraveled me as if I were a spool of thread, and now I came rolling out, wildly, much too fast, all my intentions and thoughts and purpose spinning away from me. Finally I was: nothing.

That night, Audrina climbed into bed late, at least an hour after me. I'd finally drifted off, after using Mother's sore-throat remedy of gargling with warm salt water, after fighting the urge to not pull my hair, after all the terrible thoughts that so tightly encircled me loosened, but then I awoke with my sister's entrance. I didn't move, just blinked my eyes, disoriented. The darkness of the room overcame me as I remembered, as the troubling thoughts began to once again close in.

I heard my sister shift in the bed a few times, like she couldn't get comfortable. Then she said, "Bee," as if she knew I was awake, even though I hadn't budged.

I didn't reply, and again she said, "Bee." There was a soft urgency to her voice, and I knew she wouldn't stop until I responded.

"What?" I managed to say.

"I don't want to fight." Her tone was conciliatory. "I'm sorry."

I remained silent. No, I thought. The ice dam between us was thickly frozen, heavy. No, I wasn't going to accept her apology. She had to know she couldn't keep treating me this way.

Yet I could sense a sudden temperature change in the air. Like the invisible cord that connected us, that had always connected us, was now alight, its coil warming. I couldn't cut it if I wanted. Darn it, Drina.

After another minute, she tried again: "Beeee. I'm just upset about Sally, and I took it out on you. I love you, sissy."

And just like that, the impossible: The ice cracked, melted. The water ran past us, a steady stream. Washing away remaining stubbornness. Cleansing us anew.

"I love you, too, Drina," I said, suddenly emotional. "And I'm sorry, too."

That was the thing with us, always the thing. We were sisters. Our fights were Cold War epic. When she hugged me—and meant it—it felt like an invitation to a secret society. When she judged me, it was a Supreme Court ruling. We were hot and cold, and both at once. Sin and virtue, and virtue and sin. An entire world war occurred within our small, confined existences. Sisters were we.

# Chapter Twenty

THE NEXT DAY—THE LAST DAY OF SCHOOL BEFORE WINTER vacation—Audrina was still very much alive. She woke early and quietly dressed herself, trying not to disturb me. I was awake, though I pretended otherwise; my throat still hurt, so I was staying home. My sister chose a pair of jeans, and I watched, through half-closed eyes, as she reached into my drawer for one of my sweaters—an older, camel-colored one I hadn't used in a while—instead of slipping on one of her own or her red dress, which she usually liked to wear around the holidays.

At school, she didn't seem like her usual self, her friends later said. She'd forgotten her bagged lunch, which contained Mother's carefully prepared diabetic meal: one turkey sandwich (two slices of whole wheat bread, three ounces of turkey, one tablespoon of mayonnaise), one cup of baby carrots, ten small grapes, one container of low-fat milk. The school aide on duty told Audrina she could have a meal, free of charge, and then, after ensuring my sister had picked up a plastic orange tray from the cafeteria line, promptly notified the school nurse. While the woman behind the lunch counter asked my sister for a second time whether she wanted a cheeseburger or chicken nuggets (her friend Lindsay said she chose the latter, though she didn't really eat that many), the school nurse dialed our home number.

I was home when the phone rang. I'd been alternating between reading in bed—when Mother checked on me—and playing with my hair in Mother's bathroom mirror—when Mother was out, running errands. A few of Mrs. Wiley's friends had asked Mother to make them holiday gift baskets, so she'd gone to collect materials.

Flashing the handheld mirror in front of the other, larger one, I'd tried on headbands and hats and even a bandana, trying to figure out the best hairdo to minimize any thinned-out areas. *It's gotten worse, Bee.* My sister's words kept quivering in me, forcing me to think about them. Then, gradually, the specifics of our argument—and Audrina's apology—also came back to me. She hadn't mentioned anything about Father and Mrs. Baker when we'd made up. Now I realized, with a flare of anger, that meant she probably hadn't believed me.

I darted from my parents' bathroom through their bedroom, bypassing the ringing phone on their bedside table, and into the hall, where I leaned over the railing to listen as the kitchen answering machine picked up. It only briefly occurred to me to answer it; I knew it wouldn't be for me.

"You have reached the Kocsis family," Mother's voice sang, in the familiar recorded greeting, and I waited for the moment of Audrina and me giggling in the background and then Mother shushing us. "Shh—we are not here right now, so leave a message and we will get back to you as soon as we can."

"Clara Kocsis," a woman's voice spoke loudly. "This is Vicky Filomena, the school nurse. I am calling because Audrina did not bring her lunch or snacks today—she said she forgot them at home. We are providing her with school lunch, and I will give her some snacks from my office, but I wanted to let you know, in case you want to bring them over. Please call me if you have any questions."

I followed Nurse Vicky's voice down the stairs and, in the silence following the end of her message, glanced around the kitchen. Audrina's lunch was nowhere to be found—not in the kitchen, not in the laundry room, nor in the closet where we kept our winter coats. It was unlike my sister; as careless as she was sometimes about her diabetes, she'd never forgotten the food Mother fastidiously packed for her each day. Where could she have left it? Perhaps in the car? Somewhere on school grounds? The anger at my sister deepened as the wrongs multiplied in my memory. Helping herself to my clothes. Saying terrible things to me. And now forgetting her lunch. Inconveniencing others. She was self-centered. Selfish. Mother was busy; she couldn't just whip up more food and pop over to school.

When I'd first gotten up, I thought about how I might later tell Audrina I'd been mistaken about Father and Mrs. Baker—it seemed long over between the two of them, anyway—but now I saw it didn't matter. My sister didn't believe me. She was too weak, too unwilling, to accept the truth.

The door to the garage caught my eye, and I walked over. Perhaps she'd forgotten her lunch while putting on her shoes, I thought. Gazing from the garage doorway at the shoe rack that lined the wall, I didn't at first notice the brown bag. But then, as I stepped into the space, I spied it: It was placed neatly in the bottom of the shoe rack, in the spot where Audrina normally kept her Converse sneakers.

One brown bag and, behind it, one Ziploc containing half an apple. Imposters of shoes.

I started to pull the food out and then stopped. What was I doing? What could I do, anyway? Mother wasn't home. The school was already giving Audrina lunch. There was nothing for me—for Mother—to do. Audrina needed to figure it out. She couldn't rely on us all the time.

And clearly I couldn't rely on her. I would be forced once again to face the burden of Father's secrets alone. Why? Why couldn't she trust me? Why couldn't she be there for me when I most needed her? I felt forsaken. My whole body came to vibrate, consumed by emotion. Now I wanted her to hurt the way I was hurting, mercury rising on a hot thermometer.

I shoved the lunch and snack deeper into the back of the shoe rack, against the wall, past where her white Converse would normally be positioned. Then I went inside, and while passing by the answering machine with its blinking red light, I clicked the message button to play, so that it wouldn't show we had a new message anymore. Mother wouldn't need to be bothered; now she wouldn't know.

Those white scuffed Converse sneakers with hot-pink laces ambled down the halls of Hillside, traveling from Señora Flannigan's Spanish class, where my sister accidentally used the word *dólar* for *dolor*, to Mrs. Dongle's social studies class, where she forgot the name of the Louisiana Purchase. In gym, Audrina complained she had a stomachache, and those sneakers rested on the sidelines while the other kids played basketball.

Not herself, her friends said. Quiet, preoccupied. Not Audrina.

As three o'clock neared, the sneakers paused at her locker, the one I would later discover had empty watermelon-flavored Jolly

Rancher wrappers strewn across its floor, homemade holiday cards from her friends stuffed onto the top shelf, and a crinkled magazine picture of Tom Cruise taped on the back of its metal door. My sister pulled out her tote and, as the final bell rang, walked down the gray vinyl hall, likely skirting to the left to avoid contact with a dark, brownish stain of dubious origin near Mrs. Dongle's classroom, a move all of us kids did. She headed to the gymnasium, which was nearly empty, save for Phil, the janitor, and only then would she realize that there was no play practice the day before winter vacation.

It was the last time she would continue onward, through the school lobby, where she would accidentally drop her fluorescent-yellow wool hat—the one Brian Roslin had lent her on a sledding trip the previous winter that she purposely never returned. She probably let go of the hat while stopping to tie a sneaker; her laces always came undone because she was never meticulous enough to double-knot. The hat would be placed in the lost-and-found box outside Mrs. Fitz's office, where it would sit for months. I would pass by the hat and look at it, but never touch it. One day it would be gone, along with the other misplaced scarves, gloves, and hats, likely on its way to the Salvation Army.

It was the last time my sister would exit through the school's double glass doors, calling out "See ya" to a friend—Samantha, a shy classmate who would later share with me how Audrina always went out of her way to be nice to her. A few people—Mrs. Wiley, Michael-the-mailman, Mrs. Rodale—would spot my sister as she made her way down Main Street, her light brown ponytail bouncing side to side as she walked. She looked straight ahead, not turning even when Hope asked her mom to do a quick beep of the horn.

It was the last time Audrina would traverse Main Street at the traffic light—the only one in our town—and continue down the intersecting Park Road. She would turn left and leave the outside world, as she entered the town library.

When our doorbell rang a little after six o'clock, I was puzzled. Whenever Audrina came home from play practice—usually catching a ride from Beth, a seventh grader who lived nearby—she entered through the garage. I peered through the dining room window drapes but couldn't make out who it was; the sun had gone down, and our outside lights were still off. Flicking the switch on, I opened the door and found, to my surprise, Officer Jimmy. He was not in his uniform but rather wore a brown leather bomber jacket and jeans. His patrol car was parked on the driveway, a few feet away. "Hello?" I asked, curious why he was at our house.

"Bee," Officer Jimmy wheezed. His face was red, and he was breathing heavily. "Are your parents home?"

"No."

"No?"

"No. Can I help you?"

He turned his head to glance up the street, like he was checking if he could see them. "Are you expecting them soon?"

"Yes, Mother went shopping but was supposed to be back by din- nertime. So any minute now. And my father's at work but should be coming home soon." Almost as an afterthought—or more to myself— I said, "And Audrina's not home yet, either."

At the sound of my sister's name, Jimmy's face blanched. He looked down at the ground, and I saw that his forehead was moist, almost sweaty. "Are you okay, Jim—Officer Fort?"

"Fine," he said, pulling a tissue out of his leather jacket and blotting his head. "Can I come in?"

I paused, unsure what to make of his request. Was he asking as a cop or as a neighbor? Was something wrong? Just then, I spotted a pair of headlights making its way down our street. I knew it was our Jeep, both from the sound of its engine and the car's motion. Mother always pushed down hard on the pedal once she turned onto Hickory, and then would ease up as she rounded the bend. "There's my mother," I said, jerking my chin in her direction.

The Jeep slowed almost to a stop when it reached the driveway—likely because Mother had noticed the patrol car. She then cautiously inched up to our house, parking right behind Jimmy. Mother stepped out of the car, into the illumination of our house lamppost, and her face slackened, the elasticity leaving it. I sensed in her a subdued fear, almost as if she knew something terrible was coming. And then the fear hit me, too, and I felt a little woozy. My heart started to beat a little faster. I grabbed onto the door frame.

"Mrs. Kocsis," Officer Jimmy started, bringing his hands halfway up and then back down.

Mother looked at me with an expression I couldn't interpret, and then her eyes traveled to the empty space behind me.

"Can we go inside?" Jimmy said, his voice cracking. I now stepped fully out onto the front stoop. Something wasn't right. The night was cold and clear, and I noticed how the dark sky was so striking. The smell of meat—hamburger—drifted toward me. The Greens—who lived behind us, on the other side of the pond, were grilling on their deck. They always grilled, no matter the weather.

"No," Mother said. "Tell me." I looked back and forth between Mother and Jimmy, my head going left to right to left to right to left. Something wasn't right, but the sky was so beautiful. My stomach grumbled; I hadn't eaten in a while. Cereal late in the morning but nothing else.

"Clara," Jimmy now said to Mother, taking a step toward her. Beautiful sky. Hamburger meat.

They say time slows down, distorts, in moments of crisis. I would read about this phenomenon as an adult, how a part of the brain called the amygdala becomes more active in emotional situations, laying down new, extra bricks of memory, in addition to the normal sets of memories we create. It's why pivotal moments are seared within us with all their sensory glory. The more memory bricks your amygdala builds, the longer you believe the event lasted. It's also why time appears to speed up when you're older—as a child you are building a brand-new brick house of memories, each one fresh and original, but as an adult your house is already built, and it just oc-casionally needs some new bricks. You live in your house—the house that memories built—surrounded by and defined by your bricks. Some might say trapped within them, even.

Mother held up her hand like a stop sign, like she was directing traffic, and Jimmy halted. Life halted. "Bee, go inside," she ordered me, but she was fixed on Jimmy.

"But Mother—"

"NOW."

Just then Jimmy's car radio crackled from his partly rolled-down window. I couldn't make out exactly what the transmitted voices were saying, but I swore I heard them say "Audrina Kocsis." Mother was still standing in the same position, her hand spread, midair, but her head was now cocked toward the car. Jimmy rushed over to fiddle with the radio, silencing it.

"Bee," Mother commanded. Still not meeting my gaze.

I slipped through the front door, as if I was acquiescing, but then turned back toward Mother and Jimmy to stand in the door frame. The house was warm and smelled like home, and outside was cold and hamburger meat and an earth that was stuck. I was wearing only a T-shirt. I stood, goose-bumped arms crossed, straddling two worlds: Outside was unknown, and inside remained safe, known. But I couldn't go inside, even though outside was both beautiful and cold and starry and terrible.

Jimmy approached Mother and said something in a low voice. It was a few seconds and it was a few hours and it was the rest of our lives. Time recoiled, spit. Mother collapsed on the ground, limbs askew, stop sign dissolved. Mother dissolved. Time, overcome, dissolved. Jimmy crouched down and gathered her in his arms as she shook, a human earthquake.

The beautiful sky. Stars twinkling and beautiful sky and night cold and clear and Audrina and oh my god oh my god oh my god no no no but the sky is so beautiful so how can that be?

There is devastation, and there is relief.

Mother's fear, the fear that was ubiquitous among all the mothers in Hammend, did not come true. One of her daughters had not been abducted, had not died in the same manner as Sally.

But her daughter was still dead. My sister—dead.

Audrina walked into the library and was wheeled out on a gurney, her body covered with a sheet. Delivered to the coroner.

Officer Jimmy and, later, Chief Riley stood in our family room, opposite us. My father sat at one end of our tan couch, the yellow flower pillow drawn across his chest, like a shield. Mother was perched stiffly at the other end—her back one long board, but her mouth moving. She kept repeating "No, no" as Officer Jimmy and Chief Riley spoke. I was standing next to the high-back armchair, but I was diminishing, shrinking into my body, my breath, my heartbeat—which was going fast, as if trying to compensate for Audrina's.

Here's what they told us: Mrs. Hatcher, the librarian, found my sister. Tripped over her, actually, in the lower-level room. The room was dark, one of the lights having burned out (Mrs. Hatcher had set aside a replacement for the handyman). She frantically called 9-1-1, and the paramedics came, but they couldn't get a pulse. They tried, they tried. Jimmy was off duty, but he heard the call over the radio and rushed over. He watched as they tried to resuscitate. They tried, Officer Jimmy and Chief Riley assured us. Like that mattered. Dead is dead is dead. Audrina was dead is dead.

"Was it her sugar?" I managed to squeak. "She—she has diabetes." All I could see was the forgotten brown lunch bag, sitting in the bottom of the shoe rack. And then: my hands pushing it farther in.

Chief Riley nodded; he seemed to already know that. I remembered Audrina's medical bracelet, worn in case of emergency. "It very well could have been," he replied. "She could've had low blood sugar and passed out. It looks like she hit her head against the corner of the bookshelf when she fell."

Mother suddenly bent forward, like she was examining something on the ground, and Father remained impassively staring ahead. *Borka Kocsis*, a woman's voice seemed to whisper in my ear, *this is Vicky Filomena, the school nurse.*

"The coroner is performing an autopsy," Chief Riley continued, "which will take a few days. So we'll get some definitive answers then."

"An unfortunate accident," Officer Jimmy lamented. "Such a shame. She was such a pretty girl. Everyone was always talking about how pretty she was."

At that moment, Mother threw up all over the floor. Orange

spews and then liquid. Father and I just watched, with a sense of detachment, and even Chief Riley and Officer Jimmy hesitated for a moment before running into the other room to grab something to help.

When she was done, she sat straight again and wiped her mouth with a napkin Jimmy handed her. The vomit was in a pool at her feet—the useless waste can Chief Riley had retrieved from the bathroom off to the side. "I used the back roads," she simply said, and at first I thought she was working out how she hadn't seen the police cars or fire truck on her way home. But when she added, in a flat voice, "Why did I use the back roads," I realized she was grasping for what she could have done to prevent this.

Mother was on the back roads and Father was at work and I was at home, burying the message on the answering machine.

"I'm so sorry," Chief Riley said, and then Officer Jimmy repeated this. Then they both said it again, like they'd come to the end of a music stanza and encountered the repeat sign. They moved toward the door, because it was clear there was nothing more to say: Our silences were now the verse.

"It's my fault," Mother said, her voice muffled, once we'd heard the door close. I sank into a chair and began snapping my head, like I could make myself wake up, like it could all go away if I just shook my head hard enough.

The three of us felt incomplete, wrong. Something—rather, someone—was missing. The Christmas tree was next to us, in the corner, wearing the ornaments my sister and I had hung yesterday. The oversized reindeer looked back at us. Yesterday—was that really just yesterday? The framed pictures on the garland-covered mantel were of all four of us: in bathing suits at the Jersey shore, crowded around Audrina's sixth-birthday cake, posing with a mall Santa.

*No*, I wanted to correct Mother. *It was my fault.* I looked over at the desk in the kitchen, where we kept the answering machine. The light was steady, red—no new messages.

"All that candy," Mother continued, in a weak voice. "She always dipped into the candy. Halloween—and now, now with the holidays. She was surrounded by candy. She was not being careful with her diabetes. I should've known. She, she—" Her voice broke off.

"Clara," Father said, and then, "Borka." I thought he was saying my name just to say it, but then he said it again, a little louder. "Borka."

"Yeah?"

"You always know when her sugar is low."

I nodded; this was true.

Was a family room still called a family room when your family no longer existed?

Father moved the pillow aside and said, his voice cracking, "Where were you?"

Where was I. Mother was on the back roads and Father was at work, and I was at home, hiding the answering machine message. "I was home, sick," I said.

He gave an incomprehensible grunt and folded his head in his hands. They were the same hands that had touched Mrs. Baker.

"Come here, Bee." Mother, tearstained, beckoned, holding her arms out.

But instead, I looked toward the kitchen. It was suddenly clear that I had made yet another decision I couldn't take back. One that would forever haunt me. How had I not realized this by now? The impact of small things. Small-very-big things. Each in-the-moment decision leading to the next. Like rungs on a ladder.

"The nurse called," I started, tears raining down my cheeks. I needed to quickly make things right. The words spilled out: "She said Drina forgot her lunch. She said the school was giving her lunch and a snack. She left a message—I heard the message. I played the message, I mean. I was in the bathroom when she called, so then, when I came out, I played it."

Mother ran over to the kitchen desk, like time somehow mattered, and crowded over the machine. Old messages rang through the air, and Mother jabbed the button impatiently, trying to skip ahead to the last—and latest—message. Father rose and moved toward Mother as the voice of Vicky Filomena filled the kitchen. They stood, frozen, until Vicky stopped speaking, and the answering machine stated, "End of messages."

Mother slumped into the seat at the kitchen desk, her body crumpling. But Father grew—his voice got loud, his actions intense, his anger palpable. He slammed his fist on the desk. "And where were you?" he demanded to Mother. "Why didn't you get this message? Why didn't you drop off her lunch? Why didn't you help her?"

"I—I was out shopping, for gifts, and—and the baskets."

"I told you not to waste your time on those stupid gift baskets! You spend more effort on them than you do on your own family, on your own daughters." He grabbed one of the nearby Santa Claus mugs that Mother had lined up on the countertop, ostensibly to add to the gift baskets, and began waving it in the air. "And now Audrina is dead! Tell me: How is this possible? How can be she be dead?!"

A wildness had come over Father like I'd never seen. Mother's mouth was open, and I waited for some venom to fly out back toward Father, but she just shut her mouth and put her head down on the desk. Father was ready for a battle; his hands were balled up, the mug poised like a weapon, his face flushed.

Suddenly I wondered: Had Audrina been so upset about Father that she'd gotten distracted, careless, with her diabetes? *Let's ask her,* I thought, and that's when it really hit me. Now I saw that even though Chief Riley and Officer Jimmy had told us Audrina died, even while Mother, Father, and I were in the family room, and now in the kitchen, I'd still been waiting for my sister to walk through the door.

There was no making it right. The ladder had already been created—climbed.

A disbelief—a fury—rose within me. "And where were you, Father?" I spit at him. We matched stares, as the emotional current came to a crescendo. Words unleashed from me, unable to be contained any longer: "Were you with Mrs. Baker?"

Mother's head promptly snapped up from the desk, and she gasped, while Father's eyes widened.

"I told Audrina about you two. She knew. She knew." My voice shook; I was no longer a sister—no longer me.

Around us, the air was so thick with our family history, our heavy secrets and lies, that when Father opened his mouth to say something, he began to cough instead. As he brought his arms up toward his face, the mug slipped. It struck hard against the Formica counter, chipping it, and then shattered onto the floor.

Dead is dead is dead.

At the coroner's office, they performed the autopsy Chief Riley had mentioned. In a few days' time, we learned how Audrina's sugar had gone low, causing her to have a seizure and knock her head against the bookshelf. How all those stresses—the low blood sugar, the seizure, the head trauma—were just too much for her body to handle.

Here's what I didn't learn: Everything else. What Audrina was thinking that school day, why she'd worn my sweater instead of one of hers, why she'd been so distracted, why why why she would have been so careless with her blood sugar. What she was feeling when her sugar went low, if it made her feel awful or if it happened too quickly for her to register. An accident, Officer Jimmy had called it. No, I now wanted to correct him. Accidents were spilled drinks and items you knock over when you brush too closely against a table and the time Audrina crashed her bike. Accidents were not this. Accidents were not death.

She was never good at managing her diabetes. I knew it. We all knew—Mother, Father, Dr. Carlogie. So it wasn't my fault, really. Stupid Drina—she'd known better.

If her death hadn't happened that day, it would have happened another day. Maybe the next week or the next year. It should have happened already, really. She was so careless.

Stupid Audrina. I couldn't always be there for her, to save her. She'd probably been binging on holiday candy for days beforehand and doing her little insulin self-adjustments. The container of chocolate-covered cherries Leah had given me a few days before Audrina died was nearly empty by her last morning, and I'd eaten only two. I remember seeing a chocolate wrapper floating in our toilet bowl sometime that week, having not flushed properly.

I told myself this—that it wasn't my fault. And then in the next breath, I would feel the exact opposite. I knew she'd been cheating on her blood sugars. I knew she'd forgotten her lunch. I knew there was a recklessness within my sister.

I knew.

*Where were you?*

# Chapter Twenty-one

THE MORNING OF AUDRINA'S FUNERAL, THE WORLD FELT REAL—
the winter settling in with a firm, jolting grip, the late December air
chilled rightly so, the way a glass of ice water feels when you first pick
it up—and my sister was dead-dead. The unfiltered sunlight made the
snow-covered ground outside look even whiter, immaculate even,
like the insides of the new furry Dearfoam slippers my sister and I
were supposed to receive at Christmas. The holiday had passed a few
days earlier, distinguished only by the gifts that someone—a
neighbor?—had carried up from beneath the tree and placed at the
foot of my bedroom door. It could have been Mrs. Wiley, or even
Leah—really any of the myriad of people who passed through our
house in the days following Audrina's death. They brought flowers
and cards and casseroles, which covered our kitchen table and counter,
and then the dining room table, and finally the coffee table in the
living room. People kept handing me plates filled with food while
inquiring, with a certain level of scrutiny, *Was I eating, had I eaten,*

*did I have enough to eat, was I hungry?*—as if I, too, were in danger of being hypoglycemic. I would just nod and move to another room to set down the untouched plate. When the plates and the rooms and the people became too much, I would slip upstairs, hiding in my bedroom closet. Burying my face in my sister's clothes, I'd cry myself to sleep.

A day earlier, Mother had appeared in my doorway, next to the pile of unopened gifts. She hadn't yet brought up what I'd said about Mrs. Baker, and I was wondering if this was going to be the moment. But instead, she cleared her throat and said, with difficulty, "Can you pick out a final outfit? You know what Audrina likes." Then she quickly corrected this to "liked." She leaned against the door frame, seeming suddenly exhausted, as if the small verb mistake had overpowered her. She closed her eyes, and the effect made her look almost ghoulish—her high, hollowed cheekbones emphasized without the offset of her large brown eyes. She was pale and thin, and I couldn't remember seeing her eat in the previous days, either. Her slight frame, her frailness, reminded me of Audrina. I felt terrible I'd confronted Father in front of her; my intention had never been to hurt *her*.

As I went through Audrina's clothes hanging in our closet, I realized that Mother was never going to address it. I knew then that she had known about Mrs. Baker, or she'd known enough in general about Father's infidelities to carve out her own reality, her own comfort level with it.

I chose the ruffled peach dress Audrina had recently worn to the winter dance, and then I began unwrapping our pile of presents. Buried in there was the leopard-print bangle I'd bought her and the pink-and-turquoise Swatch watch from our parents. I studied the Swatch and then pulled out the crown to rotate it, setting the current time. What time was it when she died? Should I instead set the Swatch to that? I knew she would have loved this gift; the bangle could have gone either way, but I put both aside. I wanted her to be buried with something I'd given her, too.

"Pipiske," Father used to affectionately call her. I remembered how his doing so would make me feel the *opposite* of girly or sweet, as I understood it to mean.

Later, as an adult, I would attempt to look up the word *pipiske*, but it wouldn't be so straightforward.

"I'm not sure it's a word you'll find in the dictionary," Father replied when I asked him about it.

But I found it; in fact, I found many meanings online for the word. I found references to a skylark bird from the lowlands of Hungary, known as a *pipiske* in folk terms; an 1800s linguist said a girl is called that when she confidently moves about like the bird. Definitions ranging from "perching on your tippy-toes"; to being a strong-willed, over-confident girl; to prancing about, striving to be pleasant and sweet. I read somewhere that in the old days it was a nickname for one who enjoys the company of others.

All this from one little word. Pipiske: a complex name for a complex girl.

I could still feel Audrina in our room; when I lay in her bed, the pillow smelled faintly of grape, remnants of the lip gloss she'd recently been wearing. Her clothes still crowded mine in the closet. She had a new ruffled purple skirt she hadn't yet worn; the tag was attached. Her hair strands clogged my hairbrush.

At Audrina's grave site there was a magical garden sprouting: peach and pink bouquets, yellow lilies, white carnations, even berried sprigs in shades of burgundy—a color my sister had never liked to wear. We were at the far end of the cemetery, opposite from where Sally's bones would eventually be laid to rest. Audrina would get a much better send-off than Sally, whose funeral would be restricted to immediate family.

Hundreds of people came to say goodbye to my sister. Maybe thousands, even—at least, that's what it felt like. Thousands of Hope Rodales. I saw Diane and Courtney, Patrick and Andrew, my third-grade teacher Mrs. Nowak. Chief Riley, Officer Dittmer, and Officer Jimmy—with his wheelchair-bound mother. All the neighbors—from Hickory Place, Oak Street, and Maple Way. All of Hillside had come—even Phil the janitor—and some from Franklin, our elementary school. They came like it was a school day, though it was still winter break. Audrina was more popular than ever, I realized as I looked around. She would have felt right at home with all the attention. This provided me with a momentary sense of comfort.

Even Max and his father stopped by for a few minutes, though his mother was absent. She was perhaps the only one who didn't come, and I wondered if it was because of Sally or because of the dissolution of her affair with Father, or both. Either way, I was relieved not to see her.

"So," Max said to me, his eyes glossy, after he'd patiently waited for a chance to approach.

"So," I replied. We just stared at each other, and I remember feeling like we were both fragments of who we once were. Broken, in the way that the young should never be.

"At least they're together now," he said as a tear escaped.

"Yeah," I replied, and then I asked, "Do you really believe that?"

"I have to." He leaned forward to hug me. We clutched each

other hard, and it felt different from other embraces we'd shared, although I couldn't pinpoint exactly how until later: It felt final, like a goodbye.

As they lowered the casket into the ground, Mother's and Father's bodies sagged like scarecrows. Mrs. Wiley anchored herself directly behind Mother, like a wooden frame, and Uncle Arpad clasped Father's elbow. I was standing in between them—on my own, I supposed; reality had skewed for me. The beauty of the wintry scene that surrounded us kept getting cut, sliced by a knife. At these moments the finality of her death—the knowledge that the box before us held my sister's dead body—would overcome me.

Audrina came to visit me the week after the funeral. *Her funeral*—those words like a sheet of sandpaper in my mouth. I could feel her: in the minutes that passed, in the space around me. Like I was in one bed, and she in the other, her breath deepening on the exhale in a familiar way while she slept. Like she was next to me in the bathroom, reaching for the same barrette I was, our hands brushing up against each other's, first softly, accidentally, and then with purpose—a small battle to claim the barrette first. Like she had been in my drawers, rifling through my shirts and plucking one without asking, making a hasty escape through our door, the scent of grape lip gloss and Agree shampoo trailing behind her.

She was so real, like if I closed my eyes and reached out, I would find her.

And then she was gone.

# Chapter Twenty-two

"HE'S DEAD NOW," MOTHER SAID ONCE ABOUT GRANDPA JOE, AND she said it again, this time about my sister, one early February morning as she stood in my room: "She's dead now." There was a hardened edge about Mother that appeared almost overnight. For weeks she'd been so sad, tired, and frail, barely getting out of her pajamas. But then that morning she dressed, put hot rollers in her hair, and applied mascara over her shadowed eyes, and I could feel that the softness in her had solidified, like a cooked egg. She clutched an empty gift basket in her hand, an indication she had some sort of plan.

I was still in bed. Since school had resumed after the winter holidays, I'd adopted a Max-like pattern of attendance—some days skipping, other days going and then hiding out in Mrs. Fitz's office. It was hard to get away because everyone surrounded me, wanting to somehow help—Leah, Hope Rodale, Gwen, Mrs. Dongle, Mr. Hoosier—everyone. But they couldn't help, and all I wanted was to be left alone. At school I'd begun wearing a black beanie I'd discovered in our coat closet, which one of our visitors must have left behind. I would tug the band down, only half caring whether people knew I pulled my hair, and wishing I could just disappear.

Father, too, had grown inward. Even when he was home, he didn't speak to Mother or me. He would go into his study and shut the door, bringing with him the dinner that Mother would leave out on the kitchen counter.

"She's dead," Mother repeated, and now she added, "and we're not. Get up."

"Mother," I protested, "I don't want to go to school."

"You're not going to school. You're going somewhere else," she countered. "We're leaving in ten minutes. Get ready."

The somewhere else was Dr. Pat, a psychologist. Mother dropped me off at the office front door so she could park, but then she didn't return until after my appointment, and I wonder if she'd done that deliberately, so I couldn't avoid going to see this Dr. Pat.

She was not what I would have thought a psychologist looked like. She was young, younger than Mother at least, and wore black jeans with a black leather jacket, like she had a motorcycle parked around the corner. Perhaps she did. "How are you feeling?" she asked, after introducing herself and leading me into her office, which looked remarkably plain, other than framed wall pictures of exotic-looking sites she'd traveled to. There was a sofa and two chairs that surrounded a wooden coffee table. A fish tank bubbled in the corner. I took one of the chairs, noticing Dr. Pat riding an elephant in one photo and standing atop a volcano in another. She sank into the other seat, across from me.

"How do you think?" I responded, irritated that I was stuck with this woman.

Dr. Pat nodded. "Shitty, I bet." Her tone was matter-of-fact.

I was surprised; I wasn't accustomed to grown-ups swearing around me. "Yep."

"Do you want to talk about it?" she asked, leaning forward across the coffee table in my direction.

"Nope."

"Okay, then." She put her feet up on the table and leaned back in her chair. "Look, I can only help you if you want to be helped."

"I don't want to be helped."

"Okay, then."

"Well, aren't you going to try? Isn't that your job?"

"Your mother says you pull your hair," Dr. Pat replied.

"What?"

"Do you pull your hair?"

I shifted, feeling suddenly uncomfortable. "My mother knows?"

"Yes."

"How does she know?"

Dr. Pat shrugged. "Beats me. It doesn't really matter, though, does it? She knows, and you do it?"

I realized she was asking me. "Yes," I whispered.

"I bet that's the last thing you care about right now, though."

The coffee table in front of me started to blur as my eyes filled with water. "Yes," I whispered again.

"Well, there's some things that might help. I had a patient once who used to pull her hair, and she would tape mittens around her hands, to stop herself."

I wiped a tear that had started to trickle down my cheek. "Did it work?"

Dr. Pat sighed. She still had her feet up on the table. "I don't think so."

"Do you—do you think it's worth a try?" I asked, wondering if there was hope for me.

Dr. Pat shrugged again. "Sure, why not. It's up to you."

"Aren't you supposed to know?" I was beginning to feel a little insulted by her cavalier attitude. "Why am I even here?"

Dr. Pat put her feet down on the ground and leaned forward. "Look, losing your sister is terrible. It might just be the worst thing that ever happens to you in your life. I can't help that. I'm going to take off my therapist hat for a moment and share that I actually lost one of my siblings when I was young. It was devastating, and I never thought I would be okay. But here I am. I can help you get through this. If you want my help."

We matched stares, and I recognized Mother's hardness within her. "So this is how it's going to be?"

She nodded. "Yes, it is."

"Okay."

"Okay, what?"

"Okay, okay." I replied.

"You have to say it."

"I don't know what you want me to say." I was feeling exasperated. This was beginning to feel like a game of cat and mouse.

Dr. Pat tilted her head. "Say what you are feeling. Right now—and don't hold back."

I thought of my sister's diary, which I'd now read in its entirety. She'd lied to me—and Mother—about diabetes camp. She'd hated it; the girls were mean, and her only friend had been Kate. *The most awful thing happened. They took my clothes and towel when I was in the shower in the bathhouse. I had to wait NAKED in the stall until the next girl came. I wanted to die I was so embarresed.* My sister had written me, after all. Multiple times. Her letters were all enclosed in her diary; she'd just never sent them because I had never sent her one. *Dear Bee, it's Day 7. 1 week done, 1 week to go. Bee, I really could use a letter from you right now . . . Dear Bee, Day 9. Do you have the wrong address? I don't understand why I didn't get a letter from you yet. I told Kate all about you and she told me about her sister. But her sister sends her letters . . . To Bee, Day 13. Bee, you suck. You suck almost as much as camp does. I'm never sending this letter. I'm never coming back to this dump, either.* I hadn't known I caused my sister so much hurt by not writing her; I hadn't known she was so vulnerable. I hadn't known my sister could ever be unpopular.

My sister's last entry was the one, though, that had nearly undone me:

> *Dear Sally,*
> *I can't believe you are DEAD. I'm so sorry. It's not fair. I can't believe it. Everything is so confusing. I think about death a lot. It's hard not to when you have diabetes. Bee said the most terrible thing about Father today. I can't even write what it was. She said it either because: 1) it's true 2) she's mad at me that I want to tell Mother about her hair 3) she wanted to hurt me 4) all of it. I don't think she is lying even if she wanted to hurt me. Maybe she just thinks she saw something. Father would never do that. Right??!*
> *Love,*
> *Audrina*
>
> *P.S. What happens when you die? Is it over, or are you still somehow there?*

"Well?" Dr. Pat prodded me.

"I don't know what you want from me," I snapped at her. "Do you want me to say that I feel responsible?" Dr. Pat just looked at me with an even expression, and emotions I didn't even know I had suddenly untwisted. "Do you want me to say that I should have helped her? That Audrina should be alive, and I feel like it's my fault she's not—not just because of that day but because of everything? That—that I was her older sister, so it was my responsibility? That—that I failed her in so many ways I can't even tell you? That I want her to know how much I loved her, and I'm afraid, so afraid, she doesn't—didn't—know that?"

A silence followed, and it struck me how the room—the air, the furniture—was exactly the same as it had been a minute earlier, even though I was now unhinged. Dr. Pat simply looked at me, and later I would associate the quiet restraint that surrounded us then with the field of medicine. This waiting that occurred, during appointments and in waiting rooms; the uncertainty that therapy or pills or tests could make you better; the unknowing of how long we had to live. Hopefulness combined with the hopelessness, in a single straight line. It was what my sister must have felt during Dr. Carlogie's office visits, and in the hospital, with the nurses flitting in and out of her room, as she likely hoped someone could bring her a crystal ball and magic potion, though she knew such things didn't exist.

*What happens when you die? Is it over, or are you still somehow there?*

I began to tell Dr. Pat the story of us.

# Chapter Twenty-three

My house of memory bricks must have been almost completely built by the time I turned fourteen, because my recollections in the years following Audrina's death are ill-defined, conforming to the already-present memories, like they were simply the mortar filling the spaces between the slabs.

Mother was tough, and Father was distant, and it was in this way that I continued to grow up. My life was filled with accidental awkward pauses, where people would mention Audrina or their own sister and then look at me and apologize, or just look at me and then I would feel the need to apologize, like somehow it was my fault they were reminding me of my dead sister.

My bedroom was cleared of Audrina's belongings a few months after her death; one day her stuff, including her bed, was there, and the next, when I came home from school, it was gone. Some of my own shirts and belongings had been inadvertently grouped into her pile, which I found ruefully amusing and wanted to share with

Audrina. That happened a lot—wanting to tell my sister things until the cold realization of her death would sweep back into my consciousness. Mother never revealed what she did with my sister's stuff; only later would I realize—when I became a mother, and she showed up one day at my doorstep with a sealed box—that she'd put aside select items for me to have, and to share with my own children. But back then, we didn't discuss the disappearance of my sister's stuff. We didn't discuss a lot of things. Among the topics we avoided: the day Audrina died, Mrs. Baker, Sally Baker, Father's withdrawal into his own world, my hair-pulling.

Trichotillomania, the official name for hair-pulling, would be formally recognized in the *Diagnostic and Statistical Manual of Mental Disorders* in 1987, the year following Audrina's death. Habit reversal training would be the recommended treatment, with the goal of performing "competing responses"—clenching my hands, for instance—when the urge occurred.

Habit reversal training would not be effective for me. Dr. Pat, who I would see for several years, gave it a royal effort. Physical force—the taping of my wrists—which I tried at night, would also not be effective. Nothing would be effective—ever. I would just get better at it, more strategic. As an adult, I would notice patterns: the urges would intensify right before my menstrual cycles and then abate afterward. When the desire was overwhelming, I would focus on pulling predetermined spots, where boyfriends—and, eventually, my husband—never noticed.

Leah and I would stay close, and Max would get sent to boarding school in Massachusetts for ninth grade, the fall following the discovery of his sister's body. Gwen, one of Hope Rodale's sidekicks, would eventually become a very close friend of mine—and no longer one of Hope's. In high school we would wear all black and dye our hair with purple and blue streaks and smoke joints during free period at the corner of the parking lot, where the teachers pretended not to see us. During senior year we would protest the notion of popularity by abstaining from voting for homecoming court, though it did not matter—Hope Rodale won by a landslide.

Soon after Sally's body was found, Mrs. Baker would enter rehab—someplace in Atlanta, or at least that's what people said: a facility where a famous baseball player had gone. Or maybe it was in Florida. The information got distorted back then, secondhand and thirdhand, like a game of telephone. When Mrs. Baker returned a few months later, she was wearing a chestnut-brown fur coat. She wore the coat nearly all the time, sometimes even in the summer, like it was her new robe. She'd be in the front yard, in ninety-degree weather, smoking her Virginia Slims, and no one wanted to associate with her. Even Father stopped his obligatory nod when we drove past. Over the years, Mrs. Baker played a ping-pong game of rehab, going back and forth, until the ball settled firmly in some other court—where, we didn't know. Dr. Baker was alone in the house, until one day during my junior year in high school, a Weichert Realtors *For Sale* sign was erected on his unkempt lawn. The new family who moved in had a baby girl, and I wondered if they'd had any reservations. They had to have known about Sally. They painted the green shutters a rather optimistic shade of yellow and completely redid the front yard. They removed the asphalt circular driveway in its entirety, filling in the U-shaped portion with green grass and colorful plants, and placed a straight, interlocking-stone driveway that ran directly from the street to their garage. I doubted its surface would accommodate chalk drawings.

Mother would channel her grief into the creation of personalized gift baskets. "Audrina's Gifts," she began calling them, and she went door-to-door, selling prearranged baskets and taking future orders. The neighbors bought them. Whether it was initially out of pity or desire, who can say, but at some point, word spread, and her gift baskets became in demand. The gourmet store on Main Street began stocking baskets in their display window, as did the antique furniture store, and then it was only a matter of time before nearly all the storefronts in Hammend had an Audrina's Gifts basket sitting front and center.

Mother struggled to fulfill all the orders, and the first time she asked me to help, she'd watched me like a hawk as I filled one basket, pulling items like candles and chocolates and bath soaps from her stash. When I started to enclose the arrangement with heavy-duty clear wrapping, Mother stopped me. "This is not nearly done," she said. "Or correct. Watch carefully," she commanded as she proceeded to reassemble the whole thing. It looked the same to me as when I'd done it, but over the course of a couple months, under Mother's careful tutelage, I began to understand the nuances and appreciate Mother's artistry. At some point, Mother felt confident enough in my basket-assembly skills that I could just show the final product to her for approval.

As her business continued to grow, Mother hired staff and took over the antique store when it went out of business, converting it to her main office, and then leased a warehouse in Etchers. Delivery personnel routinely drove through Hammend and our neighboring towns in vans labeled *Audrina's Gifts*.

Father would look away if we were in the car together and passed one of the vans, as if it pained him to see my sister's name. He had never returned to normal after Audrina's death—his personality flattened, as if life no longer held the possibility of pleasure. The interactions we had with each other were short, direct. Necessities. It was as though the day I lost Audrina, I also lost my father. Or maybe Father and I had mutually lost each other, unwilling to carve out a relationship that could stand on its own and move forward, unfettered by the past.

The only times Father seemed to resuscitate himself were when he was out in the backyard in the warm weather, or in the garage or basement in cold weather, making furniture, with the thick, hearty aroma of wood surrounding him. Every few months a new chair or table or dresser would appear, pushed against the basement wall or side of our garage. I don't believe Father made the furniture in order to sell it, but one day, when the furniture had infringed upon our parking spots, Mother arranged for her drivers to move a few pieces to the Hammend office, where they rested in the old antique display window, manila price tags attached. They went fairly quickly, and from then on, Mother periodically offloaded the furniture.

Audrina's Gifts would pay for my four years of college education, which I completed in upstate New York at a small liberal arts school, majoring in history. I was fascinated—and reassured—by the study of events and people who'd lived and died long before I was ever born, the way we continued to exist, as a society, despite and because of our past tragedies. During the summers, I would return home and help out with Audrina's Gifts, which, as it entered the internet age, only continued to expand. Mother remained as meticulous as ever about the presentation of the baskets; though she had long since ceased to assemble them personally, every single one still needed her visual approval—and so I went from apprentice to teacher, instructing others to carefully watch as I redid their baskets, time and time again, until they, too, became proficient. I also helped oversee the fulfillment of the company's online orders and, after my graduation, became involved in the nonprofit arm Mother decided to create. It wasn't automatically assumed I would go into the business, but I felt like it was my responsibility to my sister to do so.

The Audrina Kocsis College Scholarship was designated for a type 1 diabetic, and each year Mother and I would travel to a high school graduation to present the award to a student who, more often than not, used an insulin pump, and I couldn't help but feel a twinge of jealousy and resentment that my sister had not lived long enough to have tried this technology, which only continued to evolve through the years.

Even as I got older, I would still feel Audrina. She would be there in a way I can't perfectly describe. It's like the feeling that someone else is in the room with you, but it was even more encompassing than that. She was a presence and a memory, with me and in me. She was familiar and natural—a sister. But she was not the Audrina I had known; she was changed, reduced—a whisper.

I remember asking Mother once, shortly after Audrina died, if she thought Audrina still existed somehow.

"You'll always find something if you are looking for it," Mother had replied.

So I guess, as an adult, I started seriously looking, because sisters began to constantly surround me. Everywhere I looked, I saw them: I recognized the way sisters walked together, closer than friends do, their barometer of personal space on a different scale. I noticed sisters at the mall who had the same mannerisms—the same way of tilting their heads, even when their noses looked different, even when their hair or eye color did not match. They sometimes wore the same colored clothes, and I imagined they didn't plan it. I recognized sisters sitting across from me on the train I took regularly in my twenties into New York City on the weekends, once I'd started dating my future husband, Sam, and before he moved to New Jersey. The giveaway was the similar manner in which they crossed their legs. They spoke in sister-language: silences brimming with inside jokes, inflections that implied either questions or statements. They were like twins without being twins, their bodies connected like fused genes, translocations of DNA.

Then I would spot the sisters who didn't walk closely together, who couldn't stand to be near each other in the coffee shop line. I once witnessed two sisters saying the nastiest things to each other.

I wondered which set of sisters Audrina and I would have been.

As the years passed, I would look around my house of memory bricks and see the history Audrina and I had shared written like graffiti on its walls. I would run my fingers along the surface, revisiting our childhood, recalling our own terrible words, the fights, the hurt. The pain—but then also the beauty. The shared jokes, the kindness, *our* unspoken language. I would try to piece together this life of mine that had been created, how I had gotten to where I was.

And where was I? I'd stayed in Hammend; I was the only one left from the old neighborhood. Everyone else was long gone, some to nearby New Jersey towns, others, like Max, farther away: Seattle. The last time I'd seen him was in high school, when he was home one weekend from boarding school and we bumped into each other at the Hammend video store. We awkwardly made small talk for a few minutes, fumbling over our words, leaving everything unsaid.

I'd more than stayed in town, though. I'd become a Hammend businesswoman, wife—mother, even, to two daughters. And I was all these things because of Audrina's Gifts. I'd met Sam when he and his brothers came into our store looking for a gift for their local ailing mother. I was struck by the warmth and consideration between him and his siblings.

There I was, entrenched in a life that had been shaped by the absence of my sister.

I wondered what my life, my "house," would've looked like had things been different. Had Sally Baker not gone missing. Cause and effect, a central tenet of history. Would I have stayed in Hammend? Married Sam? What would have led to what?

And the big question, the one that always lingered: If I hadn't taken the charm bracelet piece, would Sally have been found earlier?

As an adult, my perspective on past events was clearer, sharper.

They still would have searched the lake first. They had to. But I recalled the question Chief Riley asked me the day we'd returned to the lake: "You didn't see anyone, or you *couldn't* see anyone?"

Was the location where I'd found the bracelet piece obstructed enough from view that someone could have snatched Sally without others noticing? I still couldn't answer that.

Sometimes I imagined going back in time to that day at the lake: My twelve-year-old self would show the charm bracelet piece to one of the concerned mothers, who would immediately scan the nearby woods—the section past the porta potties. Then she'd take off, racing through the woods with a protective maternal instinct—the search party masses following behind—culminating in a successful rescue of Sally.

And, if I had not taken the charm bracelet piece, would my relationship with my sister have been better? Probably not. Distance from events contracts them, but when you stretch them out, an accordion of actions, you see they are all still related, intertwined by the connecting bellows.

We would not have fought about the bracelet, but other issues would have stepped into its place. She was beautiful in a way that made me not. She was Father's favorite. She was complex, and we were complex, in that terrible religion-of-sisters way.

I didn't step in to help her the day she forgot her lunch. But what, really, could I have done? Tracked Mother down? I wouldn't have known which store to call. Tried Father at work to tell him—what, exactly? How Audrina had forgotten her lunch, but the school was providing it? He would have been annoyed that I bothered him. And it's not like I would have thrown Audrina's lunch in my bag and biked on over to Hillside to drop it off. Or accompanied Audrina to the library, forcing sugared orange juice into her mouth once she'd started to display familiar hypoglycemic signs.

But I could have. I could have done all of that. And I would have, had I known the outcome.

These thoughts were insidious, festering in me, growing alongside my daughters when their bodies bloomed inside me. So, like many people do when troubling thoughts preclude sleep, I went online. I tried to construct a timeline of it all, hoping that would help me to organize my thinking, to help me understand how it all came to be, these rungs on the ladder. I started at the beginning, the very beginning—which meant Sally Baker: searching for newspaper articles the day Sally went missing, the theories surrounding her disappearance, the specifics of when she was found. The lack of possible suspects; the mystery of who had killed her. The deconstruction of the Lake Girl, the origins of the Boston Family. For a fee of $29.95, I purchased a six-month access to the online archives of our New Jersey paper.

Sally's disappearance had been covered thoroughly, and I became fully immersed, swimming in it all. While our customers were online, buying the Audrina's Gifts "Picnic Time" basket, with the upgraded bottle of pinot noir, or the "Supreme Country Time" basket, with the organic option, I was in the world of dead and disappearing children. Some of the articles about Sally were familiar, my twelve-year-old eyes having previously digested them. Others were new to me. I didn't really learn anything I hadn't already known, and my internet searches would invariably pull up news stories about other children's abductions and disappearances. There were so many.

I would move on to a search for Audrina, which would only produce things related to the company: the brief description Mother had posted of Audrina in the company's "about" section (though no photograph), news detailing the recipients of the Audrina Kocsis Scholarship. Nothing, frustratingly, about my sister's life on its own. Nothing about her death. Not even her obituary. The local town paper had gone out of business years earlier, and there was no online access to their archives. Perhaps the public library would have microfilm rolls, I thought. But I had no plans to ever set foot again in Hammend's library.

The dearth of online information about Audrina felt imbalanced, somehow unjust; there should be something about her, just like there was something about Sally. A tugging sensation inside me made me feel as if Audrina were agreeing. But I wouldn't know where else to look, what else to do.

In my mind, certainly, Audrina and Sally were connected, though back then we were all connected in the neighborhood. Back then we were just regular kids, getting through another summer, one day impatiently waiting for the rain to pass, the next sweating under the hot sun. Chalk-smudged fingers and chlorine-tinged swimsuits. Kickball and crushes.

During the summer of '85—back before everything changed—we were all alive, in our little world, our front doors less than one hundred feet apart.

# Epilogue

# THE NEW JERSEY LEDGER

## POLICE OFFICER DEAD FOR YEARS LINKED TO 1985 MURDER OF LOCAL 4-YEAR-OLD GIRL

### *Genetic genealogy was used to connect crime scene DNA to the suspect*

HAMMEND, N.J., Oct. 3, 2018—On July 25, 1985, four-year-old Sally Baker vanished while swimming at Deer Chase Lake, a popular public swimming grounds at the time.

Her degraded remains were found the following year on a local farm, two miles from the lake. It was determined Sally had died of blunt force trauma, and sexual assault couldn't be ruled out. The community of Hammend, a tight-knit, 5,000-person New Jersey town, was rocked. There were no leads, and the case went cold.

"For 33 years, Sally Baker's death remained a mystery. Today, thanks to our hardworking investigators, DNA, and genetic genealogy, we are finally able to identify the suspect," said Merris County Deputy District Attorney Robert Bank, head of his office's cold case unit, at a news conference.

"The department never gave up hope that we would find Sally's killer," added Bank.

In 2013, investigators decided to take another look at her case. They sent clothing obtained from the crime scene to the lab, where scientific advances were able to detect new biological evidence. From that, a DNA profile of her suspected killer was created and entered into the Combined DNA Index System (CODIS), a national computer database that stores DNA from convicted offenders and crime scenes.

Unfortunately, CODIS did not find a match. It was a start, but it wasn't enough—at least not yet, said Bank. "We had the suspect's DNA, but no suspect."

Four years later, a match was made, with forensic DNA obtained from a decades-old rape crime.

"In 1997, a six-year-old girl in Arborville, Pennsylvania, was assaulted while walking home from school," said Bank. "The rape kit failed to show workable evidence, but twenty years later, the investigators took a second look and found what they needed." Pennsylvania police still had in their possession the clothes the girl had worn to the hospital. Investigators sent these clothes to the crime lab, where forensic DNA was obtained and entered into CODIS. The DNA of the rape suspect matched the DNA of Sally Baker's suspected killer.

"So here you have two crimes, one in New Jersey and one in Pennsylvania, that occurred twelve years apart. We knew we were dealing with the same suspect. We were getting closer. But we had only the suspect's DNA profile. Still no actual suspect," said Bank.

Enter genetic genealogy, the same technique that was used to crack the Golden State Killer case earlier this year. Genetic genealogy compares unknown DNA forensic evidence to public genealogy databases, such as GEDmatch, where family members may have voluntarily uploaded their DNA.

Merris County investigators used an online public genealogy database to trace the family relatives of the suspect and identified former Hammend, New Jersey, Police Officer James Fort.

Fort, a former resident of Hammend, served on their police force for six years before moving to Pennsylvania shortly after Sally's body was found. He had lived in the same neighborhood as the Baker family.

Fort joined the police department in Winchester, Pennsylvania, where he lived for twenty years before dying of cancer in 2008, at age 50. Winchester is located seventy-nine miles west of Arborville.

His body was exhumed in September of this year, and his DNA was found to be a match.

"While we can't prosecute Fort for these horrendous crimes, we hope that his identification brings the families and towns of both Hammend and Arborville some closure," Bank said. He added that while the investigations had been ongoing, the families were kept apprised of developments.

Bank noted that during Fort's time with the Winchester Police Department, he was convicted of an off-duty DUI and temporarily placed on administrative leave.

Bank suspects there may be more victims uncovered as cases continue to be reopened amid DNA advances. "It makes you wonder who else is out there, what else we'll find."

*WHEN DOES THE OBVIOUS BECOME THE OBVIOUS?*

When the story broke, our town shuddered. It was all anyone could talk about, even those who'd moved here after Jimmy left, even those who hadn't been alive at the time. At Franklin Elementary, where I dropped off my daughter Emily, and at the preschool, where I deposited my other daughter, Mia, the teachers and parents were grouped together, clutching the children with tight fingers. They gossiped, aghast. In disbelief.

But those of us who'd known Jimmy were quiet at first, processing. Struck by the obviousness of it.

I read the story over and over again, in its entirety, every time it was sent to me from the old neighborhood kids: from Diane, now a real estate agent down the Jersey shore; from Courtney, a New York–based writer; from the Wiley brothers—Andrew, a gastroenterologist in Chicago, and Patrick, a fifth-grade teacher in Etchers. We reached

out to one another, some of us connecting for the first time in years
No one looped Max into the conversation; I'm not sure we could have,
even if we wanted to. He'd fallen out of touch with everyone.

We all posed the same rhetorical question: *How did we not realize
about Jimmy?* We needed to know that we were not alone in our prior
obliviousness.

It had been right in our faces, almost too convenient to ignore:
Jimmy the cop. Jimmy the neighbor. Jimmy the caring son who never
had a family of his own. Jimmy, who'd skipped town at the perfect
time.

"Did you ever suspect him?" Leah asked when she called from
California, where she now lived.

"No," I truthfully replied. "Never."

I remembered now Jimmy's mother's fixation on Sally, which
we'd attributed to her dementia. All of the clues had been right there.

How did we miss it?

Then I realized: "The obvious" could have been any of us. Mrs.
Baker, with her eccentricities and troubled past. Dr. Baker, with
his surgical skills and conveniently parked Porsche. Michael-
the-mailman, who knew our patterns of coming and going. Mrs.
Abbott, with her busybody ways and suspicious desire to retire to
Vermont. Vittorio the pizza guy, a bit too friendly, hiding behind his
family-man facade.

The obvious was the obvious, hidden by not being hidden.

Anyone on my list—anyone in Hammend—was the obvious,
using this logic.

And that was what was so deeply troubling, that danger had
lurked among us, completely overlooked.

Now that I knew this, I couldn't unknow it.

Now I would closely examine every single adult male in my

daughters' lives. Each time a man moved to our neighborhood, or my children had a male teacher or coach. Anytime one of my girls even casually mentioned an adult male's name, my skin would prickle.

Who else out there was like Jimmy? Who else that I knew or had known? How many more were there? How many who my daughters hadn't yet encountered?

Could Sally just as easily have been me, or Audrina? Diane or Courtney? How close had we each come to being touched and murdered, left discarded in a tree?

These questions are haunting. These questions pervade. These questions will always be unanswered. These questions—*they* lurk.

Gradually, over weeks—not months—the disbelief and horror about Jimmy Fort began to fade in our town. In its place grew an absurd righteousness, a skewed lens. Hammend did, after all, have a history of self-preservation.

*That was a long time ago,* people said (as in, what a shame, but it was before our time).

*We drove him right out of here* (as if we kicked him out, instead of him voluntarily leaving).

*I don't even remember him* (as in, he's not one of us).

*One could never get away with that now* (not with today's DNA advances).

*Kids are smarter and more aware these days* (that would never happen in Hammend nowadays).

*Good thing we don't have his kind here anymore* (that would never happen in Hammend nowadays).

*Nothing like that has ever happened since* (that would never happen in Hammend nowadays).

*That would never happen in Hammend nowadays.*

"Mrs. Wiley said she always had a bad feeling about him," Mother texted me, and then texted it to me again several hours later, like she'd forgotten she sent the first message.

Chief Riley came out of retirement to issue a statement both denouncing Jimmy and distancing him from the Hammend Police Department. "James Fort was with the Hammend Police Department for six years, during which time Sally Baker was murdered. Using DNA technology, the late Mr. Fort has now been named as the primary suspect in Sally's death. Like all of Hammend, I am shocked and saddened. In my thirty-two years with the department, we never again experienced such a morally reprehensive crime. Our hearts go out to the Winchester community in Pennsylvania, where Mr. Fort served on the department for the rest of his career, and to the Arborville community, where he is suspected of committing yet another heinous crime."

It was now Jimmy-from-Pennsylvania, just like it had been the-Bakers-from-Boston.

Hammend, like many years earlier, was ready to move forward, to mark this as an anomaly, to extricate itself. More "pressing" news occupied the county paper: the upcoming holiday parade, the ongoing public objection to a proposed Dunkin' Donuts drive-thru on Main Street, the news that a local resident was awarded a merit scholarship to Cornell Law School.

Even the neighborhood gang—Diane and Courtney, the Wiley brothers, and I—who continued to keep in touch on a WhatsApp group chat that someone named The Hickory Kids, returned to exchanging Jersey-themed jokes instead of messages about Jimmy and Sally, as if we preferred humor to the sharp edge of our history.

But I couldn't move on; I'd been there that day at the lake. I was still stuck, trying to reconcile the Jimmy I'd known with the one who had been in the news. Because Jimmy *had* been one of us; he and his mother were our neighbors. He was one of our police officers. And I'd known Sally. I was perhaps one of the last people remaining from that day: Audrina was gone, Mrs. Baker gone, too—if not physically then mentally—and Max had distanced himself long ago from Hammend, leaving even my Facebook friend request from a couple years back unanswered. I was a living testament; I remembered all of it: the lifeguard, the sandcastle, the bracelet. And the aftermath— the searches, the fear it created, the way it temporarily stopped us from breathing.

And all things Sally, of course, led to Audrina.

Jimmy was the one who delivered the news that my sister had died.

We were all linked together, an incestuous relationship.

Sometime after the news about Jimmy had broken, I went into the attic of my house and pulled down the box of Audrina's childhood things that Mother had brought over for me years earlier. I'd been through them all numerous times before: my sister's light pink belted dress from her role in *Peter Pan*, a glittery headband, her fifth-grade writing assignment on the Lenni Lenape tribe, her Cabbage Patch doll, her medical bracelet. Finally I found what I was searching for: a small book, with little baskets of flowers against a pink gingham background. The lock was attached, its key still inserted from the last time I'd read it.

Through the years, I'd revisited the diary, whenever I worried Audrina was starting to fade away. Now I felt a need to open it again, but for a different reason.

I cracked it open, running my fingers over the inscription: *Dear Audrina, I hope you find this useful in recording your thoughts. Love, Mother.* And then I read. And read.

After coming to my sister's last entry, I turned the page to a blank one, creased the spine, and picked up my pen. In light of the recent revelations, I had things I wanted to share with her. It also felt like a defining part of our story had finally come to a close.

> Dear ~~Diary,~~ Drina,
>
> I don't know where to begin, so I'll start by telling you about my daughters. Emily is seven and Mia just turned five. Emily is named Emily Audrina, after you. And Mia is a just a name that I thought was pretty.
>
> They are sisters. They are we.
>
> Emily looks like you: She has your golden-brown hair, the green sea in her eyes, a popsicle-stick figure.
>
> Mia is all me: brown hair and brown eyes, a sundae shape.
>
> They are crafty, my daughters. Girl-crafty. The other day, Emily stole Mia's childhood stuffed animal, a lamb named Bah-Bah. Just because she could. Because she wanted to cause her sister angst. I had found Bah-Bah wedged in between the dryer and the wall, when I went to retrieve a fallen sock.
>
> Emily first proclaimed she didn't do it, and then later, after she admitted to it, protested that Mia was too old to have a stuffed animal, anyway.
>
> Mia retaliated by dumping out Emily's entire bottle of Taylor Swift perfume into the drain. I didn't do it, she

*mimicked and pranced around with a towel she'd saturated with the scent.*

*And then, that very night, I found them pressed together, watching TV, the same blanket wrapped around them. A sister sandwich.*

*They are amazing, and they are complicated. They are we.*

*Can I tell you something? I didn't want daughters. I wasn't even sure if I wanted kids. I was afraid I'd be a terrible mom. Not have a clue what to do. But when I got pregnant, keeping the baby seemed the logical thing to do. The expected thing. It seems like all the big decisions in my life have been safe, boring even: working for Audrina's Gifts, dating Sam—who is as levelheaded and rational a person as I've ever met (a lawyer, for goodness' sake!)—living in an apartment and, then, a house not far from our childhood home. I've crafted a carefully organized existence.*

*When the obstetrician asked Sam and me, over the ultrasound probe at our eighteen-week appointment, if we wanted to know the sex, I managed to nod. But inside I was thinking: Pleasedontbeagirlpleasedontbeagirl.*

*Then, later: When I became pregnant the second time, I already knew it was another girl, before they told me.*

*So maybe it's my chance at a redo. I don't want Emily and Mia to be us. I'd like to think that I can alter their course, that if I intervene enough, they won't make the same mistakes we did. But I worry and fear that my genes carry the imprints of our tangled history, that you and I have already unwittingly infected them.*

*At some point, as a mother, you shamefully remember how you didn't want them, before you met them, and you wonder if they've also inherited this dark secret. You hope they won't realize you have already failed them.*

*But when they arrive, motherhood is promising: their skin—their skin! Creamy, smooth, a tub of butter. Their smell, the one you sniff after they've gone to sleep, when you lean down for one last nuzzle. The smell of just skin—the best way to describe it.*

*You remember the days before they learned to speak and then the days after that. They didn't notice your coffee breath, your middle-of-the-night breath. Your sleepless-nights breath.*

*You still remember how they needed you before you needed them.*

*But then one morning one of your daughters crinkles her nose, putting wrinkles in that tub of butter, but even then, they are perfect wrinkles—fine, surface wrinkles. Made with a butter knife. You smell like fish, she says. You laugh because it's funny. And true. But then later you cry.*

*Drina, I'm sorry. Two inadequate words. It's all I can offer. I can't escape our past. There are so many things I wish I'd done differently. I would have told you every day how much I loved you, even when we fought. I knew you struggled with your diabetes, but I swear I didn't know how difficult it was. So I would have helped you as much as you needed, to the point of annoyance; I would have chased you all around town that last day of your life, force-feeding you if necessary.*

*Your absence left a hole in our family, and in me. In
everyone. You may have thought Brian Roslin wasn't into
you, but he sobbed at your funeral. All the boys did.
Everyone loved you. You were perfect, despite your diabetes.
Because of your diabetes. Because you were so brave—and
so very stupid—trying to manage it on your own.*

*It's not fair that I'm here and you're not. That I got to
grow up. Drina, we were so young. We thought we
understood the world. We thought it was our world—and I
suppose it was, then—but we didn't know what else was out
there. And that hurts my heart, that you didn't get a chance
to know.*

*I'm trying, Drina, with my daughters. I try, for our sake,
to right my wrongs. Our wrongs.*

*I went by your grave last week. Mother, not surprisingly,
has done a stellar job with its upkeep, like she's in some
best-grave competition. And she just might be—Mr. Wiley
passed last year (cancer), and Mrs. Wiley returned from
Florida to bury him in the church cemetery, and then she
decided to stay. So you and Mr. Wiley have had some
impressive grave decorations lately. You guys are buried just
two rows apart. Mother's got the edge, though; I think she
slips Fred extra money. Do you remember Charlotte Prime?
She was two years below you. Her father, Fred, is the
caretaker now. Anyway, I'm talking excessive flower
arrangements that almost encroach on your neighbors,
grave blankets around the holidays, the whole nine yards.
Mother's the one who does the flower ordering, but Fred
helps with the planting and upkeep. Mother even purchased*

*some special stone cleaner online for marble kitchen countertops and uses it to polish your stone.*

*Mother and Father are still together, after all these years. But he pretty much died when you did, Drina. You should know that.*

*I'm so sorry you had to know about him. I'm so sorry I told you.*

*Do you have any idea how many times a week, a day, I have these mini conversations with you? There's a constant dialogue in my head. I've collected thousands of stories over the years to tell you again one day.*

*Damnit, Drina.*

*It's okay—he's dead now, Mother said when Grandpa Joe died. Did you know she said that? She locked herself in the bathroom to cry—I think—and then she came out and said it. Well, she said it again, after you died. The morning she took me to Dr. Pat.*

*Of course, it's not okay at all that you're dead now. But I understand what Mother meant. She meant, you're dead, and we're not, so we have to keep moving forward, or trying, at least. There's no other way.*

*Sometimes my daughters, when they dare—they know I don't like to be asked too often (it makes me sad)—beseech me to tell them about you. Emily, in particular.*

*I occasionally agree, but tell them they have to come sit on my lap.*

*They acquiesce, even though at seven and five, they are nearly too big to both fit. They sit on me, squashed, each perched on a leg, until one of them elbows the other and the other retaliates and then they both slide off. Before they do, though, I squeeze them, the way I once wished, long ago, that Mother or Father would squeeze me.*

*Who's Sally? Emily interrupted me once, mid-story.*

*Sally? I repeated.*

*You said Sally.*

*Did I?*

*Yeah. You said Sally liked to put make-up on.*

*I didn't mean to, I replied. I meant Aunt Audrina. (Sally slips into my consciousness like that once in a while.)*

*Tell us the rest, Mia piped in, a second voice—always a second voice.*

*Their faces looked at me, and I had a sudden, wild desire to be the Operator of Time. To wind the arms of a grandfather clock backward, reversing life, undoing all the things I've done wrong. And then to be able to swing the arms forward in the opposite direction, as if I were flicking a board game spinner. To travel into my daughters' futures, to stop them from doing wrong things, too.*

*Promise me something, I said, with an urgent fierceness.*

*They heard it, the tight plea in my voice like a rubber band stretched thin, and they exchanged looks before replying, in drawn out voices, Okaaay.*

*Promise me you will always be there for each other, I said. Promise me you will always look after one another.*

*Okay.*

*Promise me, I repeated, my voice rising. Promise. Me.*

*We promise, Mom, they said, in a chorus of innocence—of unbroken water.*

But then the water breaks; a man suddenly surfaces and sinks back down, his lungs full once again. Other people appear in the lake and materialize in the woods. The search dogs run ahead; the mothers bake their casseroles. They are all looking for Sally. I helplessly watch, from where I am trapped on the beach next to you, my feet stuck in a quicksand of our memory.

# Acknowledgments

This book could not have been written without the support of many.

Thank you to my agent, Stacy Testa, for believing in this book, and in me, and for your steadfast guidance. It is beyond comforting to have you in my corner.

I'm deeply indebted to my editor, Lexy Cassola, whose enthusiasm, vision, and critical eye truly brought this book to its fullest potential. Thank you for giving this your all.

I am grateful to everyone at Dutton who helped to usher this book into the world, including Maya Ziv, Isabel DaSilva, LeeAnn Pemberton, Elke Sigal, Susan Schwartz, Ryan Richardson, and Mary Beth Constant. And thank you to Megan Beatie, my publicist.

For over ten years, I've met monthly with a group of Boston writers. To Betty Yee, Shelley Berg, and Ted Robitaille, and to Theresea Barrett and Jane Deon: Thank you for sharing your words with me, and for critiquing mine, and for your insight and honesty. Our time together has always been a haven. Shelley Berg, thank you also for proofreading.

Thank you to my longstanding online writers' group: Lada Marcelja, Paula Mirk, and Carol Schneider. This book might not exist at all had it not been for the "portable magic" that we four somehow create together.

Special thanks to those who read earlier drafts and gave invaluable feedback, including Kathy Rice, Nicole Lipson, Katherine Taylor, Kate Racculia, April Cowin, Ann Sather, Arthur Winn, Jennifer and Eric Aronson, and Rebecca and Chris Matchett. Thank you to Ellen Akins, my former thesis adviser.

There are so many others who have encouraged and supported me over the years in different ways. Thank you in particular to Katherine Steinberg, Morgan Crooks, Alan Dorfman, Matija Cale, Ranella Saul, Melissa Schwab Wright, Kristen and Jonathan Keith, Ly Nichols, Paula Restrepo, Sachiko Sato, Alina Wolhardt and Jay Gordon, Zoey Gulmi, Rachel Miriam, Elizabeth Bell Rakela, Nancy Daly, Natalie Favaloro, Bernie Dunphy, Kristen Bernstein, Sarah Tufano, Veronica Ward, Laura and Mike Kern, Amanda Bruno, Emily Holland, Marlen Caduff, Cassandra Foster, Bron Volney, Megan Dunnigan, Lorena Sanders, Bo Hunter, Maria DeSales, and Talita Teixeira. Thank you to the "Awesome TI Moms" and to the Mother-Artist Collaborative. Thank you to my Hoboken nurse friends who supported me from the early days, and to Edit Knowlton for assisting me with Hungarian. Thanks to my other friends, unnamed—you know who you are.

I'm grateful to the Writers' Room of Boston for providing a place where I could focus and write, and to Inked Voices for providing a virtual workspace. Thank you to Grub Street for fostering my creativity. Thank you to the Vilna Shul for providing a sense of community. To Mehmet Ozturk and the staff of Bristol Lounge: Many thanks for allowing my Boston writing comrades and me to linger for hours.

A special note of gratitude to Elin Hilderbrand, who kindly took the time to read and blurb my book when it was at an early stage. And many thanks to Jennifer Sleeper, who graciously made the introduction.

Last but not least, I am incredibly grateful for my family, whose love, support, and encouragement carried me toward my dream. To my mother, who meticulously combed through every draft I presented her and who patiently answered every editing question, and to my late father, whose faith in me continues to sustain me. To my siblings, for whom this book is dedicated: my sister, who also read multiple drafts and who believed in this book from the beginning, perhaps before even I fully did, and my brother, who always patiently listens to my storytelling and with whom I love discussing creative endeavors.

To my husband, Gil: Thank you for the painstaking hours you spent reviewing my manuscript, fielding my questions, and discussing and debating the finer points, time and time again. You are my Bostonian, my partner in crime, and my best friend. You know more than anyone how much I rely on you, both with writing and life. You and the kids are my everything.

To my children: Thank you for making my life, *life*.